TERROR SWE
CROWD LIKE
THE SEARCH
STENCH OF
FILLED THE
SOUGHT ESCAPE, BUT THERE WAS
NOWHERE TO HIDE.

A man moved too slowly out of Alla's path and with a casual flick of her wrist she thrust the cattle prod into his chest. There was a brief sizzle and then his limbs were taken over by a puppet master manipulating hundreds of strings in jerking, uncoordinated chaos. The St Vitus's dance lasted for perhaps five seconds, accompanied by the smell of burning flesh and the strangulated scream of a mind consumed by pain. Finally, he collapsed, a jumble of broken limbs. Without a glance at her victim, Alla moved towards her goal ...

ABOUT THE AUTHOR

James Adams is Washington Bureau Chief of the *Sunday Times*, and a leading authority on intelligence, covert warfare, terrorism and weapons. Born in Newcastle upon Tyne, he now lives in Washington, DC, with his wife and two children.

He has written several works of non-fiction about terrorism, unconventional warfare and, most recently, *Sellout*, a book about Aldrich Ames and the biggest spying scandal ever to hit the CIA, published by Penguin. His other two thrillers in Signet, *The Final Terror* and *Taking the Tunnel*, are also a blend of fact and fiction, giving extraordinary insights into the closed worlds of intelligence and terrorism.

HARD TARGET

JAMES ADAMS

A SIGNET BOOK

SIGNET

Published by the Penguin Group
Penguin Books Ltd, 27 Wrights Lane, London W8 5TZ, England
Penguin Books USA Inc., 375 Hudson Street, New York, New York 10014, USA
Penguin Books Australia Ltd, Ringwood, Victoria, Australia
Penguin Books Canada Ltd, 10 Alcorn Avenue, Toronto, Ontario, Canada M4V 3B2
Penguin Books (NZ) Ltd, 182–190 Wairau Road, Auckland 10, New Zealand

Penguin Books Ltd, Registered Offices: Harmondsworth, Middlesex, England

First published in Great Britain by Michael Joseph 1996
Published in Signet 1996
1 3 5 7 9 10 8 6 4 2

Printed in England by Clays Ltd, St Ives plc

To Frances,
who would have enjoyed this,
and to René

If we perceive our role aright, we then see more clearly the proper criterion for success: a toolmaker succeeds as, and only as, the users of his tool succeed with his aid. However shining the blade, however jewelled the hilt, however perfect the heft, a sword is tested only by cutting. That swordsmith is successful whose clients die of old age.

Frederick Brooks, 'Grasping Reality Through Illusion: Interactive Graphics Serving Science.' Proceedings of the Fifth Conference on Computers and Human Interaction, 1988.

Hard Target: *A term used in clandestine and covert intelligence to describe a secret and closed society where penetration is exceptionally difficult. It is contrasted with 'Soft Targets', which are the open societies of neutral and allied nations.*

Author's Note
and Acknowledgements

THE TRADECRAFT AND descriptions of places in this book are generally accurate. For example, the inside of the new headquarters of the Secret Intelligence Service, MI6, is as described, as are the CIA headquarters in Langley or the Russian Intelligence HQ outside Moscow. But this book is fiction and the people are creations of my imagination.

It is customary for novelists to invent names to accompany particular jobs or tasks – the British describing their American intelligence counterparts as 'the Cousins' for example. I have not invented any new espionage terms but have relied on those I have heard used.

A NUMBER OF people, who wish to remain nameless, have been helpful in providing details of tradecraft and in describing the situations inside and outside the Office which they have encountered in the course of their work. I am grateful to them all. Current and past members of both Russian and American intelligence have also given generously of their time.

Kyle Olson of the Chemical and Biological Warfare Institute helped me fill in some of the gruesome details. Much against their peaceful instincts, Christine Holt and Bill Harris, two eminent experts in their field, helped me put their scientific knowledge to terrible use.

Bob and Marnie were generous with their house in Weekapaug and gave me the time and space I needed to get this done. Jaimie Seaton and Blair Weigle helped find answers to some difficult questions and always did so with great good humour.

Authors tend to see their editors as a blessing or a curse and I am very definitely in the former camp. Richenda Todd has been by my side for some years, always encouraging but also driving me to do better. Her comments are tough, to the point and invariably improve the final product. Even more important, everything she says is done because she cares about what she does. She has my respect and thanks.

Finally, I must thank René. All authors must invest themselves in the characters they create and to do that it is sometimes necessary to dig deep. René has provided the encouragement that I needed and at every turn; as I tried to bring the vision of Nash to the page, she was there drawing me out. She is my most loyal supporter and I love her very much.

Prologue

THE TRUCK WAS dying, it had been dying for years, but somehow Genrikh Grigoryevich Yagoda managed each night to get one more wheezing, gasping, lurching journey from the ancient Kamaz. It was almost as cold inside the truck as outside. Only one heating vent still worked and in the perversity of such things it was stuck in a position that sent an intermittent blast of tepid air over the top of his head before it was absorbed by the dominant cold currents.

Yagoda was used to such privations. His was not the lot of the new entrepreneur, the slick hoods who had made so much from the new Russia. He had no produce to sell at outrageous prices in the big city, no way of getting hold of the American dollars that now seemed to rule his world, no opportunity to get out of the endless cycle of cold, poverty and emptiness in which he found himself each night.

Yagoda was at the lower end of the Russian social spectrum, ranked alongside the body washers at funeral parlours and the collectors of sewage from the decaying high-rise apartments that ring Moscow. He was a *metelschik sovak*, a dog collector His mission was to roam the darkened roads looking for dogs that had been run over or simply died of malnutrition or old age. He would toss them into the back of his truck, carcass piling on carcass as the night wore on. The skinny ones he would take to the council and receive two roubles for each body. The fatter ones he would deliver to

Black Igor who would pay a few kopeks more. Yagoda had never asked what Igor did with the remains, but he suspected the carcasses were butchered, the flesh being sold as horse meat or, to the really gullible, as beef.

Passing through the small town of Klin, ninety-seven kilometres north-west of Moscow on the bank of the Sestra, a tributary of the Volga, Yagoda was approaching the northernmost point of his patrol. He would turn right at the junction just ahead and begin his circuitous return towards the outskirts of the city. It had been a bad night. Too many farmers out here either buried their dogs or fed them to the pigs, in contrast to the city folk who just couldn't be bothered to clean up their own mess. Occasionally, however, he would have a bit of luck finding some carcass before the locals got to it. Rarer still, he would come across the remains of a portly family pet. Now that was a real triumph. It meant he could afford a glass or two of the good stuff.

Dimly, through the washed-out glimmer of his headlights, he saw the rounded mass of a body. His foot urgently pumped the brake pedal and the Kamaz jerked to a halt. Yagoda could see by the bulk that this was a good one. Even from the cab, he could see that the fur was healthy, there was no sign that it had been run over; aside from the pool of mucus by the nose glistening in the watery glare of the light, it almost seemed as if the dog was asleep.

He squeaked open the cab door and stepped on to the ground. Reaching into the back of the truck, he pulled out the broad shovel he used to prise the carcasses from the road. His feet crunching softly on the Tarmac, he approached the dog cautiously. Five years earlier, he had come across a dog just like this one. It had seemed dead enough, but when he had slid the shovel under its body it had suddenly sprung to life, wakened perhaps by the pressure of the shovel on its bruised ribs. It had turned on him and taken a sizable chunk out of his leg. Six weeks that had taken to heal; it had almost been enough to put him off collecting dogs for life.

He bent over the animal and gently put his hand out first to feel for air around the muzzle. Then he ran his hand along the fur to feel for a heartbeat. The fur felt almost sticky in his hands, but it was misty so that was hardly surprising. What had looked like mucus he now saw was the darkness of blood mixed with a lighter shade, presumably vomit. Some kind of heart attack, perhaps.

Stretching, he brought the shovel around and pushed the blade under the body. As he began to raise the dog from the ground, he felt the first itch in his hand. Before he could lift the shovel, the itching had turned to a vivid burning sensation. He dropped the shovel and lurched back, his left hand reaching to his right as if a simple touch could make the pain go away. Stumbling backwards, he squatted in front of the truck and thrust his arm into the yellow beam.

The boils appeared stark in the light, their redness against the white of his flesh. As he watched, another, and then another appeared, seeming to rise to the surface like some awful, bubbling gas. Before he had time to scratch, or even think about tending the wounds, the first bubble burst, sending a stream of yellow slime across his skin. In the wake of the rivulet, other bubbles appeared, spreading faster than he could follow, down one arm and then, where his fingers had touched to his other hand, along that arm, too.

Yagoda's mouth opened in a scream of horror, his neck muscles cording. It was too late now. Instead of a scream, his stomach spasmed and an uncontrollable spume of vomit projected from his mouth, arcing through the headlamp's gleam to splatter on the roadway three feet away. In a reflex action, his arm swept over his mouth to wipe away the residue. In its wake, a line of boils suppurated across his face.

Another spray of vomit and then the wrenching, gut-

3

twisting pain tore through him. It seemed to be everywhere at once: in his stomach, in his legs, in his head. He had no strength now to stand, could only fall to the ground, distracted for a moment from the agony of his body's disintegration by the icy cold of the road against his face.

But there was no escaping the poison which filled his body. A moment of acute sensation and it seemed as if he could feel his blood pumping. A flash of horror as his imagination ran ahead of the pain to picture the evil he knew had invaded him being carried to his every extremity. A brief feeling of warmth as his organs ruptured and blood flowed out of his mouth and down his chin. Then, suddenly, the pain faded.

There was little to distinguish the office of Mikhail Skobelev from the other low, dun-coloured buildings lining what passed for a main street in Klin. The second Russian revolution had largely passed the town by. The shiny new western-style buildings, the wide roads and the statues were found in the few big cities where the tourists visited, where the western industrialists found workers to exploit and where the local gangsters plied their trade. There it was important for the results of the revolution to be visible. Here, life went on as before.

Skobelev's office was, conveniently enough, next to the police station which was the only really modern building in town, its forest of rooftop antennas a constant mute testimony of the need for the heart of even this reduced Russian empire to feel the pulse of the people.

It was to Mikhail Skobelev that Yagoda's body was brought some five hours after his life had oozed on to the surface of the road. A truck heading for the capital from one of the many small farms that had sprung up under the liberalization programme had come across the vehicle and then the

4

crumpled body of its driver in the last frigid moments before dawn. Now his body lay spread out on a slab in the small back room of the man who was coroner, undertaker and the nearest thing to a mayor that Klin possessed. He was big, with all the muscle and fat of the caricature so beloved of nineteenth-century Russian novelists. Like a sepia photograph, Skobelev, with his dark, bushy beard, curling moustache and wild eyebrows, seemed to recall a prouder Russian past. But his hands, which should have been calloused and rough to fit his tough face, were smooth, the long fingers topped by perfectly trimmed fingernails. These were the hands of someone who used his fingers as precision instruments, wielding scalpel and forceps with a delicacy that belied his bulk.

Skobelev laid Yagoda out immediately, cut off his clothes and began the clinical probing and cutting that was required so that he could fill in the form for the Health Ministry down south.

Humming an unrecognizable tune as wound after terrible wound was exposed, Skobelev paused only to make brief notes on the form pinned to the clipboard beside him. As he wrote, the pen made a small squeaking noise, plastic moving against the rubber of his bloody latex gloves. He had recently developed a passion for pirated videos of a Russian-dubbed US television show called *Quincy*, which had become popular among an audience with a taste for anything American. For him, the attraction was in the artistry of the eponymous star's work: all high-tech laboratories, clean morgues and case-solving revelations. No chopping and cutting for him. Now that was how a coroner should work, he thought for the hundredth time.

It was the smell of death he disliked most. He didn't mind the blood and he had grown used to the smallness of death that reduced even large men to a sad and somehow hollow shell. But the smell lingered with him for hours, sometimes days, after these sessions. And this one had a smell all its own. It reminded him of a pheasant he had trapped as a boy. He had taken it home and drawn it, gagging at the sharp, pungent smell of the guts as they spewed on to the table. This man smelled like that and he hadn't even opened him up. It was as if the pustules on his face and arms had sucked the very essence of him to the surface.

Skobelev worked quickly, wanting to be rid of the grue- some cadaver as quickly as possible. The sooner the autopsy was over, the sooner he could wash off, wrap the body in a cheap cotton sheet and then, donning his undertaker's hat, take it to the burial ground on the edge of town. Beginning to end, the job shouldn't take more than a couple of hours and he could then settle down with his collection of travel brochures which would transport him far away from this place to the summer warmth of the Caspian, or perhaps even the Caribbean.

As a matter of routine, Skobelev had called the police station next door to alert them that a corpse had arrived. He doubted that they would be interested. Occasionally, if the cops had been directly involved – a knife fight, for example – one of them might wander over but mostly they stayed away, happy to let him get on with his grim task.

He wondered now whether he should have requested a police presence. He had never seen anything like this before. Clearly the body had been afflicted with a terrible sickness but the sores, the rigidity of the limbs, the strained agony in the facial muscles was like nothing he had ever seen. To make the body lie flat he had been forced to break the spine, the small snapping sounds punctuating the stillness of the room and the horror of his task.

His thin scalpel was poised to make an incision into the stomach wall when the door to his office opened quietly. A phalanx of four men entered, three dressed in light-brown fatigues. Their green epaulettes identified them not as members of the FSB the internal security police, but of the Glavnoye Razvedyvatelnoye Upravleniye or GRU, the Russian military intelligence organization.

Their leader wore an elegant woollen suit, cut in the Italian style that had become so popular recently among senior officials. His hair was swept back from his forehead and was slick with brilliantine, the dark features made even darker by an unseasonal tan, a clear sign that this was a man with access to all the privileges of the new élite.

A moment after the quartet entered the room, the smell reached Skobelev, carried imperceptibly on the draught created by their entrance. It was a sickly, sweet smell that he had experienced once when he went to Moscow and had walked among the crowds of the rich and the very rich. It was the perfume of the powerful. He felt bile rise in his throat.

'Mikhail Semyonovich Skobelev?' the civilian asked. Skobelev merely nodded, awestruck at his first direct confrontation with the vast and frightening Russian security apparatus.

'I am Colonel Nikolai Muraviev, responsible for military security in this area.'

He spoke very softly, his voice almost a whisper, but Skobelev had no difficulty in hearing each word, his terror magnifying the sounds in the stillness of his refuge. He watched as the colonel stepped up to the body, picked up the discarded scalpel and flicked casually at one of the dried sores on the face of the corpse. Skobelev noticed irrelevantly how unnaturally long and claw-like the colonel's fingernails were.

'I am sorry you have been bothered with this man. An oversight. This is a security matter.' He turned to the men behind him. 'Remove it,' he commanded.

Two of the men hurried forward, rewrapped the sheet around the body and carried the corpse out of the room.

7

Skobelev watched as the colonel reached inside his jacket and pulled out a thick wad of banknotes. He peeled off several and casually threw them on to the slab amid the mucus and gore.

'That's for your trouble and your silence,' he said. 'Perhaps you will be able to take one of those trips to the sun you've always dreamed about.'

It was as Skobelev had feared: they knew everything; everything. He felt his legs begin to give way and he reached out to the table for support.

The colonel's voice sank even lower and now Skobelev struggled to catch the words.

'But money may not be quite enough,' he continued, talking even lower, as if convincing himself.

For the first time, the coroner looked at his visitor. The soft mouth smiled gently now, a brief glimpse of the humour he found in the situation. But his eyes told the real story. There were no crinkles at the edges, no laugh lines to match the mouth. Instead they were recessed deep into the skull, dark pits that told of the cruelty they had inflicted and the horrors they had absorbed. Suddenly the scalpel appeared between the two men and the colonel reached out to pinch Skobelev's ear lobe between his left thumb and forefinger.

'You see, my friend,' he began conversationally, 'Mother Russia may be a generous and firm guide to us all, but you have to understand that for her and for me, loyalty is absolute. Understand also what will happen if you talk about what you have seen today.'

Skobelev felt a tugging at his ear and then the scalpel moved out of his line of sight. There was a brief flash of pain and then the sensation that he knew so well of blade slicing through flesh. Almost immediately he felt the warmth of blood trickling down his neck. A hand reappeared in front of his eyes holding a piece of flesh – his flesh – with a few

8

droplets of blood clinging to the edge. He felt no real pain, only a slight stinging sensation, but the casual nature of the violation and the sight of his severed earlobe broke through all the barriers he had built up over the years to immunize him against the gore of his work.

He bent forward and retched, vomiting on to the floor in front of him. The colonel took a small step sideways out of the line of fire, and regarded his victim with the paternal affection of a master for a pupil who has learned his lesson well.

1

EVERY TIME NASH walked into the shambles of Daemon's office he found it difficult to repress a quick shudder of revulsion. He needed order to keep himself sane, while Daemon purposely produced chaos to make himself comfortable, apparently relishing the distaste that it created in his visitors. Papers were piled high on every surface. The jumble of computer printouts stacked on monitors and chairs looked like a collection of hieroglyphics but were, in fact, the binary codes that he claimed to understand. The monitors themselves contributed to the impression of bubbling anarchy. Instead of sitting still and silent, each one was lit up with a different Screensaver program. On one, flying toasters cascaded across the screen, another showed fish swimming in a coral sea while a third had a complex web of geometric shapes spiralling one into the other in an unending progression.

Daemon was sitting with his back to the door, black cowboy boots propped up on the corner of his desk, keyboard perched on one knee, his fingers idly drumming a staccato beat on the plastic frame. The gold earring in the shape of a saxophone that dangled to one side of his black ponytail suggested his love of the mellow notes of Dixieland jazz and the yellow headphones he wore emitted a scratchy threnody that Nash assumed was creating the rhythm in Daemon's fingers.

Sensing Nash's arrival, Daemon pushed the keyboard back on to the desk and turned slightly in his chair.

'David. Come in. Grab a seat.'

He pushed a bunch of papers on to the floor and pulled the chair closer to the largest monitor that sat in the middle of his desk.

'Have I got something for you,' he continued enthusiastically, his fingers beginning to flick across the keyboard. Daemon's excitement was infectious and despite himself, Nash felt drawn towards the screen and the secrets that lurked within. He was an unwilling victim but the ultimatum from upstairs had left no room for argument. In today's world, computers were the backbone of the sources and methods that kept the intelligence machine humming. They were also the lifeline that could make the difference between life and death in the field. So it was learn or leave.

Nash leaned forward to stare at the screen as if eye contact alone would help him unlock the secrets that Daemon was about to unfold. The flying toasters vanished and the image was replaced by a simple menu with no logo and no identifying headline. Daemon keyed in a password and placed the cursor on the letters DSNET and then clicked again on Intelink.

'You are now entering the glorious world of interactive intelligence,' Daemon announced proudly. 'This is the Defence Systems Network, the Americans' way of keeping themselves in touch on line with all that good classified stuff they don't want anyone else to know about.' He clicked the mouse again. 'And now we are into Intelink, which is the intelligence information software that allows all those US agencies and bureaus who normally don't speak to each other to access the same intelligence on screen.'

'So how come we're in there?' David asked.

Daemon held up his hands to protest his innocence.

'Not guilty,' he insisted. 'They offered and we gratefully accepted.'

Nash's suspicions and Daemon's protestations were an indication of the computer expert's well-deserved reputation. Other people's information was his business and the more secure the database, the more interesting the challenge. From the Chief down, he was known in memos and in person as Daemon, a nickname he happily accepted as it suited his own perception of himself as a kind of satanic figure inside this most righteous organization. The nickname had arisen from one of his early lectures, in which he explained that Daemon is the label used in computer-speak to describe the utility programs that lurk in the background of most software systems. It had seemed to his audience that Daemon described not just Frank Cory but the dark arts he was supposed to practise for the Office.

He was prophet and poet, teacher and master technician who tried both to enthuse and to guide the neophytes of the Secret Intelligence Service through the opportunities that the relatively new world of computers presented to the old world of spies. He had come to the attention of one of the spotters at Manchester University when a query had arrived from the Pentagon about an unauthorized penetration of the computers at Bolling Air Force Base that devised and monitored the launch codes for the Inter-Continental Ballistic Missiles. The Americans had also discovered that the same hacker, tracked to the computer lab at Manchester, had been surfing through the Internet injecting password sniffers in dozens of different networks to steal codes and logons in a giant Hoovering operation.

Confronted with the evidence Cory had readily admitted everything, describing it simply as an intellectually challenging exercise. There had been no intent to spy or corrupt any of the systems, he was simply fascinated by the complexities of the problems confronting him. The spotter had seen the potential and contacted the Office. One of the recruiters had gone to Manchester and taken Cory out for a quiet drink. A delicate dance had followed, with the recruiter opening the door of opportunity to a world which he hoped would fascinate the young hacker: the best computers, the opportunity to cruise the Internet devising ways to pluck information from reluctant and well-defended providers. And no, he wouldn't have to wear a suit.

Since Daemon had signed on, he had become something of a prize pupil, a showpiece demonstrating just how right-on the Office could be. His ponytail was fine, so were the headphones, even the spoof e-mail that appeared around the building in the Chief's name complete with his personal code was seen as just part of the price to be paid for having such a genius on board. There was no one who doubted his brilliance, even if few really comprehended. To try and bridge the cultural divide between the computer literate and the rest, Personnel and Training had decided that Daemon should conduct regular one-on-one seminars with selected operatives, and Nash had made the trek to Daemon's eyrie to embark on one of his guided tours through cyberspace.

'So what does this stuff let you do?' Nash asked.

'Do?' Daemon replied sarcastically, as if the very size of the word were an insult to the power of the system now at his command.

'Crop production in Russia?' He flicked through a country menu, clicked on Russia, scrolled down another menu to Economy, brought up Agriculture and then Grain Production. The CIA estimates for that year appeared with a linear graph comparing it with the previous ten years (the decline in production since the demise of communism was evidently going to continue, Nash noted).

A few more touches on the keys and the Russian production

was compared with production in the Ukraine and then with Argentina and finally with the United States, first by tonnage and then by production per acre. It was all very pretty, Nash thought, but he had pored over similar material in the briefing books.

'I can get all this from the public library,' he needled, wanting to drive Daemon to really strut his stuff.

'Well, how about this?' Daemon replied, first clearing the screen and then working through a different series of menus.

Graphics appeared that showed a topographical map of Bosnia. Daemon moved the cursor to a spot which marked one of the confrontation lines between the Serbs and the Muslims.

'You want to see what's been happening in the fighting in the past twelve hours and what we think will happen in the next twenty-four?' Daemon asked. 'Watch.'

The map was replaced by pictures taken from an aircraft flying over the ground. The film showed artillery pieces shelling trenches and then troops advancing along a wooded valley where they were met by heavy fire from dug-in machine-gun positions.

'What you see is the product of thousands of satellite photos taken over the past day which has been synthesized with on-the-ground reports from the UN troops and CIA assets. The computers have taken the information and created a movie that makes the fighting comprehensible to even the stupidest political mind.' Nash nodded, impressed. 'And if that's not enough for you,' continued Daemon, 'then I can offer you this.'

Once again his hands began their complex dance. He continued talking as his commands and responses were shuttled back and forth across the Atlantic via satellite in fractions of a second.

'You know they've seven acres of computers over at the

National Security Agency – another three at Langley,' Daemon explained helpfully. 'Four trillion bytes of secret information – equal to a stack of paper about thirty miles high. Intelink gives us access to all that. Makes most of our records downstairs obsolete and cuts down the research time on any project by weeks, maybe months. Take you, for instance. You've been doing some work on trafficking, right?'

Nash nodded. For the past two weeks he had been drawn into an effort to crack a move by the Cali cartel in Colombia to make a $50 million property investment in Prague using funds that had been laundered through one of the newly privatized banks in Moscow. He had been the co-ordinator in the Office while a team had been at the sharp end in the Czech Republic trying to bring the local intelligence people up to speed. So far it seemed that too much cash had been spread among too many officials to scupper the deal.

'One of the things you guys try and do is monitor the shipment of the chemicals used to refine cocaine. Stop the chemicals and they can't make the drugs, yes?' The way Daemon described it, the task was simple but in fact it was very difficult to monitor the movement of the chemicals, in part because sifting the different intelligence and bringing together the knowledge on chemicals, shipping agents who fronted for the drug producers and the ships and aircraft that carried the raw materials was a logistical nightmare.

'Give me a chemical,' instructed Daemon.

'Try toluene,' Nash replied.

The computer scrolled through a list of all the manufacturers of the solvent worldwide.

'OK. Now we need to set a few more parameters,' Daemon explained. 'We'll cross-ref that to the shipping manifests of every vessel registered at Lloyd's that is either at sea or has notified them of a cargo. Then we'll look for any intelligence that matches any of those ships or any of the companies that own those ships with links to any of the cartels. Then we'll add the final kicker of any intelligence on manufacturing plants in any of the countries of destination.'

Almost as soon as his fingers had stopped their work, a list of fifteen companies, ships, cargoes and destinations that appeared to fit the profile appeared on the screen.

'*Et voilà*,' Daemon exclaimed with the pride of an owner whose dog has just performed a spectacular trick. 'Months of work for you, a few seconds for me.'

It was the power that was so impressive, thought Nash. If he could just understand how to get at the information, his life might become a lot easier. Daemon made it appear so simple, but Nash knew that appreciating the potential and knowing enough to take advantage of it were two concepts separated by a gulf of ignorance and a typing style that had yet to move beyond the hunt and peck.

He glanced at his watch.

'Sorry, Daemon. Gotta go. Late for the Agency. Yet another bloody slide show from the button-down boys of the CIA. Still, a bit more help from you and I'll be free of that as well,' he said with a grin. Daemon waved a casual goodbye and moved his headphones back into place as Nash closed the door behind him.

'This is now a business that generates some $500 billion a year, ladies and gentlemen. That's billion with a capital B. More money than the total GNP of sub-Saharan Africa. Or, to bring it closer to home, it would take at least a millennium of saving your budget pennies before you managed to approach the annual budget of the drug barons.'

There were a few polite chuckles from the audience and for a brief moment a smile flickered across the face of the speaker, who was struggling to woo the audience and clearly failing.

Why was it that these Agency guys always needed to bond? Nash wondered. A lecture is a lecture but somehow they always wanted to make it into a meaningful experience where everyone had to share their pain or even their bad jokes. It must be all those human relations courses they go on, he thought. If it was, they had done nothing to improve their style, which was invariably tight assed and buttoned down, even to the regulation Brooks Brothers shirt.

Nash looked around the lecture hall, reflecting on its deterioration in the short time since the move from Century House. At the beginning, it had been filled with light and the clean smell of new paint. But the room had no owner, just a succession of temporary tenants who were there for an hour or two and then gone. Someone had tacked cardboard over the windows to keep out the light which interfered with the smooth running of the slide show. The room smelled of old cigarettes and even the paint appeared dull, as if the cares of the audience had somehow leached through the floor to the walls to tarnish everything.

He rolled his neck from left to right and winced as he felt the strain of the session in the gym. It was all very well getting fit for the field, but the Marines were brutes and particularly seemed to relish putting civilians through the wringer. Nash stretched his legs out in front of him and leaned back in the chair, feeling his vertebrae ease in their sockets, grateful for this respite.

'At the Agency we've been trying to convince the policy-makers that the problem can be contained and then rolled back,' the CIA man continued. 'But as you can see from this graph,' he clicked a button and a chart with three wiggly lines, one red, one green and one blue, appeared on the screen, 'we have not been successful. The blue, line shows the level of funding which has been unchanged for the past five years. The red line is the amount of cocaine and heroin seized inside the United States over the same period. You can see it's been rising steadily, reflecting the lack of resources and a drug policy that's devoted to the politically correct ideal of prevention on the streets rather than going after the dealers. The green line is our estimate of drug income worldwide.' His pointer flicked briefly at the screen but Nash could see the bad news clearly enough. The green line began as a gentle curve upwards and then made an almost vertical climb.

'The traffickers reached critical mass some time ago and everything they get now is real gravy,' the speaker continued. 'The new drugs coming in from the former Soviet Union have pushed the price down a little but the Colombians, the Russians and the Sicilians have carved up the market. There's more coke and heroin on the street and more addicts. The profits have just gotten bigger and bigger.'

The light level in the room increased, imparting a flat yellowness to everything. There was some shuffling and coughing. Nash looked around, taking in his colleagues. As always, they seemed so young, although most were around his age which should have given them a faint air of maturity. It was hard to believe that the fate of the nation rested in the hands of these people. Or rather it rested in the hands of him and his colleagues from the Human Intelligence Tasking Centre.

These days there was no stereotypical intelligence officer. The very world they worked in had changed dramatically in recent years and they had had to change with it. The upper-class Brit who had casually and often amateurishly ambled his way through the diplomatic gossip circuit had been forced to give way to men and women who felt as comfortable in the backstreets of Cracow as in the boardroom of a multinational. If they were bound by anything it was a kind of gregarious ruthlessness; the ability to mix with all sorts and yet be prepared to exploit apparent friendships with hardly a second thought because it was the job and not the person that really mattered.

The post-lecture questioning followed the usual pattern of specific probing and vague answers with the home team, as always, wanting to know just what the Agency knew and the Agency, as always, reluctant to share, particularly in such a large group. As the meeting broke up, Nash moved forward, still enthused by the time he had spent with Daemon.

'I'm David Nash,' he began, shaking the other man's hand with the crisp up and down movement preferred by Europeans. Sure enough, he was met with the macho muscular grip that was taught in all the American management courses as a sign of a man who had real sense of purpose and an ego to match.

'Philip Thomas. Good to know you, David.'

'We've been covering the same beat and I've just been looking at some of your computer data,' said Nash, extracting his hand. 'Stunning stuff. Should help to offset some of the gloom that you were talking about.'

'Maybe,' Thomas replied, his tone clearly sceptical. 'We've seen all this before. Every advance in technology seems to be matched by a change in direction from the White House or the Drug Czar or some other piece of political cover. It's an uphill struggle, but maybe you can make better use of the data than we have.'

Nash took in the deep-set, dark eyes, the creased forehead and the mouth that had the downward curve of the true cynic and divined that Thomas was another of the Agency folk who had fared badly in the recent revolution. Since the Ames case in '94, everyone had been on the Agency's back and the new Director had been orchestrating a purge. Dozens had been fired and hundreds more, perhaps thousands, faced the axe. Thomas was clearly feeling the strain.

Their conversation was interrupted when Pat Angel, the

Mother Superior and fount of all wisdom to the men and women in HIT, pushed through the crowd at the door and grabbed Nash's arm.

'Binsted wants you,' she said urgently.

'Any idea what's up?' he asked, knowing full well that Pat's own private intelligence network was certain to extend to any plans his boss might have for him.

'You leave on Tuesday,' she replied. 'Russia, I think. Drugs.'

2

NASH RUBBED HIS eyes, thumb and fore-
finger coming together to squeeze the bridge of his nose, his
brain registering the ridge of broken bone, a reminder of his
misplaced confidence on the unarmed combat course at the
Fort. The gesture did little to relieve the gritty tiredness
stinging his eyes. He took a deep breath and exhaled slowly,
watching his breath plume briefly on the air to be snatched
away by the bitter wind. He huddled deeper into his overcoat,
hoping for protection but knowing there was no refuge. This
was now a matter of endurance.

'Jesus, David. This reminds me of waiting for one of those
late night meetings on Hampstead Heath,' Yuri said. He
chuckled lightly. 'The wind came straight from Siberia. It
was bitter.' He shivered theatrically.

Parashvili spoke with that accent peculiar to those who
have learned a foreign language from a teacher whose knowledge is stuck in a time warp. He had been taught at the KGB
headquarters at Yasenevo by Peter Feaver, a minor figure
from the British Foreign Office who had defected in 1953.
Almost a nonentity in intelligence terms, Feaver had been
lionized by the propagandists as a major player and so had to
be given a job that appeared substantial. He would turn up to
work in a nearly new Zil every morning, dressed in what at
that time passed for decent clothes in Moscow, and spend all
his time teaching English. His accent was post-war English

middle class: all strangulated tones and elongated As. Yuri had taken the affectation and added a few of his own, the most prominent of which was the word Jesus, used not as an imprecation to a God he did not believe in but as simple punctuation.

'Perhaps you were watching me from one of those little flats MI6 used to maintain on the Heath,' laughed the ex-KGB man, apparently delighted not just with his little jibe but also with the opportunity to tweak so directly the tail of the organization he had spent most of his working life combating.

'Not my area,' Nash replied. 'Anyway, from what I gather, whoever it was you might have been meeting would hardly have been worth our trouble. The Chinese were much more of a challenge back then.'

The sparring done and predictable positions taken, the two men turned aside. Parashvili strolled over to the men wearing the dirty brown uniforms of the FSB, the Russian internal security police, who were lounging against their cars parked by the side of the two-lane road. Nash moved to the centre of the road and looked south. Over the horizon, the glow of its lights still visible as night gave way to the first cracks of dawn, lay the port of Odessa. Somewhere out in the darkness, their quarry was moving towards them.

This was a bizarre business, Nash reflected. Here he was, stuck in the middle of nowhere waiting for God knows what and doing so at the behest of a senior officer in the SVR, the body that had taken over all the functions of the old First Chief Directorate of the KGB. Sometimes, he thought cynically, it was difficult to tell where the old ended and the new began. But for now, the Russians were on the side of the white hats.

Nash hunched deeper into his thermals, seeking some

illusory comfort, eager for action. It wasn't just the cold that affected him. The fluttering in his stomach, the watery feeling in his bowels were tell-tale signs of either fear or the anticipation of imminent action – he had never been able to decide which.

Six months earlier, when he had first been assigned to the Human Intelligence Tasking Centre at the Office, it had seemed like an end to the grind of collection and analysis that occupied so much of an intelligence officer's daily lot. A brief refresher course down at the Fort, the Secret Intelligence Service's training centre in Portsmouth, a day out with the SAS boys at Hereford, and then off to Moscow with a three-man SIS delegation to discuss co-operation with the transformed KGB. His leader was Richard Littlejohn, a veteran of the Cold War and one of those promoted in the 1992 Christmas massacre that had swept away a layer of the older generation. The SIS team was the last of the major western intelligence agencies to make the pilgrimage. MI6 thought the changes in the KGB – the elimination of the First Chief Directorate, the establishment of the Sluzhba Vneshnei Razvedaki or SVR, and the appointment of the academic Yevgeni Primakov as its head – were purely cosmetic. As far as they and their counter-espionage colleagues at MI5 could see, it was very much business as usual.

Nevertheless, Russo-western working groups were established in Paris, Bonn and Washington, and the intelligence chiefs serving in the different countries were individually named. There had been no sale in London, however, where the political pressures on SIS were less and the old suspicions remained strong.

Then Rick Ames had been unmasked at the Agency as a long-term agent first of the KGB and then of the SVR. He had betrayed at least ten American agents, all of whom had been executed. A further one hundred agents had been identified, along with virtually all covert CIA operations in the former Soviet Union. There was some satisfaction in SIS that their caution had been proved justified in such a dramatic fashion. Not so their political masters, though, who had decided that, Ames notwithstanding, Russia was a friend who deserved some help. SIS was left with little choice but to travel at least some distance along the road towards reconciliation.

There was common ground in combating a new wave of drug trafficking through the countries of the former communist bloc: both Britain and Russia were faced with the problem of cocaine being produced in Colombia and smuggled to Europe. British customs had provided the first real lead. A Polish émigré living in London was arrested trying to smuggle fourteen kilos of cocaine into the country. Customs had asked SIS to investigate further and the trail had been followed back to Gilberto Orejuela (also known as the Chess Player), the leader of the Cali cartel in Colombia. He had needed a new outlet for his supplies once the American market became saturated, and had found it in Eastern Europe. Working with the CIA, SIS had uncovered two trails. The first, via the Polish port of Gdynia and the Czech town of Hradec Králové, had been destroyed. The second entryway was the port city of Odessa. Nash's brief was to watch and report back. Ideally, he would uncover the pipeline all the way back to Britain.

The Russians saw the situation differently. The SVR, mindful of budget cuts, needed a high-profile success. There was to be no lengthy covert operation, simply a trap. Any intelligence that might be produced would be a bonus.

So far, the operation had been smooth enough. The pallets of tinned meat had been unloaded from the Polish vessel *Polonia* at around midnight and the truck had set off accompanied by two civilian cars, presumably loaded with local hoods. Tailing the convoy was a single unmarked police car which was keeping in touch by radio – in this country, where relay stations were few and far between, a disturbingly unreliable process.

The radio in Yuri's hand crackled and he held it up to his ear for a moment before nodding and muttering 'Da' twice into the mouthpiece. He bent down, put the radio next to him on the seat of the car and then shouted in Russian to the police who were lounging around their cars. Immediately there was a burst of activity. The spiked chains that lay coiled by the side of the road were dragged across to form a sharp barrier to any vehicle trying to drive through. Ahead of them four of the police cars made a W across the road, effectively barring progress. Yuri turned to Nash.

'They are just a few minutes away. We'd better get out of the way. And you might need this.'

David felt the coldness of a pistol butt against his palm. Looking down he recognized the 5.45 mm PSM, standard issue for the Russian security forces.

'I know you British don't like these things, but this is not St James's,' Yuri laughed. 'Here they shoot you first and wish you good morning afterwards.' He snicked the safety catch off and then reached under his parka to produce a similar weapon of his own.

'It's ready to go. Make sure you are too.'

Nash followed Yuri off to the side of the road behind one of the police cars and opposite the spiked barrier. The chill of the gun in his hand seemed to suck out what little warmth was left in his body and Nash felt the beginnings of that deep trembling that is the precursor to hypothermia. Then, he saw the lights in the distance and suddenly his body was flushed with the warmth of fear and the adrenaline rush of imminent action. As the convoy approached, the police cars simultaneously turned on their blue lights, washing the ambush with an intense oscillating colour bath. The vehicles, which seemed so far away one moment, were upon them an instant later. The driver of the lead car – a Moskva, he registered irrelevantly – had clearly received none of the training that a bodyguard would have had in the west. He expected to see the nose dip as the driver applied his brakes - perhaps even the beginnings of a fishtail spin as he spun the wheel in an effort to evade the obstacles ahead. But there was no attempt to slow down. Instead, the driver aimed directly at the point where the two cars nearest to Nash met, clearly hoping to force them apart and clear a path for the truck bearing down behind.

Nash saw the flashes of gunfire from the first car and then the second. There was a rush of air around him as the shots carved through the stillness, intermingled with the staccato sound of AKR sub-machine-guns on automatic and the crackling of the bullets as they passed nearby. There was no cover, nowhere to hide and nothing he could do. Real fear gripped him now, reaching deep inside him, taking his stomach and twisting it into a tight fist. He hunched closer to the road as if that slight movement would create the reassuring illusion of greater protection.

He heard a scream from his right as a policeman was hit and there was the deeper sound of the AKR as the police returned fire. The lead car seemed to accelerate towards the point of impact and then with a grinding screech of metal, the three vehicles met. The cars seemed to levitate under the shock and then lurch backwards towards the waiting police. The roadblock disintegrated as the gangsters' car drove the middle police car towards the far side of the road, shunting the one next to it and pushing it, too, away from the centre. Under the initial impact the car nearest Nash spun around in an impossible pirouette before hopping sideways off the road directly towards him. He watched the car coming, unable to move, frozen in place by the suddenness of the violence. He felt a massive blow in his side, thought that he had been hit, and then felt himself thrust clear of the oncoming car. He let out a huge 'whoomph' as the breath was forced from his body. It was the garlic smell from the revolting sandwiches Yuri had eaten for breakfast that helped David make the connection between the impact and the weight that now lay upon him.

'Jesus, David, this is no time to go sightseeing.' Yuri levered himself up and then dragged Nash upright. The lead vehicle had done its job. The truck now had a clear path through the ambush and was rushing towards them, engine screaming. In the reflection from the still-rotating blue lights, David could see the rictus on the face of the truck driver as he hunched down over the flat disc of the steering wheel, peering intently through the windscreen, face full of purpose and focus.

The truck scraped one of the police cars, but so powerful was it that the forward momentum was unaffected. Then the driver saw the chains straddling the road and his mouth opened in the beginning of a cry of horror or hate. There was no time to change course or to slow down and the truck powered straight over the spikes. There came a rapid series of pops as each tyre in turn was punctured, followed by tearing, flapping sounds as the rubber shredded. The bottom of the truck was shrouded in brilliant streams of red and orange sparks as the wheel rims met the Tarmac, and it shuddered to a halt 150 metres from the ambush.

As David moved to get up from his knees and run after the truck, he felt Yuri's restraining hand on his shoulder.

'Wait here,' Yuri gestured back towards the ground.

The gangsters' second car had been perfectly positioned. Far enough back for its occupants to see and avoid the trap ahead but close enough to learn from the mistakes of the others. Engine screaming at maximum revs, the driver veered to the side, trying to slot between the crashed police car, the road and the end of the chains. It was a course that brought the car directly towards Nash and Yuri. Nash brought his gun up in the classic firing position, arm stiffly extended ahead of him, body slightly turned to one side. The words of the Royal Marines instructor came unbidden into his head – 'squeeze, don't pull' – and the little gun bucked in his hand as the first round hit the car. He heard Yuri firing and sound and movement blurred as the vehicle raced towards them. He could see the muzzle flashes from the oncoming car as the smugglers emptied their magazines as if bullets alone would clear them a path. Each barrel seemed to be pointing right between his eyes and he could almost feel the impact of the first bullets in his body. The windscreen of the Moskva starred and then disintegrated as the non-reinforced glass shattered under the impact of several bullets. David could see the driver, eerily blue in the half light. His face was peppered with shards of glass like some macabre sculpture. A brief glimpse of blood, a shattered eye, a sliced nose, a mouth wide in agony and the car was past in a swirl of gravel to collide head on with a pine tree.

The gunfire and the noise of colliding vehicles had stopped. In its place were the screams of the wounded and dying and the ticking of hot engine blocks cooling. Yuri and Nash rose from their knees. David was surprised at how heavy his limbs felt, as if he had just emerged from two hours of weightlifting in the gym. Following Yuri's lead, he forced himself into a shambling trot in the direction of the stationary truck. Guns ready, they advanced on the cab and Yuri jerked open the door while David covered him. The two men inside were unconscious.

Two enormous doors at the back of the truck were secured by a padlock. A policeman appeared with a long tyre lever and soon the padlock popped off the doors, which swung gently open. The two men peered inside, at boxes piled four high blocking the view of the rear. Yuri stood on the tailgate and levered a box from the first row down. In the darkness of the truck it was impossible to distinguish what lay behind and Yuri reached in to take down another box.

There was nothing that could be defined as movement; no person or face. Later, David replayed the moment and couldn't decide what it was that made him fire. Perhaps it was the change in air pressure as the guard, the final backstop, moved slightly to get Yuri more firmly in his sights. Perhaps it was simply his nerves playing tricks. But instinct brought his gun hand up and he fired three times directly over Yuri's shoulder and into the truck. There was a cry of agony that quickly became a burbling wail as the blood from a punctured lung bubbled into the victim's mouth. There was a brief feeling of revulsion at this, his first killing. There would be time for reflection later. For now, he simply followed the questing snout of his pistol as he searched for the next threat.

Yuri jumped down from the tailgate, mouth open wide, laughing.

'That was close. Another couple of inches and I would have had a new parting in what's left of my hair.'

Yuri gestured two of the policemen forward and while one trained his sub-machine-gun on the truck, the second unloaded the first line of boxes. Yuri produced a knife and cut open a box. Inside, the cans of meat looked innocent enough. He cut through one of the lids and prised it open. Inside was a small ingot of metal which was designed to make the can's weight equal to that shown on the label minus the three bags of white cocaine powder that lay underneath. The trap had closed.

The police moved to interrogate the living, the dying and the wounded with equal ferocity. David moved away, but he could still hear the blows. This was a country that had embraced the ideals of democracy but had yet to shrug off the expediency that comes with the support of a police state. After a huddled conversation with the police chief, Yuri told Nash what had been learned.

'They were taking this cargo to Moscow,' Yuri explained as they strolled along the road. 'It's just one of several shipments that are arriving around the same time. Unpack, refine where necessary and then either sell locally or ship out to Europe or America. It seems that these people's masters in Moscow are getting over ambitious. One warehouse, one refinery. We persuaded the truck driver to give us the address.'

'I suppose you only had to ask him nicely,' said David.

The Russian ignored Nash's sarcasm. 'This isn't just one gang but a new network,' he continued. 'Part of the new world order that's been constructed in the last year or two as the gangs try and find ways of working together rather than just killing each other.'

His fist punched into the side of Nash's arm, excitement bubbling over.

'Just think, David, my friend. What an opportunity. We could deal these bastards a real kick in the balls.'

'Easy to say, Yuri,' Nash replied, his cautious tone reflecting, he hoped, just the right mixture of measured enthusiasm leavened with sufficient doubt to stop this before it went any further. 'We are here and this place, wherever it is, is miles away. Anyway, our orders were to gather some intelligence down here and not go off on some mad scheme.'

'Ahhh, you worry too much, my friend,' Yuri reached into his pocket and brought out his SVR identity card. 'This can still get us where we want to go. And just think how much better things might be for us both if we don't just start filling in the forms now but follow the trail and do some real damage.'

His arm moved across Nash's shoulders and drew him closer, embracing him into his enthusiasm and his conspiracy.

'These people,' his other hand swept wide with the smoke from his cigarette appearing to encircle the carnage of the ambush, 'won't be missed for several hours. We have the chance – perhaps the only chance we'll ever have – to get there ahead of them and into the heart of a major operation.'

It was difficult to refute either the logic or Yuri's enthusiasm. Nash knew that if he went forward, he would lengthen his own odds against survival – never volunteer was always the best maxim in combat – but then again, Yuri was right. It was an opportunity and he was supposed to show initiative in the field.

'What's the plan?' he asked.

'Plan? Plan?' Yuri replied sarcastically. 'We go there. We find the place. We take them out. We get a medal. We retire. Plan? Don't talk about a plan. Let's decide to do it and then we'll worry about what comes next.' He assessed the hesitation in his new comrade in arms and pressed forward. 'So, you're with me, David.'

Without him, Yuri was certain to do something and, whatever that something was, the chances of the results being shared with the Office would be close to zero. If he went along, he would at least have the opportunity to gather more intelligence, which, after all, was supposed to be what this was about.

'OK. Let's do it.'

The shouted commands came too fast for Nash to follow as Yuri rounded on the nearest policeman and then on his colleague and each in turn bent over their radios to shout orders at the next people down the line. The Russian turned to Nash with an apologetic grin on his face.

'Old habits die hard, my friend. Particularly when you need to get something done.'

A policeman came up to them and began a babble of excited Russian which Yuri swiftly translated.

'There is an army air base about forty kilometres from here. We should be able to arrange a helicopter from there. The base will have secure communications and I can speak to Moscow and see what we can organize at the other end. Let's go.'

David surveyed the bloodbath they were leaving behind, wondering how much more would be shed before this thing was finally over, and how much of it would be his.

3

FIFTEEN YEARS EARLIER, the Hind-A was the helicopter that every intelligence officer wanted as a scalp. Around the world both MI6 and the CIA tried to beg, borrow or steal one of the choppers which had secretly entered the ranks of the Soviet and Warsaw Pact armies. It was a flying armoury, as capable of ferrying troops to the front line as of shooting down enemy helicopters or destroying tanks and armoured personnel carriers. The American Defense Intelligence Agency had eventually obtained one for $15 million from a corrupt Polish general. What they would have given to be seated where he was now, Nash thought, as he took in the landscape that was rapidly changing from the aridity of the Southern Ukraine to the lusher green of the territory south of Moscow.

Nicknamed the Dragonfly by the Mujahedeen in Afghanistan, it had looked the part waiting on the Tarmac at the air base. Yuri's magic card had done the trick and they had been airborne with the minimum of fuss.

'Jesus, David, these guys have nothing to do except count the days to retirement,' he had muttered in a stage whisper as they walked to the aircraft. 'Most excitement they've had all year.'

'How did you get on with Moscow?' Nash asked.

Yuri had spent half an hour on the phone talking to God knew who in the capital. The conversations had begun badly with an angry exchange and then a slamming down of the phone. But clearly things had improved after that until a smiling Yuri had emerged, thumbs in the air.

'I tried the police, which was a mistake,' Yuri explained. 'They don't want to know about this kind of thing. Anyway, they've all been bought off.' He rubbed his thumb and forefinger together in the universal symbol of corruption. 'But the President's office is another matter. They know where their loyalties lie.'

Two years ago it had been a combination of SVR and internal security troops which had saved the President during an abortive right-wing coup. Traditionally, the KGB had control of the President's security but this had supposedly been transferred to civilian control. It was the intelligence services, though, who knew the location of all the secret tunnels running underneath the Kremlin and during the coup it was their special forces that came to the President's aid. Critically, too, it was the SVR and the FSB – the internal security police – which warned off the military, telling them that it was a coup doomed to failure. Since then, there were favours to be called in and the President's office had never failed to respond.

'There's an Alpha group waiting at the other end. They've already sent out the recce team. So by the time we get there, everything should be ready to roll.'

Nash had heard of the Alpha teams: paid assassins or the backstop of the forces of law and order, depending on who was telling the story. Since the breakup of the Soviet Union, the teams had been used in Georgia, Uzbekhistan and Chechnya to counter terrorism and to suppress civil dissent. They had done some joint training with the German GSG9 and he had heard that the SAS had come over to observe some of their operations. Nash supposed that, like the SAS, they were the blunt instrument used to carry out the tasks that the politicians wanted done but didn't want to spell out. He was glad they would be on his side.

'You mentioned back there,' Nash's thumb jerked back in the direction of the ambush, 'a new world order. What did you mean?'

'It seems to have begun in '93 in the Caribbean,' Yuri explained, his voice distorted through the headphones in Nash's flying helmet. 'The Colombians own much of Aruba, and they called a summit to talk about the future. Russians, Japanese, Nigerians, Americans, Sicilians – they all turned up wanting to get a share of the pie.'

'But I thought these people were all scrabbling in the same gutter,' Nash protested.

Yuri shook his head and went on to set out a terrifying scenario of a world carved up among different gangs with the Colombians controlling cocaine production, the Russians handling drug distribution in Europe, the Sicilians co-operating with them for a share of the profits, the Nigerians masterminding financial fraud. It was a vision of a world gone mad where laws, borders and sovereignty meant nothing. Only profit and expediency mattered.

'You make them sound unstoppable,' Nash replied.

'Well, look at the facts, David,' Yuri responded. 'One, they have more money than many of the governments who are trying to catch them – $500 billion in illegal cash being laundered each year.' Noticing the scepticism in Nash's eyes, Yuri continued. 'A trillion dollars in turnover, more than most countries' GNP and enough to make them a real world power – if they ever choose to exercise that power together. Two, these groups have absolutely no scruples. What matters is getting what they want. They are unbelievably violent – did you know that we had more people killed by gangs last year than in the whole nine years of the Afghan war?'

'Let's not get carried away here, Yuri,' Nash interrupted.

35

'Criminals have always been part of life. Sure, they're a bit richer and they have guns and power, but we've heard all this before. Remember the terrorism of the sixties and seventies? We were all on the brink of revolution. Yet here we are. Democracies have survived and life goes on.'

'Jesus, David. You people are all so fucking complacent.' Even through the tinny relay of the microphone, the anger in Yuri's voice was clear. 'The end of the Cold War broke down all the barriers. There's no structure any more. Democracy? What fucking democracy? You think my country is democratic because we had a few votes and elected some people? You think there's democracy in Poland? In Ukraine? These countries are barely managing to survive and every one of them is a target of the gangs.'

Yuri began to tick off points on his fingers. 'Moscow: forty thousand businesses owned by gangs; the southern republics: three million acres of marijuana and half that of opium poppies, all new crop and around a quarter of the current world supply; Russia: $10 billion a year in lost exports siphoned off by the gangs; New York: five hundred Russian immigrants in the past three years, all from Moscow gangs. The seeds of chaos are being planted everywhere and now we have the new alliances. This is not terrorism. It's not the old-style robber barons. It's a threat to us all and we have to fight it.'

Suddenly, as if exhausted by his passion, he stopped himself and then reverted to the congenial figure that Nash knew better.

'Forgive me, David.' He laughed. 'Too much excitement for one day. I'm losing my balance.'

In perfect counterpoint to his words, the helicopter began a long looping turn that brought the city into clear view through David's window. He could see the two wide beltways ringing the city, the tall, grey apartment blocks that mark

36

each suburb and the trough of socialist architecture. But the treasures were visible too, the cupolas of the churches that had been deserted during the communist era and were once again filled to capacity; the parks that made Moscow one of the world's most attractive cities and, finally, the massive structure of the Kremlin itself with the Moskva river curling gently along its southern walls.

Flying low, they traversed the city and passed over the inner loop road and then Nash picked up the distinctive twenty-two-storey white building that was the headquarters of the SVR at Yasenevo. (It was one of the secret jokes of the Cold War that the KGB had modelled their own headquarters building on the CIA's at Langley, even down to the marble entranceway and the commemorative stars for those who had died on duty.) They landed in the senior officers' car park next to the Y-shaped older building.

There were four black vehicles waiting for them and, as Nash walked down the steps from the helicopter, the biggest man Nash had ever seen eased himself out of one of them: a Ford Explorer – the Rolls-Royce of the special forces world.

'David, this is Captain Dmitri Yerokhin.' Nash felt his hand engulfed. He expected a crushing grip but felt a brief spasm and then he was set free. Looking into the captain's deep-set, dark eyes, he thought he detected a crinkle of laughter. A man who had to prove nothing, Nash thought.

The Russian opened one of the Explorer's rear doors and ushered Nash and Yuri inside. Nash's senses were immediately assaulted by that mixture of cordite and camaraderie that men accustomed to combat seem to ooze from every pore. The six other men crowded in the back were all dressed for battle in the standard one-piece neoprene suits and heavy body armour common to all special forces. The silent watchfulness and the sense of coiled tension was common, too. What was different about these people was that they all seemed so huge. It was partly the bulk of weapons and armour but also simply that they were big men. If this had been the SAS, Nash's six-foot frame would have blended in nicely. Here, he felt both vertically challenged and inferior.

As soon as the doors closed, the small convoy moved off. There were no blaring sirens, just an orderly progression out of the SVR compound and then due south towards the centre of the city. It was one of those magical Moscow spring days when winter is finally over, the blossoms are out on the cherry trees and the weather is warm enough to believe that summer is just round the corner. Another time, Nash would have spent the day strolling the Arbat or admiring the cosmopolitan women who were now a feature of Tverskaya Street. Yuri's voice dragged him back to the harsher realities of the present.

'They've recced the building. It's just behind Ulitsa Povarskaya which seems appropriate enough.' Seeing Nash's quizzical expression, Yuri went on: 'Cook Street. It's where the Czar's cooks once lived and I guess our targets are continuing the tradition, only using different ingredients.'

A rumble from the front seat indicated some kind of interpolation from the team leader. Yuri listened and then turned back to Nash.

'That area is filled with large houses. No front gardens so we have to go in straight from the street. Lots of traffic in and out but we've no idea of numbers inside. Watchers on the roof and at the front gate. Dmitri says getting in is no problem. Getting out might be a bit more difficult.'

'Wouldn't it be safer to wait for dark and move in then?' Nash asked.

'Waiting is too risky,' Yuri replied with finality. 'The team we intercepted probably had some check calls to make. The longer we wait the more likely the whistle is to blow. We go in now.'

38

They had left the sparsely populated outer suburbs some minutes earlier and were now closing on the centre with their driver maintaining a steady seventy miles per hour, apparently oblivious of traffic lights and other vehicles. It was the typical arrogance of the professional soldier who is totally confident in his ability to survive shot and shell and come out the other side. Fine for them, Nash thought to himself. He felt no such security and merely wanted to get to journey's end and get all this over with.

The car made a left turn and Yuri leaned across Nash to point out the sights.

'We're on the Garden Ring. The Gorky Memorial Museum coming up on your right in a couple of minutes,' he said conversationally. 'Nice area this. Bit like Hampstead. Lots of artists, actors, authors, that kind of thing. Quiet neighbourhood. Good for what they want.'

Dmitri gestured with a chopping motion off to his left and the car pulled in to the kerb.

'Is this it?' asked David.

'Not quite, but we're not far away,' said Yuri. 'Time to get suited up.'

Men lugging equipment began to pile out on to the pavement and Nash followed Yuri to stand on the concrete, squinting in the bright light after the tinted windows of the Explorer. The other vehicles had all pulled up behind them and in moments the pavement was festooned with black-suited men busy with all the checks that can make the difference between a successful mission and dead friends.

Nash accepted a piece of body armour which he was pleased to note covered both neck and crotch, unlike the standard British army issue which seemed to assume that bullets somehow only headed for the chest. He shrugged into it and immediately felt his shoulders sag under the weight. He felt Dmitri's hand drawing him towards the rear of the second vehicle. The tailgate was down, displaying an array of weaponry fixed to clips along both sides and on the back flap. Nash recognized many of the weapons including several variants of the AK-47, a 9 mm Makarov, and plenty of the more familiar western guns like the Heckler HK53 and two of the CAWs assault guns favoured by the Americans. As usual, Nash thought, the boys liked their toys. He had never been one of those who can sit in the bar after a bit of range practice discussing the merits of this or that type of ammunition round or the different rates of fire of pistols. He had hoped he would never need such knowledge.

'We will stay in the background,' said Yuri. 'No sense in us two getting shot. We'll leave that to the heroes.' He picked up a 9 mm Beretta with a laser sight fitted underneath the barrel, unclipped a holster from the rack and handed them both to Nash.

Behind him the men in the last two vehicles had been busy bolting ladders on to the roof racks. The Russians had grown so used to observing the extraordinary behaviour of those in authority that none of the passers-by thought or dared to come and question them. Instead, a small band of curious onlookers had gathered at a respectful distance to watch as two men climbed up each of the four ladders while a further six men clung precariously to the roof itself.

'With the house being on the street, we can go in fast on the ground floor and these guys will go in through the first-floor windows,' Yuri explained. 'That way we should be able to clear the house before they manage to get properly organized.' He gripped Nash's arm and shook it. 'We hope, eh, David? We hope.'

They piled back into the vehicles. This time, there was no chatter and none of the snickers, burps and grunts that mark the preliminaries for action. Each man was focused on his mission, thinking ahead to the operation and what it might bring. It was a brief moment for reflection – not about the agony of the gaping wound or the darkness of death; there lay hesitation and failure. Instead each man knew with total certainty that the mission was going to be a success. They were the best and the best win. There was no room for doubt.

Looking around at these fierce warriors, Nash felt very alone. Oh sure, he had been trained, but the day down at Hereford had been more of a jolly jape with the secret warriors. *He* would never actually have to do any of that stuff, that was *their* job. And now here he was, bowels turning to water, throat constricting, mouth parched. But there was no turning back. Nervously, his hand dropped to the butt of the pistol, as if the feel of the metal would provide the reassurance he needed.

The driver gunned the engine as they sped through the streets. There was no attempt at stealth, just a lurching, speeding crazy run that seemed to go on for hours but in fact lasted only a couple of minutes. Nash heard Dmitri shouting into a small microphone around his neck. The words were impossible to decipher but the sense of exhortation and command was clear. The mission was a Go.

As they rounded the final corner, Nash saw two men standing in the street, weapons pointed like thin sticks up towards a building on the left. He saw the small puffs of smoke as each man fired several times and then, like a parody of a John Ford western, three men came into his vision describing perfect curves as they arced through the air to hit the pavement. There was no sound, just a jumble of broken limbs and the spraying of blood from skulls that had splintered on the hard ground. The guards had been taken out.

The lead vehicle came to a stop in the middle of the street, the second immediately behind. Without pause the third mounted the pavement and passed them on the inside to halt against the wall. The two ladders on the car's roof pivoted forward until they lay against the wall. As Nash followed Yuri out of their car, he saw the first Russian dive head-first through the first-floor window, his Kevlar helmet breaking the glass and his body armour clearing the debris for those who were following on his heels. Immediately, there was the sound of gunfire and screams as the dreadful business began of clearing one room after another.

He felt Yuri's hand on his arm pulling him forward through the wreckage of the wooden front door that had been felled with four rounds from the CAWs. In different circumstances, this might have been a great house to visit for a dinner party. High ceilings, with the angles and curves of art deco that gave this part of Moscow its distinctive style. But it was fear, not fashion, that was uppermost in Nash's mind. He withdrew the pistol from its holster in his waistband and used it to nose ahead of him as if it could smell out danger before it found him. Dmitri's large back was ducking and weaving in front. The Russian's huge hand made an underarm throw to his left and an egg arced into a room off the main passage. There was the thunder of an explosion and then a blinding light as the flash-bang did its work. A man emerged from the room, hands over his ears and was then pushed back by a burst from the Russian's stubby machine-gun. Now was not the time to take prisoners. Now was the time to survive.

Now that action was driving him, Nash, too, felt caught up in the adrenaline rush. His fear had gone, replaced by a tingling, stirring sense of place and time. Here he was alive. Now he was ready to kill, to defend, to attack. But everywhere he turned, the Russians had been there before him. They were the professionals and he was simply the passenger.

Treading over debris and bodies, Nash worked his way slowly to the back of the building. There appeared to be one main hallway with rooms to right and left and a central staircase leading to the other floors, from where there were sporadic gunshots that grew less and less frequent as the threat was negated.

Nash found himself at the far end of the house looking through a miraculously still-intact glass door out on to a lovely peaceful, daffodil-filled garden. The glass of the door was spotted with blood.

'The building is secured,' Yuri walked up to him, a pistol dangling loosely from his hand. 'Fifteen of theirs dead or wounded, two of ours down, but they'll live.'

'What about the drugs?' Nash asked.

'Ah. The drugs.' Yuri appeared discomfited. 'We expected a factory and we've found a house. A few bandits, certainly, but in Moscow these days that's not unusual. No drugs. No factory.' He ran his left hand through his hair and then wiped off the sweat on his trousers. Pulling in favours for a successful mission for which everyone can take credit was one thing. Being responsible for a daylight raid on a quiet suburban house that produced nothing except dead bodies was quite another.

Nash looked around, taking in the decoration and the style of the building. He remembered the ambush on the road and the way the drugs had been so carefully concealed. His subconscious made the connection even as he began to reply to Yuri.

'Surely, all these old houses had a basement, somewhere for the servants to live,' he said tentatively.

'Of course!' Yuri shouted and yelled something in Russian at Dmitri who was standing talking to one of his men further down the hall. The big Russian grabbed a weapon from the man and walked back towards them, the gun muzzle-down. As he walked his right hand squeezed the trigger of the shotgun and each step was punctuated by a loud 'boom'. The solid shot powered through the wooden floor, leaving fist-sized holes through which bright light flowed. Dmitri fired one last time as he reached Nash and, peering down through the smoke, Nash could clearly see another room. As he looked closer, he could make out the terrified face of a man who was hunched against the wall, waiting fearfully for the next bombardment from above.

Dmitri's deep rumble echoed along the passage and through the floor.

'He's warning them to come up or grenades will drop down through each hole in the next ten seconds,' Yuri explained.

There was a moment's pause and then a hidden door in the wall behind the stairs opened and the man Nash had seen through the hole in the floor walked out with his hands raised in the air. Even without the white coat he was wearing, this bespectacled middle-aged man was no gunman. He looked exactly what he was: a terrified lab technician.

With Dmitri leading, Nash and Yuri descended the twelve steps to the basement and found the treasure they had been searching for. It was a single long room with benches lining both walls and the paraphernalia of a laboratory littering the tables. Nash strolled down the room with Yuri and watched as the Russian's despondency of a few minutes earlier was replaced by the elation of a man who has gambled and won.

'This time we got them right where it hurts,' Yuri exclaimed, his left hand coming up and miming a fist closing around a man's balls.

On a large bench lay hundreds of *matryoshkas*, the nesting sets of dolls that are so popular among tourists in Russia. Inside one there is another and then another until the tiniest is a delicate piece of wood carving. Yuri picked one up, carefully opening each doll until he reached the carving, and then opening that up, too. Nestling inside the little fat body was a small sachet of white powder.

'Perfect,' Yuri said admiringly. 'Every tourist who comes to Russia buys one of these. Great distribution system.'

A few minutes' exposure in the space had made Nash want to vomit. The smell of chemicals, particularly the ammonia, was overwhelming. The technicians had clearly tried to combat the stench by festooning the walls with small containers of air freshener. The effect was a sickly sweet aroma that clogged his senses. He breathed as shallowly as possible and longed for some fresh Moscow air.

'Look,' Yuri exclaimed. 'They've been bringing in the cocaine as paste and then refining it here.' He pointed out boxes labelled GARLIC PASTE – PRODUCE OF FRANCE, and the hundreds of empty jars that had been discarded. There were flagons of sulphuric acid, drums of ether and hydrochloric acid and box after box of powdered baby milk which Nash supposed were all used in the processing of the coca paste into cocaine.

Yuri pulled open the door of a freezer that stood against one wall. Aside from a shelf filled with meat labelled USDA PRIME it was empty.

'Maybe they've just shipped out a load,' he said, half to himself. 'Still, there's enough here to put a decent dent in the market for the next few months.' He turned to Nash.

'Thank you, David. I know you went out on a limb to come here. But it worked, didn't it?' he enthused. Maybe people will look back on the past few days as an example of what might be possible between us now. This' – Yuri's hand encompassed the laboratory, the piles of material and the papers that littered a number of the desks – 'will take us a while to go through, but I'll keep you informed.'

'Thanks,' said Nash.

'Oh, and David,' said the Russian, 'I owe you one.'

Now that was a marker that might be worth calling in, Nash thought to himself.

4

WITH THE DRUGS bust completed and the
Russians' interrogation of both the smugglers and the chem-
ists under way, Nash had reported back to the Moscow
Embassy where the SIS station chief presided over a smaller
office and a larger number of outlying undercover officers.
While the interrogations might have produced pure gold, SIS
wanted none of its people anywhere within range while it was
taking place. The SVR might have become more democratic
in some ways but its interrogation methods remained brutally
efficient. For Nash even to observe the kind of behaviour the
SVR team would adopt in the cause of extracting information
was not a sensible move. If it leaked out that someone from
the Office was present, heads would roll and the first to go
bouncing down the hill would be Nash's.

He had filed a brief report and then caught the morning
flight to London, risking becoming another Aeroflot statistic
in order to answer the urgent summons home. The Underground from Heathrow had dropped him at Victoria and
then it was a short walk across the bridge to the south bank
of the Thames and the new headquarters.

There was never a committee to welcome the weary hunter
home from the field, just a casual hello from whoever was in
the Centre at the time. The exact nature of the assignment
was always secret so there was never any specific gossip, just
the general camaraderie of an élite unit. The first task was the

written report which was sent directly upstairs to Diana Binsted, the Director of the HITC. Using internal e-mail, she would either distribute it without comment or issue the summons for something a little more personal. Nash knew the call would come; with Russia, it always went that way with Diana.

He had hoped to escape to get a decent night's sleep before having to confront the realities of the debrief but it was not to be. The fatal hesitation as he was leaving his work area was his undoing. The phone rang and, as usual, he was simply unable to resist picking it up to see who was on the other end. The summons was gruff and immediate, so putting his coat and bag back down, he headed for the lift.

His knock on the Director's door was answered with a curt 'In.' Nash sat before his boss's desk and waited for the storm to break.

Diana's forefinger hit the Execute button on the keyboard, which flashed green and then darkened as the type vanished. She turned in the black swivel chair to face Nash who was watching her carefully over the rim of a china cup filled with coffee.

'This was supposed to be a WAR mission, not some kind of free-for-all shoot 'em up,' she accused. 'Watch, Analyse and Report means just that. As it is, we have a few more dead bodies, a bust to keep the Russians happy and not much more intelligence than when we began.'

Nash said nothing and swallowed another mouthful of coffee. At least this was the genuine stuff and not that processed filth from downstairs, he reflected. Whatever else you might say about Diana, she did try to keep the barbarians at bay.

Diana pressed forward accusingly. 'Well?'

'You've read the report,' he replied. 'This is Russia we're talking about. It's bedlam out there. Their country's falling apart and there's damn all between them and the hoods who want to take it over. I'd have preferred something a little simpler too, but you can write all the rules you want back here – out there it's a different game. The boys want results. Long-term operations are out, instant fixes are in. And they don't give a damn what I or anyone else think.'

He shrugged, the movement expressing all the frustration and hopelessness of dealing with people who wouldn't play by the same rules.

'We got the best we could out of the operation. We smashed one smuggling ring, shut down a lab and established new links between the Russian gangs and gangs overseas. Seems to me that's a pretty fair return. If you think we can roll up an organization, you're living in fantasyland. The best we can get is a bit of aggravation for the opposition and some int on routes, people and future plans. And that's just what we got. As far as –'

Diana's hand slapped down on the surface of her desk.

'No, David,' she interrupted. 'That's not the best we can get. The best we can get is the intelligence we need without having one of our officers acting like some kind of cowboy. Nobody from the Office has been killed in action since the Korean War and I'm not about to allow you to break the record through some macho action that you think is fun but I know is just plain stupid.'

Nash recalled the gut-wrenching fear as he came under fire. If she thought that was fun, she was crazy.

'My job was to work with the Russians,' Nash replied, the anger clipping the words and giving his voice a sharp, abrupt edge. 'They say "Come with us" and I say "Terribly sorry, but I have to stay at home minding the shop"? These boys want commitment, not a bunch of bloody rules. As it is, we've got real cred with Parashvili and his people and that's going to be worth gold in the future.'

He paused, understanding that there was genuine concern behind Diana's aggression.

'I'm sorry if I went too far but you know that's what it's like in the field. Think on your feet, go with the mission, all that stuff. I think we got a result. And I'm here to talk about it.' He grinned, hoping to engage her in his success. He was relieved to notice a slight quiver at the side of her mouth and realized that he had weathered the storm.

'Yeah. Well, at least the Russians came through,' she conceded.

Parashvili had shared what intelligence had been gleaned so far from the interrogation and he promised that there was more to come. Nash passed it to Diana who shared it around the building. After that, it might even reach the Joint Intelligence Committee and thus an audience that really mattered in the political corridors of power. The important thing was that there had been something to pass on.

'Parashvili is keen enough and after this he owes me one.' Nash smiled slightly. 'Primakov has clearly decided that he needs us to keep in with the politicos back home. The more business he does with us, the better their intelligence and the more kudos he gains. So far, it's been a reasonable trade.'

Diana tapped her black Mont Blanc pen reflectively against her teeth.

'Well, I suppose we can sell this little operation as another triumph of light over darkness. At least the Minister will be grateful that we've managed to keep another shipment off the streets. One more small success in the never-ending war to keep our masters on side and the Treasury in its kennel.' She laughed softly, cynically.

The Secret Intelligence Service had survived the cuts in the early nineties which had decimated the MoD, the Foreign Office and just about every other government department, but only just. And the move from Century House (or Gloom Hall, as it was known) to their brand-new £450 million home near the Houses of Parliament was a mixed blessing:

every time a minister or a critical MP drove by on their way to work, they only had to glance to their right to be reminded how much money intelligence was costing the nation. Small wonder then that Diana needed every crumb she could get.

The Director rose from her desk and moved over to a window. The sun was shining outside, a perfect English spring day. But no windows opened and every pane of glass was covered by blinds to deflect the lasers of anyone trying to listen to the conversation inside. Just in case anyone should raise a blind, the glass was covered in a copper overlay to prevent cameras seeing through. Additional protection was provided by the waterfall of Muzak which cascaded down the inside of every window, inaudible to the human ear but enough to deflect any microphone. If only those MPs knew, Nash thought. Far from being a palace, this was a sealed prison. And what was visible was just the beginning of the bars. All the silicon-encased computers were housed in lead-lined rooms to prevent electronic eavesdropping. Special telephone, fax and computer cables were vacuum sealed so that any attempt to interfere with the lines could be instantly detected. All access points to the building were covered by high resolution cameras with zoom, night vision and 24-hour recording capabilities. Rumour had it that every corridor and every room, including the cubicles housing the coffee machines, were as carefully monitored as the outside of the building. So, there was little of the humanity that affects most office relationships.

Diana levered two slats of the blind apart and peered outside, eyes squinting slightly in the sunlight.

'We've heard from Spitz,' she said. The long fingers of her right hand toyed with a large purple brooch pinned to her cream shirt.

David felt the beginnings of a knot gathering in his stomach at this tell-tale habit that betrayed nervous tension. It usually presaged trouble coming in his direction. He guessed that he would soon be back in the world of NOC – Non-Official Cover. It was known as the School of Hard Knocks, which these days was a pretty apt description of what the business had become. Instead of using the diplomatic cover of the Embassy as a base from which to work in a foreign country, SIS now increasingly used NOC. What SIS wanted was local businessmen, low-level government officials who might get promoted and produce some real gems in the years ahead, or simply academics and journalists who knew what was going on and were well plugged in to the gossip circuit. At various times in recent months, Nash had been a visiting businessman selling sanitary ware (known in the Office as the loony cover), a tourist, a management consultant and a banker. He also had a cover with the Embassy that worked perfectly for his relationship with Parashvili, and one as a writer research-ing a new tourist guide to Russia that the Office felt would allow him to travel freely without suspicion.

'GCHQ passed us a message last night,' Diana continued. Spitz wants a meet, as soon as possible. He suggests Kiev.'

David had met Spitz twice in the past. He was a well-placed salesman in the defence sales network run by the Russian Ministry of Defence who had been recruited three years earlier. Of course, Spitz was not his real name but a codename provided by Miss Piggy, the Centre's mainframe, to conceal his identity from everyone except the handful of people who either met him or handled the raw material he produced before it was sanitized and passed along.

'Why the urgency?' Nash asked. 'There's a routine pass in a couple of weeks. It's not like him to get excited.'

'He doesn't say. But he's given us the crash code so I want you out there tonight and we'll try for a meeting in two days.'

Nash walked out of Binsted's office, turned right towards the atrium that rose eight floors at the front of the building facing the river and then descended one flight of stairs to the IT Department on the third floor, sandwiched between Personnel and Proliferation. The recent move had quadrupled the size of their empire and IT had been given one of the choice locations, reflecting the new status of technology in the organization.

Nash inserted his card into the lock, punched in the four-digit code and waited for the security camera to match face with code and card. There was a click and the door swung open. He pushed open the swing door to his left and entered Alex's office.

It was difficult to tell that this was the new heart of SIS. Two computer screens sat on the desk in front of her, one an ordinary Apple Mac, the other an unmarked screen and plain keyboard. It was this system that really mattered, that linked this office with the mainframes six floors below. With the power to handle 575 million calculations a second, the system could decrypt intercepted messages, encode transmissions for rebroadcast in fractions of a second and, in the right hands, send electronic pulses around the world to unlock the most secure database doors.

To the left of the terminal stood a small rubber figure that Nash recognized as Saddam Hussein. Hit his head and, after a few moments of being squashed flat, he would bounce back to his original shape. A Buddha, stomach shiny from good luck rubs, stood to the right and a single cream telephone with a dozen speed-dial buttons completed the furniture on the simple, light wood desk. The walls were plain except for a large, framed silk flag with Lenin and Stalin stitched in profile and the words 'Workers of the World Unite' in Russian over their heads. A souvenir of Moscow, it was a small joke and a reminder to everyone just how far they had come.

Alex had her back to him, her fingers clicking softly over the keys. The sun was coming in the window at a slight angle to hit her face from the side and highlight her dark, wavy hair which fell in a fashionable bob to her neck. Her eyes were focused on the screen, the small crow's feet indicative of a slight squint as she tried to screen out the sun. She looked so lovely, so gentle, a welcome contrast to the stark efficiency he had experienced three floors above and a glimpse of the reality it was so easy to forget in the cycle of briefing, mission and debrief that had become the pattern of his life.

Noticing his reflection in the glass, she spun her chair round to face him.

'So, David. More trouble?' She turned towards him, her mouth opening in a welcoming laugh.

'How did you know that?'

'You forget I can use the IMP to access all the ARs and, given Diana's views about you and the Russians, she was clearly going to be pissed off.'

David groaned and put his hands to his head in apparent agony.

'Christ almighty,' he protested. 'First Daemon and now you. I thought we had agreed that you would keep the jargon to a minimum. I'm just a Neanderthal from HIT, you know. Not one of your own.'

Alex turned back to the terminal, her fingers starting to move over the keyboard as she began speaking. If Daemon was the explorer testing the frontiers of cyberspace, Alex was the practical guide to the available technology. Where he flew with flights of fantasy, she was firmly planted in the Office to make sure that the system worked, that the officers had the technology they needed to do their jobs.

'The Interface Message Processor gets me in to the master system.' She typed four digits. 'A code gets me into the Agent Report sub-directory, another code for your personal directory and there we have it.' A final flourish and Nash saw his report of the Russian mission flash on to the screen.

'Very clever.' He glanced at the screen and saw Diana's initials and then a space indicating she had put in her personal code to show that she had read the file. Ominously, there were several blank lines to follow, evidence that she had added her comments for others with a similar clearance to read.

'What gives with Diana?' he asked. 'I was lucky to get out of that Russian trip in one piece and all she gives me is grief.'

'You know about Moscow?' Alex asked.

In 1984 Diana had been stationed in Moscow running Brass, one of SIS's assets in the Russian Ministry of Defence. He was young, enthusiastic, the son of a minister and exceptionally well placed. Their relationship was never sexual – that would have been unforgivably unprofessional – but it was clear that there was mutual attraction between the source and his handler. It was never discovered exactly what had gone wrong, but a brush pass at the Petrovsko-Razumovskaya Metro stop had been compromised. Suddenly they were both surrounded by goons from the KGB and whisked off to the cells behind Dzerzhinsky Square.

This was just after Oleg Gordievsky had left the country, courtesy of an SIS escape pipeline. Gordievsky had been the designated head of station in London for the KGB and was flagged for promotion to major-general before he had been fingered by Ames and the sleuths in counter-espionage. The KGB had been furious that MI6 had penetrated so deep into the heart of their own organization and wanted revenge. Diana and Brass provided the perfect outlet for their fury. She wasn't tortured – a diplomat and intelligence officer was immune from such acts in case it provoked an underground war that nobody wanted. Instead, she was forced to sit in the room while Brass was put through the wringer. Nash had never heard just what it was they did to him but he assumed it had been the usual round of drugs, electric shocks and simple violence. He died and she was released two days later, a shadow of her former self.

It had taken a year of therapy with Mike Reiss, the SIS shrink, before Diana was back at her desk. Outwardly, she was the same aggressive, intelligent and committed person she had always been. But now there was a patina of darkness. There were moments when she appeared obsessed about the new Russia, as if the old regime had scarred her so deeply that she found it impossible to accept that things really were different.

'Sure, I've heard the history,' Nash replied. 'But there was no need for her to take it out on me.'

He moved over to one of the black swivel chairs that sat to one side of Alex's desk.

'Now how about telling me about Spitz. What's got him so excited?'

Alex cleared the screen, fingered the keyboard once more and another file was called up from the HotSit or Hot Situation message centre. The coding at the head of the message showed it had arrived at GCHQ that morning, been decrypted by Cray 3, read by analyst 3725 and sent to SIS at 10.50.

'I wonder what Spitz has to say that's so urgent,' Nash said. 'The only thing that matters to us in Russia right now is denuclearization and an imploding economy. Those are hardly Spitz's turf.'

In Russia, Spitz was one of the best. Sources are recruited by a foreign intelligence agency for reasons known by the acronym MICE for Money, Ideology, Compromise and Ego. Spitz was the most reliable kind; motivated entirely by ideology, specifically his belief that gangsters were destroying his country by buying everything within in it and selling it abroad. It was he who kept SIS apprised of arms movements, allowing them either to encourage their political masters to take action or to let the competition in the Defence Export Services Organization of the MoD know just where the Russians were hoping to sell their surplus tanks and missiles. In the tough international market, which was currently awash in surplus weapons, SIS had managed to give DESO a key edge.

'The only way we can find out is by setting up the meet,' Alex replied. 'Let's go and get the HAA set up.'

They walked down the corridor and into one of the interior, windowless, rooms, only the four two-inch holes in each wall giving a hint of its purpose. This was where the source handlers in HIT prepared the messages for onward transmission to their people in the field. Gone are the days of radio contact; SIS had decided that the only secure method of message transmission was the encrypted hologram.

Nash stepped to the centre of the room and, speaking directly into the lens of the camera facing him, he told Spitz where and when to meet him. The message would be transmitted from GCHQ in Cheltenham that evening for onward transmission to an SIS cover operation in Paris, and from there reach Moscow.

Alex watched the performance on the video monitor, inserted the floppy disc with that day's encryption codes embedded in it and watched as the codes transformed David's face to a mass of indecipherable squiggles. Only Spitz, with an identical code, would be able to make sense of the message.

'What about something to eat?' Alex asked him as they made their way back to her office.

'Why not?' he replied. 'A chance to catch up before I hit the road again.'

After months of meeting, gossiping and sparring, Alex and David were colleagues making that journey from business into the more complex world of friendship. For David, the meal was another chance to get to know this fascinating woman who understood a technological world that remained mysterious to him. But there was more to Alex than bits and bytes; he wanted to find out just how much more.

David had had no one since Jaimie and work had become a substitute for what might have been. In recent months, he and Alex had grown close. She was one of the few anchors in his unstable world, yet she was so difficult to handle. Life, work, missions – they were the challenges he had learned to manage – but Alex? She was her own boss.

'So what happened with Diana?' Alex began, leaning forward expectantly. 'Every word.'

'Oh, the usual drama,' David shrugged. 'I can't decide whether she sees me as herself when she was younger and is jealous of my being in the field, or whether she really thinks I'm a complete wanker who shouldn't be allowed out without a white stick. Today, it seemed more like the latter.'

'Well, if it was that bad, I'm sure she'd be keeping you back at the Office,' Alex reassured him. 'Moan if you like, but travelling is your life these days. Three times in less than a month; much more and you may as well not come home.'

'I like to travel,' he protested. 'It keeps me busy.' Another flight, another hotel room, another brief adrenaline rush and then on to the next crisis. But there were times like today when the contrast between the out there and the here and now was just too stark.

'I could do with a few days doing nothing down at the cottage instead of being pushed off into the deep water yet again.' He leaned back in his chair, arms meeting above his head in a stretch. 'They never told us about any of this when we joined. You remember those chats in Carlton House Gardens?' She nodded, smiling at the shared memory of a procession of men and women wheeled in to tell them about how wonderful everything was going to be. There had even been 'The Magical Mr Memory' – a.k.a. George Higgins, circus performer – who could recite the players and scores of every football team since the year dot. He taught them the tricks of recalling conversations and data, all great fun but of little value when faced by a terrorist with murder in his heart and an AK-47 in his hands.

'For all you macho guys, it was as much about image as substance,' Alex teased. 'You all thought you were following Bond down the path of sex and saving the world.'

Nash snorted in disgust. 'I wish I'd had his job. You knew the enemy; the weapons were guns and fists with the odd gizmo thrown in to give you an edge. A martini at White's or Boodle's at the end of a bruising day. No computers, no nuclear proliferation, no biological weapons and none of the bureaucratic crap that rules our lives. God, we didn't even officially exist back then and now we have parliamentary oversight with a bunch of ignorant MPs breathing down our necks.

'When I go out there,' he gestured airily towards the Thames and the horizon, 'I have no idea where the threat is coming from. I'm supposed to co-operate with our new pals, the Russians. These days, the grenade is as likely to be lobbed from America as from Russia. And as for the gorgeous women – well, I've yet to see them. Present company excepted, of course,' he added hastily, taking a drink to cover his embarrassment.

Alex laughed, unoffended. She knew that every time Nash left the Office, he did so alone and he survived because of his quick brain and tough training. He might dismiss the legacy but it was clear enough to her.

'Don't ignore your heritage,' she mocked. 'If you look on your map you'll find that the Office is located at the end of Bondway – a message from our masters to remind us of the best recruiting agent the Office ever had. I for one am glad I wasn't around back then. All those boring old farts sitting around in their clubs talking about how they were going to change the world and never really doing anything.' She made a grunt of disgust, consigning the years of the Cold War to the scrapheap of history.

'Well, I *was* around back then,' Nash replied. 'Or at least for the back end of it. The difference is night and day. I was trained to work in a structure with sources we knew and methods we'd used for years. You could go to Moscow and everyone understood – the KGB and us – how the game was played. Go there now and it's anarchy. Ex-KGB running the gangs, the gangs running the country and us scrabbling around trying to keep pace with the chaos. It's madness.'

'So why bother?' Alex asked. 'You're young, single. You can do what you like. Take the money and run.' For the past four years, SIS had been running an early retirement scheme to bribe people to leave rather than having to fire them.

'It's not as simple as just taking the money,' he protested. 'It sounds trite maybe, but there's a job to do. We won the Cold War but there's plenty of other bastards out there who are just waiting to try and take us out. It would be easy enough to pack up and go into insurance or something but it would feel like quitting.' He grinned. 'Anyway, it's fun. Lots of travel, good expenses. Interesting people. Getting shot. You know, join the Office, see the world and die.'

She laughed. 'I thought movement was supposed to be what it's all about for you people: action, drama, the pace, the thrills.'

'It's not like that,' he protested. 'Or rather, it wasn't like that. I don't want to just sit on my arse form-filling, but you can have too much of a good thing. I'm not sure people understand how much our world has changed out there. And I'm not sure I can change enough to stay alive.'

Alex knew more than most about the people in HIT and their assignments but David had always been the odd man out. Most of the others seemed to fit the profile of the hired gun: men drawn in from the SAS and the SBS, a few others left over from the Cold War who had done interesting work in Northern Ireland or Hong Kong. But David was different. Just how different she wasn't sure but she sensed a depth in him that she found surprising and interesting. Curious, she had hacked into his file. There had been the usual reports from training, an assignment to Northern Ireland, a posting as the junior man to Moscow. But it was all very flimsy, with too many unexplained gaps. Her curiosity had been aroused. Now, she hoped to get some answers.

'Your file has been carefully sanitized,' Alex continued 'Not much personal stuff . . .'

The question was left hanging in the air, the question the Office had tried to avoid his being asked. Only the few who needed to know the truth actually did. The rest could only wonder. Alex was the first one to take the bull by the horns and ask him to his face. Nash paused and took a slow swallow of the Chardonnay.

'I went to Exeter to read languages originally, not because I knew what I wanted to do but simply because I had travelled with my parents and spoke some French and Spanish. I was approached there by an Office talent spotter. It was all very tentative. Typically British.' He smiled, remembering. 'Once I understood what was going on, it sounded very attractive. I liked the idea of belonging to something different and doing something worthwhile. It sounds very naïve now, but I really wanted to do my bit.

'In the old days,' he stopped himself, laughing. 'God, that makes me sound ancient. Let me rephrase that. A few years ago before the world turned, they had so many crazy rules. We could never admit who we were − not even to our families. Now we have MPs keeping an eye on us and there's even some poor bastard delegated to answer questions from the few favoured press who have the right phone number.'

Alex laughed. 'Well, you moles may not like the bright lights but it suits me just fine. All the gizmos I want and then some.' She leaned back in her chair, arms open wide. 'Now, this is the life.'

It was so easy for her, he thought. She never had to confront the fear of exposure, the terror of a discovered meeting or a compromised source. But perhaps that explained why he had joined SIS rather than settle for the humdrum world of the Foreign Office.

'A couple of years after I came out of the Fort,' he went on, 'they sent me to Northern Ireland as liaison with Five. The Province has been some kind of proving ground for us for years and I suppose they thought it would do me some good. Frankly it was pretty dull stuff. As usual Box were very protective of their turf and my remit was simply to open doors for them if they needed it. The reality was that they only asked once in the two years I was there. So, I spent my time on familiarization trips, seeing different units, finding out how the system worked over there, getting some understanding of just how impossible it all was.'

She leaned forward, nursing her glass, sensing that he was about to reveal the reason for the pain which she could feel inside him. Her eyes ran over his face taking in the lines at the corner of his mouth, the prominent cheekbones and jawline, the pale whiteness of the scar on his forehead. There was a tautness to him, she thought, a tension that was both attractive and disturbing.

'Damn,' said Nash, reaching into the pocket of his trousers and producing the bleeper which had begun to vibrate, indicating an incoming message. Opposite him, Alex was making similar movements. They both laughed, caught out by the dreaded umbilical cord that kept them attached to the office.

Nash read the small message screen and saw the number 1909, the date of MI6's founding and a modest joke by someone who wanted a signal that, if intercepted, would mean little or nothing to anyone outside the Office. There were other numbers for different emergencies but this was the most common, a signal that he needed to return to the Office immediately. He looked at Alex.

'The Office?' she asked. He nodded and gestured to a waiter for the bill.

Diana was waiting for them, a cup of coffee at her elbow. 'I'm sorry to drag you back like this,' she began. 'Particularly you, David. I know you've got a plane to catch, but I wanted to see you before you left and it seemed sensible to get you both in here at the same time.' She nodded in Alex's direction.

Nash saw that Diana looked tired and tense. The combination of long hours, coffee, cigarettes and, he suspected, whatever it was that had brought them here now, had drawn the skin tight across her face. The artificial lighting accentuated her greyish pallor. It was one of his more macabre habits but he sometimes thought he could see cancer in people: the drawn skin, slightly hollow cheeks and the colour were all tell-tale signs of a body's imminent betrayal. Now he thought that the pace would eventually make Diana a victim. What must have been an attractive profile when she was younger was looking increasingly worn.

'So, what's the panic?' he asked.

'It's the Americans,' she replied. There was not exactly a collective sigh from her audience but the shuffling and stretching showed what David and Alex both thought of this piece of news. Diana smiled ruefully, acknowledging their reaction.

'Yes, yes. I know. *Crise de jour* and all that. But this time they claim to have some good intelligence of trouble ahead that will directly affect you, David. They seem convinced it's both A1 and very serious,' Diana continued. 'Just how serious, we remain to be convinced. But if they're right, the civil war everyone has been predicting for the Ukraine since the end of the Empire is about to happen.'

They had all read the traffic over the past couple of years and the analysis had been uniformly gloomy. Ukraine suffered from runaway inflation, a basket-case economy and no prospects. Most of the eastern half of the country claimed Russian and not Ukrainian heritage and the Russian bear was waiting to pounce, with the military still decrying the loss of Empire and the political leadership terrified of civil war in its largest neighbour. All in all, a recipe for disaster. Nash recalled a report from the Joint Intelligence Committee a couple of months earlier that talked about the possible consequences of a real breakdown in law and order. It had been an apocalyptic scenario with dark talk of war spreading through Europe, NATO being dragged in and huge loss of life.

'Where do we fit in?' Nash asked.

'You're off to see Spitz,' Diana replied. 'We need to know anything he may have on the situation in the Ukraine, anything on Russia's plans, anything at all we can take back to the Americans. Washington thinks this might all go belly up in short order and if the Russians are going to intervene, we need a heads up a.s.a.p.'

She turned towards Alex.

'There may be information the Americans have missed and I want you to get on to GCHQ and have them trawl through the material for the past month or so and see what's there. You handle the liaison with them and try and bring me something I can offer to my masters.'

She nodded in the direction of Parliament which glowed in the distance. It was a still night and Nash could see the perfect reflection of Big Ben in the waters of the Thames. It was a romantic sight, a whole world away from the real darkness they were confronting.

'So, just who is this guy Kuchma?' The President leaned back in his brown leather armchair and looked at the Director of Central Intelligence. The DCI had grown to hate these moments: the President, unlit cigar clamped between his teeth, making the Cupid's bow of his mouth appear more like a landed fish gasping its last; shirt open and bare forearms crossed behind his head. It was not the casual nature of the dress that he disliked – the DCI himself was wearing the Washington uniform of dark shirt, boring tie and dark suit – but the intimidating nature of the man. The DCI was quietly spoken with the demeanour that reflected his training as a lawyer. He spoke softly in measured tones, his eyes sharply focused behind the wire-rimmed spectacles.

The President by contrast was sharp, tough and aggressive, subject to mood swings. An affable chuckle might be followed a minute later by one of the President's legendary eruptions; a three- or four-minute tirade filled with profanities and personal abuse. It was the uncertainty that the DCI had come to hate and, like all bullies who see themselves as moderate conciliators, the President sensed the weakness and did not hesitate to exploit it.

'As you know, Mr President, Leonid Kuchma was elected leader of the Ukraine in July 1994. He is pro-Russian – or at least more pro-Russian than his predecessor – and has taken some steps to bring his country closer to Moscow. Oil deals, some barter, talk of joint military exercises, and so forth.'

'And where does he stand on the nuclear issue?' the President asked. This was the key, the lynchpin of America's relations with Ukraine and the one issue that mattered above all others to the President. In early 1994, he had negotiated with President Kravchuk the destruction of all 1,600 of the Ukraine's nuclear weapons in exchange for $5 billion in aid.

But now there were signs that Kravchuk's successor Kuchma would renege on the deal and demand more money before signing the nuclear Non-Proliferation Treaty.

'That's unclear, Mr President,' said the DCI. 'Our information is that Kuchma is under severe internal pressure. Inflation is running at thirty points a month, the economy no longer resembles any known economic model and there's still considerable tension between the Russian supporters in the Crimea and the east and the nationalists in the west. All in all, it's a mess.'

'Frank was telling me there have been some problems around Romny,' the President said, his eyes flicking towards the National Security Adviser who sat off to his left. The DCI wanted to scream but kept himself in check so that none of his emotions showed in his face. For months, the President had not been reading the intelligence summaries that were faithfully delivered by the courier from Langley at 06.00 every day. These had been the touchstones on which previous incumbents had formed their policies but this one paid them almost no attention.

The President had promised that things would be different after the DCI took on the unenviable task of cleaning house at the Agency in the wake of the Ames affair and the revelations about the CIA's involvement in the murder of an American citizen in Guatemala. It had been the President at his smooth-talking best: arm around the shoulder, the low, honeyed voice promising instant access to the Oval Office, a Cabinet position and unwavering support. In part that is what had persuaded the DCI to take the job. But, of course, nothing had really changed and he had found himself becoming as frustrated as his predecessor.

And not reading the daily intelligence brief was simply insulting. Had the President done so, he would have known that, for the past two weeks, there had been reports of fighting in and around Romny, near Ukraine's eastern border with Russia. It was the headquarters of the 56th Guards Regiment which was mainly made up of Ukrainians from the east although commanded by officers of Russian origin, like most of the country's armed forces. The Guards Regiment had been sent east to ensure that pro-Russian sentiments there were kept in check. Now, apparently, the military had been failing to keep order. Troops were in the streets, there had been shooting and looting, the deadly combination that often marked the beginning of civil war.

'Some problems indeed, Mr President,' the DCI acknowledged with irony. 'We have hard evidence of at least fifty deaths in the last two days. There are indications that the riots may spread to Kharkov, Ukraine's second city. If that happens then Kuchma is sure to cancel next week's visit to the White House and we could be in for some very tough times.'

'Any sign of the Russians moving?' the President asked.

'Not so far. We know there are elements in the Russian military who would like to see the annexation of eastern Ukraine. Most of the people living there owe more loyalty to Moscow than to Kiev, but the President's kept them in check so far and we presume that he'll be able to hold the line.'

The President nodded and then swivelled in his chair to look out of the window on to the Rose Garden. His face, reflected in the glass, wore the look of a first-year schoolboy presented with a university examination paper. The DCI almost pitied him.

The Agency man looked round the room which had seen so many great men make decisions that have shaped the world. The recent redecoration of the Oval Office by an out-of-town friend of the First Lady had produced what to the DCI's jaundiced eye was something between a Turkish brothel and East Coast gangster chic.

The President, in a move that had since been the subject of many Washington jokes, had chosen the presidential desk first used in the Oval Office by his hero, John Kennedy. It was known as the Resolute Desk, an unfortunate name given that this incumbent was generally considered to be one of the most irresolute men to have sat at it. As usual, his In tray was impressively empty and the desk was uncluttered apart from a clay paperweight with the word DAD inscribed by his daughter, a pair of scissors from a recent ribbon-cutting and a miniature version of the campaign bus; mementoes from happier times, when the promise of the future was unsullied by the realities of the present and the recent past.

The President swivelled back to face his audience.

'And what is the state of their nuclear arsenal?'

This was the key issue and the one that the DCI hesitated to address. Once again, he was going to be the messenger bearing the bad news that one of the President's few foreign policy triumphs was going sour.

'Since your agreement with Kravchuk, the Ukrainians have only gotten rid of around a quarter of their SS-19s. At that rate it will be well into the next century before even that part of the arsenal is destroyed. And they've done zero about the SS-24s which are the real menace.'

'So what do I tell Kuchma next week?' the President asked.

'I'm afraid that's not the worst of it,' the DCI continued. 'Officially, those weapons are under Russian control, but we now have credible information that the Ukrainians have succeeded in getting access to some of the SS-24s, which is very bad news indeed.

'We believe that Kuchma will raise three issues with you. First, he'll argue that the time is still not right for him to sign the NPT. Second, he'll complain about the slow progress towards denuclearization, arguing that it's all the fault of the Russians. Third, he'll say that he's under great economic pressure and that his country urgently needs more assistance or the nuclear weapons might get into the wrong hands.'

'Christ. You're telling me he's coming to town with a gun to my head?' The President's round face reddened as he began to work himself up into a fury. 'That fucking little shit. I won't eat dirt from that bankrupt sonofabitch. He has nothing, he is nothing and he'll stay that way!'

The passion died as quickly as it had swelled. He took the cigar and put the chewed and soggy end in the ashtray as another thought occurred to him.

'Ukraine with nukes. Jesus, Congress will eat me alive.' He passed a hand across his face. 'So, what are we going to do?' he asked the CIA chief.

'Well, first of all you'll need to discuss all this with the Secretary of State and with Defense,' he replied. The two men were the architects of the President's Russian policy, and had consistently argued for a soft approach to Russia. 'But my advice is to play hardball,' he added. 'Kuchma doesn't yet have access to all the missiles. For now, you hold the purse strings and Russia controls the missiles. In the short term, your problem is going to be keeping the civil unrest under control and you'll need Russia's help for that. In the longer term, you have to force both Russia and Ukraine to do business together and disarm in the process.

'The one thing you must avoid is civil war in the Ukraine with Russia watching on the sidelines waiting to intervene,' the DCI warned. 'Civil war would mean we would have to do something. Ukraine is not Georgia or Chechnya. We would have to intervene if the Russians got involved. That could start a new Cold War and none of us wants that.'

The President leaned back and pivoted in his chair. Once again, he took in the peaceful sight of the Rose Garden, his thoughts reaching out, seeking a way forward to avoid the nightmare unfolding before him.

5

JUST BEHIND THE Morisa Embankment on the south side of the Moskva stands a nightclub called Hell, a totem to the new degeneracy that has hit Moscow in the last five years. It is here that the young toughs from the gangs come to flaunt their gold jewellery, their thick wads of American dollars and their brassy women, and where well-heeled foreigners come to pick up one, or perhaps two, of the prostitutes who gather around the tables near the entrance. It was also one of Pyotr Sakharovsky's more visible investments.

Like its counterparts in the west, Hell served high-priced drinks, terrible food and a very loud diet of rock music. It also made Pyotr a great deal of money, giving him status and access in a city where visibility helps produce both. The men he controlled were known as the Lubertsy gang, or the Lubers, after the suburb where Pyotr lived and from where most of the recruits still came. The years of reform under Gorbachev saw a rising curve in the Russian crime business. The Soviet Union was falling apart, central control had all but disappeared and the old Moscow-organized and officially sanctioned corruption of the Brezhnev era had given way to almost pure capitalism – albeit capitalism backed by a gun.

Under Pyotr's careful guidance, early adventures into protection had expanded to embrace prostitution, then drugs, then import–export – consumer durables in, antiques, arms and art out – so that Pyotr had become one of the *vory v zakone* (thieves within the code), as the godfathers of the gangs are known. In the few short years it took for Russia to fall apart, Pyotr and his fellow godfathers prospered in ways that were almost unimaginable outside the country. He had become a leader among the 5,000 criminal gangs, known as the Organizatsiya, that employ around three million people whose sole business is corruption – of people, commerce or the country – a business which pervades every level of Russian life, from the 20,000 police officers fired for corruption each year to the state factories now owned by the gangs. Sakharovsky's was a raw power, hard earned on one of the new frontiers of capitalism.

On his second stroll of the evening through this small part of his empire, Pyotr basked in the approbation of his guests. Those who knew him reached out to shake his hand, squeeze his arm or whisper the latest piece of gossip. For the less fortunate, without access to the great man, it was clear that he was someone of importance and they watched with interest as he moved from table to table, occasionally raising a hand to bring a waiter bearing yet another bottle of Louis Roederer Cristal to a favoured guest. It could have been a scene in any nightclub in Europe. Only the two watchful bodyguards trailing in his wake, their right hands permanently under their jackets ready to pivot their folding-stock Ingrams into a firing position, suggested this was a more dangerous environment.

It was the time of night when life for the two bouncers on the door became boring. The club was full so they had little to do except turn away guests or eject drunks from inside. The best part of the evening – the arrival of the gaudy tarts, some of whom were extraordinarily beautiful – had long since passed and both men were now just waiting until dawn when they could head home.

There was a scream of tyres which competed with the sound of the rock music blaring from inside the building. Four Volvo saloons pulled up in Indian file outside the club entrance. There was a brief pause, an apparent stillness, despite the incessant muffled pounding of the music, and then the ordered world of the bouncers disintegrated.

As the cars settled, the two doormen moved as one, their hands reaching under their jackets for their weapons, but they were far too late. Before their hands had even touched butts, there was the coughing of a silenced machine-gun firing through the open window of the lead Volvo. The bullets moved from left to right in a slow traverse across each body. There were no screams, no sounds even, apart from the click of the gun-slide moving rapidly back and forth to expel one round and chamber another. The bullets made a hard slapping sound as if a fist were being driven repeatedly into the palm of a hand, their deadly force shredding flesh and bone, spraying the front door and wall of the club with a slimy cocktail of grisly matter.

To those familiar with the gangland scene in Moscow, the Volvos were a giveaway. Imported cars were a must for any organization wishing to establish an image of status and wealth. Just as the Lubers preferred the Mercedes Benz, the Boolas – named after the gang's first headquarters in an old bakery – drove Volvos. They were followers of Alla Raikin, a former prostitute known as Golden Arm, criminal slang for the successful tart she once was. Attacked by her pimp when only fourteen, she had slipped out a knife secreted between her buttocks and plunged it up beneath his chin and into his brain. At a stroke, she had taken over his network which was now the most powerful in Moscow. Like Pyotr, Alla had real ambitions and almost enough ruthlessness and flair to make it happen. She, too, was into drugs, weapons and protection. She had just expanded into the lucrative pizza delivery market adding her own personal twist known in town as a P and P or pizza and prostitute. With every large order, a whore came free, a service that had proved extraordinarily popular.

But however innovative she might be, there was always Pyotr and his cursed Lubers blocking her at every turn. In theory, they each had a clear slice of the Moscow pie to call their own, but reality meant that ambition squashed every agreement and she had been at war with Pyotr for months now. Tonight was going to be her night.

Stepping out of the lead car, she took her station at the head of a solid phalanx of gunmen who were fanned out behind, crowding the pavement and anxious to go to work. Her men were dressed in the fashion of the street: baggy suits, linens and silks demonstrating that these were not just musclemen but money-men too. The shirts were buttoned at the neck, the shoes expensive Italian leather. Only the guns, a mixture of Ingrams, Steyr-Aug semi-automatics and a sprinkling of more exotic weapons, would indicate that this was more than a fashion shoot.

Alla herself had done everything she could to shrug off her street background. The expensive clothes, the carefully coiffed hair, the manicured nails all testified to money. But they had not bought her taste or style. The black catsuit might have passed muster were it not for the swelling thighs and growing stomach that evidenced the advancing middle age which, in another life, would have made her the perfect grandmother. The gold hoop earrings and the patently bleached hair were a reflection of bad taste rather than poor professional advice. In her left hand she carried the golden cattle prod that had in part given rise to both the legend and the nickname.

The silenced shots which had so swiftly cleared the door had done nothing to alert the party inside Hell. Alla strode into the club, her bodyguards rushing to fill the entrance behind her. The music was so loud and the attention on the dance floor so focused that at first nobody noticed the new arrivals. It was the prostitutes gathered in ambush near the door who saw the invaders first and the recognition of Alla was instant. A sharp upward movement of her left hand stilled the trigger fingers to allow the few who had thought that this evening their luck had run out to make a hasty exit. Then the firing began.

Advancing at a steady pace past the bar lining the left-hand wall, the Boolas began firing to left and right. This was no orderly execution but a series of random killings designed to terrify and to warn. There was no need for silencers now, and after half a magazine destroyed the sound equipment the rattle of machine-gun fire interspersed with the heavier boom of an automatic shotgun dominated the room.

Terror swept through the crowd like a wave, spread by the searching bullets and the stench of blood that swiftly filled the room. Everyone sought escape, but there was nowhere to hide.

A man moved too slowly out of Alla's path and with a casual flick of her wrist she thrust the cattle prod into his chest. There was a brief sizzle and then his limbs were taken over by a puppet master manipulating hundreds of strings in jerking, uncoordinated chaos. The St Vitus's dance lasted for perhaps five seconds, accompanied by the smell of burning flesh and the strangulated scream of a mind consumed by pain. Finally, he collapsed, a jumble of broken limbs. Without a glance at her victim, Alla moved towards her goal at the far end of the room.

Within thirty seconds, the carnage was absolute. Bodies were everywhere, the cries of the wounded and the terrified interspersed with shorter bursts from the guns as a Boola found a particularly tempting target. But for now, their job of spreading terror in Hell was mostly done.

Pyotr had watched Alla's arrival on the closed-circuit television in his private quarters at the back of the club. It had been a silent horror movie, the images somehow rendered more painful by the absence of colour and sound. For once his intelligence network had failed and he was impotent to defend himself or his club. He watched as Alla advanced purposefully towards the door to his quarters and he realized that he was her real target, not the club. He called to his two bodyguards, pressed a button with his foot and a gap in the wood-panelled wall appeared, to reveal a flight of stairs. As the panel closed behind him, the door to his office blew apart under the attack of a magazine of solid shot.

Alla's eyes swept the empty room and understood at once that her quarry had escaped. She turned, pushed her way through her Boolas and led them back to the club entrance. Her golden arm thrust angrily to left and right, her passage marked by jerking, squirming bodies, the electricity shocking the dead and the living indiscriminately.

No one spoke on the drive back to Alla's headquarters. Tough as they were, none of the gangsters dared to face the backlash of her seething frustration. Alla's base, a bizarre mixture of utilitarian Swedish and gilded Louis XIV French, was in the suburb where she ruled and where the people felt fiercely protective of her and her wealth. She knew enough to look after her own and the new football stadium, the cinema, a modest park and a group of high-rise flats surrounded by flower-beds were all results of her apparent largesse. The fact that all these ventures turned a profit and were useful methods of laundering money was something that concerned her subjects not at all. The centrepiece of her empire was hidden behind large metal gates and a high wall topped with razor wire. The cameras clearly positioned on tall metal poles every fifty metres around the perimeter were specifically designed to discourage the casual visitor; the microwaves, geophones and infra-red sensors were there for the serious professionals who wished to try their luck.

As the gates opened silently at the approach of the cars to reveal the perfectly arranged flower beds that swept up towards the portico at the front of the house, a footman in the house uniform of brocade and leggings – an affectation she considered appropriate for her style – descended the steps to open the car door. Like all her employees, he carried a handgun in a holster in the small of his back and a knife in a sheath strapped to his forearm. He could and would defend his mistress with his life.

To her left she noticed a black Benz with diplomatic plates. At least something was going to plan, she thought. Through the hallway and past two enormous oils painted in the socialist-realist style of the old era that showed workers toiling heroically in fields and factories, she turned left into the panelled study that she used as her office.

A man rose as she entered and bowed with the short little deferential bob that is the Japanese equivalent of the western handshake. Nodding in reply she moved across the room to sit behind a mahogany desk with a bare, highly polished surface. To one side, on a functional light wood workstation, sat a single computer. The contrast was jarring and some-how offensive, as if a waiter had poured salad dressing into a glass of Mouton Rothschild. She addressed the Yakuza boss peremptorily.

'So, Mr Yamana, you bring me good news, I hope.'

There was a fleeting expression of distaste across the face of the visitor at this rush to business before the courtesies had been addressed. But, Golden Arm was a legend, and on her own turf, so perhaps convention could be ignored for once.

'Madame Alla,' he began formally in his stilted Russian, the Japanese cadence giving his voice a Bugs Bunny quality as he tried to wrap his sibilant tone around the guttural Russian syllables.

'I am very pleased to see you here,' she interrupted, a brief crack in her lips suggesting a smile of welcome. 'Some tea perhaps?' Without waiting for the invitation to be accepted, she moved her right hand below the desk to press a hidden bell. Moments later, another butler appeared pushing a trolley laden with delicate Sèvres china and the sweetmeats so loved by the Russians.

After the ritual of pouring had been completed and the pastries handed round, the butler departed, leaving the remainder of the pastries on the desk by Alla's right elbow.

'I assume that your presence here signifies that we have an agreement?' she asked between mouthfuls.

Both host and guest knew each other better by reputation than in person. For both of them, there was the kind of wary mistrust that two predators exhibit when manoeuvring past each other in the jungle. They had met for the first time two years earlier as honoured guests on the Caribbean island of Aruba where they had been invited to a meeting that was destined to create a new international crime organization, the dire implications of which Yuri had described to David in the skies above Alla's power base.

It had been a convivial occasion. All those invited were there because they were thought to be the most influential of the gang leaders operating in their region. Some, like Yamana, were simply powerful while others brought a particular skill or product to the party. These were men who were at the top of their form, dealers in death who had perfected their business. Alla had been the sole female representative.

The only item on the agenda was to carve out the existing criminal turf to restrict competition, maximize profit and marginalize the influence of the law enforcement agencies lined up against them. The proposal from the Colombians was simple: first, they would be given access to the European markets for their cocaine while the European production of heroin would be allowed into the American market. That was the easy part. The complicated negotiations came with Yamana and Alla Raikin, who found themselves offering expertise without much product. Yamana-san had unparalleled access to the legitimate market which made him both an ideal launderer and a perfect outlet for the growing Far Eastern business. Raikin understood the opportunities that existed in both Russia and the former communist bloc for the enterprising criminal. Both Yamana and Raikin were happy to allow access to their areas for a take of the profits, but they also wanted to look to the future.

She had pointed out to the Colombians and the Sicilians the huge potential of the former Soviet Union and the Far East, offering immediate assistance in some of those areas in return for guarantees of future access to the others' existing markets.

There had been a shuffling of papers at that, a noticeable chilling of the atmosphere at the effrontery of this woman. Then she had pointed out the three million acres of marijuana and around one and a half million acres of opium poppies she controlled in the southern republics. Alla had noticed the widened eyes and hurried swallows as her audience absorbed the true dimension of the figures she was reporting. Their choice was clear: keep her out and see their market collapse, or take her in as an equal partner.

Yamana, who considered himself a cut above the others at the meeting, had been impressed. He had visited her in Moscow and gained first-hand knowledge of just what she could offer him. Both understood that this was truly a marriage of need and convenience. It was she who had come up with the vision that would bind them together. It was her masterful plan that she sketched out to him during his second trip to Moscow and it was his quick mind and long experience of international politics that honed and refined the raw product into a brilliant piece of brinkmanship.

77

The potential rewards for each of them were huge, large enough to satisfy even the most voracious ego – at least for now. There was little discussion about the details of control and divisions of the spoils. It was as if they both understood this was dangerous territory that, if explored, might expose cracks in their alliance which would swiftly become unbridgeable fissures. Instead they reassured each other blandly that 'of course' both parties would remain equal and that unity was everything. Such clichés were enough for now.

Yamana sipped his tea. 'At this time,' he began tentatively, 'we are prepared to agree to the first stage of your plan.' He held up his hand to forestall an angry exclamation from Alla. 'But I need some assurance that you have the support of the military and that, when the announcement comes, there will be no opportunity for either the government here or the western powers to act.'

She wanted to reach across the desk and strangle the little shit. Instead she took a savage bite out of a *millefeuille*, squeezing the custard out of the sides as if she were squeezing Yamana's neck. In recent years, there had been no reason to reassure anyone of anything. What she wanted, she took, and any who questioned her authority, she killed. Simple and efficient. Now, she was having to cut deals, to justify her actions. Then again, perhaps this time the stakes made an occasional explanation worthwhile.

'You know the level of discontent among the military,' she replied. 'They have been reduced to selling not just their uniforms but their guns, their missiles and even their nuclear weapons. Except those always seem to go straight to the CIA or MI6,' she laughed derisively.

'Worse still, they have lost their status. Nobody cares about the military any more. They have become an irrelevance to Russia and a costly burden on the people. I'm pretty sure they want what we have to offer – a place back in the sun where they feel they belong.'

'That may be,' Yamana replied. 'But we are risking every-thing here. Do you really expect us to rely on what you *think* the military will do? That is hardly reasonable.'

'Reasonable?' Alla snorted. 'None of this is reasonable. This is a simple calculation. If we do as I suggest, will some of the military follow my lead? Yes. Will the rest move against us? No. And why not? Because they are powerless.'

She moved away from her guest and Yamana disguised a grimace of distaste as he watched her buttocks roll with the movement of her legs. The door at the far end of the room opened quietly and a man dressed in the uniform of an army colonel strode purposefully into the room.

Yamana had spent enough time in the firing line to sense menace instinctively and he felt his hand move automatically towards his hip and the small gun he had concealed there. He quickly controlled the gesture, recognizing that there was nothing personal here. This man was simply dangerous.

'This is Colonel Nikolai Muraviev,' Alla gestured towards the visitor. 'He will be able to reassure you.'

Muraviev moved to a comfortable armchair, drew on the creases of his trousers and sat down before crossing one leg over the other. He reached forward and picked up a cream cake from the tray, devouring it in three precise mouthfuls. It was a process of precision matched with a sensuality that was both compelling and revolting. Muraviev wiped his hands and then drew out a small knife, and began flicking it underneath his fingernails to extract imagined dirt. Yamana noticed that the habit had driven the flesh back from his nails so that they appeared unnaturally long, almost claw-like. As a man who admired control in all its different forms, the Japanese gangster was filled with admiration. The power centre in the room had subtly shifted. Where Alla had been the dominant force, the new man had taken some of her space. Just how much, he would be interested to see.

'I assume you speak for the military?' Yamana asked.

'We none of us can speak for the military these days,' Muraviev replied with a slight smile. The colonel spoke so softly that Yamana found himself leaning forward to catch the answer.

'But the people I represent control significant sections of the armed forces. Significant enough for you to achieve your goals without difficulty.'

The colonel seemed so confident that Yamana wanted to reach out and burst his bubble of self-satisfaction.

'You surprise me, Colonel. To a humble foreigner, the situation seems less clear-cut. You talk of control and I see the shambles in Chechnya, officers deserting their posts, generals resigning, troops disobeying their orders. I look at Bosnia and I see Russian soldiers running the black market and looking like a Third World rabble, not part of a first-class army. Just why should you be able to deliver anything better than that?'

As he was speaking the colonel stilled in his chair, his right leg stopped its gentle swinging movement and his jawline tightened.

'What you describe are not the Russian armed forces,' he replied, his voice still soft but its tone now clipped and abrupt. 'They are political operations by political leaders in Moscow. Chechnya and Bosnia' – he made a dismissive gesture – 'Political sideshows. You Japanese have enough reason to remember the Russian soldier. He has not changed and neither have his leaders. The Empire may have gone, but we understand the needs of our country and we have the men and people to do what is necessary.'

'Forgive me for saying so, Colonel,' Yamana continued, pleased with the soldier's reaction, 'but you make strange allies – the gangster and the military officer. What brings you together?'

'A good question,' the colonel replied. 'These are difficult times. My country has fallen apart. There's no leadership. We've sold our country and our souls to McDonald's and the IMF and we are slowly being strangled by the American opportunists who use their dollars to buy up what is left. Some of us believe that there is a better way, an opportunity to create a new nation from the old, a nation that will once again be welcome at the top table not as beggar but as royalty. To achieve that, a measure of compromise is necessary.'

'Colonel Muraviev is right,' Alla intervened. 'The country is collapsing and what is left is now controlled by people like me.'

She got up from her desk and began to pace, as if the movement alone would give her words some convincing volition. Yamana watched her carefully, trying to gauge the strength of the words against the cold analysis of his cynical judgement. Sourly, he reflected that if control of her waistline was indicative of strength of will, then they were all in trouble.

'We control much of modern Russia and we could eventually have what's left,' she continued. 'But, what our President laughably describes as his government will try to stop us and so will the Americans and their friends, who seem to think they have the right to tell us Russians how to live our lives. For now, we prosper. But our enemies at home and abroad are massing against us. Alone, we might not survive. And alone, the military is dying of neglect. Together, we can achieve a great deal.

'Consider this,' Alla spoke through a mouthful of yet another pastry. 'We are now harvesting enough opium from the southern republics to increase the world supply by a quarter; we have enough marijuana going through the Black Sea ports to satisfy existing demand in the rest of Europe; we have more investments in Wall Street, the Bourse and the City of London than any African nation. And this is just the beginning. We are truly a country within a country.'

She sat down again, and used a napkin to remove a smear of custard from the corner of her mouth.

'But, we are operating not as a country but as criminals. Yet, in America when the Rockefellers, Carnegies and Mellons began they, too, were just like us. America understood that they needed people like us to help build the nation. Now, it's their heirs who see us as a threat to the world. Only this week, I lost a major shipment of drugs on its way to Europe – the third in two months. And that led to one of my warehouses here in Moscow being raided. The Americans want to bring their agents here to fight us in the way they have fought the Mafia in their own country. And our beloved President uses us as yet another reason to go cap in hand to the Americans for more aid. Instead of being recognized as entrepreneurs, we are treated like dirt.'

She saw a small smile flicker briefly across Yamana's face as if he were amused at her preoccupation with legitimacy. She rose again and moved towards him so that she was standing looking down at the Japanese as he idly swung one crossed leg against the other.

'You laugh,' she sneered, 'but you Japanese already have it all – a corrupt government, a corrupt country and a corrupt people.'

Yamana stiffened at the insults and made to rise from his chair as Muraviev's soft tones forestalled the slanging match about to ensue.

'We are forgetting why we are here,' he said. 'If we achieve our goals, then none of us will have to worry about what others think.'

Yamana sank back into his chair and waited for Raikin to continue her explanation of the way ahead. For the next ten minutes Alla spoke uninterrupted, outlining her plan. By the time she had finished, the eyes of the two men facing her showed all the greed and ambition she had hoped to inspire. Individually, each of the three was a formidable force. Together they would be irresistible.

Marat Balagula checked his mailbox and felt the sudden tightening of his stomach as he saw the familiar padded envelope. Walking up the three flights of stairs to his apartment on Priorova in the Ipatovka district of Moscow, he waited until he was inside the door before he opened the package and slid out the single CD – Beethoven's Symphony No. 9 with Solti conducting. In other circumstances, he would have relished the opportunity to listen to such a wonderful performance of one of his favourite compositions, but there were other priorities now.

Balagula combined three careers: arms salesman, senior official at the Russian Ministry of Defence and British spy, codename Spitz. The last of these had been embarked upon, ironically, as a result of Russia's westernization. Under the Old Guard there had been a certain structure to his work. The Soviet Union used arms transfers as a way of gaining influence and useful foreign exchange. This was no different from the way America, Britain or France behaved and in his view it was perfectly acceptable to sell weapons as part of a foreign policy which, although expansionist, at least had an underlying moral code.

The collapse of the Soviet Union had turned a controlled market into a free-for-all. All bets were off in the scrabble for cash and the struggle for survival. He had seen missiles go to Tehran, ballistic missile guidance systems to Pyongyang and even the designs for the still secret T-94 tank to a front for the American Defense Intelligence Agency. Everything was for sale. He could foresee no conclusion but anarchy.

In 1990 he had begun feeding small bits of information to the British in an attempt to counter some of the worst excesses of this new trade. Of course, he had intended to control the relationship with the British but, of course, before long it was he who was subordinate. Stories from the west of an arms shipment seized here or an arrest there were sugar on the pill of betrayal. His life as a traitor had evolved into a familiar though frightening round of summons, clandestine meeting and relief as he returned to the safety of his lair.

He had met Nash only once but they had hit it off immediately. They were the same age, had the same spirit and shared a love of American cars (the Office had promised Spitz a Camaro when he eventually came out).

This was the first time he had called for a crash meet. But it was also the first time that he had been confronted with the reality of his spying. This time, it wasn't another plan for a new piece of equipment or even some details about the machinations among the power élite. This was danger, real and immediate danger. With the knowledge had come the raw terror of a man who has seen through the darkness and understands the horror that lurks there. He had to share what he knew, as if the unburdening would somehow relieve the pressure. Now, as he held the small padded envelope with its Classic 4U label in his hand, he hoped that he was about to be relieved.

Classic 4U, a CD club based in Paris on the rue Vendôme, was an MI6 front. It did plenty of real business and, in fact, to the surprise of its sponsors and to the embarrassment of the accountants, had actually turned in a modest profit in the past couple of years – a bureaucratic nightmare because the Treasury always took the money and the paperwork just wasn't worth it. But its main purpose was message transmission. So far, its codes had never been broken and its delivery system was almost impossible to penetrate.

Carefully holding the CD in his left hand, Spitz moved across to the wall where his Aiwa player sat on a shelf. Powering it up, he watched as the dials illuminated and then he slotted home the disc. There came the familiar soft whirr as the CD was sucked into the machine and then the music began to flow from the speakers.

Spitz held down the Play and Reverse buttons. The music stopped and a small red light that glowed on the front of the machine flickered and then changed to white as the laser probed for the CD's embedded hologram. The light became a projector and Nash appeared in the room, life size and apparently floating in mid-air. Spitz listened carefully to the instructions for the meet.

6

NASH HATED FIELD meetings. Every lesson at the Fort was designed to reinforce the message that face-to-face is fatal. Never meet the source, avoid all contact, rely on dead-letter boxes and if you do have to meet make sure you have plenty of back-up and minimal margin for error. It was easy for those buggers to write the script, he thought to himself. They should try it out here sometime; find out what it's like when reality meets the rules.

Nash had flown into Kiev that morning on the Air Ukraine flight from London. There had been no time for the usual niceties of a zig-zag route to confuse watchers: Ukraine was a basket case and flights were sporadic and unreliable. A lurching, nightmare journey of coughing, ragged engines, coughing, ragged stewardesses and execrable food had been the price he had been forced to pay to be certain of making the meet.

For Spitz, of course, Kiev was perfect. A foreign country with no visa required and an easy journey from Moscow.

As soon as he arrived in the city, Nash visited a dead-letter box near the tomb of Prince Yaroslav the Wise in the north-western tower of St Sophia's Cathedral to collect his gun, careful to ensure that he was being neither followed nor observed.

Until three years earlier, it had been Service policy that officers in the field go unarmed as guns tended to blow a cover both literally and figuratively. That had changed when Billy Dunlap from counter-narcotics had found himself on the wrong end of a drugs bust in Budapest and he had had nothing except his fists to defend himself against two well-armed killers. The drug barons observed none of the conventions that ruled the spy world during the Cold War: never kill an officer from an enemy service; never fire a weapon if it can possibly be avoided; no gratuitous violence and absolutely no fingerprints. Frank had been brutally tortured, for information and as a warning, and there was ample evidence the torture had continued long after he had told them what little he knew, even after he had been beyond feeling.

The lesson had not been lost on the sixth floor and carrying a weapon was now a routine requirement. This had led to all kinds of logistical problems as it was impossible to travel armed. A series of dead letter boxes had been established all over the world with the idea that people like Nash coming into a strange country would never be caught short. The quality of the weaponry likely to be deposited therein could be variable, to say the least, but this time Nash had been fortunate and he now had the comfort of a Browning 9 mm under his left arm.

Nash began the slow and circuitous route to his spy. He took the Metro and exited at Maidan Nezalezhnosti. Then he walked up the hill towards the old part of town heading for the Zoloti Vorota, the Golden Gate built in 1037. The arches covered in beaten gold had long been stripped bare. But it remained an impressive entrance to the old town with its narrow winding streets, ancient wooden and stone buildings and people who looked as they must have done at the time of the 1917 revolution. There was none of the emerging rich in their Hermes, Givenchy and Hugo Boss – just poverty and the sense of despair common to many Third World countries.

In the shadow of the Golden Gate was another Metro stop

and ten minutes later he was deposited at Arsenalna station. A mercifully short journey on a rattling, creaking No 20 trolleybus took him to the whitewashed walls of the Kievo-Pecherska Lavra, the Monastery of the Caves. Looking around idly, as if searching for the entrance he knew was 150 metres to the south, Nash felt sure there were no watchers and that he had not been tagged.

The trouble with the Office, he thought as he surveyed the ancient ruins, is that there were too many classically trained scholars earning some pin money in their retirement by scouting out suitable places for clandestine meetings. SIS had dozens of these folk whose remit was to go to countries they knew well and find places that would work. The requirements of a good rendezvous were simple: approachable from a number of different directions; in a public place, preferably where tourists visit; several exits; and well-enough known that locals could find it easily.

An expenses paid trip to the site of a dig or a lecture or simply a well-remembered holiday was too good for many of the old buffers to turn down. But the result was a range of RVs that favoured museums and ruins over cafés and corner shops.

The Monastery of the Caves had been founded in 1051 by a monk called Anthony who liked the hilly site, in part because it was easily defended and in part because the caves which dotted the hillside were ideal for contemplation and seclusion. They were also humid enough to preserve perfectly the bodies of all the monks buried there – a feature which the superstitious locals thought miraculous and which added to the monastery's reputation. Beneath it were miles of underground passageways, many of which were uncharted and unsafe.

'The most important thing for you to remember is that you meet in the upper caves, the Dalnyie Pechery,' the Office had advised. 'If trouble starts, there's a wooden bridge that connects you to the near caves, the Blizhnyie Pechery, and from there it's just a short skip to the street and safety.'

The caves had the smell of old socks combined with rotting fish. The only light was provided by the candle that had been supplied with his ticket, the flickering flame of which created more shadows than illumination.

The rendezvous was for the third of three churches that had been carved out of the hillside and he made his way slowly along the stone corridor towards the shape that was dimly discernible in the distance. As he approached, a figure stepped out of the shadows and moved towards him. He was surprised to notice his right hand reaching for the 9 mm, a nervous reflex brought on by the oppressive, disturbing atmosphere of this dank hole. As the figure came closer, Nash saw that it was Spitz, but a Spitz who looked very different from the confident and polished spy he had met in the past.

The erratic light from the candle in Spitz's trembling hand exaggerated the lines on his face and highlighted the obvious fear in his eyes. This was a man close to breaking, Nash thought.

'Thank God you come,' Spitz said, his left hand reaching out to grip Nash's arm. His English, which was normally fluent and Americanized, sounded guttural and halting as nerves brought his natural accent to the surface. 'We must move away from here.'

He pulled Nash with him along the tunnel that led down and away from the church towards the caves and the network of burrows below. Spitz's agitation was contagious and Nash could feel himself growing wary.

'Relax, Spitz.' Nash forced his voice to be calm, reassuring. 'Nobody knows I'm here. I assume nobody followed you either?'

'No, no. I did everything correct. The bus, the train,

walking, doubling. Everything I learn. But, this is very dangerous, I know. I know.'

'OK. Let's keep moving.' They continued down the corridor that seemed to descend steeply into the distance. The candlelight was so dim that it was impossible to discern the end of the tunnel. They walked forward arm in arm, two old men shuffling along an unfamiliar path.

'What's so urgent, anyway?' Nash asked. 'Don't tell me you're blown?'

Although his tone was lighthearted, he dreaded an affirmative answer.

'No, nothing like that. Or at least not so far as I know,' Spitz replied. 'Is much more serious.'

Nash could see Spitz's head turning from side to side as he looked nervously into the blank walls of the tunnel, as if expecting something or someone to jump out at any moment.

'You know that some of the military have been involved to sell equipment to make money?'

Nash grunted assent. This was hardly news.

'Last week, I am invited to see General Kuntsevich.' Nash knew of Kuntsevich, the head of the programme to destroy Russia's chemical and biological weapons. He had been the architect of the arsenal during the Brezhnev, Andropov and Gorbachev eras. A staunch believer, he had somehow survived the revolution and Yeltsin had put him in charge of destroying all the equipment he had created. Not surprisingly almost nothing had been done since his appointment and there was even evidence that new research and development work was being undertaken.

'He told me he was very pleased with the work I do, that I am one of the few who had made the transition good from old order to new. How I clearly understand the new economic and political reality. For me this is very flattering, you know,

David? This Kuntsevich he is a legend. One of the great survivors from old days.'

'So what did he want?' Nash prompted.

'For me to use my connections to sell for them a new weapon that's been developed. He says it is of the "less conventional nature".

'That night, he take me for a drive to some kind of laboratory outside of Moscow. He showed me around; so many rooms filled with test tubes and cages of mice. Then we have a demonstration of this new stuff, this RD-74.'

'Which is what, exactly?' Nash asked impatiently.

'Some kind of biological weapon. Genetically engineered from the plague germ so that a handful can kill a city and a bucketful would destroy all of your country.'

Spitz described an experiment using a goat, a cow and two dogs in a sealed room which was pumped full of an invisible and odourless aerosol containing microscopic amounts of RD-74. After three minutes the smaller dog began to twitch and then to tear at its skin. Before it died, the pain-demented creature had bitten clean through its own leg. The other animals had died equally gruesomely in what had been a revolting and wanton spectacle.

'It was worse than you could ever imagine,' Spitz said. 'And this stuff is designed for use against people. That sick old fool actually expected me to go and sell it. It's madness, madness.'

'Jesus Christ,' said Nash, horrified. 'If something like that were to get into the wrong hands . . .'

Spitz was almost beside himself. 'There's no "if" about it, David. This isn't just a madman's plan. It's practically already out there. We have to stop it. We have to!' The Russian's voice was becoming louder and louder as his hysteria grew.

'Calm down man, for God's sake, or you'll blow us both,' said Nash in a harsh whisper. 'Now, what do you mean, "already out there"?'

'Sorry. Sorry. It's just . . .' Spitz took a deep breath and regained a little of his composure.

'Kuntsevich said one of the crime gangs that run Moscow these days had offered $50 million for a single vial of RD-74. He was very happy. Said this stuff was more valuable than any nuclear bomb and much cheaper to make. He wouldn't say why they wanted it. Just dropped some hints that I would know soon enough and that the world was going to have to listen when people like him talked. Nash, you have to do something. Millions could die.'

'Is there still time?' Nash asked. 'The deal is done, from what you say.'

'The handover's been delayed,' said Spitz. 'An infected dog escaped a couple of nights ago and there was panic in case the security people would find out what had been going on. RD-74 doesn't officially exist, you see. That delay might buy us some time.'

Nash could hear the shuffling of someone coming from behind and the vague echoes of footsteps ahead.

'I think we may have company,' Nash observed in a tense whisper.

Spitz picked up on his tension and slipped rapidly back into panic. 'This way. Hurry.' He gripped Nash's arm in a tight fist and pulled him downward towards the steps that were farthest away, but Nash pulled back.

'Wait. Stay still. They'll be expecting us to make a move. Let them come to us.'

He leaned forward and blew out Spitz's candle and then extinguished his own. The sudden darkness was absolute and all his other senses seemed to sharpen as a result. He could hear not just the approaching steps but the drip of water on the walls, Spitz's ragged breathing and the thumping of his own heart.

Nash freed the Browning, its solid weight providing a

fleeting reassurance. He slid the sleeve back over the barrel to force a round into the chamber and pushed up the safety catch. Backs pressed against the wall, the two men waited, hearing the steps coming closer and closer.

With shocking suddenness, a bright white beam pierced the darkness to their right. It wavered briefly and then, detecting the shadows their bulk cast against the tunnel, locked on to them. This was the moment to decide between action and reaction, whether to play by the rules or go for the jugular. Nash pushed away from the wall, dropped to one knee and squeezed the trigger twice.

The sound of the shots was like a train crash in the narrow confines of the tunnel. He felt numbed by the sound waves that reverberated down the corridor. He saw the torchlight waver and then drop to the floor and roll over and over before coming to rest, its beam illuminating a tiny patch of floor and wall. One bullet at least had clearly found its mark.

In the security of darkness once again, he grabbed Spitz and propelled him down towards the lower caves and whoever lay below. As his hearing returned, Nash could hear Spitz sobbing. They made terrifying, stumbling, fumbling progress down a slope that became steeper by the moment. There were no handholds, no sense of what lay ahead. Nash felt irrationally certain that every step would be the one which would take them both tumbling into a bottomless abyss.

The light behind them was moving steadily downward once more. Obviously, Nash thought to himself, there must be more than one above and God knows how many below. He kept his gun pointed firmly forwards, ready to fire at a reflexive twitch of his trigger finger.

His left hand, which had been feeling the solid wall as they rushed onward, suddenly lost all contact and he almost fell. Thinking that he might have found a side tunnel, he dragged Spitz to a halt. He reached tentatively into the gap and felt something light, ephemeral, more solid than a spider's web, more like old paper, yet softer. He jerked back, unable to prevent a cry of revulsion escaping his lips.

'Christ. It's a body!' he exclaimed.

The monks had been laid to rest in open-sided chambers hollowed out of the walls. The holes were sometimes deep enough for two or three monks to lie forever side by side. Grimacing, Nash put his hand back to the hole, trying to get a sense of exactly what it contained. He could feel the rotting skin of whoever it was that lay in there. He pushed a little and the skin gave way to the bone underneath and with it the stench of the flesh that had been gently rotting for perhaps two centuries came wafting over him. It was a smell so strong that he immediately retched, doubling over in a spasm, his stomach contracting in disgust as his mind absorbed the shocking message from his senses.

Steeling himself, he moved forward again, this time to push deep inside the hole, feeling for depth, height and width. It was enough.

'Come on,' he urged Spitz. 'Take your shirt and hold it over your mouth. Climb in.'

Spitz, too, began to gag as soon as he put his head inside the hole but Nash shoved him forward. There was a series of soft cracks as already brittle bones collapsed under the weight of the intruder. Nash levered himself up behind Spitz and forced himself into the space, which was now holding three people where one was expected to lie at peace for eternity.

Nash whispered to Spitz to be quiet while he himself tried to control his breathing. It seemed only moments before the light of the torch was probing the path in front of their refuge. As the tracker moved past, Nash could see reflected the stubby snout of a sub-machine-gun probing forward, seeking them out. A few paces further on the hunter met with the other half of the team, evidently to the surprise of both. There was a hurried conference, the gist of which was clear enough, even without Spitz's whispered translation.

'They don't understand how they've missed us,' Spitz mouthed into Nash's ear. 'They know there are two of us. They know your name.' His voice rose an octave at the realization that if Nash was marked so personally then in all probability so was he.

'How many?' Nash asked.

'I've counted three voices so far,' Spitz replied.

That would make sense, Nash thought. Two teams of two minus the one he had taken out. It was surely only a matter of moments before the hunters realized that their quarry had only one place to go.

Nash's fingers probed the body beneath him and found what felt like a femur. Hefting it carefully in his left hand, he reached out, swung twice and then threw the bone as far as he could back up the tunnel. There was no satisfying crash as it hit the tunnel floor but a whisper of sound as the bone landed and then disintegrated into a million fragments of dust.

The noise was enough to alert the hunters and their torches flickered and then pointed back up the tunnel. There were running footsteps and then they were past. Immediately, Nash slid out of the hole and pulled Spitz after him.

'Run and keep running,' he whispered.

Spitz headed off down the tunnel, his steps covered by the noise from the retreating footsteps of the hunters. Nash turned and ran after Spitz. Speed and not stealth was what counted now as they raced for the underground wooden bridge that connected the two sets of caves. The faster they went the wider the gap and they propelled themselves forward, crashing off the walls, stumbling at misjudged steps and cursing each fumbled footfall.

It was Spitz who destroyed their chances of escape. A

badly timed step combined with a lurch into the right hand wall sent him careering forward, arms windmilling and out of control. His balance lost, he fell, his forward momentum driving him hard into the rock of the tunnel floor. His wrist took the full impact and snapped with an audible crack. If the hunters hadn't heard that, they certainly couldn't have missed Spitz's scream of agony as the broken bones ground together.

Nash stopped and bent over his fallen spy. He put his hands underneath Spitz's shoulders and heaved, trying to drag him upright.

'Get up, man,' he shouted, all caution gone. He looked back over his shoulder and could see the torches heading towards them. The hunters, too, had abandoned any attempt at stealth and were shouting encouragement to each other as they ran towards them.

Nash pivoted around and squeezed off four shots in rapid succession, moving the gun slightly after each round so that the width of the tunnel was effectively bracketed. One of the torches fell. Two down, two to go, he thought.

He saw the flashes of an answering burst of fire and felt the bullets go by, their shock waves strong enough to alter the air pressure against his face. They were either very lucky this time or the hunters were aiming off, seeking prisoners and not corpses.

Spitz was on his knees now and Nash thrust him to his feet so that he could drive him forward. A few more stumbling steps and then the texture of their flight changed. There was a sense of space and then the clack, clack sound as their steps met the wooden planks of the bridge connecting the caves. A few moments more and they would be safe.

He should have anticipated the blocker. Any good ambush always had one and this was no exception. They were halfway across the bridge when another torch came on ahead of them and a voice came out of the darkness behind it.

'Tell your friend to stop, Nash, or you're both dead.'

Nash fired twice and then rolled twice, out of line of any return fire, so that he was at the edge of the bridge, one leg dangling over the abyss.

The voice in the darkness laughed gently.

'You don't think I would do anything so stupid as to hold the light in my hand?' it asked. 'Come, come, we're all professionals here. Put down your weapon or I'll shoot your friend in the kneecap.' Nash noted that the owner of the voice spoke perfect, unaccented English.

A single red beam came out of the darkness, hovered briefly on the wood next to Spitz's leg and then the gun fired. The bullet followed the laser to its target and tore a five-inch gouge out of the planking.

Nash tossed his gun away.

'Good. Very sensible. Ah. I see my colleagues have arrived. Wait where you are.'

Nash looked behind him and watched as three men moved out on to the bridge, their shapes shadowy in the reflection of the torchlight from the other side. His mind raced, searching for a way out, a solution that might save him and his source. But there was nothing to be done. The trap had closed.

The three men reached them and stood a few paces back, out of reach of flailing arms or legs, their faces invisible behind the blinding glare of the torches. Their anonymity made them somehow much more frightening than if he could see them clearly. But it was the guns in their hands that made the menace palpable.

'Your friend is a traitor, Mr Nash,' said the voice. 'My instructions are clear – betrayal has only one punishment.'

There was a brief, barked order and one of the men took a short step forward. Spitz looked up at the killer and clearly knew that he was marked for death. His mouth began to open in a final and futile imprecation, while his hands moved in front of his body to repel the assault he knew was coming.

With the casual disdain of the true professional, the man raised his gun – a Mac-10, Nash registered automatically – and let off a burst that lasted no longer than two seconds.

The spew of bullets from the stubby barrel lifted Spitz up and threw him over the edge of the bridge. There was no sound except the slap of bullets hitting flesh and then the raindrop sound of blood dappling the wooden bridge. Finally, moments after his destroyed body had disappeared into the darkness, there was a strangely musical and innocent tinkling as the spent shell cases hit the ground.

Nash made to rise up, fury overcoming caution at the sight of his source being so casually murdered. But he had no time to make even that empty gesture.

'This is a lesson to you, Mr Nash,' the voice said. 'Keep out of our affairs. Next time my orders will be less generous.'

There was a brief sense of disturbed air, an impression of a descending shape and then a flash of pain and he felt himself falling.

7

THE ROCKS THAT surrounded the All-Union Research Institute of Applied Microbiology at Klin were just part of the terrain. The ground outside the perimeter fence that surrounded the huge complex had been cleared of all shrubs and trees to provide a clear line of fire for the guards who patrolled with dogs and machine-guns inside the grounds. Not that anyone would have been stupid enough to come too near. Every 100 metres, large white boards with red lettering announced BIOPREPARAT – SCIENTIFIC RESEARCH ESTABLISHMENT. KEEP OUT. For Russians, conditioned by generations of subservience to the orders of the state, such an instruction was as good as an electric fence. The guards had little to do at Klin. The cleared area remained so only because the orders said that was how it had to be.

Except for the rocks.

They were low-lying and grey, formed from the granite that lay just a few feet below the surface. The fact that one of these rocks was not quite what it seemed was the doing of Vladimir Pasechnik, the former Director of the Institute of Ultra Pure Biochemical Preparations in St Petersburg, though it had been known as Leningrad in Pasechnik's day. Pasechnik had defected to Britain in December 1989 and brought with him the revelation that the Soviets had been secretly working for more than twenty years on a massive programme to develop a new generation of biological weapons.

The whole enterprise had been established under an organization called Biopreparat, a supposed offshoot of the Academy of Sciences, which was officially conducting medical research. Pasechnik revealed that, in fact, the whole venture had been paid for and run by the Russian Ministry of Defence in what was perhaps the largest and best-kept secret programme of the Cold War. He brought out with him the formulas for sixteen different biological weapons, variants of pneumonic plague and tularaemia. There was no antidote to any of these strains in the west and their release would have had a devastating effect.

Pasechnik's information was corroborated when two more defectors from the Biopreparat programme reached America and Britain in 1990. The second delivered the disturbing news that not only had the Russian President's instructions to close down the programme in the wake of the Cold War been ignored, but that newer, even more lethal weapons had been developed.

The west's response was a rock codenamed Little Nell, devised by a small team of scientists working for a CIA front company called MicroGraphics Inc., which was based in the hospitable surroundings of Aspen, Colorado.

Little Nell was a marvel of microengineering, containing cameras, sensors and solar power packs that could see, hear, record and transmit everything that happened within its operating radius of around a quarter of a mile. It had been secretly planted by Harry Maskowicz, the second counsellor at the Embassy and one of the many Agency operatives in Moscow, one winter's night. It had been simple enough. He had to slide just a few feet inside the cleared area, scrape a small depression, plant Little Nell and then pack the earth back around along with a potent weedkiller at the front of the rock and a few flower seeds at the back to both give a clear field of view and make the rock look as natural as possible. The Agency did try to think of everything.

Little Nell had acted as a silent spy ever since, picking up telephone conversations from inside the building, recording the pattern of the guards and routinely photographing every vehicle going in and out of the plant day or night. At 1800 EST on every fifth day, in a single digitized burst lasting no longer than seconds, Little Nell relayed all her stored information via a KH-11 satellite back to Fort Meade in Maryland and from there to Langley.

One night, an unmarked car arrived at the gates of the laboratory just before midnight. Little Nell faithfully recorded its arrival and its departure forty-five minutes later. Just after the vehicle left, a telephone call was made from the complex to a number in the Ministry of Defence in Moscow, ninety-seven kilometres to the south-east. The conversation was short: a grunted 'Da' at the Moscow end and the simple message 'It is done' before the caller hung up. Knowledge of that single conversation could have prevented all the tragedy that was to follow, but it was to be two days before the KH-11 came on station and the two-second burst headed back to Langley. By then the conversation would merely be a useful clue in unravelling events already spinning out of control.

'That was a complete bloody cock-up.' Diana was almost shouting, her anger visible and visceral.

'Well, if you hadn't suggested an RV chosen by a myopic geriatric then I might have been able to do something,' retorted Nash. He, too, was furious at himself for losing Spitz. He had been storing up the anger for two days and Diana's attack had brought it all to the surface. 'An RV lit only by candles. No proper escape route. Trapped like ducks in a barrel. Hardly surprising it turned out as it did!'

Diana turned to her computer and began re-reading Nash's report for the umpteenth time, needing the distraction to calm her down and prepare her for the next step.

'The Inquisition's convened upstairs. You raised some pretty serious questions which the Chief wants to talk to you about. We should head on up.'

They took the lift to the sixth floor which is home to all SIS's central management, turned left and then through a door marked simply 'Director'. The outer office, guarded by the faithful Joan and her two assistants, was little different from every other executive suite in London, with light-wood furniture, computer terminals and filing cabinets. The single noticeable difference was the combination locks on the cabinets, a hint of the secrets hidden within.

David Spedding had replaced Sir Colin McColl as Chief. He was an Arabist who had cut his SIS teeth first at the spy school in Cairo and then in the souks of Damascus, Baghdad and Beirut. Like so many of SIS's better officers, he appeared unassuming, cultured and in many ways the perfect product of a public-school education. But like all those who lived in the shadows, he had both darker and lighter sides.

Nash had met him only twice, one occasion being the traditional drinks party before the SIS choir set off to perform its annual concert of Christmas carols in St Columba's in Pont Street. It had struck Nash that the idea of intelligence officers singing 'Silent Night' to an audience who thought they were simply a bunch of well-meaning government clerks was a truly British concept. Nash had noted intelligence and toughness in Spedding's eyes; dark brown, deep, impenetrable and shadowed by the light.

Spedding rose as Nash entered and came round his desk to greet him.

'Nash. Do come in and sit down. How's the head?'

In a brief reflex, Nash moved his right hand up to touch

the bandage that still encircled his head. He had lain unconscious in the tunnel for three hours until a party of German tourists had come by and helped him down the passage to the open air. To buy time, his attackers had emptied his pockets, taking his wallet, money and all forms of identification. With typical Germanic efficiency, his rescuers had insisted on calling an ambulance and the police. That had caused all kinds of other problems as he had been unable to use any form of diplomatic immunity and instead had to rely on his cover identity of a Manchester businessman. That had tied him up for a full day. By the time he was freed, Spitz's deadline had long passed.

The only visible memento of the incident was the white bandage which the doctor had insisted on while the ten stitches in the back of his skull had a chance to take hold.

'I'm fine thanks, Chief,' he replied.

Spedding's deputy, Richard Teller, was also in the room. Teller was an old SovBloc hand and one of the legendary players in the field who had helped run Gordievsky when he was active in Moscow. He had also been responsible for setting up the Penguin network, the foundation of counter-proliferation intelligence gathering in the ex-Soviet bloc after the Cold War, a flash of genuine brilliance from which SIS was still reaping the benefits. He was also a staunch Republican, which went down well during a stint as station chief in Washington but was seen as rather suspect in Whitehall. Within the Office, where every little eccentricity was treasured as part of the payment for entry to their élite band of brothers, a dash of anti-Monarchist sentiment did wonders for his reputation.

'Shall I be mother?' the Chief asked, picking up the pot to pour. The tea was Harrods No. 51 Darjeeling, the china was decent Wedgwood and the sugar the special lumpy stuff that came from Fortnum's.

Nash mentally sniffed the air. Not a hanging, he thought with some relief, it's all too informal. He still anticipated something nasty coming in his direction at the end, though. There was too much high-priced talent in one room for his liking.

'First, David, it's a great relief to have you back safely,' Teller began. 'It's a great pity about Spitz, though. He was a brave man; we should have served him better.'

Nash nodded. Teller shrugged as if to dismiss the past. 'Still, it's the lessons that we have to learn from this that concern us,' he continued. 'I'd like your impressions of the team that were after you. Professionals, do you think? Nationality?'

He left the questions hanging, the generalized queries supposedly giving Nash the opportunity to answer as fully or as briefly as he wished. Nash was uncomfortably aware that his response would be analysed unmercifully by the three veteran interrogators whose focus of attention he now was.

'Obviously, I've thought of little else since I recovered consciousness in the tunnel,' he began. 'Professional? Certainly. I didn't make them on the way to the meet and neither did Spitz. We don't know which of us they were following, but clearly they knew their business. Also, that operation in the tunnel was classically pro. Send the ferrets in at one end to drive the rabbits towards the trap at the other.

'They weren't just goons either. The kit was good and they knew how to use it. That first burst was fired downhill, in the dark, and they managed to fire deliberately wide, which was a pretty neat trick. I'm glad they were good enough to miss.' He tried a smile. It wasn't returned.

'What about nationality?' asked Spedding, his hand gently patting the top of his head to ensure that his bald patch was covered by the hair he always combed over from the side. It was slightly disconcerting, Nash thought. He rather expected a wig to sprout wings and levitate to hover somewhere over the Chief's head.

'I've thought about that too,' Nash replied. 'The first team talked in Russian which Spitz translated. Doesn't make them Russian, of course, but it's a reasonable assumption given the location and the nationality of our source. But the backstop? Now he's a real puzzle.'

'Just because he spoke in English doesn't make him one of us,' said Teller.

There was something about Teller's tone, Nash thought. A hint of nervousness, perhaps. Careless phrasing? Surely not. There's something adrift here and I'm in the bloody life-raft, he thought.

'You may be right,' he said. 'But you know how native British English sounds; it's a very difficult thing to mimic. Just look at the awful job Hollywood makes of it. The Russian and English accents are chalk and cheese, that's why their people operating undercover here never pretend to be British. This guy's accent was flawless. Either he's the best-taught foreign intelligence officer we've ever known or he's a Brit. And I would go for the latter. In which case, he might indeed be one of us.'

'That's hardly likely, Nash,' Spedding interrupted quickly. 'There have been no rogues out of here that I've heard about. Could be one of those rejects from the SAS though. They're always turning up in the wrong places. Should call themselves the Special Assassins Service.'

There was polite laughter at the weak joke. These days with the redundancies spreading through the armed forces, there was more than a little truth behind the Chief's words.

'I don't know,' Nash reflected. 'There was something about what he said and the way he said it. As if we were both in the same boat.' He paused, recalling once again the conversation.

'No. That's not right. But certainly there was some kind of bond – or at least I got the impression he thought there was.'

Suddenly the room went dark as the lights turned off. There were muttered curses as once again the automatic sensors failed to do their job. The designers had built sensors in to each of the offices that turned off the lights if the room was empty. They had never worked properly and every meeting seemed to be interrupted by sudden bouts of darkness. It was Teller who got up to turn the lights back on and he continued talking as he moved.

'That's all a little fanciful, David,' said Teller dismissively. 'I think we should focus on what went wrong and not get sidetracked to irrelevant issues. Anyway, you'll have plenty of time to go over all this in due course. The internal affairs people will be in touch shortly and you'll be able to discuss it with them.'

Teller stood up and the general shuffling suggested that the meeting was over. Nash felt the cold anger that had been fuelling his body over the past two days again rise to the surface. This meeting had an agenda he didn't understand and Spedding certainly wasn't going to explain. On the surface, the brass weren't really interested in the killers, and hardly seemed to care about the loss of one of their best sources. But Nash knew that the compromising of even a single agent was considered by the Office to be a mortal insult to their professionalism. None of this rang true. He was being screwed around for God knew what reason. Well fuck them. If they thought he was going to be fobbed off by a cup of tea and a few honeyed words from the top, they could think again.

That Spitz had died just to become another inconvenient statistic made Nash's throat constrict with fury. The bastards were just going to let Spitz go, as if his information and his death mattered not at all. Well, damn them all.

'Before we brush this all the way under the carpet' – the three senior personnel in the room turned as one in Nash's direction, taken aback both at the audacity of his intervention and at the anger in his voice – 'there are two things we are forgetting here. First the information that Spitz passed on and second the fact that the team knew not only about the RV but also my real name.

'As far as I'm concerned that means we have a leak and I want to know what you're doing to plug it. Holographic communication is completely secure so that's not the problem. Who knew about the meeting?'

'Half a dozen people here and nobody in Moscow had the precise details,' replied Spedding. 'We've checked them all and they're clean. If there's a leak, it's not from us. Perhaps Spitz spoke out of turn at his end. Perhaps you . . .' he left the accusation unmade. 'Face it, David, we'll probably never know.'

'And as for the biological weapons programme,' Teller jumped in before David could respond, 'we've been following that pretty hard for some years. We managed to publicize it a couple of years ago in the hope that it would be shut down. Thatcher raised it first and so has everyone since then. Same thing with the Americans. Each time the Russians promise the moon and deliver bugger all. There's a limit to how far we can push them without de-stabilizing the President, and we've just about reached it. There would need to be some pretty compelling evidence for us to go in to bat again. And what Spitz had to say is hardly that. Nevertheless, we'd like you to go over to Washington and have a chat with the Agency about it. Brief them and see if there's anything they can add. After that you're scheduled for Moscow. Apparently Parashvili says you're the first civilized Englishman he's met in years. He wants our help on some organized crime issues. Now, unless there's anything else . . .?'

Nash shook his head, deciding that discretion was the wiser course. Meeting over.

As the four of them headed for the lift, Nash found himself walking next to Diana. He made as if to tighten a noose around his neck.

'That was no lynching, David,' she replied, her voice low. 'They wanted to hear for themselves just what you thought.'

'I got the impression I wasn't telling them anything new.'

'I'm not sure,' she responded thoughtfully. 'But I know one thing: if I were you, I'd watch my back. Somebody's marked your card, David, and whoever it is knows their business.'

She moved ahead to join Teller and Spedding. Nash took the stairs down two floors to where his office was located. He hesitated and instead of turning right moved off to his left towards the counter-proliferation centre. Like so much else at the Office, this was a relatively new department. Bill Watts, the Yorkshireman who headed the department, had brought common sense and a remarkable intuition to a job that required sifting much more than the usual dross from all the intelligence that flowed in from around the world. CP was a priority task these days and covered everything from nuclear materials to conventional weapons systems. Everywhere you looked, new countries were trying to make or buy chemical and biological weapons. It was a Herculean task to block all the routes and all too easy to make the stuff.

SIS had recruited a few of the men and women who had the particular attributes needed for the hunt and Frank Taylor was one of them. Nash had attended one of Frank's lectures about chemical weapons and had been impressed not just by his breadth of knowledge but by his laconic style which did little to disguise his clear commitment to the task. Most of the analytical boys tended to become so absorbed in their subject that any conversation was baffling. Frank was different. He actually relished the chase and treated as an intellectual challenge the job of pulling together apparently random facts to make a complete picture of perfidy by one country or another.

Nash knocked on Frank's door and, hearing a muffled grunt from inside, walked into the office. He stopped with one foot in mid-air just inches from Frank's heaving chest. He looked down into the round, red and sweaty face and thought for a minute he was witnessing a man undergoing cardiac arrest. Seeing the look of alarm on his face, Taylor quickly pushed Nash's foot to one side and sat up.

'Don't worry, lad. I'm not dead yet.' He stood up and dusted down his baggy, black corduroy trousers as if this simple action would return them to some kind of pressed and pristine state. 'Bloody doctors. Bad back. Hurts like hell after sitting at the infernal machine for too long.' He gestured towards the computer. 'So, they have me doing these exercises twice a day. I feel like a constipated duck most of the time but they tell me it's very, very good for me.'

He moved over and sat in the swivel armchair, picked up his half-moon spectacles, put them on and then peered at Nash over the top of the lenses.

'Well, sit down. Sit down,' he swung an arm towards the second chair in the office. 'What can I do for you, David?'

'I've come across something that might run across some of your territory and I wanted to get myself up to speed.'

'Well?' Taylor said impatiently.

'It's to do with BW – specifically Russia's BW programme,' David continued. 'I wanted your five-minute Cook's tour.'

Taylor leaned back in his chair and stared at the ceiling for a moment, collecting his thoughts.

'People talk about nuclear weapons as the threat to the world. Rubbish. Chemical weapons are far more devastating in their effects and biological are even more dangerous.' Seeing the look of disbelief on Nash's face, he hurried to explain.

'Oh, don't get me wrong. Nukes are bad enough and the idea of nuclear war is beyond our worst imaginings. But that's not the point. If we get to the stage where Washington and Moscow are exchanging nuclear arsenals then it's all over for everyone. What is much more of a threat is if Tripoli or Tehran decide to play with the big boys. They might go for nukes because it's sexy and has status but what they really want is something that will work for them; that's easy and cheap. Most of them already have CW which is essentially a manufactured product like a deadly form of fertilizer.

'BW is a whole different ballgame. It uses living viruses or bacteria which are reproduced in the laboratory and then delivered by bomb, shell or even the simple household aerosol.'

'Like Japan?' Nash prompted, recalling the nerve-gas attack in Tokyo's underground railway system.

'Precisely,' Taylor replied. 'There you had a bunch of loonies working in their own backyard and then planting a few small containers of sarin which should have killed thousands but by pure chance only took out a handful. That showed how easy it is, and sarin isn't even on the front line of BW these days.

'You can make BW from just about any virus you like, from Lassa fever to plague to encephalitis provided you have the laboratory – and just about any child's chemistry set will do provided you understand how to use it.'

'If it's that simple, why doesn't everybody have the stuff?' Nash asked.

'Plenty already do. The South Africans developed a virulent strain of the malaria virus and used it to kill hundreds, maybe thousands, of people in Angola and Namibia in the 1980s. The Libyans and the Iranians both have programmes and so do the Iraqis. Name me a bad guy and I'll find you a secret BW programme.

'The problem is not the BW itself but what you want to do with it. All viruses have a short life and most have antidotes, but the bad guys use genetic engineering to give them longevity and immunity to all defences. Designer BW, if you like.'

Taylor got up from his desk and began pacing his small office, punctuating each of his sentences with a stabbing forefinger.

'You want to overfly London with an aerosol and kill everybody within two weeks; I'll give you a variant of the Ebola virus that caused such a scare in Zaïre a while ago. You want to make everyone so depressed that all they can do is weep rather than fight; I'll refine the Rift Valley fever virus to retain that particular symptom. You want people to die? No problem. To have chronic diarrhoea for just twenty-four hours? It can be arranged. You want it airborne? Carried in the drinking water? We deliver.'

'Christ almighty,' Nash exclaimed. 'If it's that easy how come Gadaffi hasn't taken us all out by now?'

'Making the basic stuff is easy. Making it do exactly what you want is much more difficult. You mentioned the Russians earlier. Well, they spent the best part of ten years trying to perfect new strains of plague and they've succeeded – but it took a lot of effort. And, of course, unlike CW, which has a shelf life of years, you can't manufacture BW and keep it for a rainy day. You have to set up the plant and have it ready to go at a moment's notice to produce the designer BW of choice. And that's where we have our opportunity.'

'By tracking the factories?' Nash prompted.

'Sort of. We have a watch-list of materials that ranges from the seventy or so viruses and bacteria that can be used for BW to the fermenters, centrifugal separators and aerosol inhalation chambers that are all part of the process.

'Trouble is, all these things have more than one use.

Freeze-drying equipment is essential to suspend the virus but it's good for freezing peas, too. Baby formula can be a good growth medium for some viruses but millions of mums have probably never heard of BW.'

'It sounds like an impossible task,' said Nash.

'It is. But we can do a lot. We stopped the Libyans buying up the South African BW experts so that slowed down their programme by a few years. We're squeezing the Russians, trying to cut out the Iranians. But at the moment it's a losing battle.'

If Taylor was right, then Spitz's intelligence was indeed vital. If the Russians had really taken the next step along the road from development to manufacture to proliferation, then they were all in trouble.

Nash walked into his office, an optimistic euphemism for the partitioned-off cubicle in which he spent his time completing a seemingly endless stream of forms whenever he was back at base, preparing for his next trip.

There were two pictures, one a lithograph of Billy the Champion Rat Killer which showed a bull terrier in the ring achieving his record of destroying 100 rats in five minutes in 1823. It had been his father's, so there was a measure of sentimental attachment to it, but he thought it amusing to display such a revolting spectacle. Even within the Office, few people had any idea of what he actually did. Sure, everyone knew of the Human Intelligence Tasking Centre, but Need To Know ensured there were no awkward questions from inquisitive colleagues.

David was one of only 400 or so people operating under cover out of a total Office staff of 1,800. The traditional spy, the diplomat at an Embassy or the occasional officer working for some other government department overseas, was being supplanted by a higher grade of field operator, one who understood the rough and tumble world of the street and knew how to survive in it. There are few terrorists to be found at diplomatic cocktail parties in Paris, or even in Moscow, these days. And while it might be useful to look for a corrupt diplomat selling fake end-user certificates to arms dealers in Lagos or Manila, he would be more likely to be spotted in an Amsterdam bar.

HIT members were the front line troops. Rumour had it that Nash was the Office's hired killer. It amused him to play up to their preconceptions and Billy the Champion Rat Killer was perfect.

The second picture was a watercolour by Fletcher which showed a boy casting a long, looping fly-line across a dark pool. The picture conveyed to him all the tranquillity, the thrill of the chase and the anticipation of the strike that fishing meant to him. It was a gift from his father, and it had come with the warning that, like the fisherman in the picture, the profession he had chosen was one where the independence he craved was just one step away from the loneliness he would come to dread. Every time he looked at the picture, he recalled his father's words.

The light on his telephone was blinking, indicating a message received. He pushed Play and the nasal tones of the head of Internal Affairs crackled back at him.

'Nash? It's Graham Smart. We need to talk about your recent trip. Call me as soon as you receive this, please. Thank you.'

Nash thought for a moment, weighing up the consequences of starting what would inevitably turn out to be a balls-aching, form-filling nightmare. He shrugged and sat down at his keyboard.

He logged on, typing in his last name and the password CUTTHROAT. His choice had occasioned a groan of mingled disgust and dismay from the people in IT responsible for authorizing passwords, though in fact it referred not to his work but to the magnificent brown trout he had caught fishing the Bitterroot Valley in western Montana some years earlier. The warm days, the wild roses growing along the riverbank, the wide, empty spaces, were where his heart went in the dark moments when he missed Jaimie or the loneliness of the work became too consuming. He typed an e-mail message:

TO: SMART

FROM: NASH

TRIED TO CALL YOU BUT YOU MUST HAVE BEEN OUT. AM LEAVING ON ASSIGNMENT FROM THE CHIEF. I WILL BE IN TOUCH WHEN I RETURN.

That should keep him quiet, he thought with some satisfaction.

There was a tap on the partition and Alex walked in. She sat down in the single chair next to his desk and looked him over.

'Hail the conquering hero.' There was neither laughter nor sarcasm in her voice, just the concern of a friend who clearly did not like what she saw. 'Rough trip, I hear. How's the bump?'

'OK. Hurt like hell for the first day. Now it feels a bit numb round the edges.' His hand reached up to touch the bandage. 'It's an odd feeling. A bit like someone has got hold of the two bits of my scalp and is pulling them together. Which is what's happening, I suppose,' he smiled.

Alex took in his exhausted expression and crumpled posture. There was a depth to the eyes, a drawing in of the flesh around his nose and neck, that made him seem almost haunted. She had read his report and knew how close he had come to death and how fortunate he was to have come back.

Within IT, Alex's specific responsibility was the men and women of HIT. She made sure their communications were the best, that they were secure and that when they left the Office they stood as good a chance as possible of returning safely. She relished the challenge but found the danger her charges faced unnerving. When she would lie awake at night after sending someone out for a meet, the image that kept recurring was of the faithful woman waiting at home while her man goes off to do brave deeds. She sometimes saw her concern as weakness, but found it impossible not to worry about people she cared about so much.

She had seen them all come and go and thought she had got used to the tension and the drama. Then Billy Dunlap had been taken. He was not one of hers but she had visited him in hospital. It had been horrible; this shell of a man sitting hunched over in a wheelchair, eyes turned inward, all fire damped out to leave just a husk. Now, whenever she sent them out, Alex thought of Billy.

David had been the only one she had got to know socially. There had been that dinner, truncated by the summons from on high, and drinks a couple of times before that. She had been determined not to date anyone from the Office, but David's appealing mix of vulnerability and toughness had made her break her own rule. At times he seemed so contained, self-assured, impregnable. On other occasions, like now, he seemed uncertain and sad. Somewhere, sometime, she was sure that life had dealt him a tough hand.

'You've moved so far into the High Risk category that the Chief should have told you to stay home and go fishing,' she said. 'Let someone else pick up the ball.'

'I'm not sure about the risk,' Nash replied. 'But I am sure that Spitz died because he had some information that he thought was sufficiently important to call a crash meeting to tell me about. It was also important enough for someone to kill him.'

He paused, thinking again about the horror of the moment when Spitz died. When he spoke again, his voice was low, reflective.

'The bastards. My source and they just blew him away.'

'But there was nothing you could do,' Alex said. Then, realizing that the simple platitude was not enough, she tried to be more reassuring. 'David, I'm really sorry. It must be so frustrating. One of your people dead and you back here.'

'That's the worst part of all this,' Nash replied, the bitterness of his tone reflecting the blame he felt for the death of his source. 'The fact that he died while I just lay there. Those guys played me perfectly. Judged what I would do and just what they needed to do to get what they wanted. They knew. They knew about me, they knew about Spitz, they knew about the meet. They knew everything. And yet the Chief, Teller and the rest of them just don't give a damn.'

'Well, what can they do?' Alex asked. 'As I understand it, Smart has begun an investigation. And you're still on the case so at least you may be able to find out just how it happened.'

'Perhaps. But if we've got a leak, then we need to find it and plug it. It's no bloody good just waiting for Smart to do his stuff. That could take months while those buffoons from Security fill in their forms. Meantime, I might be dead and God knows how many other sources will be at risk.'

'At least some of Spitz's information is being put to good use,' Alex said. 'I got the message that you're off to Washington. I'm to give you a new gizmo to take with you so that you can keep in touch. Come with me and I'll take you to the latest marvel of modern technology.'

They walked out of Human Intelligence to the stairs which faced the central atrium that soared the full eight storeys of the building. Two minutes later they were in Alex's office.

Alex sat down at her desk. 'Did Daemon show you the Intelink?' she asked.

'Sure,' Nash replied. 'On one of his short bursts through cyberspace. Fast, exciting and incomprehensible.'

'I know what you mean,' she laughed. 'Well, here's my version. A bit slower but you'll need to get used to it. For you guys in the field it's a stunning resource. Intelink is the Top Secret version of the Internet that allows policymakers, soldiers in the field and intelligence officers to tap into the CIA's database and draw all the classified information from different databases into one file. It's already revolutionizing the way the intelligence community works. Now, name a country,' Alex ordered.

Nash paused for a moment and then said 'North Korea' and watched over her shoulder as she began to manipulate the data.

'This system is entirely encrypted and gives us access at the Top Secret level,' she explained. 'There are other higher codeword levels but the Americans haven't shared them with us yet. We're working on adding our own data into the system so that the intelligence we want to share can be accessed in the same way.'

A few clicks on the mouse led her to the latest footage from the previous month's military display on Revolution Day. The colour was excellent, the quality as good as ordinary film. After a few moments, she exited the show and asked for satellite imagery. That series showed the film taken of Pyongyang by the KH-11 satellite on its routine daily pass overhead. Nash was always astonished at the detail these pictures could produce. He could see the people walking in the streets, hunched over in the cold. He could even see the plumes from the car exhausts as they navigated through the crowd.

'I can get you profiles of all the military leaders, a break-down of their economy, the size of the President Kim Jong-Il's underwear and how often he changes it. It's all here. Stuff that would have taken weeks to collate I can access in seconds.'

'Very impressive,' said Nash with the feeling of a man

who doesn't begin to understand just how what he has seen can be possible. 'I hope I'm not going to have to learn that before I head out.'

'Hardly,' Alex laughed.

The sight of the satellite imagery recalled the memory of Spitz's hurried instructions about the biological weapons. Some of the intelligence traffic he had seen on the Russian BW programme had come in from remote sensors. Maybe some of the answers he wanted might be hidden in there.

'Can you get into the Keyhole stuff on the Russian BW programme?' he asked Alex.

'Sure,' she replied, clicking her way through a series of menus that refined her query until she reached Russia/military/R&D/BW/KH-11. A click of the mouse brought up different imagery from the dozen or so different sites that both the British and the Americans were convinced were being used to develop the new strains of plague virus. David peered closer to the screen as the colour footage showing different factories played. But there was nothing out of the ordinary: smoking chimneys, mostly silent buildings; a few cars coming and going, just the normal workaday routine of any lab anywhere in the world.

'There must be something,' he muttered to himself. 'What about the signals people? We must have targeted the BW programme for intercept.'

'Daemon's the master at that,' Alex replied, reaching for the telephone. 'I'll see if he's around.'

A few minutes later, Daemon's lanky, shambolic form ambled into the office. He greeted them both with a casual 'Howdeedoody' and sat down in the seat next to Alex. He laced the fingers of both hands together and pushed them out to produce an alarming cracking noise and then held them up like a surgeon preparing for an operation.

'What magic would you like these perfect instruments of

pain and pleasure to perform for you today?' He looked around expectantly.

Alex briefly ran through the BW problem and Nash's search for some answers to a vague proposition that had been put to him.

'We need anything that's been picked up recently that might give some new information into the BW programme,' she said.

''Kay,' Daemon replied hunching over the computer, fingers beginning to fly across the keyboard. 'We need to use the Intelink to get across from Langley to the NSA and then into their Home Page for BW to see if there's anything on the open intercept.'

A succession of different images flashed on to the screen to be cleared by a series of keystrokes and then replaced by yet more images as the computers refined the search. He turned towards Nash.

'The way this works is that the boys at Fort Meade will have entered a number of key words – BW, Biopreparat, stuff like that – into the dictionary and then each time those words occur in an intercept, the whole conversation or message will be downloaded for further scanning.'

'What about other languages?'

'No problem,' Daemon replied. 'Five years ago we just worried about Russian and Arabic. Since the sarin attack in Japan we've expanded it to include just about everyone. Anyway, the computer doesn't care much. We record it, the computer translates from the original and brings the message on screen in English.'

Daemon had begun scrolling through a list of messages that included the first three lines of each message, a note of the original language, where and when it had been recorded, who had accessed the data and if any action had been taken.

'The trouble with this is that we get so much crap. Look at

this.' Daemon's finger pointed at a message apparently recorded in Arabic a week earlier in a conversation between Damascus and Tripoli.

'The computer thought it was great. It's got "biological", "Libya" and "Syria", so we're hitting the right words. Trouble is, you've got Mrs Diplomat in Tripoli talking to her mother back home about the difficulties of getting the right washing powder. It's that sort of thing that keeps people like Alex and me in business. Thank God.'

After the first thrill of seeing the awesome capacity of the computers, Nash swiftly grew bored with this list of the mundane and the bizarre. For the experts, it might provide a nuance here and a hint there but for him there was none of the real juice that would take him down a new road.

'Isn't there anything else?' he asked, the disappointment clear in his voice.

'Well, as you ask, there is a little something we might try,' Daemon said, his voice taking on the timbre of an excited schoolboy about to commit some frightful prank.

'We're in Top Secret at the moment and the Americans have Special Compartmented Information above that with designated codewords for individual projects. Their way of keeping prying eyes off the really sensitive stuff.' He gave a satisfied laugh. 'But you wouldn't expect me to have wasted my trip to the States, would you?'

The screen cleared once more. This time, a much shorter list appeared and Daemon called them up one by one. Nash leaned forward to read over Daemon's shoulder. At first, there appeared to be nothing; a useless batch of data, much of it confirmation of intelligence already known: a report of a discussion between the Russian President and some of his top officials which reflected his frustration with the military and their refusal to obey his orders and shut the programme down; a report from a construction site at Lakhta, near St

Petersburg, which was part of a new, and very secret, Russian military effort to enhance further their BW capability.

There was just one report that originated in Vladivostok that sparked his interest. It wasn't so much the details – a port official reporting that a cargo of aerosol inhalation chambers, interfacial polycondensers and phase separators had arrived from Japan – but the notes that some Agency analyst had written at the end of the file:

Although consistent with previous Russian shipments for their BW program, all this material suggests the construction of a whole new facility to manufacture BW. This is inconsistent with other intelligence. Also, they have either manufactured their own hardware or bought it from Sweden. This material appears to have originated in Japan. Original source and final destination are unknown.

There had been no action recommended and none was necessary. In these days of computer searches, the material would simply rest in the database until a query produced the cross-reference that would bring the file back up. Until then, it would remain a small piece of a still-shapeless jigsaw.

'That may be interesting but it doesn't tell you much,' said Daemon.

'Tells me bugger all,' replied Nash. 'But it's the only inconsistent piece of information you and your wonderful computer have managed to produce.'

'Well, excuse me,' said Daemon, piqued. 'I can open the doors but I can't guarantee what's in the rooms. That's down to you spy boys and once again you seem to have dropped the ball.' He rose to leave. 'Nothing personal,' he added as he strolled out of the room.

Alex watched his departing back for a moment and then turned back to the computers. She double clicked to exit the program and moved her chair slightly. Alongside the two desk computers was a small black box. She sat down, flicked the catches on either side and lifted the lid. A full-size screen was in the top with a normal computer keyboard in the bottom half.

'This, in case you didn't know, is a laptop computer,' she explained helpfully. 'We 've made one or two modifications which you might find useful.'

She pressed a small switch on the left-hand side and the screen lit up and then began loading files. After a few moments, the screen was fully lit with a grey background. At the top of the screen were two layers of small icons.

'Now this is just a normal laptop and you can type letters to friends, write your memoirs, keep a diary or do anything else you might want from a word-processing package. But you can use this little red button here to move this pointer on the screen and if you click here, you will see what else this can do for you.'

Her thumb delicately manipulated the little button that was recessed in the centre of the keyboard and brought the arrow over an icon that looked like a letter going into a mailbox. A click of the space bar and the screen cleared. A moment later a different image appeared, this time a series of larger icons with the words VIDEO, SCRIPT, ENCRYPT written in green inside red boxes.

'This gives you the ability to talk directly to the Office through this microphone here,' she pointed to a rectangle of tiny holes at the top of the keyboard. 'This will give you a live video link so that you can see the person at the other end. You will also be able to read in real time maps that we store in the database here or satellite imagery as it is being relayed back to us. You can do searches across every existing database that can be accessed from the Internet.'

Noticing his bemused expression, she laughed. 'Or we can do the searches for you.'

She tapped the keys, there was a clicking noise of a telephone dialling and then the screen cleared once again. She typed in Mallard.Int@Compuserve.Com and then typed: *We believe that the Russians are experimenting with a particle beam weapon, codenamed Pyramid, that can kill by simulating a heart attack. Do you have any information on this? Hale.*

She pressed a key, the screen cleared. She clicked the pointer on a small telephone icon and the link disconnected.

'That was a message to a forum composed entirely of former intelligence officers from around the world. It's rather like a café in Montmartre where the old spies gather for a gossip except that it's done entirely on computer. Most of us have never met the others on the forum and the way the Net works it's virtually impossible to find out just where a message is coming from in the world. I happen to know that Mallard is really Sasha Nikonorov who works in the GRU while he thinks I think he's an ex-DIA man.'

She laughed. 'This is just a new version of the wilderness of mirrors. The difference is that our computers are better than theirs. He thinks he knows, but I know he doesn't know, *ergo* I have the real knowledge.'

'If you've got Russians, Americans and God knows who else playing around on this, how can it be secure?' asked Nash. Already concerned about his personal security, the last thing Nash wanted was to have his computer conversations monitored by the enemy.

'Don't worry, cryptography has come a long way since you were at school. These days the Crays downstairs do the work for us and each of the crypto systems we have is generated specifically for the user and relates to the date and time of each day. The Cray produces a crypto using a prime number and that code is automatically generated for you each time you create a message. At my end, the system reads when the message was created and then applies a particular key to decode the message. The ciphertext is uncrackable unless you know the original method that was used to create the cipher and that would require access to the IT department.

'All you have to do is create your messages and talk to me. The coding and decoding all happens automatically at either end. Simple.'

'Ha,' Nash grunted his disagreement. 'This all sounds impossibly complicated to me. How on earth am I going to retain all this and make it work?'

'Think of it as liberation,' Alex replied, her voice full of the pleasure that an expert has when explaining something to the ignorant. 'This is telephone, television, video and satellites all rolled into one. And, I've added a little something that just might help you in a crisis.'

She clicked on a yellow icon of a smiley face. The screen cleared again and she was into a separate program called Alex.Com.

'This is a package for you to talk directly to me, laptop to laptop. It'll work just like a dedicated phone line so that when you send a message to me, I can pick it up without it ever going through the mainframes here. We can have a conversation on screen and I'll be able to send you answers back in real time.'

'But won't that cut off your access to all the other systems?' Nash asked.

'Not at all. I can put you on hold, dial in to the mainframe and access anything I want. Then I can patch you in through my machine. That way, you get the information you want and you have a direct line that will help you scythe through the bureaucratic jungle around here.'

'Sounds good to me,' Nash replied. 'Maybe I can use the trip to Washington to test it out. If there are problems, you can walk me through the answers when I get back.'

'Perfect,' said Alex. 'What's your schedule?'

'DC tonight. The Agency tomorrow and perhaps the next day and then back for the weekend.'

How would she ever get to know this enigmatic man?

There had been no opportunity to talk about anything but work since his return from Moscow, and now he was off again. She decided to be bold.

'Look, David,' she began tentatively. 'Why don't I take the laptop down to your cottage for the weekend? When you come back, you head straight there and I'll meet you. You can show me around and we'll go over any problems you might have been having with the system.'

She could see both speculation and the beginnings of a rejection forming on his lips.

'Don't worry, I'm not planning an invasion,' she continued. 'And I'm not offering my body either. You need some help. I want to make sure you get it. We can combine work with a bit of fun. And I'm sure you have a spare bedroom.'

His relief was evident as his expression changed from concern to appreciation. He reached down, picked the laptop off the desk, zipped it into its case and headed for the door.

'Fine, see you there,' he said with a grin. 'The key is in the nesting box by the front door. I'll send you directions via this infernal machine.'

The vulgar stretch Rolls-Royce turned through the Karamon Gates leading to the Nijojo Castle, Yamana's inner sanctum. Alla Raikin looked through the smoked windows with envy; the Castle made her palace in Moscow appear like servants' quarters. Inside Yamana was seated on a gilded throne in a magnificent room, filled with glorious colours and beautiful, delicate, priceless works of art. To his right sat Kim Jong-Il, the North Korean President, in a damask-upholstered chair, angled so that the two men could see each other.

Alla knew that the two Orientals had more in common than slanted eyes. Yamana was the owner of the *Mang-yongobong-92* that, three times a month, made the twenty-seven-hour journey from Niigata on the west coast of Japan to Wonsan in North Korea, carrying around 250 passengers and a mixed cargo which invariably included a few special orders for the ruling family, a very profitable sideline for the Yamaguchi-gumi, the branch of the Yakuza that Yamana controlled.

Alla took a seat to Yamana's left. Yamana cleared his throat.

'So, to business,' he said, in the hard voice of a man used to command. 'How are things proceeding in Moscow?'

'We have the support of the required military units, Muraviev has seen to that. There is no question that the naval fleet will join. They have not been at sea for nearly two years and the ships the admirals command will be rotting hulks in another two. They want a country that can offer a real possibility of running the kind of navy they once joined.'

'And the Army? The Air Force?'

'At worst they are neutral and at best they will come over to our side.'

'What about afterwards?' pressed the Japanese. 'Even assuming the President does nothing, the international community will not stand by and let a new empire emerge that they might see as a threat. The Americans will move against us and so will the United Nations.'

Kim gave Yamana a look that mixed disdain with what appeared to be astonishment. 'America? The UN?' he asked. 'The one led by a gutless idiot who wants everyone to love him and the other a bunch of powerless bureaucrats who will take six months to make a decision which even then will be worthless. We have nothing to worry about from them.'

'I disagree,' Yamana said to the North Korean. 'Colonel Muraviev may be able to secure for us the nuclear weapons that our plan demands, but getting the launch codes may take months, perhaps years. I have no doubt the Americans and the others on the Security Council will move fast – or at least fast enough to take action before we can defend ourselves properly.'

'We've discussed this before,' Alla interrupted. 'We agreed that what was required was something that would shock, would make any thought of moving against us impossible to contemplate. I have found that violence is an effective deterrent,' she continued. 'Particularly if it is applied with great force to cause maximum suffering in the shortest possible time.'

There were enthusiastic nods from her listeners as Alla went on to explain her proposals in detail. But their satisfaction with the plan was suddenly disturbed when Alla spoke again.

'I'm afraid we have had a leak,' she began, hesitant to be the bearer of the news that they all dreaded. 'The British had a spy in Moscow who learned that somebody has been buying product from the Biopreparat programme.'

'How the hell did that happen?' Yamana demanded.

'A fool of a general got greedy and tried to recruit a salesman. As luck would have it, the salesman was also a British spy. The general didn't identify us, so we still have some cover. But the fact remains that the British know about the product.'

'Damage limitation?' rapped Yamana.

Alla held up her left hand and began to tick off her fingers.

'First, the spy has been eliminated so he won't talk again. Second, the general has also met with an accident so there will be no more freelancing by him. Third, there is no sign of any further breaches from the plant, so I think we've shut that door.'

'So we have nothing to worry about,' said Kim Jong-Il.

'That's not quite correct,' Alla said. 'Before we eliminated the spy, he contacted a British agent called Nash, David Nash. We have to assume that the spy told him what he knew.'

'What do Spandau say?' Yamana asked.

'We got them to take out the spy and they did their usual efficient job. They were unable to kill Nash at the same time, of course, for reasons you will appreciate. They have referred it back to us instead. I received some additional information from them today. Despite his masters' apathy, Nash is determined to follow it up. He's going to be a problem. How we deal with it is up to us.'

'Then there is no choice, Madame Raikin,' said Yamana without hesitation. 'Kill him.'

8

 span style="small-caps">As he drove through the white entrance
gates to Langley and over the anti-terrorist barriers buried in
the surface of the road, Nash reflected that at least in Washington SIS operated in style. A few years ago, he would have
stayed the night in some grubby apartment. But Richard
Teller had somehow managed to convince London that a
larger Georgetown house was required for entertaining in
the style the Americans expected instead of the apartment near
Rock Creek Parkway. It was nonsense, of course, but at the
Agency so much emphasis was placed on style and a decent
entertainment allowance was a clear signal that the visitor was
somebody of significance. No wonder Teller was now deputy
director, Nash thought sourly. Anyone with the ability to
finesse that one deserved to be.

The SIS station in Washington is perhaps the most important outpost the Office has. It does not have the largest staff —
that honour goes to Moscow — but it is the one responsible
for liaising with American intelligence. Intercepts by GCHQ
are shared with the National Security Agency and vice versa.
Similarly, information from sources is also shared but with
their origins generally disguised to protect the spy.

With their $28 billion budget and tens of thousands of
employees, American intelligence was always going to be the
gorilla on the block and the British were conscious that they
were tolerated only because they could bring something to

the party. That something was an ability to recruit and run sources in key countries such as Russia and China. In return, good intelligence from the Americans gave Britain knowledge that would otherwise be lacking and allowed the small island nation to punch well above its weight in the international arena.

Langley was a mix of the best and brightest that America's building industry had to offer. The impression of scale began with the entrance hall to the main building. Nash walked across the sixteen-pointed star set in marble in the vast entranceway. He passed beneath the engraved inscription that read AND YE SHALL KNOW THE TRUTH AND THE TRUTH SHALL MAKE YOU FREE. To his left the bronze statute of William 'Wild Bill' Donovan, founder of the Office of Strategic Services, the forerunner of the CIA, peered endlessly at his legacy.

Nash moved to his right and up a short flight of steps to the visitors' reception.

'Mr Nash?' The voice belonged to a small, round woman whose eyes appeared enormous behind thick glasses. He nodded and obediently followed her to the lift, which took him to the sixth floor. As the door slid open, a tall blond man with the broad shoulders and tight waist of an American football player stepped forward. Here there were no hand-shakes. These were the trained gatekeepers who needed to keep their hands free. And they were all supposed to be Harvard or Yale graduates, too.

'This way, Mr Nash.' The giant gestured ahead and then fell in behind. Nash passed through a narrow door which he assumed was a disguised X-ray detector and then into the inner sanctum of the DCI. The view of the wooded Virginia countryside with the Potomac river in the distance was stunning, giving the Director's office a sense of remoteness and privacy that was altogether lacking in London. No other building was visible, just the green of the woods and the distant shimmer of sunlight on the water.

'Dave, great to see you. Jim McConnell.' The hand reached out to engulf his even as he was taking in the dark suit, white Brooks Brothers button-down shirt and red tie. The beefy face over the fleshy neck was broken by a wide, even-toothed smile that was meant to embrace with its warmth. Nash instinctively recoiled from the affected bonhomie. He disliked the instant abbreviation of his name by a man whom he had never met and he immediately distrusted the cold, unsmiling brown eyes.

'A pleasure to meet you, Mr McConnell. David Nash.' He could hear himself begin to elongate his vowels and heard too the emphasis on the 'David', underscoring the reality of his name, whatever this oaf might think. There was a brief pause as McConnell registered the correction, but smile intact he steered Nash over to a small group of deep armchairs to the left of the Director's desk.

'The Director's on the Hill this morning. Another grilling by the oversight committees,' he grimaced in disgust. 'But he particularly asked me to pass on his apologies and told me to make sure you know that we are entirely at your disposal.'

It was a fiction, Nash knew. The Director had probably never heard of him and the drawbridge would come up just as soon as he tried to test the generous offer. But the Americans were so good at the smarm stuff. Despite himself, he could feel the charm having its effect.

'I've been asked to take you through what we think is going on over there and then I know you want to discuss some thoughts you have.'

So, this was to be a hardball session. The Director's office to impress, the heavy mob to greet and now the soft soap of the usual slick presentation to wrap him up and send him back home. Any nonsense and they'd bring on the heavy brigade who would try different, tougher, tactics. Nash sat back and waited for the show to begin.

McConnell reached for a remote control pad on the table in front of him and clicked a button. The wooden panel in the wall in front of them retracted into the ceiling, carrying with it a painting of Indians offering the hand of friendship to some white settlers while other whites were coming behind them, clearly about to gun them down. Political correctness had reached deep, Nash thought.

The screen flickered briefly and then the image of the first slide, headlined 'The Russian Economy' appeared on the screen. It had always seemed to Nash that slides were the first refuge for the ill-prepared teacher or the inadequate briefer. Somehow the props were supposed to make the subject clearer. In fact, they simply raised the boredom threshold. He settled into the chair and prepared for the onslaught.

'OK,' McConnell began. 'As you know, I am Director of European Operations which these days takes in Russia and the countries of the former Soviet Union. We also take an occasional look at the French.' He laughed lightly and Nash dutifully smiled at the in-joke. Some years earlier the French had been discovered trying to steal economic secrets from America's defence industry and their activities were now monitored closely.

'You can see from this chart that the Russian economy is now in pretty good shape,' McConnell continued. He picked up what looked like a pencil, flicked a switch and a red laser beam lanced out from his hand to dance over the graph and the accompanying figures.

'Monthly inflation, which was running at forty per cent, is now down to around three per cent. This make Russia less of a terminal patient. Out of the ER and into the recovery ward. But the local Mafia now accounts for around half the economy and seems bent on pillaging what remains. Our view is that, over time, they will come to see that it is in their long-term interests to plough some of their cash back into the local economy. Most big bad guys in the US now have their houses in Long Beach, their private jets and their strings of girls. Even for them, there has to be a saturation point for the physical and material needs and we think the Russian mobs have about reached that so we're upbeat about the future.'

He flicked another switch.

'Now this is Ukraine. You can see that inflation, assuming we can really measure it at all, is around sixty per cent a month. Industrial production is still falling at rates that suggest every factory still open soon won't be and those that have folded have folded for good. Investment from outside is zero and even the Mafia is having a tough time making a go of it. There is simply no money around.'

'So what's going to happen?' Nash asked.

'Ah. Now there you have the key question which your masters and mine want answered,' McConnell replied. 'It's a tough call, real tough. By all normal standards, the Ukrainians should have risen up in revolt at the incompetence of their masters. But for some reason the peasants are reluctant to kick ass. Years of conditioning, I guess. The military, though, are a different ball game. Every second officer has a Russian babushka telling him how much better things are in the Motherland. Many of them don't consider Ukraine their homeland at all. They would prefer to be ruled by Moscow than by Kiev, especially now the Ukrainian economy's in the toilet.'

'But that problem has been around ever since the Union collapsed and there's never been any serious indication that things are going to explode,' Nash interrupted. 'On the contrary, life goes on. All the alarmist reports that were being put out three or four years ago have proved wrong. Here we are, still having the same conversation and nothing has changed.'

It was a sore point. The Agency had prepared a series of

assessments known as National Intelligence Estimates or NIEs following the 1991 failed coup that had eventually brought Yeltsin to power and each of them had predicted looming calamity. That winter there were going to be food riots; widespread starvation was predicted; the returning soldiers from eastern Europe had nowhere to live and would use their guns to take what they wanted. None of it had proved accurate and the Agency had been licking its wounds ever since.

'I hear what you say, David,' replied McConnell. 'I have someone I'd like you to meet.'

He pressed another device on his remote control and a few moments later, a tall, almost unnaturally lean man walked into the room.

'David, I'd like you to meet Philip Thomas. Phil, this is David Nash from SIS.'

Nash escaped with some difficulty from the lush embrace of the chair and took two steps across the room to accept the offered hand. They had met before, of course, at the lecture on international crime and drugs a couple of weeks earlier. Nash paused, waiting to see whether the other man would remember and if so, whether he would acknowledge the meeting.

'Dave. Great to see you again.' The hesitation was so slight it might almost have gone unnoticed if Nash hadn't been watching for it. 'I'm sorry we didn't have time to talk for longer. Maybe this time.'

'Fine with me,' Nash said shortly. His initial impression of the man was reinforced at this second meeting. Despite the firm handshake and the apparent 'go get 'em' approach to life, Thomas had the tired air of a man either exhausted or unhappy or both. But then, from what he had heard, that was not too unusual around the Agency these days. Budget cuts were not a purely British phenomenon.

'David, Phil is with our Moscow station working in deep

cover attached to our trade mission. His real job has been to monitor ethnic unrest. He has come across some interesting stuff which he is going to share with you.'

McConnell gestured with an open hand, encouraging Thomas to take up the slack. Seeing Nash's questioning expression, Thomas smiled sheepishly, a boy caught in an innocent prank.

'Drugs are part of my remit, David,' he explained. 'I was passing through London to keep you folks up to speed and it was thought that a talk about the problems might be helpful. These days, we double up wherever we can.'

He glanced over at McConnell to see if there was any response to this blunt barb. None was forthcoming so he moved back to the main topic.

'Yeah, well as I'm sure the Director has told you,' Thomas began, 'Ukraine is so far down the pan it's practically invisible. That itself might not matter but we've picked up some interesting signals in the last couple of weeks that suggest others might be about to take advantage of the situation.'

'The military?' Nash prompted.

'Noooo.' The negative came out in extended form, as if there were one answer with underlying sub-clauses. 'We don't think it's the military directly but we do think that some of them may be involved. Perhaps I should explain.

'As you know from your own experience, the Mafia in Russia today are everywhere. They control many of the businesses, most of the action on the street, whether it be prostitution, drugs or the corner kiosk, and increasingly they control parts of government. But the major players know that to survive they must expand. The question is where? They are doing what they can in the former communist countries like Poland and Czechoslovakia, but they're up against reasonably successful and well-established capitalist economies. There are big western investments in eastern Europe now and they will be protected by the investors and the host government.

'The target of opportunity is Ukraine. It's virgin territory, just like Russia was a few years ago. Control by central government is minimal. Investment from outside is as close to zero as makes no difference and both the people and the military are seriously pissed. This is primo ground for the Mafia to exploit.'

'But how?' Nash asked. 'You say there's no money there, no investment, just a bunch of hungry peasants and disgruntled military. So what's the attraction?'

'The people who've made all the money in Russia have got billions to invest,' Thomas replied. 'They have a cash machine going in Russia and it's working so hard they just can't keep pace. They're awash in dollar bills and they've nowhere to go. Ukraine offers them real opportunity – provided they can gain power. With power comes access to whole new markets, not just in Ukraine but outside. They could start to reap really serious money.'

'And then there's the nukes,' McConnell prompted.

Thomas nodded, both recognition and hesitancy in the single, simple gesture.

'That's the real problem,' he explained. 'In Russia, control of the nukes has remained remarkably solid. In the Ukraine things are different. Officially they are still supposed to be under Russian control. Unofficially it's a fudge with the Ukrainian military doing their best to crack the access and launch codes. Success is only a matter of time. For the Mafia, control of that arsenal will give them serious power. They could not only sell what they wanted to the highest bidder but they would have their own perfect blackmail weapon.'

'That's all very apocalyptic,' said Nash. 'But what is the evidence that any of this is going on? We have picked up nothing with a nuclear flavour. On the contrary, we think there are serious threats inside Russia.'

'Yes, we'd heard that you had some concerns in that area, David,' said McConnell smoothly. 'We'd like to hear about those in a moment. But first, let's hear Phil out.'

Thomas levered himself out of the chair and began to stalk across the square of dark brown carpet in front of the slide screen. He reminded Nash of a giraffe packed for air shipment with only a tiny space to contain its long legs.

'We have done some interesting work with the Mafia in the past year or so,' said Thomas tentatively. To Nash this translated that the Agency had developed some good sources inside the gangs. There was a paranoia about revealing the existence of sources, particularly after the Ames case when hundreds of operations had been burned because of loose talk. The language had taken on a new, distant, tone where it was all 'interesting work' or 'useful developments' or 'helpful information' and never 'sources', 'assets' or 'agents in place'.

'In the past couple of weeks we have gathered some reliable information that one of the Mafia leaders is planning a major assault against the Ukraine. He has been subverting the Russian officers in the military, laying out huge sums to buy loyalty and he appears to have a commitment from enough senior people to make a difference. We also know that he has been in touch with both the Iranians and the Libyans with a view to passing on some of the nukes he will get when the trouble starts.'

'And what chance of success do you give this?' Nash asked.

'Pretty good,' Thomas replied. 'A military takeover with the promise of a closer alliance with Moscow, free elections within six months and a guarantee of lower inflation and bread on the table will win over enough people to make it happen. The unknown is the ultra-nationalists in the west of the country. But if the coup is ruthless enough, there shouldn't be any meaningful opposition – or rather no opposition that will last longer than a few days.'

Nash knew what that meant. Widescale butchery to eliminate anybody who might stand in the way of the new order. Tough tactics which the Slavs had grown used to down the centuries. In a strange way they even seemed to welcome authoritarian regimes and be uncomfortable and uncertain with the freedoms that developed nations largely took for granted.

'Just how credible do you think all this is?' asked Nash, the scepticism evident in his voice.

'Oh, we think it's credible enough,' said McConnell. 'We sent a SNIE to the President two days ago and he is probably meeting with the Principals group' – he paused and looked at his watch – 'about now at the White House. I'm not sure that we will actually do anything,' he smiled slightly, his disdain for the politicians and their lack of leadership clearly evident. 'But, they can't complain that they haven't had the information.'

If the Agency had committed itself to a Special National Intelligence Estimate, then things were indeed serious. These days, the President paid so little attention to the intelligence community and was so disenchanted with the information it supplied that rumour had it that the SNIEs had virtually dried up. The Agency preferred to keep well below the parapet rather than risk getting sniped at again for intelligence failures that were more usually a failure of the political leadership to listen when they were told.

'So, who's behind all of this?' Nash asked.

'Now, there we can help you,' McConnell replied. He clicked the remote control, the screen cleared to be replaced by a film. It had that grainy quality that even the computer enhancement couldn't disguise, a clear indication that it had been shot with a micro-camera, probably hidden in a button or the top of a walking stick or a cap badge. The film showed a man walking along a Moscow street – Nash recognized the elegant mansions of Kropotkinskaya district and his judgement was confirmed when the neon lights of the Tren-Mos Bistro filled the frame. It had been founded in 1992 by a couple of American businessmen from Trenton, New Jersey and it served pizza and cheeseburgers at extraordinary prices. It had become a favoured haunt of the local gangsters who were among the few who could afford the prices and the standard demand for payment in US dollars.

The man being photographed was clearly prosperous. His camelhair coat looked as though it came from Bond Street or Madison Avenue and probably cost a small fortune. The dark shoes seemed expensive but it was the barber and the bodyguards that showed this man was one of the city's new élite. Instead of the usual Muscovite pudding-basin cut, the man had a perfectly coiffed head of hair, each greying strand in place, the whole layered to present the shape of the small but elegant head in its best light. This man had money. He seemed familiar to Nash, a half-forgotten face from some distant briefing.

The four thugs who surrounded him, two in front and two behind, were standard Moscow fare. Large, very tough and with their gun hands permanently in place under their coats. There was no pretence here that they were unarmed. The idea was to send the strongest possible signal: mess with us and you're dead meat. They bulled their way through the queue outside the restaurant, clearing a path for the man who walked unhurriedly to the head of the line, a place he clearly considered his by right.

'That is Pyotr Sakharovsky, head of the Lubertsy gang, or the Lubers as they are known locally,' Thomas continued. 'He's one of their top men, part of the group known as the *vory v zakone* or thieves within the code. He controls protection, drugs and prostitution in his Moscow sector but he is also a little more imaginative than some of his colleagues in the Organizatsiya. It was he who organized the great rouble scam and he who first understood the possibilities represented by the privatization programme. A smart boy, is Pyotr, and he clearly has ambitions that reach way beyond Moscow.'

It came back to Nash. Pyotr had been identified to him in the past as one of the few Russian gangsters who had been of some assistance to the British. Not an asset exactly, more an occasional help when their interests coincided, or a desperate last resort. Did the Americans know that? he wondered. He for one wasn't about to tell them if they didn't. Anyway, the Americans had always been more squeamish about who they dealt with, as if spying was part of some moral crusade: only good Christians need apply.

'So, if I understand this right,' Nash said, marshalling his thoughts, 'you suspect a Mafia-backed coup in Ukraine which is being organized by friend Pyotr here,' he gestured at the screen. 'That coup would threaten the stability of Russia and the Ukraine and could well embrace the other former communist countries and spill over into western Europe. Correct?'

The two men nodded.

'Any idea of timescale?'

'Our information is thin on that so far,' McConnell replied. 'We think sometime in the next two weeks, things will begin to happen. But there is no date certain as yet. We're working on it.'

There was a pause. Nash watched the interplay between the two CIA men. Now, we get to the heart of this, he thought. There was no signal that he could see but it was Thomas who picked up the ball. The light division first, Nash thought, the heavy to follow if the first assault doesn't work.

'We understand you have some concerns about Russia's BW programme,' said Thomas. 'We've been working very closely with SIS on this, ever since Pasechnik came over, and it remains a top priority. Give us an outline of where you think we are and I'll then share our thinking with you.'

'We believe there has been a leak from the Biopreparat programme,' Nash replied. 'That that old bastard Kuntsevich is preparing to sell some of their genetically engineered plague weapons to the highest bidder. We know that some of the material is already out there, sold to one of the gangs.'

'When you say "we know", what exactly do you mean?' Thomas asked.

Nash hesitated, turning over the options in his mind. This was always the trickiest moment in a relationship that involved the sharing of intelligence. Give too much and the source would be compromised. The fact that Spitz was dead made little difference as even a dead source can reveal valuable tradecraft. Too little information and his clearly sceptical audience would remain unconvinced.

'We have what I believe to be very credible evidence that there has been seepage and that there will be more in the immediate future.'

'You say "evidence", David. Is that single source or is there collateral?' Thomas pressed.

'Single,' David admitted reluctantly.

There was an almost audible relaxation in the tension. Nash groaned inwardly. Single source was deniable. Whatever game was being played here he had lost.

'You see, David, it's like this,' McConnell said. 'We've made a major investment to track the programme and the product and we have taken the Russians to the mat. Reagan to Gorby, Thatcher to Gorby, Bush to Gorby, Major to Yeltsin, Clinton to Yeltsin and on down the line. They've been fronted up and they've admitted it and promised to shut it down.'

'But they haven't,' Nash pointed out.

'As you say,' McConnell admitted. 'Now there are two

problems with this issue, the general and the specific. At every summit for the past five years, the subject has been discussed and the Russians have promised every time to try and shut the programme down. Now you and I both know that's not good enough.' McConnell smiled slightly, embracing Nash into the conspiracy.

'But this is international politics, right? And we're in the sewer receiving all the shit which the politicians are shovelling down at us. State and the NSC have convinced the White House that raising the profile on this one will expose the Russian government's weakness, piss off the military and maybe provoke a confrontation that none of us wants.'

He held up both hands, palms out towards Nash as if to ward off the protests he knew were coming.

'Now I know that sounds like a crock to you. And it does to me too but that's the politics. So that's the general. Now to the specific.

'When we first heard about the possibility of increased BW activity from you guys, we immediately launched our own investigation, both here and in Moscow.'

'We have some technical means that keep an eye on this, David,' Thomas added, though he offered no further details about Little Nell. 'We've checked and come up with nothing.'

David wondered what 'technical means' the Yanks had come up with now. No doubt satellites, or lasers, or mikes or some other bloody gizmo. The Americans always believed the equipment and never the people. Unbidden, a brief image of Spitz's bloody body arcing away from him flashed before his eyes. Spitz believed what he was saying, Nash was certain.

'We have also checked on other information sources that are available to us. Reliable sources. We are assured that there is nothing happening in that area we don't already know about,' McConnell added.

There was a note of certitude to the Americans' assertions

that Nash knew would be pointless fighting. The Agency seemed as uninterested in the whole affair as Spedding and Teller had been. McConnell stood up, clearly anxious to move on.

'I'm truly grateful that you took the time out to have this little chat,' he said, his hand reaching around Nash's shoulder to draw him close. 'I feel we've cleared the air and we all know where we stand. Incidentally, you and Phil will be seeing a lot more of each other. He's leaving for Moscow tonight to keep an eye on things for us. I hear you're going to be heading in that direction, too. Be sure and keep in touch.'

Nash felt like a pinball with absolutely no control over his own destiny. London had clearly sent over a very detailed briefing in advance of his arrival, complete with future travel plans. Aside from such an obvious breach of Need To Know, it was no bloody American's job to mind his back or tell him what to do.

He shook McConnell's hand at the lift, waved a farewell to Thomas and headed for the ground floor. Whatever the pressure, it was not the honeyed words from the CIA men that he took with him into the car. It was the memory of Spitz leaning over in that dark, damp cave and muttering the words of warning that were to cost him his life. Nash had failed him then. He would not fail him now.

At Dulles, he had taken the PeopleMover shuttle bus to the outer terminal and laid up in the Executive Club lounge. It had been full of the instruments of modern executive warfare: fax machines, photocopiers, telephones and even dedicated modem lines. None of the machines looked as if it had ever been used but it seemed an ideal time to try out the link with Alex via the laptop. The woman at the reception desk seemed to have even less clue than he did about the array of machines but one of the telephones had a small screen on which appeared instructions for every conceivable action.

Nash placed his credit card into the right slot, waited for the prompt and then plugged his modem cord into the outlet and turned on his machine. A few moments later, the screen lit up and, following Alex's instructions, he moved the cursor to the icon that looked like a letter being posted in a box and pressed the key. There were some satisfying whirrs and clicks, the sound of a dialling tone and then the connection was made.

GOOD MORNING, DAVID. HOW ARE YOU? printed out across the screen in blue letters on the grey background.

It was eerie. He knew that nobody was at the other end, that it was simply an automated computerized response, but he wanted to say or even type FINE THANKS, HOW ARE YOU? as if mere words could make the inanimate more accessible.

Using two fingers, he typed in the details of his flight time, some directions and the ETA so that Alex would know when to expect him at the cottage. He clicked on the send key. A flashing message ENCRYPTING appeared on the screen and then both the information and the message vanished, presumably to reappear on Alex's terminal in London. He was about to turn the machine off when a message flashed on the screen: SWITCH TO VOICE.

He clicked on an icon of a red face, mouth open wide in a shout, and moments later the screen filled with Alex's face.

'I'm glad I caught you,' she said. 'And impressed that you've got this up and running.'

He paused and then leaned forward to speak into the microphone.

'Can you see me as clearly as I can see you?' he asked.

'Not that time. All I saw was the top of your forehead. You don't have to lean forward. The mike's sensitive enough to pick you up at normal distance and if you move forward then the camera can't follow you. It's that little orange button in the line of lights underneath the screen. It used to be a battery warning light until our people made some changes.'

He glanced down and saw the light, resisting the temptation to lean forward and chop his face in half once again.

'Did you get my message about the cottage?' he asked.

'Sure,' she replied. 'I'll be there when you get in.'

There was a brief pause as they both waited for the other to fill the gap, the distance and the mechanics of the conversation draining it of any intimacy. Inevitably, they started to speak at once and laughed in unison.

'This hasn't been much fun,' he continued. 'The same scepticism here as in London.'

Encrypted the conversation might be, but training and natural caution ensured that it was kept to vague generalities. But Alex still picked up on the undercurrent of frustration.

'Poor David,' she replied, her evident sympathy cutting through the banality of the remark. 'You can tell me all about it when you get back. Don't let the bastards grind you down and remember there are some of us back here in your corner.'

It was the reassurance he needed and wanted to hear directly. After the bruising meeting at Langley he wanted to reach through the screen and embrace the familiar face and its welcoming smile. But the physical separation compounded his natural reticence to produce a stiffness that afterwards he mulled over, kicking himself for missing the opportunity to say what he felt.

9

Driving with the roof down, Nash used the journey along the M25 and M3 to clear the grit of the transatlantic flight from behind his eyes and enjoy the sheer exhilaration of speed and noise. The soaring trumpets of Hummel's concerto drove him forward, the doubts left from the trip and the uncertainties about the way forward pushed to the back of his mind by the pleasure of the moment and the thought of Alex awaiting him. They trained you to always look for the opposition – in shorthand CYS, or Check Your Six, a hangover from the days when vigilance had been compared with an RAF pilot watching his back – but England was England and nobody ever did anything on the home turf, so after the obligatory glance or two in the rear view mirror, he paid no special attention to what was going on behind. Even if he had checked, he probably would never have noticed the dark green Rover which picked him up as he entered the slip road to join the motorway and manoeuvred to stay in touch, at first from far behind, then ahead, then behind again, always two or three cars away.

Nash, on the other hand, was virtually unmissable in the sky blue 1967 Ford Mustang with which he had fallen in love on sight and bought on impulse for its classic lines, its smell of old leather, the feel of raw power from the engine and the soft top that freed the spirit in summer. Jaimie had considered it a mad indulgence and secretly so did he. When she had become pregnant, he had resigned himself to replacing it with something more practical. Now, he kept it partly in memory of those happier times and partly because it was a simple pleasure in his increasingly complicated world.

Nash considered the turn from Winchester on to the A272 the beginning of journey's end although the last stretch always seemed to take longer than he expected. The cottage was something he and Jaimie had always talked about – the place in the country where they might raise a family; a spot where they could escape the pressures of work and the horror of a polluted, gridlocked London. Now, it was merely a monument to what might have been.

He pictured the security of its timbered walls, its thatched warmth and the green chaos of a garden he always meant to dig but never got round to. His fingers drummed the steering wheel, his impatience to be home matching the swelling rhythms of the trumpets. Suddenly he noticed a tiny red dot dancing on the fingers of his right hand. A refraction of the sun through the rear window? The realization that with the top down there was no rear window gelled with a distant memory driving him instinctively to force the wheel to the right in a sudden, jinking motion.

The dot of the laser sight jerked away and then swiftly moved back into the car, searching out the back of his head, his shoulders, anywhere that presented flesh and bone. Frantic now, he jinked again, dragging the protesting car over to the left and on to the verge. The wooden fascia of the car disintegrated, shards of wood flying inside the compartment with a sound like a buzz saw. One of the shards knifed through the softness of his cheek and he immediately felt the warmth of blood flowing down his face.

Glancing in the mirror he saw the shape of a green car on his tail, fishtailing as it tried to follow his swerving moves. The barrel of a gun was poking from the passenger side of the car, the bulbous torpedo shape of the sight clearly visible. Nash switched his focus back to the road ahead.

He knew with such certainty that he was marked for imminent death that he could almost feel the flesh of his back parting to make way for the metal entering his body. He imagined the beginning of the flood of pain and then the violent wrenching crash as the end came. He found himself hunching over the wheel, as if by making himself smaller, he could improve his chances of survival.

He moved the wheel again and the dot suddenly appeared on the rev counter of the instrument panel. Nash realized that, seconds earlier, it must have been focused on his back. The dot was immediately replaced by a line of bullet holes marching from the instrument panel along the top of the fascia and then through the windscreen. There was a crack as the unlaminated glass shattered and he brought his right arm as best he could over his face and clenched his eyes shut. Pieces of glass like tiny arrows drove through the thin protection of his shirt and into his arm, peppering his skin with barbs of pain. The car lurched, suddenly directionless, and he drove his fist forward through the starred pane, clearing a line of vision.

He pulled the car back on to the road and floored the accelerator. The long bonnet of the Mustang rose as if its equine namesake were reaching to jump a fence as the engine smoothly responded to the extra pressure. This was what the car was for, speed on the open road, but it had been designed for the wide open spaces, not the twists and turns of an English country road.

As the speedometer moved towards ninety, he saw the Rover creeping closer, the better drivability of the modern vehicle more than matching the Ford's brute power. Speed was not going to save him. He needed an edge. And that edge was knowledge.

He had driven this route a thousand times. He tried to

unfurl the road before him, seeking any feature he could use. Blood from the hundreds of tiny cuts in his forehead was running off his forehead into his eyes, creating a red film over his vision. In a series of jerky movements, he swept his arm across his face trying to clear the blood and his sight. The blood on his hands coated the wheel with what felt like a thin slick of oil.

The turn on to the A32 into the Meon Valley provided his first opportunity. He kept well over to the left, leaving it until the last moment to flick up the handbrake, spin the wheel and slide across the road in a squeal of tyres to power south towards home. But there was no hesitation from the car behind. It had clearly anticipated the manoeuvre.

'The bastards know where I live,' he muttered, cursing his own impotence. It was not just survival that was at stake now. It was Alex's future, too. If the chase were to end at the cottage they would take her out as well. He had to leave the main road.

He turned off, heading for East Meon where a sharp right on a blind bend just before the village pond might provide the bolt hole he needed. The twisting and turning of the tiny lane at least made it harder for the shooter in the chase car to find a steady mark. His eyes flicked to the mirror and he saw that the barrel had vanished from the side window. Clearly, they were biding their time, waiting until he led them into a better killing zone.

The brief lapse of concentration nearly killed him. The blind bend began at the top of a short rise which curved left and then right in a short chicane. Straight ahead was a pond which the road passed on the right heading off towards Ramsdean. A flick to left and right and he was through the chicane, dragging the wheel to the right with both hands, the car hopping across the road as the tyres lost their traction. But he'd overdone it. The back end was slipping away and he was heading for the water, the tyres clacking as they hit gravel and then touching the grass. He pumped more fuel to the carburettor and turned into the skid, praying that the defensive driving instructor at the Office knew what he was talking about.

Hesitating only briefly, the nose of the Mustang followed the line of his leaning shoulder as he willed the car out of the turn and back on to the road. The wheels gripped the solid Tarmac surface and he was away, powering towards the next turn.

From somewhere behind came a rending of metal and a hiss of steam. Looking back in the mirror, he saw that the opposition had not done their homework. Clearly caught off guard by his sudden manoeuvre, they had tried to slide through the turn in his wake and failed. The bonnet of the car was in the water and he could see the driver slumped over the wheel, unconscious.

He gave a snarl of satisfaction and slowed to a more manageable speed, heading for the cottage. He hesitated for a moment. Go back and check that the driver was out or keep going? At the cottage was Alex, a weapon and a phone for the call that would summon all the help he needed. The decision made, his foot stabbed down on the accelerator. He thought ahead to what should be done: first, check on Alex; second, call the Office and give them the CB code, warning them that he had crashed and burned. There was training for this kind of thing but you always expected it to happen in St Petersburg or Saigon, never southern Hampshire. That was the province of the other mob, MI5, and even they never really had any trouble in England, only in Northern Ireland. So what would they do? Fence him off, keep him quiet, give him some protection and then get him the hell out. Not a very welcome prospect. Still, there was no choice on this one. Someone was bound to have seen the shooting; they had passed too many cars and the Mustang always attracted attention. The blood on his face would have been enough to provoke some nervous calls to the police that a madman was on the loose.

The black and white sign announcing the entrance to Hambledon village came up on the left and he felt a brief uplifting of his spirits at the welcome sight. He passed the Bat and Ball and turned up a narrow, single lane track, right again and into the short gravel drive to Hunter's Lodge – a pretentious name for a tiny place, he had thought when he first heard about it. He pulled the car up in front of the garage, eased the door open, and got out. He was suddenly extraordinarily weary, the adrenaline now long gone to be replaced by post-combat lassitude. Ahead lay the Lodge, its thatch coming low over the wattle and daub walls, looking storybook peaceful in the midday light.

The front door opened and Alex stepped out, her laughing, smiling greeting fading first to concern and then horror at the sight of him.

'My God, David,' she cried. 'What on earth's happened?'

'I was attacked on the way down here,' he said as she came up and placed an arm round his waist as if to carry his larger bulk over the threshold. 'Some guys with a rifle and a laser sight nearly cut me off in my prime.'

The dim kitchen with its Aga giving off powerful heat in the corner was almost claustrophobic after the open road but he sank gratefully into a chair next to the dining table. She stood back from him, her jeans and open-necked check cowboy shirt speckled with blood. If it weren't for the blood, she would fit in here perfectly, he thought to himself.

'What do you mean, attacked?' Alex demanded. 'Who did it? Why?'

He shook his head wearily. 'I have no idea. It came out of the blue just after I'd left Winchester. This bloody red dot from the laser chasing me for miles. God, it was terrifying, Alex. I thought I'd had it.'

He pushed his hand up to run it through his hair and they both noticed he was shaking.

'Stay there. I'll get you a shot of something to restore you and then we'll get some hot water and a towel to clean you up,' Alex said, her commanding tone brooking no argument.

'First I must call the Office,' he said. 'They have to know. This wasn't just some kind of drive-by shooting. It was me they were after and they know where I live. They may be back.'

He reached out for the phone and began to dial the duty officer in London, then stopped.

'What's the CB code?' he asked Alex.

'I've no idea, sorry. Something to do with the stars at the moment, isn't it? Great Bear? The Plough?'

As usual, the Office had a sequence for these things, developing a theme for a six-month period, which allegedly made the codes easier to remember, so that an agent who had been compromised and was at risk – crashed and burned in SIS jargon – could sound the alarm. There had been one memorable period when the theme had been tea. Some poor guy had been burned in Warsaw and had to ring up the duty officer and shout 'Crumpet' down the line. Legend had it the reply had been a helpful 'Where?'

He could hear the phone ringing at the other end and the urgency combined with Alex's prompting focused his mind.

'Saturn. No. Apollo. Apollo, that's it. They're going through the American moon shots.'

The phone was picked up at the other end with a gruff 'Hello'. There was no identifying phrase. If you knew the number, you were assumed to be on the side of the angels.

'Apollo,' Nash said.

'Who?' the voice answered.

'Cutthroat.'

'Where?'

'Home.'

'Action?'

'Terminal.'

'Stand by.'

He could imagine the duty officer picking up the phone, calling the duty director, the startled querying, the recognition that Nash had not only called a CB from his own house but a Terminal as well. Exposed, attacked and attempted assassination. It was unprecedented. He thought with some satisfaction of the consternation this call would be causing.

'The Cleaners are on their way. ETA thirty.'

That sounded too fast for anyone from the Office. Must be the standby unit from Hereford, chopper to the naval base at Waterlooville and then drive up. Then all the boring stuff would begin: the debrief, the police report, the endless questions to see where and how he had been compromised, the search for some lessons to be learned. The prospect numbed him.

He thought briefly about the mess he had left behind, recalling the scene he had fixed in his mind through the rear-view mirror. One down and the other probably out. Time enough for that later. He felt a glass in his hand and looked up to see Alex smiling down at him.

'Will ye tak a wee dram, sorr?' The Scots accent was so awful that he smiled, a brief break in the tension that was still knotting his stomach. He gulped the whisky down, feeling its liquid warmth spread down through his chest.

'Ahh, that's better.' He gave a sigh of satisfaction. 'Help is on its way,' he continued, 'but it wouldn't hurt to take some precautions. Under the bed in the main bedroom you'll find a leather gun case.'

She left the room and he heard her moving around upstairs

to return a moment later with the tattered gun case he had inherited from his father. This was the first time he had put the gun together in years. He locked the stock to the barrel, broke the breech and inserted two cartridges and then placed it carefully to one side, butt on the floor and barrel resting against the drawers containing the kitchen cutlery.

'Let's get you cleaned up,' said Alex. 'Come into the sitting room where I can see what I'm doing.'

Nash allowed himself to be guided to an upright armchair next to the window. Alex placed a bowl of steaming water on the table beside him. This was his favourite room in the house. The large bread oven dominated the inside wall, the familiar old armchairs that he knew from his parents' house alongside, the pictures and the beginning of his collection of ancient maps hanging on the wall, each one with a story of adventure, hope, triumph and failure hidden beneath the cracked vellum or creased silk. Hanging from the wooden beam running over the fireplace were a few of the huge sea-angling hooks he had used while fishing in various parts of the world. They were too big to fit anywhere else and in a moment of tidiness, he had placed them there, where they had stayed.

Alex drew up a stool and began her work. As the bowl turned red with his blood so the extent of the damage became clear.

'Most of this I can take care of with tweezers and some plaster. But this one here' – she touched his cheek – 'is going to need some stitches.'

As she drew out shard after shard of glass and then cleaned the wounds, David could smell her body and feel the pressure of her breast against his shoulder. After the terror, it seemed as if all his senses were heightened. It was intoxicating and intimate. Despite the pain, he felt himself becoming aroused. But he said nothing, slightly embarrassed to feel so much and too frightened of rejection to do anything about it.

To make room for the bowl Alex had pushed aside a picture that sat on the table. She had not really looked at it but now as she dipped the cloth into the water, she took in an image of a young and very beautiful woman.

'Is that the wife you've been hiding from us all this time?' she said jokingly. The wince she detected in Nash was not, she realized, one of physical pain. God, there was a wife. Bad joke. Bad timing. She cursed her naïvety.

Perhaps it was the association of cars and death that triggered the need to talk. Perhaps it was just the proximity of a woman who was showing the kind of sympathy he needed. Whatever, he wanted to share himself with this woman in a way that was both cleansing and reassuring.

'You asked me once about my file, the blanks in it,' he began.

She paused in her dabbing and looked at him directly, surprise and curiosity in her eyes.

'The blanks arose because of what happened back in Northern Ireland. You remember I was sent there a couple of years after leaving the Fort?'

She nodded.

'I was married back then and I had taken Jaimie over with me,' he gestured towards the picture. 'She was American. I wanted her to see the place. We'd only been married a couple of years and I saw no reason why an apparently innocuous civil servant at the Northern Ireland Office should be at any kind of risk.'

He went on to explain how they had met while he was on an exchange scholarship at the Kennedy School. The year abroad in an academic environment was thought to be good for young SIS recruits and he had leapt at the chance. He had loved the American thirst for knowledge, enjoyed the relaxed atmosphere and fallen in love with Jaimie Seaton, a young student at the school who was writing a thesis entitled 'The

New Right: Russia's Nemesis or Nirvana?' It was exactly the kind of pretentious alliterative title that got Kennedy's professors excited and they had debated long and hard about the issues. That intellectual foundation was enough for them to begin a relationship.

She had seemed wondrous to him: full of spirit and energy with all the enthusiasm that makes some Americans so attractive to their reserved British cousins. In bed, too, she proved to be more giving, more adept and more experimental than anyone he had met in England. She told him that she liked his quiet style, admired his strength and found him a welcome contrast from the nerds and jocks who walked the halls at the Kennedy School.

It was a meeting of minds and bodies that culminated in her moving to England with him for a research position at the International Institute of Strategic Studies. He had proposed in the kitchen in the middle of making dinner – hardly romantic but she had not hesitated. It was only then that he explained the true nature of his work. His revelation mattered little to her; there was no difference between the man she had met and the spy she now knew. It was, he explained, just a job. No James Bond antics, no George Smiley intrigues.

The posting to Northern Ireland came shortly afterwards. Jaimie had loved the place, with its gentle greens, soft colours and extraordinary people. And, of course, as an American she had been made to feel especially welcome. Heavily pregnant by this stage, she had travelled round the province absorbing the local culture and joining him whenever she could at the different official functions he attended. In many ways it was an idyllic posting: they had all the time together they needed; life was set fair.

They had been staying with friends in Newry. Jaimie had gone off to Armagh, while he stayed behind for a meeting with RUC Special Branch. Two hours later, he was driving to meet Jaimie for lunch when he came across a police roadblock. These were routine in Northern Ireland and he thought nothing of it until the crawling traffic brought him closer to the cause of the hold-up. It was not, as he expected, a security roadblock but something much worse. The ambulances, the fire engine and the army bomb disposal unit were evidence enough of that. It was only when he saw the rear of a Rover car sticking out of the ditch by the side of the road that he began to fear the worst. Getting out, he had run the two hundred yards to the car.

Afterwards, he would always associate feeling breathless with tragedy, as if the racing heart and gasping lungs recalled the agony of the moment with complete precision. He, who had difficulty remembering the colour of his own eyes, remembered each frozen frame of the moment of discovery and loss: the breath of the policeman gathering on the cold air; the young age of the bomb disposal men working calmly in the wreckage; his stomach squeezing him so tight that he could hardly suck the air into his lungs as suspicion edged into certainty; and finally the voices, each with that edge of distress and pity that people can only whisper.

Jaimie's car had been casually flicked from the road into a ditch by a massive car bomb that had been detonated by a command wire. Her body was still inside, untouched for fear of a booby trap. The IRA's real target had been the police patrol ahead of her car but there had been a small delay, enough to allow the target to escape and Jaimie to be killed. During the flight from road to ditch and from life to death, the car had been split in two, its engine still lying absurdly in the road. The memory that remained with him was not the sight of Jaimie's face, which looked remarkably peaceful. What stayed with him was the vision of her legs, severed at the hip and lying locked to the front end of the car, small pools of blood gathering at the stumps. The baby inside her –

a little girl – was delivered stillborn by Caesarean section at the scene. It was so cruel, so brutalizing, so completely unnecessary.

The numbness had insulated him for a while. He had been called back to England, naturally. The Office was very protective of its own and was small enough that any loss affected the whole family. And of course his mental state had to be assessed. He had done well enough for a while and then found himself breaking down at the oddest moments. His whole upbringing had been typically British and he had always thought that strength was demonstrated by suppressing emotion rather than showing it.

Mike Reiss, the Office shrink, had set the crisis in context, explaining that grief was the healthy part while suppression was simply stockpiling emotional trouble. Only much later did David realize that Reiss had also been using their sessions as a way of conducting a much deeper evaluation. The trauma of Jaimie's death had hardened David, steeled a youthful enthusiasm for a secret world into a recognition of the true realities of covert war. The crucible had toughened him and focused his aggression. What Reiss detected was not a thirst for revenge – that would have made Nash simply a dangerous man – but a determination that, with proper direction, would produce a ruthless energy that could be harnessed to real effect.

Reiss had learned over the years that the men and women in the field who suffered most and were the least effective were those who acted out of a sense of duty. Duty alone was a poor foundation to support the emotional extremes that death and, on occasion, dishonour could deliver to an agent in the field. Such an agent had to be hard enough to do the job, with sufficient motivation to underpin the emotion and sensitivity enough to remain stable. Nash was such a person, reported Letts.

The reorganization of 1992 provided the excuse the Office needed to pull his evaluation and tap him for a transfer to the newly established Human Intelligence Tasking Centre. Six months of refresher courses at the Fort plus a few more that were new and he was ready for the field.

'I'm so sorry about Jaimie,' Alex said when he had finished. Her hand reached out to touch his, a gesture of both sympathy and intimacy. 'What I don't understand is why you didn't just leave after that. I think I'd have quit and gone to grow marrows in Scotland, or at least got out of the firing line. Why continue?'

It was a question he had asked himself often enough in recent days.

'I don't know. After Jaimie died I needed something and this seemed to be it – what the shrink described as a focus for my inner rage.' He shrugged. 'He may be right about that although I don't feel angry most of the time, just sad.'

She reached out and rested her hand on his.

'You know, David, there are friends out in the world who are there to help if you want it.'

He was unused to such sympathy and Alex immediately sensed his uncertainty. She delicately moved the conversation back to firmer, more neutral territory.

'So, how was America?'

'Interesting,' he replied, marshalling his thoughts. 'It was rather like the meeting in the Office that sent me there in the first place. Everyone had their own agenda and a careful script that had been worked out as the best way to warn me off any further inquiries in Russia.'

'But why should anyone care?' Alex asked.

'The argument seems to be that what Spitz had to say was rubbish, that the real focus is on the Ukraine and that I should just do what I'm told and everything will be all right.'

He winced as a particularly long sliver of glass was teased

from the flesh near his chin and dropped with a small splash into the bowl of water.

'Perhaps they're right,' said Alex. 'It's possible, you know. Spitz had been operating under great stress for some time. The attack in Kiev may have been the last straw, pushing him over the edge.'

'I think about Spitz often,' Nash replied. 'Relive that moment in the tunnel. Sometimes I wake up in the night and it's so real I can reach out and touch his arm, turn it back, make it different. I can remember the smells, the taste of fear, hear his voice. I've played our conversation back again and again in my head and each time I come up with the answer that he was telling the truth.'

'Sure, but that may be only the truth as he understood it. Perhaps he was simply wrong.'

'No.' The word was strong, final. 'He was calling it as he saw it all right. But there's something else going on here. First there was the attack in Kiev, then whoever was after me just now clearly knew when I was flying in, which airline, which terminal, where I was heading – everything. That tells me that not only is there a leak big enough to break the dam but whatever it is people think I know, makes me worth killing.'

'That's exactly right. And I'm here to finish the job.' The voice came from a man who had entered the sitting room from the connecting door with the dining room. There had been no sound to alert them, no noise as he eased open the back door. The surprise was absolute, just as he had intended. David automatically reached for the shotgun before realizing he had left it in the kitchen. He cursed his stupidity while the assassin laughed.

He was dressed in jeans and a dark shirt with a brown leather jacket. The zipper was undone letting the flaps of the jacket hang open, the downslung shoulder holster clearly visible. It was empty, the gun filling the man's right hand, its barrel pointing between the two of them, bulbous with its black silencer. Nash realized that the assassin must have continued his journey from East Meon on foot, determined to fulfil his contract. This was not just a professional, this was a fanatic. But how had he arrived so quickly? The guy must be some athlete, Nash reflected. He wasn't even breathing heavily.

'You British were always such soft targets,' he said. 'That little trick in the village may have caught out my partner but I had no problem getting a lift. People are so helpful, don't you find?' It was said with the sneer that the strong reserve for the weak.

Nash couldn't quite place the accent. Not English certainly. But good linguistics training with a slight sing-song undercurrent. Scandinavia perhaps?

He wanted to search for a weapon, an escape route, a distraction, anything that might buy a bit of time and postpone the inevitable, but he dare not break eye-contact with the man for fear that he might miss the slight tightening of the eyes that would signal that a bullet was about to be fired. It was a slender thread, and would give him a millisecond of opportunity at most, but he was damned if he would simply give up.

Nash felt a slight movement at his left side and sensed rather than saw Alex's hand moving away from his leg towards the bowl. There was no heat there, no scalding water to burn the man's face and drive him screaming from the house. He needed a distraction. He tensed, visualizing the room, marking off distances, judging the moment.

He saw the man's eyes begin to narrow and knew that the end was near. He tensed, ready to spring.

There was the crunch of tyres on gravel as two vehicles raced up the drive and screeched to a halt. It was enough.

The man's eyes flickered to the window. Alex snapped her wrist and the bowl went arcing in a parabola of drops and splashes. The metal container clattered satisfyingly against the wall and then smashed into the window, breaking the glass with a crash.

The assassin squeezed off the first shot towards Nash even as his eyes swung back to the room. There was a soft pop as the silencer did its work but Nash had driven himself up, reaching towards the fireplace. His right arm swept across the lintel, fingers closing around one of the fishing hooks that hung there. He completed the forward movement, sweeping his arm along and down, sinking the barb into the flesh of the man's cheek.

The man reeled back, the pain instant and overwhelming. His head crashed into the low doorway, the impact snapping his head back towards Nash. Nash pulled downwards, using the gunman's own momentum to sink the hook deeper. He pulled, dragging his prey forward, desperate to overwhelm him with movement and agony. The man overbalanced and Nash followed through, now suspending him from the hook like a marlin. Unable to support his bulk, the flesh simply peeled away from his jawbone in a long bloody strip, drawing the skin down so that it hung like some monstrous, misplaced tongue.

The man gave a roar of agony. Driven almost insane by the pain he swept his gun arm up and dealt Nash a massive blow on his wrist. It was enough to numb him and his fingers spasmed, opening to drop the hook.

It had been his best shot, his only shot, and he had blown it. The man levered himself upright, his gun level in front of him. There would be no hesitation now, no second chances. Alex screamed as she saw his trigger finger beginning to lever backwards.

There was a shattering blast and Nash felt the air quiver

around his face. The assassin was lifted bodily as if by a great wind and slammed back against the wall. A second blast followed and his chest became a mass of matter as the heavy solid shot tore it apart. He made no sound as he slithered down the wall, legs splayed out in front of him, pistol now dangling from a limp wrist.

Nash felt arms grip his, spin him round and propel him back and out through the kitchen doorway. He looked round and saw Alex being similarly manhandled. The only sound now was the shouts of the men in brown fatigues doing what they did so well: secure the perimeter, check for back-up and get out as quickly as possible. Nash allowed himself to be carried along on the tide of efficiency and discipline. His rescuers obviously knew exactly what to do next and how to do it. He wished that he could say the same about himself.

10

'HE WAS AN Israeli. Name of Yossi Melman,' Diana said. 'One of the Shin Bet people kicked out after those shootings on the West Bank. Been operating as a freelance ever since. We have no idea who he was working for.'

That would explain the accent, Nash thought. Plenty of the Israeli intelligence people did their training in Scandinavia for reasons he had never really understood. Maybe it just gave them some acclimatization and access to their networks in Russia. Anyhow, they seemed to feel comfortable there. Nash shuddered inwardly as he relived Melman's demise twenty-four hours previously. That awful scream and the sight of that bloodied face would remain with him for a long time.

'So we haven't a clue how he came to be after me?' he asked Diana.

'Not so far. The second man had vanished by the time the police reached the crashed car. We've tracked Melman back through the videos at Heathrow. He came in via Paris using a Norwegian passport in the name of Larsson the day before you arrived back from the States, but apart from that, nothing.'

Nash and Diana were sitting in the Office restaurant, the normally stunning vista across the Thames obscured by driving rain which cut visibility to the edge of the river and sent wide streaks of water running down the one-way glass. They had both finished their Caesar salads and Nash was embarking on a salmon fillet.

'This all smells of a set up to me,' he said. 'First the Kiev business and now this. And just how did this Melman character know where I lived and when I was coming back?'

Diana chewed reflectively on a mouthful of pasta.

'You can take it that you were well and truly blown after Kiev,' she replied. 'You can take it, too, that they probably knew you were coming well in advance and that you were meeting Spitz. Either that, or they followed Spitz to the meet. But they certainly had some good intelligence. They clearly knew enough to make you and to know where you were headed.

'All of that adds up to some very good sources. The Russians certainly don't have that kind of information in their standard files, so there must be a leak from someone involved with either the Americans or the Russians.'

'Which is more or less what I said in Spedding's office and got laughed out of court,' Nash said.

He paused, wondering just how much Diana really knew. It was rumoured that the business in Russia had compromised her status among the top echelons. Although the shrinks had given her a clean bill of health, there would always be lingering doubts that the ordeal had damaged her irreparably. She would never make Director now. How bitter did she feel about that? Bitter enough to go over? Nash doubted it. Diana still carried enough clout to provide a fair degree of job satisfaction – and to make her a useful ally, he reflected. He recalled her anger after his return from the drugs bust and the Kiev trip. She had been hard on him but maybe that was only because she cared. Whatever, she was worth the risk.

'We keep dancing round this, Diana, but the truth is that someone here is feeding intelligence to God knows who and nobody seems to care.'

Diana hesitated, taking in the man in front of her. She understood what it was like to be alone in enemy territory. She knew that she was at times over-protective of the people like David whom she sent out there. She felt for each of them, travelled with them and wished them home safe. Sometimes, when things went wrong, she was forced to relive her own experience moment by painful moment, imagining what might be happening to her man in the field. Her anger after David had exceeded his brief and gone on the drugs bust with Yuri had been that of a mother whose child's life had been endangered.

Since losing Spitz, David seemed more contained and watchful. Sad too, she thought, as she took in the dark pouches under his brown eyes. She ached to give him the reassurance he both wanted and needed. But there were deep political pools here which even her well-developed antennae were having trouble probing. Certainly, he deserved more than the casual brush-offs he had received so far.

'It's not that they don't care, David,' she said. Her thumb jerked upwards in the direction of the sixth floor. 'They know there may be a leak and they know the quality of your information. The question is what should be done about it? You have to appreciate the politics: Russia's relationship with the west, ours with the Americans, the Office's with our ministers. And then there's the specific problem of Russia's BW programme. We've been telling the Americans for ages that the Russian bear is still dangerous but they don't want to listen. And of course no one wants to upset the apple cart by pushing Moscow too far on the bio weapons issue – there's too much money at stake to risk being frozen out of the new markets in the east.'

'So, where does that leave me?' Nash asked.

'In the brown stuff, I'm afraid. I think they're just going to let you go your own way and see what happens. If you're right about the BW, the Mafia, the right-wing aggression, they'll take the credit. If you're wrong, then they're covered. You were a loose cannon; what could they do?'

'Well, fuck them,' Nash spat, the anger clear in his voice. 'I'm buggered if I'll be walked over by either the thugs out there or those bastards upstairs. I want the people who killed Spitz and I want the people who ordered me dead. If that plays into some grand plan, fine. If it doesn't then that's just too bad.'

It was exactly the response Diana herself would have given. Covert operators were all loners, iconoclasts used to working outside the established order. The greater their isolation, the more combative they became. Nash is one of us, she thought.

'As for the leak,' she continued, 'it's under investigation. Finding a mole can take months, though. Certainly longer than we've got. Smart, in Internal Affairs, is apparently giving it his full attention.'

Nash snorted derisively. 'That buffoon. He was transferred from Croydon Met when the local skinheads got too tough for him. Putting Smart on the job is the equivalent of tackling an oil slick with a box of Kleenex.'

'I hope you don't mind if I join you.' David looked up to see Richard Teller hovering nearby. David wondered how much of their conversation he had heard. As usual, there was nothing to be read in those cold eyes, just the usual calculating assessment of his audience.

'I'm sorry to hear about the trouble you had down in Hampshire, David,' said Teller, biting into the Biscotti that came with the coffee. 'You clearly seem to have upset some people.'

'In my job I expect to upset people,' replied David. 'What I don't expect is to be blown by my own side.'

Teller had a nervous habit of drawing in his upper lip

and sucking it lightly between a gap in his teeth, making his lips pucker like a fish gasping for air. It was both unattractive and an indication that he needed time to formulate a careful answer.

'I know that must be how it seems,' he said. 'But Smart has found no supporting evidence so far.' He held up his hand to ward off the rebuttal he could see forming on David's lips. 'Say what you like about him, but he does get the job done. Eventually.'

'And while he's plodding along, people are trying to kill me in my own home,' David shot back.

'I understand your frustration, David. But I'm not prepared to order some grand inquisition that will shut down your department and half the others on the basis of one or two incidents that might or might not indicate a leak here. Don't forget that we share a lot of our information with the Americans. It's perfectly possible that whoever was involved in Kiev might have followed you back here and then to Washington. Just how well were you checking your back?'

It was an awkward question to which Teller probably already knew the answer.

Teller drained the rest of his coffee with a finality that suggested the conversation was drawing to a close. 'I read your report from Washington, David.' Teller leaned forward, his face serious. 'We share their concern. If events unfold as they believe they will, then we're all going to be dragged in. Ministers are most unhappy at the prospect of civil war in Ukraine. One Bosnia is more than enough.

'You're liaising with Philip Thomas in Moscow, aren't you?'

David nodded, remembering the CIA man with distaste.

'Work with him, David. The Americans could be very useful to us. However, there are also one or two lines of inquiry we would like you to pursue for yourself when you get out there. Alex will fill you in. And see what you can get from Parashvili too, yes? He knows his way round the Moscow cesspits, I'm sure.' Teller glanced at his watch. 'Meeting. Must go. Keep in touch, won't you?'

He rose from the table and headed for the doors. As briefings go, it was one of the shortest and least helpful Nash had ever experienced.

Alex was waiting for him as he stepped out of the lift and they walked together down to Science and Technology. They had been separated soon after the rescue for debriefing, not so much to find discrepancies as to pinpoint any facts that might have been forgotten by one but not the other. They had not seen each other since. He looked at her anxiously to see if there were any signs of the effect of such violence on a woman who was used to battling with inanimate gigabytes, not armed gorillas.

Nash would not have been surprised to see red eyes and tear streaks, a grey pallor that would indicate lack of sleep, but there was nothing. She looked her usual serene self in white linen trousers, a cream blouse and an orange wool jacket, a light blue brooch with a swirly abstract design pinned to the lapel. There were no signs that only the previous day they had been fighting for their lives. He marvelled at how resilient the human mind could be.

'Look, Alex,' he began tentatively. 'I wanted to apologize for getting you involved in the drama at the cottage. I would never have gone there if I'd thought there was a risk to you.'

He broke off, realizing how feeble it sounded. Alex put her hand on his arm, forcing him to a halt and bringing him round to face her in the corridor.

'Don't be ridiculous, David,' she said. 'There was nothing you could have done. It wasn't as if you set me up or anything.' Her voice was firm but her face seemed to fall back on itself as she replayed the scene in her mind. Despite a pill to help her sleep, her previous night's dreams had been filled with colour and the feeling of raw terror that she had experienced in the room. She had woken feeling exhausted and on edge. She had had time, too, to reflect on David. He had reacted to the assault with a concentrated savagery that she found both exciting and terrifying. Every time she thought of the scene, it was the sight of the fishing hook tearing flesh that dominated. Every time she had woken in the stillness of the night it was to hear the dying screams echoing in the dark corners of her bedroom. She viewed him with a new respect, and was a little frightened by the rage that she now knew lurked within him, waiting to be unleashed in another bout of furious, focused violence.

She had thought in recent weeks that they might possibly have a future together. He was physically attractive and smart enough to hold her interest, but her confidence had been shaken by the events at the cottage. Could she divorce the ruthless protector from the gentle lover she had imagined? Fear was no foundation on which to build a relationship.

'I wanted to thank you for saving my life,' she said, the cliché sounding trite to her as she spoke. As if reading her mind and embarrassed by the sentiment, he shrugged off the remark.

'It was mainly self-preservation. I was the primary target, remember. Anyway, for what it's worth, now we both know what it's like at the sharp end. Teller tells me you've got some material for me,' Nash continued, switching the conversation to more familiar ground.

'Had, not have,' she replied. 'I've sent over an HAA and some other kit in the bag which should be waiting for you when you arrive at the Embassy.'

'What's in the HAA?' he asked. Hologram Agency Activators were normally only used for messages between controller and source. This internal usage was bizarre.

'I don't know.' She frowned. 'I was simply handed the disc already encoded. I tried the database to see if I could find out who it was from but access was blocked by the Chief's private code. Even I can't get inside that. I'm afraid you're on your own on this one. Be careful, David,' she cautioned, laying her hand on his arm.

'At least we've got the laptop,' he replied. 'I'll let you know just as soon as I find out what's happening over there. If you find out what's going on over here, you do the same.'

'Deal,' she smiled. Where David was going, he'd need all the help he could get.

Nash was thinking about Alex's smile as he walked back to his office. Thus distracted he had entered the cubicle and almost reached his desk before noticing that his chair was already occupied by someone idly fingering through the mail in his In tray.

'What the bloody hell are you doing?' he shouted.

The chair swivelled round to face him and Nash saw that it contained Graham Smart. The head of Internal Affairs was a small man – ferrety was the adjective which always came to mind – with the large paunch of a policeman who has spent too much time drinking beer with his snouts. He was one of the most despised men in the building, someone whose presence always indicated trouble and whose questioning invariably cast aspersions on their recipients' loyalty.

The fact that he had been headhunted by the Office from the Met after a career spent hunting terrorists and crime gangs meant that he couldn't be all bad, Nash supposed, but the man was his own worst enemy.

Perhaps he tried to cultivate the image of an outsider because it helped his work or perhaps he was genuinely obnoxious. Either way, Nash was certain there was more to this man than met the eye. His small, startlingly blue eyes oozed cunning and his tight mouth was perpetually pursed in a moue of disapproval. The fact that he had emerged from his lair usually meant trouble. Nash was in no mood to tolerate interference.

'I'm just on my way to catch a plane,' he said. 'Whatever you want, you'd better make it quick.'

'That's what you said last time, Mr Nash. And then you disappeared,' Smart replied. 'This time, I want some answers.'

He produced a small, spiral-bound notebook and a pencil, crossed one leg over the other and paused, pencil hovering just above the paper.

Nash moved past him and began to gather up a few requisites for his trip to Moscow.

'Mr Nash, you and I both believe that we have a leak in the Office. If that's so, it's very much in your own interest to identify the culprit as soon as possible. Now please take this seriously, I have a job to do.'

Nash's response was partly a result of the anger and fear which had been building in him since the attack at the cottage and partly due to the growing isolation he was feeling in the Office. Yes, there was a leak all right, but by the time Smart's plodding investigation got round to plugging it he would probably be dead. Nash's only salvation lay in his own hands. Zipping up the laptop he turned to face Smart, his mouth a tight, angry line.

'I think we should understand each other,' he said, his voice barely controlled. '*I* have a job to do too, part of which is to find the people responsible for killing one of my sources and almost killing me. That is something I take very seriously indeed. What I don't take very seriously is some second-rate retired plod wasting my time going over information that is already in the reports.'

He dropped his bag on the floor and turned to the computer on his desk.

'There. You want to know what happened? There it is. You want to know what I think? There's a leak bigger than the Amazon somewhere in here. Read my report and go and plug it. Meanwhile leave me the fuck alone.'

Picking up his case, Nash stormed out of the office. The investigator licked the end of his pencil and jotted down something in his notebook, completely unfazed by the outburst. Methodically, he closed the book and returned his attention to Nash's In tray.

11

THE FLIGHT TO Moscow had lasted the scheduled four hours and it had taken Nash a further two hours to clear customs and security, the delay due to the incompetence of a system completely overwhelmed by the consequences of liberalization rather than the security-inspired paranoia of old. Sheremetyevo II had been built in 1979 when the state expected about 5,000 passengers a day to be processed. Now, 15,000 a day were travelling in and out of Moscow on international flights. The deep fissures in the walls and the cracked floors reminded Nash more of a small, failing, African nation than one of the world's superpowers.

Once upon a time, he would have been met by an Embassy driver who would have bribed the right people to ensure that there was no interference by the riff-raff on the smooth journey via diplomatic passport from plane to limo. The cuts had seen to the chauffeur and travelling under cover meant there were no favours from anyone.

As he walked out of the customs area, he moved into the bustling chaos that is the entrepreneur at work in Russia's free market. In theory, all Moscow cab drivers are licensed. In practice, it is a free-for-all with the most enterprising taking the spoils. Nash was immediately engulfed by a crowd of ragged-looking drivers all desperate for his business. He moved his case protectively in front of him and began to force his way through the morass, turning down offers as he went.

He felt an insistent tugging at his sleeve and looked down into the face of a young girl, no more than twelve and with the cherubic beauty that some Russian women attain early but rarely manage to hold on to.

'Don't listen to those peasants,' she said in perfectly modulated English. 'They're scum. You deserve the limousine that is waiting for you outside. Cheaper than these crooks, too.'

Nash had no doubt that if he had been French or German, she would have switched with equal fluency to the appropriate language. As scouts go, this one is a cut above, he thought, deciding that her enterprise deserved reward. He nodded and, with a wide, impudent grin, she led him off, the cries of disgust from her competitors falling behind them. The kerbside was a bedlam of honking cars, shouting policemen and the polyglot of people that make up Russia: the smart army officers, the fashionable *nouveaux riches* complete with bodyguards, the peasants with their bundles stacked high on their heads heading home to visit relatives in distant parts.

The hand of one particularly filthy example of this last group reached out to pluck the suitcase from Nash's grasp. He moved forward angrily, prepared to do battle, when the young siren piped up.

'No. No. This is your chauffeur,' she shouted. 'He will take you to Moscow.'

The unshaven face, the torn trousers and tattered leather jacket were hardly reassuring. The man's voice, a gruff parody of an American gangster movie, seemed to complete the picture of a rogue hard at work in a crooked business.

'Waal, buddy. Mighty fine to see ya. Mighty fine,' he turned, leading Nash forward, giving him no opportunity to back away. 'Right this way. The limo is parked just over there. Five minutes we'll be on our way. Fifteen we'll be downtown.'

They pressed through the crush to the 'limo', a cavernous, ageing Chevrolet cab of the type once popular in New York before gas guzzling became unfashionable. Some enterprising American had spotted a new market for the ancient rejects in a country that was anxious to embrace all things western.

Nash opened the front passenger door and sat down on the patched leather seat. His driver got in next to him. There was a grinding whirr as the starter motor tried to engage, then the engine caught, issued an enormous explosion and began to tick over with a steady rumble.

'Easy apple pie,' his driver said with satisfaction. He stretched out a hand. 'Vlad. How're ya?'

'David.' Nash shook the offered hand feeling the hard callouses of a man used to manual work.

The girl waved her goodbyes and headed back to the terminal.

'My kid,' Vlad said proudly. 'Trained her myself. She'll be out in a coupla minutes with someone else for my brother, then another for my cousin and then I'll be back. A breeze and better than growing tomatoes.' He laughed a deep, gut-wrenching rumble that made his stomach wobble alarmingly. Nash found himself smiling an endorsement of this engaging man.

'Wanna hear a joke?' Without waiting for Nash to respond, Vlad carried on.

'Boris Yeltsin is standing on his balcony outside his bedroom. He's just got up and he's having a stretch, you know, scratching himself. Suddenly he hears a booming voice. "Good morning, Boris," it says. He looks around and can't see nobody. The voice speaks again. "Good morning, Boris."

'This time Yeltsin sees that it's the sun speaking to him. Polite as ever, he replies: "Good morning, Mr Sun."

'That afternoon the same thing happens. The sun wishes

Boris a "good afternoon" and Boris replies "Good afternoon, Mr Sun."' Vlad honked the horn and a group of cyclists dispersed hurriedly from the speeding taxi's path.

'Goddam factory workers,' cursed Vlad. 'Where was I? Anyway, that evening, Yeltsin decides to get in first. "Good Evening, Mr Sun," he calls out.

'"Fuck you," says the sun, "I'm already in the west."'

Vlad laughed uproariously, delighted with himself.

They had left the airport complex and were heading south towards the centre of Moscow. Since he had last been here, the road had sprouted ads for McDonald's, Burger King and Ben & Jerry's Ice Cream. The international conformity of the mass market, he thought cynically.

'So, David. Where ya stayin'?'

'The Metropole.'

Vlad whistled a long single tone of appreciation.

'You guys have money to burn.'

It was hardly the time or the place to disabuse his driver about the source of his wealth. Anyway, Nash knew that with the slightest provocation he would have received a barrage of Vlad's worldview and that was more than he could take right then.

The road from the airport, once a four-lane highway showpiece, had fallen into disrepair and so had the cars that used it. The journey was a continuous obstacle course of potholes and abandoned cars which Vlad handled with the insouciance of the consummate professional.

The ambush came without warning. Only an evasive move taken by Vlad to avoid yet another pothole saved them. Instead of hitting them broadside, the truck merely crunched the rear wing of the cab, spinning them through two complete circles. Nash was flung against the side of the door, his head crashing against the jamb.

'What the fuck?' Vlad cursed and continued swearing more

expressively in Russian as he wrestled with the wheel and struggled to bring the car back under control. For a moment Nash's vision was blurred from the crash. Then it cleared and he searched for the source of the impact, taking in the ancient truck that had clearly swung across the central reservation in an attempt to take them out. His head swivelled, looking ahead and behind for other sources of danger.

A black Mercedes Benz drew up alongside the cab and Nash turned just as the rear window came down to reveal the face of a black man. The man's eyes were fixed steadily on Nash but it was the barrel of the shotgun that held Nash's attention.

'Vlad. It's a hit.' The words galvanized Vlad, who had been prepared for this moment by years of gangster movies. A pump of the brakes and a spin of the wheel and they were behind the car even as the gunman pulled the trigger, the shots whistling in front of the windscreen and scoring a series of lines on the yellow paint of the bonnet.

Nash felt a surge of anger. The bastards were doing it again. He'd had enough. He heard a rumble from his side and looked over to see Vlad's mouth open in a laugh, the yellowed teeth clearly visible. The bloody man was enjoying himself!

Vlad reached into the glove compartment to pull out the biggest revolver Nash had ever seen. He saw the look of surprise on Nash's face.

'It's tough being a cabbie in Moscow. Crooks everywhere and all wanting to steal my money or my daughter.' He thrust the weapon at Nash. 'Here. You're going to need this. Those fuckers have messed up my car. Let's kick ass.'

The gun – pre-World War I, Nash guessed – was heavy enough to brain anyone who came within range, but whether it would fire if he pulled the trigger was quite another matter. He was about to find out as Vlad accelerated directly towards the back of the Mercedes.

'These pussies,' Vlad snorted dismissively. The switch from defence to attack caught the assassins completely by surprise. They had clearly expected to choose their moment and the force of the huge Chevrolet connecting with its rear end caused the Benz to lurch to the right. For one brief, terrifying moment, they were locked together, bumper to bumper as the Mercedes moved towards the embankment and then over it. The jolt separated the two cars and Vlad spun the wheel, just avoiding the drop. A scream of brakes, the smell of burning rubber and they came to a halt fifty metres from where the Mercedes had disappeared from sight.

Vlad flipped the lever on the steering and the automatic box shifted into reverse. Another scream of tyres and they were back at the point where the other car had left the road. The two men jumped out and ran towards the verge. The Mercedes lay on its side at the bottom of a short incline, its nose buried in a pool of muddy water. Nash ran down the bank and wrenched open the rear door. The impact of the crash had concertinaed the front of the car, pushing the dashboard back. The driver was clearly dead, his chest crushed by the steering wheel. The assassin had been flung forward by the impact and hung over the back of the front seat. With strength born of the adrenaline rush of an escape from violent death, Nash put both hands on the man's belt and pulled, jerking him out of the car. He fell with a whoomph of expelled air, arms and legs splayed.

Nash knelt down and slapped him hard across the face. The man groaned and his eyelids fluttered as consciousness began to return. Nash hit him several more times until the blows registered sufficiently for the man's eyes to open.

'Vlad. Translate for me, will you?' asked Nash.

The Russian came over and knelt by the man's head.

'Who the hell are you?' Nash demanded and then had to wait a frustrating few seconds while the anger was translated into a burst of Russian. The hint of a smile appeared round the man's mouth. The idea that he should find this situation funny drove Nash over the edge. He lifted up a foot and brought it down with crushing force into the man's testicles. There was a cry of agony and the man tried to sit up but was pushed down by a blow in the shoulder from Vlad.

The cab driver clearly realized the message that Nash was trying to get across and joined in enthusiastically, shouting at the man, underlining each sentence with a heavy blow to the chest and shoulders. When that tactic failed to produce the desired response, Vlad reached inside his jacket. There was a soft slither as a long, straight-bladed knife reflected the beginnings of real fear in the man's eyes.

'The little fucker thinks he's tough,' said Vlad. 'Well, I'll show him tough.'

He began to talk in a softer, almost caressing voice as he explained to the assassin just what he was about to do. The man started to squirm but Vlad moved his bulk so that he was straddling his chest, pinning the man's arms by his side. One hand came down to hold the man's head still, the other brought the knife point down so that the tip pierced the skin at the corner of his eye. His intention was clear and if the words hadn't made it plain enough, the pain of that first prick certainly did.

'Call off your dog, Nash.' The voice was neither a cry for help nor a shout of anger but a request issued in the tone of a reasonable man caught out by unreasonable circumstances. And the voice spoke English not Russian.

'Who the hell are you?' Nash repeated, now that he knew he was understood.

'Raffet. Olivier Raffet.'

'Who are you working with? How did you know I was coming? Why me?'

'Just leave him to me, David. I'll have him singing in two

'seconds flat,' Vlad interrupted, pushing his knife in a little further to underline his point.

'Look, Nash,' Raffet continued while trying to pull his head away from the knife, 'it all went wrong. I'm sorry. There's nothing personal. I get my orders. I carry them out. It's as simple as that.'

'First Kiev, then England, now here. That's personal. And if you don't give me some answers, I'm going to turn Vlad the impaler here loose on you. It's personal for him. You messed up his cab.' He gave Raffet a wolfish grin completely devoid of humour. 'So let's start at the beginning. Who hired you?'

There was a scream of pain as Vlad drove the knife a little further home. It had yet to touch the eyeball, but blood was now running in a continuous thin stream down the side of his face.

'Spandau. I work for Spandau.'

'And who or what is Spandau?' Nash asked.

'People like you and me. A group of ex-intelligence people. Spies for hire. We work for whoever pays us. Kind of Spies 'R' Us. You name it, we do it.'

'And why me?'

'No idea. I got a message in Lisbon yesterday to head out here. Met one of our local people.' His eyes flicked in the direction of the crashed car. 'The truck was supposed to take you out. I was only back-up. As I said, it's nothing personal.'

'Well, my life's pretty personal to me,' Nash assured him. He had been listening to the voice, trying to pinpoint the slight accent. French, he decided.

While the interrogation had been going on, Raffet's hand had been easing its way towards the pistol he kept in a holster on the back of his hip. He plucked it loose, flicked off the safety catch and gradually brought it round so that the barrel was facing upwards.

There was a muffled bang and the flesh of Vlad's inner thigh exploded as the bullet entered and then exited trailing blood and flesh. There was a roar of anger from the Russian and before Nash could move, he had moved the knife a few inches and plunged it deep into the gunman's upturned neck. The blade pierced the roof of Raffet's mouth and entered his brain. Death was instantaneous.

To Nash, the British Embassy on the Naberezhnaya Morisa Toreza had always seemed a bizarre place, a throwback to a different era when the Raj ruled the world. It was situated on the banks of the Moskva river directly across from the Kremlin. Legend had it that the balcony of the Russian President's private apartment looked directly on to the Embassy and successive ambassadors took great pleasure in flying what was generally thought to be the largest Union flag in the Foreign Office inventory at every conceivable opportunity. This used to particularly annoy Leonid Brezhnev, a noted Anglophobe, who had tried to force the British out of the building without success.

The main building was all old wood and baroque carvings with stunning tapestries depicting Russian hunting scenes hanging from the walls. The reception rooms were filled with ornate scrollwork in gold leaf surrounding enormous mirrors in which the various members of Moscow's diplomatic corps could preen themselves. The first sign that the Embassy was actually a place of work came in the driveway. With typical Foreign Office parsimony, a Portakabin had been sited there to handle Russian visitors wanting a visa to Britain. Behind the main building, in stark contrast, stood a sixties monstrosity completely devoid of aesthetic appeal. It was here that SIS had their offices.

Inevitably, they had got the worst deal. This was partly because the regular FCO wanted to put a stick in the eye of those they used but privately despised. It was also partly that the Office always insisted on maximum security and the best place to be was either underground or inside a building where there were no windows to open or for others to try and penetrate. Thus, SIS's Moscow station was a Stygian pit where no one ever saw the light of day. In the summer, when the hours were long and the opportunities for recreation few and far between, there had been concern over the years that SIS operatives going to meets would be picked out by their pallor. A long memo had been fired off to London which had resulted in the establishment of a tanning room known to everyone as Hyde Park. The reminder of home appealed to those in the know and officers were able to pretend that they, too, were able to have some fun in Moscow.

A wounded Vlad had dropped Nash at the Metropole the night before. He had decided not to report the attack, Vlad being easily placated by the bundle of dollar bills he had offered to effect repairs to his cab. Any contact with the Office would simply give the mole more information to pass on. There was no point in changing hotels. You were vulnerable in every city as soon as you checked in and in Moscow that was doubly so. Every concierge was in the pay of someone. He knew the Metropole well and at least it was territory of his own choosing. He also knew that any further attempt on his life would take time to set up, time that he intended to use to good effect.

The Metropole had been a welcome refuge. New German money had restored the fading Art Nouveau building to all its former glory. The British Embassy had a deal with the owners, who welcomed such an establishment clientele with open arms. The diplomats discovered that the place had become a favourite meeting spot for Mafia leaders. Everybody who was anybody, or at least everybody who thought they were anybody, visited the Metropole sooner or later. As places went it was the place to be. Just about every known language was being spoken, usually at the same time and all with the same message: there was a fortune to be made out there and boy, have I got the deal that's going to do it.

Nash strolled the ten minutes to the Embassy from the hotel, which was just down the road from the Bolshoi and the old KGB headquarters at Dzerzhinsky Square. So far as he knew, nobody was following him. Then again, given his recent record, he wasn't sure he would have been able to spot a tail if one were there.

The SIS complex – more a series of interconnected rooms – was accessed through a single door with a camera over the lintel and a key pad off to one side. The pad operated not with a code but with palmprint recognition. Nash placed his hand on the dark screen and looked at the camera, imagining the guard on the other side looking at him. Thank God access did not rely on the Marine deciding if he fitted the profile of an SIS officer. Instead, the database would do the work, comparing his print with what was already in the file, checking to see he was still current and finally matching palm print to the face. The whole process took just five seconds and there was a satisfying thunk as the bolts withdrew and the door opened.

That was almost the extent of the high-tech wizardry at the station's disposal. The real work of the outpost was done in a separate part of the main building just under the roof. There, a large contingent from GCHQ used their knowledge to try and pick up every conversation that went on in the Kremlin across the river or in the Ministry of Defence building three blocks to the east. There was intense competition between the British and the Americans' NSA team who were both pursuing the same mission. But down here was where the planning was done for operations, where the information from sources was processed and where attempts were made to satisfy the endless queries from London. In theory, Moscow station was a promotion and a positive step on the career ladder to the dizzy heights of the sixth floor. In reality it was a hell of impossible demands, scarce resources and, more recently, a fantastic volume of product which was rapidly overwhelming the limited staff's capability to process.

It was no wonder, Nash thought, that Nick Bayes looked so wiped out. A man he had seen leave for Moscow a year earlier with the fitness of a 43-year-old golf fanatic was now haggard and pale – visits to Hyde Park notwithstanding. Clearly the Station Chief was cracking under the pressures of the job.

'Christ, Nick, you look like hell,' Nash said. Bayes groaned theatrically.

'Tell me about it, David,' he said. 'We have more defectors queuing up to sell us their life story than we have people to even meet with them. Men, women, young, old, SVR, MoD, you name it, they all want to move to Surrey.'

He ushered David into his office, a large cubicle with modern, light brown furniture and a computer terminal on a stand off to one side. A set of dusty golf clubs were propped in the corner. Bayes picked up a piece of paper from the desk.

'Look at this,' he said. 'We're even getting e-mail into the Embassy with offers from defectors. It's madness. We just don't have the resources to cope with this stuff. The sooner this tour ends and I can get back to the Office and tell stories about how tough it was and how well I did, the happier I'll be.'

It was a familiar tale of man-in-the-field versus the bureaucrat back home. There were always too few resources and always too many demands. The measure of a good Station Chief was the ability to keep all the balls in the air while producing something that resembled a useful intelligence product. Despite the moaning, Nash knew that Bayes was well regarded back home.

'Anyway, my troubles are hardly your affair,' said Bayes. 'I received a signal about you yesterday and something arrived in the bag for you today. Seems you're on most favoured nation status at the moment. I'm told to render you every assistance, no door to be left unopened, blah, blah, blah.' Bayes made a salaam. 'You wish and I'll make a command.'

'I don't know much more than you,' Nash replied. 'Let's have a look at the HAA, see if that can tell us what's going on.'

The two men walked along the corridor to the second door on the left. 'The signal made it crystal clear that I'm not welcome in here, so do your stuff and I'll see you back in my office,' said Bayes as he gestured Nash inside.

Nash turned on the CD player and inserted the disc. He typed the word CUTTHROAT into the small key pad that rested on the top of the machine. There was a click as the laser connected with the disc and then the image of the Chief floated in front of him.

'Sorry about all this cloak-and-dagger stuff, Nash,' Spedding began, 'but until we catch our mole . . .

'Three things we want you to do, David. One,' the Chief held up a finger, 'check out Spitz's story about the BW programme. The Americans are playing down the BW angle but it's my guess that Spitz was killed because of what he knew and that you were attacked for the same reason. Be careful, they'll probably try again.'

'Oh, do you think so?' replied Nash with sarcasm, remembering Olivier Raffet.

The hologram continued. 'Two, try to find out whether there's anything in what the Americans are saying about trouble brewing in Ukraine. And three, find the leak.'

'Just like that,' said Nash.

'Easier said than done, I know,' continued the Chief, as if

he had heard Nash's comment, 'but we're getting nowhere at this end. Perhaps you'll have more luck.

'Apropos Ukraine, the Americans have sent in Philip Thomas and you're to liaise with him. We also have an asset in place in Moscow that I would like you to meet. He'll be in the bar of the Metropole at six this evening. He will find you.

'Keep us informed. You can report back through Alex Wright.'

There were no farewells, no attempt to bestow good wishes on a mission the Chief probably felt was doomed to failure. The image simply faded to leave a few dust motes hovering where he once had stood.

In a small room off the Oval Office the face of the Russian President shimmered on to a screen. His American counterpart sat facing the monitor, a tiny camera on top of it projecting his image back to the Russian leader. He wore a small earpiece that was invisible to the Russian so that he could listen to comments from his aides who were sitting outside.

'Good morning. Or should I say good afternoon?' the American began, pausing briefly for the translator to do his work.

'Good afternoon it is. And how are you today?'

The niceties dispensed with, it was the American who set the agenda.

'We are concerned at information we have received that there may be trouble brewing in Ukraine, trouble that will directly affect your relationship with your neighbour. I wanted to discuss this with you.'

The Russian's face reddened and his already swollen features appeared to grow larger. Ukraine had produced nothing but problems for him ever since he moved in to the Kremlin.

First it was the nuclear weapons, then the requirement for oil subsidies, now some other trouble.

'I thought the money you promised Kuchma at your last meeting and his agreement to speed up the transfer of nuclear weapons had dealt with any problem from that direction,' the Russian replied.

'So did I, my friend. So did I. But we understand from normally reliable sources that there are efforts under way to provoke a civil war in Ukraine. We also understand that some of your military officers may be involved, indeed that some members of the Russian armed forces may be prepared to join the fight on behalf of the rebels.'

The American paused again. He could see that his opposite number was getting even angrier and he continued swiftly.

'I fully understand that you knew nothing about any of this,' he reassured the Russian. 'But of course you will want to take all necessary steps to contain the problem.'

'You talk of "provoking a civil war". What exactly do you mean?' the Russian asked. 'And just who are these "normally reliable sources"?'

It was an obvious question and one which the American was not prepared to answer.

'You will understand that I can't be more specific at this stage . . .'

The President heard the DCI's soft voice in his earpiece muttering 'Aid. Play the Aid card.' Giving no sign of the outside advice, the President continued.

'I am sure you appreciate that I have my critics here at home who would welcome the opportunity to take some action against anyone who tried to interfere with the process of democracy. If Russian soldiers were to become involved in some kind of action in Ukraine, it would be impossible for my country not to respond. For instance, Congress might demand reduction of aid to Russia, maybe ask NATO to intervene. I don't think either of us wants anything like that, do we?'

As the translator finished his work at the other end, the Russian leaned back from the screen, the bully and the browbeater replaced for a moment by the calculating politician who understood exactly what was required to ensure his own survival. He had been a careful gambler all his life and he knew when the deck was stacked against him. He leaned forward.

'Thank you, my friend. Your warning will be heeded.' The screen cleared as the line was cut in Moscow.

The door opened behind the American President and the DCI crowded into the narrow space with Steve Dorsey, the Deputy Secretary of State.

The President swivelled in his chair to look at the DCI.

'So just what do we know?' he asked and then continued to answer his own question. 'This guy Pyotr Sakharovsky is planning a military coup in Ukraine and we estimate that it stands a fair chance of success. Right?' The DCI nodded. 'Then we have the problem of loose nukes, a hoodlum running the country and God knows what kind of problems with the Russians.'

'We've been running some probabilities through the system and our best guess is that there's little chance of Russia interfering and a fairly high chance of civil war in the country,' said the DCI.

Game theory had long been in vogue at the Agency, but found little favour with the State Department – particularly after the mixed results it had given recently (military success in Somalia, civil rights would be restored in Haiti, a Bosnia peace accord). Dorsey jumped in, his spectacles jerking with the angry movement of his head and reflecting off the fluorescent light.

'If you're prepared to bet that Russia will keep out of this once the shooting starts you're crazy,' he said. 'This is what the Russian military have been waiting for: a civil war on their doorstep; a large group of ethnic Russians; the prospect of bringing the country back into Moscow's sphere of influence. Look what they did in Georgia, in Chechnya, in Azerbaijan. Whatever he may say, there'll be nothing the President can do to stop the military. They'll want action and he'll have to give it to them or he's history.'

It was a bleak assessment but one with which there was common agreement. They had all watched as Russia either provoked insurrection or stepped in to put it down in several of the former Soviet Republics. The US President had granted the Russian his wish to control peacekeeping operations in the near abroad rather than provoke a series of confrontations over countries about which he cared little and NATO cared not at all. The Ukraine, however, was too big and too visible. Do nothing and they would both be history, he reflected sourly. For now, though, it would be enough to brief the allies and make sure that the military had got their act together to respond if necessary.

'Get me the Chairman,' the President commanded. The computer operator moved his mouse over one of the icons that read CJCS for Chairman of the Joint Chiefs of Staff and clicked twice. The link to the Chairman's office across the Potomac river in the Pentagon was completed in seconds. The President swiftly briefed his military commander on his conversation with Moscow.

'I've told him that unless he can control his people, we'll have to respond,' he added.

'How did he react to that, Mr President?' the Chairman asked.

'He got the message all right but whether that means he can do anything remains to be seen. Personally, I'm doubtful. If the Russians are unable to contain the crisis, then we must be ready. I want NATO to begin contingency planning for a series of specific military responses from containment to intervention. Speak to the British, the Germans and the French. See what support there is and make sure that our people here are ready to move if I give the order. I'll have State work up their end and we'll meet tomorrow morning to go over the options.'

The soldier nodded.

'And General,' the President added. 'Make sure you look at *all* the options, including nuclear release.'

The President sat back in his chair and reflected on the two conversations. He was supposed to be the inheritor of a peaceful new world which he believed could be shaped to provide a better home for his children and the children of generations to come. Now he found himself planning for the unimaginable.

12

ON THE BRIEF ride back from the Embassy, Nash found himself starting at the sound of car horns and flinching as yet another mad driver scraped by at a junction with fractions of an inch to spare. Logically he knew that they – whoever they were – wouldn't have had time to set up another operation but self-preservation had honed his instincts to razor sharpness.

With a cheery wave, the driver dropped him in the small parking area in front of the Metropole. Before he had even turned towards the lobby entrance, he felt a hand grab his forearm. He whirled, foot raised to drive down his assailant's shin in the classic opening manoeuvre to break a close hold. Before he could make contact he recognized the laughing face of Yuri Parashvili.

'Christ, Yuri,' he half shouted. 'A man could get himself killed that way.'

'David. David,' the Russian chuckled. 'You shouldn't allow a little attempt at assassination to upset your day.'

'How the hell did you know about that?' Nash asked.

'You forget how close we are these days. Your office kindly alerted me to your planned visit. I'd intended to meet your flight but,' he shrugged, 'Moscow traffic.' The gesture consigned drivers, pedestrians and the erratic traffic lights to the scrapheap of missed appointments. 'Then I heard of the incident on the way into the city, made a couple of calls and here we are.' He grinned. 'It seems that you have upset somebody a great deal.'

'You might say that,' Nash replied. 'But exactly who remains to be seen.'

Yuri drew Nash away from the hotel entrance and towards a black Volkswagen Golf parked amid a line of Mercedes saloons, each with a chauffeur standing alongside.

'Come, David,' said Yuri. 'There are things we need to discuss.'

When they were both settled in the car, Yuri reached inside his jacket and withdrew a sheaf of papers. The sight of documents always sent a slight quiver down Nash's spine. They were the real gold, the traceable, checkable, factual strands of intelligence every officer wanted in his hands. Better than verbal descriptions, more exciting than intercepts and much, much more difficult to obtain.

'When I last saw you, I promised that we would go through the material we found in the warehouse and that I would let you know if there was anything interesting,' Yuri continued.

'And was there?'

The Russian paused to light one of his foul-smelling cigarettes. Nash immediately rolled down his window in a silent protest. The move had little effect except to draw the smoke through the open window via Nash's face.

'There was plenty of good stuff about the drugs business. Shipments in, shipments out, traffic patterns, connections, that kind of thing. Nothing of much interest to you. But there were two things I thought we might talk about. One piece of information and one question.'

'Shoot.'

'You remember all those raw materials we saw?' Nash nodded. 'It seems that the warehouse was run by one of our local gangs, the Boolas. Nothing too surprising about that –

all the gangs are into drugs of one kind or another. What was different is that the material had arrived by an unusual route. There was no obvious Colombian connection. All the processing supplies had arrived from Japan and the shipping manifests indicated vessels owned by the Hirano Shipping Line.'

'Is that supposed to ring any bells?' Nash asked.

'No, it didn't to us either, but we've been doing some checking. Hirano has an interesting history. Involved in big business with North Korea. We've tracked it moving Korean exports to Iran. It's also been in the people business taking Vietnamese to other parts of South Asia.'

'Why should that be of interest to me, or to you for that matter?'

'It's who's behind Hirano that matters. We think it's the Yakuza. If that's the case then we may have a new alliance between Russian and Japanese organized crime.'

'You told me before that these people were carving up the world between them. This is just one more example, isn't it?' interrupted Nash.

Yuri flung the stub of his cigarette out of the window and exhaled noisily.

'Right. But this alliance spells big trouble. The Boolas are big in opium production down south and they've apparently cut a deal with the Colombians on cocaine. The Japs have the amphetamine market wrapped up. If we do have a new alliance, between them they cover just about every major drug around.'

Nash whistled.

'I'm assuming you knew nothing about this?' asked Yuri. Nash shook his head. 'OK. Then we come to the second problem. Some of the material in the warehouse was not going to be used for processing the drugs. It was heading east, not to Japan but to Vladivostok.'

'What kind of things?' Nash asked. Yuri flicked through the papers once again and paused at one sheet.

'Two tons of baby formula, dry ice. A bunch of other stuff had been sent before we arrived – acids, some lab equipment and so on.'

'That's a hell of a long way round,' Nash pointed out. 'Japan to Vladivostok is a two-day journey. Japan to Moscow by ship would take weeks.'

'True. But we think this was a single cargo from a ship that loaded up in Europe, not Japan. The drugs were brought in from Colombia to Antwerp and then loaded on board the Japanese vessel which took on the other cargo at the same time. Then everything would be broken down here and the Boolas would shift the stuff east through their own network. Efficient and almost impossible to trace.'

It was the mention of the baby food that had rung some distant alarm bell in Nash's subconscious. He pictured the distinctive yellow and white tins that he had seen on the supermarket shelves and then, suddenly, the memory came flooding back. Frank Taylor, the BW man in counter-proliferation, had said that baby formula was used as a growth medium for some types of BW. And Vladivostok had come up in the intercept that Daemon had pulled up on the Intelink. So what the hell did all that mean? Organized crime making BW? Was that the dark secret everyone was trying to stop him finding out? If true, they were all in the shit and sinking fast. He needed to get on to London and do some checking of his own.

Despite the thoughts racing through his mind, Nash remained poker faced. Yuri saw none of the excitement and horror that Nash felt. Nash looked at his watch and realized that action would have to wait. He was almost late for his rendezvous with the Chief's 'asset' at the Metropole.

'Thanks for that, Yuri,' he said, putting his hand on the door and easing it open. 'I'll run it by London and see what I can get.'

He walked the few paces across the car park and pushed open the swing doors of the hotel entrance. The bar at the Metropole lay at the end of the long marble-floored reception area. Convention had it that, if exposed, make a virtue out of the exposure. So, Nash had selected a table for two in the front where everyone could see him and his expected visitor. He nursed his lager which at ten dollars a pop still tasted like the watery stuff that was a fraction of the price back home.

The Chief's briefing had been extraordinary. No proper chain of command, no back-up and no escape route. That meant big trouble as far as Nash was concerned. The Chief suspected a leak so high in the Office that he couldn't trust the information to anyone. Alex, who had nearly died in the attack, was obviously safe, but apart from her the suspect list could include anyone. Unbidden, the picture of Teller came into his mind. That calculating, watchful face, those cold eyes. He had been in every briefing, knew every move. Nash turned the thought over like a sour lemon, disliking the taste and yet unable to resist the flavour.

He was being cut loose from the support system that the Office claimed to value so highly. 'Never Alone', that was the message that was drummed into you again and again. In trouble, the Office will get you out; exposed, they'll find the cover you need. It was a sound enough motto to bolster morale but here he was confronted with the reality and it was not very comforting.

The package Alex had sent over in the bag from London had included the gun that now nestled securely underneath his suit jacket. It was a Glock 22 automatic pistol with a 15-shot magazine, the biggest you could have on a pistol without it appearing so bulky as to be visible even to the untrained eye, made not from metal but from polymer which saved a full 10 oz in weight while sacrificing none of the stopping power. The Glock used bullets of a Federal Hydra-Shock design. Once the bullet left the barrel, the spinning motion would peel an outer layer of the round back from the central body so that it looked like an aircraft propeller. The spinning blades would slice and dice tissue as the bullet penetrated. Officially outlawed by most governments for use in warfare, it seemed to Nash that if it came to actually firing the gun, then he wanted to make sure of killing whoever was causing him a problem. There would be no opportunity to discuss the niceties of international conventions – or at least not if he intended to be the one who walked away.

A second variation on the standard weapon was the tiny laser sight that fitted in front of the trigger guard. As he knew from recent personal experience, the sight could be deadly.

A shadow fell across the table. Nash looked up from his drink and saw a pair of long legs encased in tight-fitting, shiny black thigh-boots. His eyes rose higher, taking in the short – very short – red leather skirt, the puffy cream silk blouse and the choker of three strands of pearls around a slim neck. The woman's face was everything her body had promised: full lips, with a pout exaggerated by purple lipstick outlined with a dark pencil line, a strong nose with wide, flaring nostrils, blue eyes and cropped blonde hair. The effect was extraordinarily sensual, an open invitation. She smiled slightly, clearly used to the effect she had on men and enjoying it. Nash smiled back, enjoying the tease and knowing that this would go nowhere. He did not sleep with prostitutes.

'David Nash?' The question came in a breathy, accentless voice. The smile dropped from Nash's lips. This was no tart. This was trouble.

'Who's asking?' he parried, trying to buy some time.

'I'm your six o'clock appointment,' she replied. 'Come with me.'

Oh well, in for a penny, thought Nash as without saying anything he placed a note on the table to pay for the beer and rose to leave. The woman led the way through the reception area with Nash following a pace behind. He could feel every eye following her and then passing on to him and knew what each guest was thinking. The concierge could not resist what he thought was a knowing leer. He knew that next morning at breakfast everyone's eyes would be on him, assessing him, wondering just how good it had been.

A black Mercedes 500SL was waiting outside the hotel with a man in a matching black chauffeur's uniform holding open the rear door. She bent and stepped into the car and Nash paused, enjoying the brief glimpse of upper thigh and hoping for more. Then he, too, bent and settled in to the comfort of the vehicle as it smoothly pulled away.

'I must apologize for the scene in there,' she said smiling. 'But nobody thinks twice about a man going off with a prostitute. It's so obvious and yet it provides a very effective cover. I'm sorry if I embarrassed you.'

'Not at all,' replied Nash. 'I'm quite used to being picked up by strange women in hotel bars.'

'My name is Veronika,' she continued and Nash watched as she moved her right hand on to her thigh and then up her skirt. He barely had time to absorb the sensuality of the movement and to speculate just what it might presage when there was a slight click and her hand reappeared to point a small pistol at his chest. Her thumb flicked up the safety catch to the left of the trigger guard. Her hand was steady, the gun small, silver and very deadly. So much for allowing hormones to overcome training, Nash thought.

'This is a Sig-Sauer P230, 7 shot .38 automatic,' Veronika explained, all sensuality in her voice replaced by a hard-edged professionalism. 'It is loaded with a hollow-point round that will make a big mess of you without doing too much damage to this lovely car. All of which is to say don't bother trying to escape. Even if you get past me, the doors are locked from the front and the glass screen before us is bulletproof.

'First I need to make sure that we continue to our meeting in a friendly way. Could you please turn away from me, lean your head against the window and kneel on the seat.'

Nash did as he was instructed. Hunched up in the back, he was effectively restrained from making any movement while she was free to explore his body. The search was thorough, intrusive and erotic. She began at his neck, her left hand feeling around his collar for the knife that some people concealed there and then moved across his shoulders and down his arm, kneading, pushing and pulling to explore every crevice. Her fingers swiftly felt the strap of the shoulder holster and then slid inside his coat to remove the gun and the spare magazine. She continued around his chest, fingers lightly touching his nipples and then his underarms before moving down across his stomach to his crotch. As someone who used sex to conceal a weapon, she was especially thorough in questing between his legs and he could feel her fingers move across his penis, squeezing and kneading, before gently touching his balls and then probing back towards his anus and between the crease of his buttocks. Despite the ignominy of his position, he could feel himself becoming aroused, the sweat beginning to break out on his brow as he tried and failed to control the automatic response to a body that was betraying him.

The sensitive part of the search over, her fingers swept down his thighs and calves and then pushed briefly inside his shoes, looking for the ankle gun that was a favourite of American undercover cops but which the British considered too obvious and too dangerous.

He heard a slight shuffling sound as she moved away from him to the far side of the car.

'You can sit down now, David. The fun's over.' He could sense the laughter in her voice and he cursed her silently. She had clearly guessed at or felt his excitement and he was furious at the ease with which she had been able to manipulate him.

'Elementary precautions. Nothing personal,' she continued when he was sitting in a more comfortable position. 'My instructions were to make sure you were unarmed, just in case you might react in an unnecessarily aggressive manner.'

'So where are we going?' Nash asked. They had left the ring road now and were heading north towards the Moscow Dynamo Stadium, reaching the outer limit of his knowledge of the city. There seemed to be no attempt to disguise their route, no doubling back or cutting across minor roads. Presumably they assumed he wouldn't be coming back.

'You'll just have to wait and see,' Veronika replied unhelpfully. 'But don't worry, you're among friends. There is no danger to you provided you do nothing stupid.'

Thus dismissed, Nash settled back in the vehicle and attempted to record the route so that if the opportunity arose, he would be able to return on his own. The car felt unusually heavy, even for a Mercedes. There was hardly any movement as it went into turns and the acceleration was almost stately. Armoured, he thought to himself. These people were serious players. But with whom and for what?

Somewhere north of the Academy of Sciences Botanical Gardens, the car turned in to one of the staid, grey apartment blocks that blotted the Russian landscape, monuments to a conformist architecture designed like the communist system itself to smother creative spirit. The only difference in this block was the large double gates and high wall surrounding its entrance, the cameras and microwave defences too small to be detected by a casual glance.

The half-dozen bodyguards lounging in the dirty entranceway eyed Nash with the hungry look of unfed piranhas. He stepped gingerly past them and followed Veronika down a passage, took a left turn and then stopped at a large black, wooden door at the end of a short corridor. His nose wrinkled in distaste at the smell of rotting cabbage and cat's pee that lingered in the hall. Veronika pressed a small section of the door which slid open with a slight hiss to reveal a key pad. She punched in a five-digit code, pressed her thumb to a small square of glass and waited. After a few seconds there was a gentle sigh of an airlock being released and the door swung open, its weight evident by the size of the hinges and its thickness. Wood covering steel, Nash thought. This place is a fortress.

He walked into a different world, filled with light and colour. It was a world of wealth and sophistication light years removed from the filth and degradation outside the door. He found himself standing in a large entrance hall that soared to at least forty feet with a black and white marble floor. A pair of elegant console tables rested against opposite walls, their scrollwork and chequered inlay distinctively nineteenth-century Russian. On one a pair of Revo sunglasses had been dropped alongside a Vuitton wallet. On the other a bunch of purple roses exuded an intoxicating perfume that swept away the last vestiges of the smell from outside the door.

Canvases portraying the social realist art of the post-war period covered the walls, depicting workers who clearly felt blessed to be toiling for the Great Union. There was even the stock portrait of the young revolutionary, hammer in one hand, sickle in the other, cresting a hill and marching onward into the sunlit uplands of the successful communist revolution. Over his shoulder the stylized images of Lenin and Marx encouraged him forward.

'I find it helpful to walk past these mementos every time I come home.' The voice belonged to an elegantly dressed man of about Nash's age who had come into the hallway from the far end. His English was almost accentless, just the occasional guttural blur indicating that the speaker was Russian. 'It reminds me of just how far I have come and how close I came to being one of them.' He gestured at the paintings. 'It was a close-run thing, you know. We need to be on our guard that the people who created the monster don't get another chance.'

The man dressed with the casual style of the seriously rich. A light yellow, short-sleeved shirt that looked soft enough to be silk, a narrow blue leather belt supporting dark blue woollen trousers cut with pleats to give them a wide, comfortable look that was distinctly Italian. Dark brown leather loafers completed the ensemble.

He was clean-shaven, lean, fit and with the hardness that comes from facing and meeting tough challenges. The penetrating sea-green eyes had a glint of humour in them, as if he could see Nash's brain working frantically to place the face with the surroundings. It was the hair that put the final brick in the wall. For a man so young it was remarkably grey, silvery even, and trimmed close to his head so that what might otherwise be an unruly tangle of curls was a fashionably close-cropped cut.

'Ah, I see my reputation has preceded me,' said the man reaching out a hand and smiling to expose a very un-Russian expanse of even, white teeth. Seeing Nash's hesitation he went on: 'And I see that what you have heard is not all good. But come, come, Mr Nash, or may I call you David? Formality between two people of our generation always seems so unnecessary, don't you think?'

'Mr Sakharovsky, I presume?' said Nash, ignoring the Lubertsy gang boss's outstretched hand.

'Call me Pyotr, please.' Sakharovsky's smile didn't falter. 'I am delighted to welcome you to my home and my headquarters.'

A butler appeared bearing champagne flutes on a silver tray, the wine's creamy yellow colour clearly indicating an excellent vintage. Nash wondered if Sakharovsky would be so gauche as to point out his extravagance and was relieved when he did not. His host gestured towards the glasses and Nash took one, astonished to hear in the deferential 'Thank you, sir' the well-modulated tones of a British butler. Now that was style, thought Nash, impressed despite himself.

'I hope you'll be able to stay for supper, David, but before that I thought you might like to have a look round.'

'Sure, why not?' said Nash, trying to recapture at least some of the initiative. 'Lead on.'

'I'm sorry that we had to bring you here by such an unusual method,' Pyotr continued. 'But I knew that Veronika would issue an invitation you wouldn't want to refuse.'

He and the woman both laughed at the little joke, clearly enjoying his discomfort. He wondered if Sakharovsky knew just how thorough her body searches were.

Nash nodded in recognition that what Pyotr said was probably true. He would never have simply walked out of the Metropole with a hood thrusting a gun in his ribs, especially if he knew he was being taken by Sakharovsky's people. Looking at him now, though, in the comfort of his own home, a beautiful woman paying court, surrounded by the trappings of a civilized man, it was difficult to make the connection with the warmonger Nash had been briefed about in London and Langley.

Nash knew Sakharovsky's history well, from poor boy to teenage hoodlum to black marketeer to gang boss. The Lubers had fingers in several pies – drugs, prostitution, money laundering, arms deals. Pyotr was a hands-on boss, known to be personally responsible for at least twenty murders, though never successfully prosecuted, for reasons which Nash could imagine all too easily. Pyotr's voice dragged Nash back from his reflections.

'When I began to gain some authority in the chaos of the Gorbachev reforms, I discovered I needed more than just an office,' he continued conversationally. 'I wanted somewhere that would keep me in touch with my people. Somewhere that would remind me of what might have been. This,' he said, gesturing around him, 'was the result.

'I own this block and everyone in it works for me. It is office, home, work and play. A fortress that looks innocent enough from the outside but is virtually impregnable.'

He turned right off the hall and Nash followed as Pyotr pointed out the offices with their Apple workstations, the accounting office where spreadsheets were following cash flow and monitoring performance of the different subsidiaries of his empire. They went down one level to the indoor swimming pool, gym and weapons range and up one level to the bedrooms, each with its own Jacuzzi, steam room and exercise area. There was a fine collection of Impressionist paintings on the ground floor, and some quite decent nineteenth-century French and Italian oils including some faintly erotic works by Munch in the bedrooms.

The one thing the complex lacked was a vista. Nowhere was there a view except in the central square around which the apartment block was constructed. There, Pyotr had planted a garden that reminded Nash of the atrium in the Office. It was filled with tall and exotic plants that grew together in wild profusion. The view from the windows overlooking this area was similar to one in the Amazon jungle, except that there were no birds, and no insects, in part perhaps because few of the plants would survive a Moscow winter. In the cold months, this must be a truly bleak place, Nash reflected.

Despite the furnishings of silk and wool, plush sofas and curtains, and beautiful modern furniture from France, Britain and Scandinavia which underlined the wealth and taste of their owner, the whole place had the oddly antiseptic feel of a workstation-cum-military base, designed for the purpose of keeping secrets in and people out. Pyotr would always be a prisoner of his money and the enemies he had made. What could be worth that sacrifice? Nash thought to himself.

The tour ended in a large room furnished in soft browns and creams with a full-sized snooker table in its centre.

'Before we move on to dinner, I thought it might be helpful to explain to you just why you are here,' said Pyotr.

'That would certainly be a start,' Nash replied sarcastically.

'You have been told, no doubt, that I am one of the biggest crooks in Moscow. That is true. But I see myself as no different from the British robber barons who began your own industrial revolution. Then they were pioneering heroes who exploited the working class. Now I am a hero to the thousands I employ and to the hundreds of thousands who indirectly owe their work to the money I invest in the new Russia.'

Nash raised a sceptical eyebrow.

'OK, so you disagree.' Pyotr shrugged his shoulders and gestured dismissively with his almost empty glass. 'I'm not here to justify myself to you or anyone else. I just want you to understand that things in Russia today are not as simple as they might seem from the comfort of Washington or London. This is the Wild West. I may not be Wyatt Earp but I'm not Billy the Kid either.

'I've heard from my own spies in the bazaars that people have been saying particularly unkind things about me recently.' He smiled self-deprecatingly to let Nash know that whatever spies Pyotr might have certainly did not just work in the bazaars. 'I suspect that you, too, have heard that I have been organizing a coup in the Ukraine with the intention of taking over the country.' He paused. 'Such rumours are complete nonsense.'

'I'd hardly expect you to admit it,' Nash replied.

'Why not? I could tell you that I am about to assassinate your Queen – what could you do about it? I have nothing to do with the Ukraine. Who would? The country is a madhouse. Its government is a shambles. Its economy is a joke. Never invest in the unpredictable if you haven't got the guns to back it up. And I certainly don't have the people or the guns to win a civil war in the Ukraine.'

'But you can't deny that the Russian black market's almost saturated. You'll have to find new outlets somewhere if you're going to expand. You don't strike me as the type to rest on his laurels.'

Pyotr laughed, a rich, full, head-thrown-back laugh of genuine amusement.

'You foreigners. You just don't understand what Russia is like today. Ten years ago I had nothing. Five years ago I was worth a million dollars, maybe two. Today, I own two hundred legitimate businesses and run dozens of other operations. I have a turnover of around $4.8 billion a year and I make nearly $1 billion in clear profit.'

Seeing Nash's scepticism at this tale of fame and fortune, Russian-style, Pyotr pressed on.

'These figures are real, David, and I am not alone. Several of my colleagues in the business have seen the same growth. This is a mad country where the lunatics are in charge and the really sane are in business and making a fortune.'

'But that still doesn't answer the fact that there is a limit to what you can do here, that you need to expand to make progress.'

'David, David,' Pyotr remonstrated. 'You've been listening to the Americans again. They have so quickly forgotten their own heritage. I have only just begun here. Five years ago, everything I had was illegitimate. Today I am forty per cent legal and in another five years that figure will be up to seventy per cent. Why? Because I am not here to rape and pillage my own country. I am investing in her future, in my future. I am in partnership with multinational concerns, household names in the west, and they are going to be my future wealth. Just as the old Russia was destroyed by the arrival of capitalism so the new Russia will be built by the new capitalists, people like me. I don't need Ukraine or anywhere else. There is no limit to what I can do here. Russia has only just begun its journey to a new greatness.'

There was logic enough in what he was saying. But for Nash to believe this man would mean that everything he had been told in Washington and by the Office was wrong. To believe an acknowledged crook – however seductive the surroundings or the staff – made little sense when the evidence against him was apparently so convincing.

Pyotr could see the questions in Nash's manner and leaned forward as if to whisper a dirty joke in a crowded formal dinner. He was close enough so that Nash could smell the champagne on his breath.

'You're worried about me in the Ukraine. That's rubbish and always has been. Take my advice. Look elsewhere. And not just for other people but other places too.'

'What do you mean by that?' Nash asked.

'Well, if the story about Ukraine is a lie then the storyteller is also a liar. Logic should tell you that the lies are being told for a reason and that reason is to expose me and take me out.'

'If you're as innocent as you claim, then who's guilty?' Nash asked. He tried to keep his voice neutral but it was difficult to keep the cynicism buried.

'I can see that you remain unconvinced,' said Pyotr. 'Look, I have a suggestion for you. My men and I are planning a little mission for later on tonight which you might find revealing. Why don't you come along? It may be a little dangerous, though. You'll need to be well prepared.'

He gestured towards Veronika who reached into her bag

and handed over Nash's Glock. He supposed this was an acceptance ritual of some sort and that Pyotr no longer considered him a threat. He also had no doubt that there were guns trained on him right now. The slightest wrong move and the servants would kill for their master.

'Veronika will take you back to your hotel after dinner. We'll pick you up there around three a.m.'

Nash found the proposed alliance of law-enforcer and gangland killer bizarre, but the logic was compelling. Pyotr might want to play the innocent but he certainly had someone in the frame, too. That made tonight's operation, wherever it might lead, the right place to go.

'I'll be waiting,' assented Nash.

'Excellent, David. Glad to have you along.'

Nash thought this might be a good time to take advantage of their new-found camaraderie.

'There's one other thing you might be able to help me with, Pyotr,' he began tentatively. The Russian looked on encouragingly, clearly amused that, despite his reservations, his guest felt that a crook like him might have his uses.

'We've been investigating a number of recent developments in Russia which are of concern to us,' said Nash carefully. 'Along the way it's become clear that we're treading pretty heavily on someone's toes. I'm not talking about our normal rivals; these guys are too violent and too well informed.'

'Sounds to me like Spandau,' said Pyotr.

'That's the second time I've heard that name in two days,' Nash replied cautiously. 'What does it mean?'

'All I know,' said Pyotr, 'comes from a visit I was paid a few months ago and what little I've been able to piece together since then.'

Pyotr had received a call from a man claiming to be a former agent for the DGSE, the French overseas spying organization. When he had arrived at the rendezvous, the man had identified himself as Paul Richardson, a former operations man for the American Defense Intelligence Agency. He was representing an organization of former spies, people who had been fired or made redundant at the end of the Cold War, who wanted to put their talents to some use. They had banded together to form Spandau, a mercenary group of spies-for-hire.

'Why the name?' Nash asked.

'You remember that Rudolf Hess, the Nazi war criminal, was held in Spandau jail?' Nash nodded. 'Well, the jail was apparently also the location of a number of meetings between different intelligence service chiefs during the Cold War. It was totally secret, totally secure. The organization seems to have been named after those meetings. A kind of in-joke to those in the know as well as a method of telling people like you that Spandau knows even the darkest secrets.'

'Who's behind it? Did Richardson say?' Nash asked, mulling over the significance of Pyotr's information. This was frightening. A group of spies who knew the tradecraft, knew the sources, knew the methods. It would be like having the best of the rest playing the first team with the first team permanently short of their trainer and half the squad. Spandau would be able to field experienced operatives from all the spy agencies, provide them with similar equipment, train them in similar ways and allow them to operate outside the law with no politician breathing down their necks. It was the kind of assignment any field agent would love.

'My visitor simply referred to the Founder,' Pyotr continued. 'No names. But he did say they have British, French, American, Israeli, Russian, even Chinese, as part of their team. Of course, how true any of this was, I have no way of knowing. But they were certainly pricey. They wanted a retainer from me to secure their services of $100,000 a month to start and then payment per assignment. Expensive, but worth it if they can deliver,' Pyotr said.

'So why didn't you take it?' Nash asked.

'I have a pretty good intelligence network of my own,' Pyotr replied. 'And you always have trouble with people like that. They get to know how you work and the next thing you find that they're working against you for some bastard who's out to screw you. No thanks. I prefer to rely on my own resources.'

It certainly made sense and would explain the professionalism of the people in Kiev. He had sensed at the time that they seemed almost too professional, as if they had read the same manual. Now he knew that they probably had. It explained the Israeli assassin in Hampshire, too. But it didn't explain who was giving them their information.

Nash thought for a moment. Pyotr had answered some of his questions but he was no nearer to finding the traitor. With the kind of money the Russian had been talking about, Spandau could afford to buy just about anybody in the Office. The question was who had sold out? The answer might lie with the mission planned for later that night.

Pyotr pushed himself out of his armchair and gestured to Veronika and Nash to follow.

'Come, it's time for dinner.'

By the time Nash returned to the Metropole, the frenetic pace of earlier in the evening had slackened and the lobby was comparatively empty. As he strolled towards the lifts at the far end, he noticed the night shift on the reception desk looking his way. The tale of his exit had clearly been passed along. Or was that just his paranoia?

'David. Buddy. Great to see you.' The call interrupted his self-absorption. He turned his head and saw Philip Thomas rising out of one of the comfortable armchairs to stride over and greet him. So much had happened since he had arrived he had forgotten all about the Agency man and his requirement to team up with him. Clearly this had not slipped Thomas's mind and he had been lying in wait.

'Philip. Good to see you, too. Hope you haven't been waiting long.' The two men shook hands and gravitated towards the bar where Thomas ordered a beer and Nash a whisky and soda. In a gesture to the lateness of the hour, Thomas had shed his CIA uniform of dark suit, white shirt and dark, dull tie in favour of casual light brown trousers and a bright green polo shirt with a sweater slung round his neck. It was as much a uniform as the suit and signalled 'American' to anyone. But then Moscow was full of Americans these days so the very shrillness of the outfit was a disguise of sorts, Nash supposed.

'How long have you been in town?' Thomas asked. Nash assumed he already knew the answer and was simply making the point that he should have been in contact before now.

'Only just arrived. Been rushed off my feet,' Nash replied. 'I'm glad you called round. Saved me the trouble of coming to see you in the morning.'

'Have you found out anything useful?' Thomas asked.

Nash hesitated. 'Nothing much,' he replied. 'I've just been getting myself up to speed, seeing the folks at the Embassy, sniffing the air. You know the form.'

'Sure. Been doing much the same myself but I do have some additional Intel on friend Sakharovsky.'

'Really?' Nash prompted.

'Yeah. It seems our original intelligence was right. He's definitely the man behind the Ukraine operation.'

Thomas caught Nash's sceptical look and his mouth tightened.

'Look, David. We've been over all this. Our sourcing is one hundred per cent. He's our man. We know what he's going to do. We know how he's going to do it. All we don't yet know is when it's going to happen.'

Looking at Thomas's angry face, Nash wondered how he could have thought it so benign in the DCI's office. This was not the congenial Ivy Leaguer he had met then. This was the hard-driving Agency operative that he should have known lurked behind the well-mannered veneer. Any thought he had about sharing what he had learned vanished in the face of the CIA man's aggression.

'What's your latest on the troop deployments?' Nash asked, sliding away from the confrontation.

'There's increased signals traffic which our people say is the beginning of some kind of limited mobilization in the west. But we have no collateral for that from overhead. Predicting timing from what little we have is not easy, but it looks like being within the next few days.'

Nash grunted, absorbing the information. If the satellites had detected nothing, it was difficult to imagine that any large-scale troop movements could occur within days. The Russian military was so incompetent now that NATO believed it would take at least two years for them to organize any kind of massive conventional attack in Europe. An operation in Ukraine would not be on that scale. Still, even getting a few thousand troops on the road would require a huge logistical effort and take a while to set up and manage. The increased signals traffic meant nothing, Nash reasoned. A classic example of making the facts fit the desired scenario.

'Are we doing anything to pre-empt?' Nash asked.

'NATO has some contingency plans in the works,' Thomas replied. 'But your guess is as good as mine as to what that means. My people say the President's preparing to act, but what he'll do is anybody's guess too. He's getting conflicting advice from all sides: let it go, give the Russians a bloody nose, draw a line in the sand, do something, do nothing. The usual political crap.'

Nash drained the last of his whisky and put the glass back down on the table.

'I'm bushed. Can we finish this tomorrow?'

'Sure, David. Let's do lunch. How about 36? Around noon?' Thomas suggested.

The Kropotkinskaya 36 was Moscow's first co-operative restaurant when it opened. Since the revolution it had been privatized and prices had gone through the roof but the emphasis on authenticity kept the customers coming back for a taste of old Russia. Best of all, it was always busy enough that quiet conversations would vanish in the overall bubble and foreigners were commonplace.

'Sounds good to me,' said Nash and with a casual wave walked off towards the lifts.

As he rode up to his room, he wondered why, from that first trip to Washington, the Americans had been so keen to implicate Sakharovsky and ignore what Spitz had to say. Pyotr's explanation of just why he wanted to have nothing to do with the Ukraine seemed plausible enough, and acceptance of the Russian gangster's explanation had been reinforced by his conduct during dinner earlier that evening.

The conversation had ranged from the political situation in Russia to the growth of rap music in the country to the recovery of the market in contemporary art in Europe. Throughout the meal, Veronika had been the perfect hostess. She was clearly no bimbo but a cosmopolitan woman with brains that could spar on equal terms with Pyotr. If the intention of the meal had been to disarm Nash, it had succeeded. He found it difficult to believe that this man was a threat to the world. He certainly was ruthless and a self-confessed gangster on the rise but his apparent frankness was appealing. Nash was convinced that here was the genuine article.

And then there was Spitz, left hanging in the wind with the chair kicked from under him. Nash remained convinced that his source had been telling the truth, that it wasn't just some piece of hyperbolic fiction dreamed up by a fantasist. But if

Pytor wasn't the BW buyer, who was? Maybe tonight would answer some of the questions.

Back in his room, he walked across to his computer, turned it on and clicked the icons that made the satellite link between Moscow and London. It was late in London, too, and he was surprised when Alex's face appeared on the screen.

'Alex, great to see you,' he spoke into the microphone.

'Yeah, another late night. Daemon and I have been trying to iron some bugs out of the system.' A hand wafted across the front of Alex's face and Nash realized that Daemon was sitting beside her. This was an opportunity not to be missed.

'Daemon, you remember the other day we went through the Intelink to look at Russia's BW programme and you picked up that message about unusual shipments to Vladivostok?' He heard a muttered acknowledgement from Daemon. 'Could you get back into the database and cross-ref that with a Japanese shipping company called the Hirano Shipping Line. Then cross-ref that to Vladivostok and see if any of their ships comes on the radar screen. Then try that list of raw materials and add in baby formula and see what turns up.'

'Sounds wild to me,' said Daemon. 'I'm just logging on to the other computer. Hang ten.' Nash heard a tuneless 'Dum de dum de dum de dum' off screen interspersed with the clicking of keys. There was a grunted 'Aha' and then a curse.

'What's the problem?' Nash asked impatiently.

'No problem,' the voice replied. 'Just a password that's been changed.' There was a slight pause. 'Now we're in. OK, we put in the parameters and wait a minute.' Another pause. 'Or two. Or three. And *voilà*.'

'The Lloyd's Register has the *Toshugu*, a merchant ship registered to the Hirano Shipping Line, docking at Vladivostok on the same date the Agency source claims the material arrived.' Nash could hear Daemon humming as he read through the data trying to cull the relevant information. 'Three more vessels of the same line in Europe in the past two months. Seems they've been all over the place. Cargoes unloaded in Antwerp and Kiev. One ship logged to New York, the other two are heading home to Osaka. Nothing on baby formula, but that's hardly high on anyone's watch-list.'

'Anything on who owns the shipping line?' Nash asked.

'Hirano is registered in Panama. It'll take us weeks to crack that. Could mean something. May mean nothing. Everyone likes Panama these days. You can hire any crew you like so there's no problem with the unions and if you have something to hide, they're happy to oblige.'

So, Yuri's idea of some kind of alliance between the Japanese and the Russians may have been right, Nash thought. But what did it mean? If the Mafia were really building a BW plant, then what the hell was it for? They could hardly be planning to market the stuff around the world. That would be suicide: no way could they be allowed to survive. But, if this linked in to Spitz, then maybe it was this he was talking about. It was all so frustrating. So much intelligence yet so little information of real substance.

'Daemon, Alex, thanks a lot. I'll be sending over a report later tonight. Gotta go.'

He broke the connection and immediately began to type a précis of his meeting with Pyotr, the mission later on tonight and the existence of Spandau. This was new intelligence and he had no choice but to pass it on. Pyotr was being run by London and God knew what he was telling them through back channels. I might want to run alone, Nash thought sourly, but the pack was always there, snapping and snarling.

And now he could add the intelligence about the BW. Surely now London would have to listen. There was clearly a connection between what Spitz had given them and the information Yuri had gleaned from the warehouse. When combined with the information in the database, the conclusion was inescapable that a plot was being hatched. At the very least, organized criminals were trying to set up a BW manufacturing facility and the consequences of that were almost too terrible to contemplate.

Maybe now London would take the leak seriously. At least now there was a real line to follow and not just a bunch of suppositions. They could check out anyone who had joined Spandau after leaving the Office, for a start, although identifying the actual mole might well be easier from the field. He had been on the receiving end of two attacks so far and the number of people who knew his exact movements on both occassions were very few.

Nash turned over what he had written, scrolling through the message, using the words to try and trigger his subconscious. Spedding? But there lay the ultimate madness where all were guilty and only he was innocent. Teller? That, too, was preposterous and anyway there was no motive that he could see. Daemon? Hardly. He was too preoccupied with his computers and had no reason to know his travel plans. Alex? He paused, mulling over the unthinkable. She knew everything and had all the right access. He didn't know her well enough to dismiss motive and she certainly had the opportunity. He recalled her face at the moment when the assassin had entered the cottage. No. She had been as surprised as he was. More so, even. If not Alex, then who at the Office was scheming to get him killed? That was the hardest to bear: the hidden enemy, unidentified but all-seeing, unknown but knowing all. When you didn't know whom to trust, there was no choice but to trust no one.

With a gesture of finality he pressed the Send key and the encrypted message cleared from the screen. Nash logged off and lay on the bed to get what little sleep he could before the three a.m. call to action.

13

As Nash restlessly faced the prospect of a sleepless night, five miles away on the other side of the city Alla Raikin was just as unhappy. This was her plan, her country and her people and she was damned if some filthy little Japanese thought he could tell her how to run things in her own backyard. What just a short time ago had seemed like a perfectly organized operation had begun to fray round the edges and so had her nerves.

'Don't tell me about the risks,' she shouted at Yamana. 'The payoff we're all going to get from this easily makes the risks worthwhile.'

She was pacing back and forth in front of the enormous baroque fireplace of her sitting room. Despite the effective central heating, there was a blaze in the grate from logs that had been laid there earlier that afternoon by the servants. She liked the effect and felt it contributed to the grandeur of the setting. Her Japanese ally may have his castle but she could comfortably match that with her Moscow headquarters. The fact that Yamana could hardly keep the disdain out of his voice at the sight of this overdecorated pile of nouveau extravagance entirely escaped her. She may have despised his Asian background, with the distaste that most Russians have for other cultures, but equally he thought her gauche wealth and complete lack of taste placed her almost beneath contempt. Their marriage of convenience was on the rocks, the honeymooners' pretence at friendship or respect now well and truly over.

'That may be so,' Yamana replied softly, the coarse Russian consonants somehow made more delicate by his voice. 'But all risks have to be balanced against both the rewards and the prospect of discovery. If our little operation is exposed then we will all suffer as a result. No risk is worth the price of failure.'

'I know that. I'm not stupid,' retorted Alla. 'But we need to keep some perspective here. The risk is a small one, really. The Americans are convinced that Ukraine is about to be engulfed in civil war. This British agent Nash will soon no longer be a problem. The Americans don't believe what he has to say and MI6 are playing their usual political game which doesn't include him. NATO is concentrating on contingency plans for Ukraine and meanwhile our own plans are right on schedule.'

'Don't dismiss Nash so easily. The Spandau people have already underestimated him twice with fatal consequences,' Yamana responded. 'He's trying to make trouble for us. We can't afford to have him digging around asking questions that could reveal our plans. I want Kiko to take care of him.' He gestured to Kiko Katsura who was standing behind the seated Yamana, a trained dog waiting to do his master's bidding.

Katsura was a small, almost prim, man dressed in the dark suit, white shirt and plain tie that is the uniform of all Japanese civil servants. His deferential mien and humble appearance was a useful disguise that fooled many and certainly disarmed most. Behind the meek façade lay a ruthless and sadistic killer whose almost suicidal bravery and unquestioning loyalty made him Yamana's most lethal and trusted weapon.

The two men had travelled from Kyoto in Yamana's private aircraft, ostensibly to discuss some new trading arrangements with the Russian government. In fact, they wanted only to have this meeting with Raikin and to ensure that the operation was on track. Yamana was a careful man and he had recruited his own sources within the Boolas and they had been reporting that all was not well in Moscow. He had decided to come and see for himself, leaving Dear Leader, Kim Jong-Il, to return home for a brief visit to reassure his allies in the military that his plans for a new and more powerful North Korea were proceeding apace.

The Yakuza leader turned to other matters. 'I hear that you have become involved in a dangerous distraction with some rival group here in Moscow,' he said.

'Pah,' Alla gestured dismissively. 'A little argument about turf which I shall win. It is nothing that need concern us here. This is merely a personal matter.'

'Even so, I would suggest for all our sakes that you keep a lower profile until our operation is completed. We need no distractions at this late stage. Personal or not, your acting like a Chicago gangster will focus attention on all of us.'

Alla sniffed derisively but said nothing.

'Now, what about our contingency plan, just in case there are any problems?'

Alla stopped her pacing and opened a hidden panel at the side of the fireplace. She reached inside and pulled out a silver Thermos.

Seeing her handle the container with such a casual air, Yamana felt a *frisson* of fear coursing down his back. The consequences of an accident were too horrendous to contemplate.

'As you can see, everything in that department is under control. Nobody is giving Nash's story any credence and it was a good decision to eliminate that traitor Balagula. Why on earth didn't Spandau kill the British agent at the same time? Sometimes those people are ridiculously sentimental about their own kind.'

Yamana knew that something more than sentiment was involved, concepts of brotherhood and bonding which the jumped-up whore in front of him would never understand. He let the matter pass, saying instead, 'Well, I'm pleased to hear that at least something is going according to plan. Now please put down that flask before you kill us all.'

He relaxed visibly as Alla complied. 'Thank you. So, we are agreed then. Kiko will attend to Mr Nash as soon as possible. I will –'

The ringing telephone was a surprising sound in that room. It was as if the control that Alla clearly exercised over her people had momentarily lapsed to allow the intrusion of the outside world. She appeared equally surprised and moved swiftly across the room to kill the trilling noise.

'Yes.' The single word was both a bark of acknowledgement and a command to speak. She listened for a moment, her brow lowering, then threw down the handset with a force that made the whole instrument jump from the wooden desk on which it rested.

'A problem?' Yamana prompted.

'It appears we are about to receive some uninvited guests,' she replied. 'I hope you will stay for the party.'

Her smile was not pleasant. Yamana, a man used to dispensing death casually and without conscience, recognized a grimace that mixed anticipation with fear – in his experience a very dangerous combination.

The car that collected Nash from the Metropole was not a Mercedes but a Volvo. It, too, hugged the ground, clear evidence of the armour that lay beneath the conventional paintwork. Aside from speaking his name, the chauffeur had simply escorted Nash to the car, opened the rear door and allowed him to step into the back. To his astonishment, Yuri Parashvili was already seated inside.

'Hi, David. How's it going? Jesus but I hate these early morning starts,' the Russian SVR officer grinned, enjoying Nash's confusion.

The Russian was all in black with trousers tucked into the high boots favoured by Russian paratroops. A Kevlar bullet-proof vest covered his chest and a pistol was slotted into a cavity in its left-hand side. Across his lap was a Heckler and Koch MP5 stubby sub-machine-gun. The twin curved magazines clipped together suggested that Yuri had come armed not just to defend himself but prepared for war.

'What the hell are you doing here, Yuri?' he asked.

'We have a common ally in Pyotr,' replied Yuri with a laugh. 'He . . . he . . .' Yuri groped for the right expression, 'plays both sides. Is that how you say it? Yes. Plays both sides. A little bit of business for you. A little bit of business for us. Perhaps a little bit of business for others as well. Who knows? He's useful to us so we allow him some rope. Anyway, he's the police's problem, not ours. As far as we're concerned he's just another source to help us protect our country. You can't deny that he's well connected.'

'So just how did you get in on this? And what is "this" anyway?' Nash asked.

'Well – and you mustn't be angry, David – I got a call from Pyotr earlier this evening. He explained that you had been visiting.' The Russian flicked his right hand back and forth and raised his eyes to the ceiling. 'A fabulous house, no? Jesus, these gangsters, they certainly know how to live.'

'Get on with it, Yuri.'

'Sorry. Where was I? Ah yes, he called me and told me about your visit; your concerns about Ukraine and so on. Ever since the American President called my President the SVR has been under pressure from Primakov to find out what the hell is going on. I wouldn't be surprised if that old bastard's behind the whole thing anyway, but even he can't ignore presidential orders so we've been working on it ever since. So far, without much luck.'

Nash knew that Yuri's criticism of Yevgeni Primakov, his boss and the head of the SVR, was just a device to draw him closer, to embrace him into the Russian's conspiracy. Primakov was an old communist from way back and had been appointed as a sop to the hard-liners in the military. Since then, he had been something of a loose cannon arguing for less parliamentary oversight of the intelligence community and for the re-establishment of Russia's influence on the near abroad. Yuri's little aside might have more than a germ of truth in it.

'We'd heard some rumblings about Ukraine,' Yuri continued, 'but there have been plenty of complaints in the military in recent years. Most of it's just mess-room gossip among people who want to turn the clock back but can't even find the winder, let alone work out how to tell the time. This time, though, sources seem to have been coming out of the woodwork in Kiev and here, eager to tell their story of a coup, a civil war, rebellion in the Russian military. All apocalyptic stuff – but I get suspicious when everyone wants to tell a story we'd normally need the thumbscrews to get. Not that we use thumbscrews any more in the new Russia,' he added with a laugh.

'Then Pyotr informs me that you're involved and that the Ukraine is all a sideshow but won't tell me the real story. Says I'd better come along tonight and see for myself. So here I am.'

Nash looked out of the window at the empty streets. They were heading south past the ring road and towards the outer Moscow suburbs. As usual, he reflected sourly, I have no idea what's going on. He could see his face reflected in the glass and saw in it a mixture of amusement at his own folly and nervousness about where it might lead. Perhaps, he thought, Yuri has some other answers.

'What do you know about Spandau?' he asked the Russian. There was a pause while Yuri lit a Russian cigarette which fizzed alarmingly as it burned. This time Nash reached across and wound down Yuri's window.

'We've heard of it but that's about as far as it goes,' Yuri replied.

'Come on, Yuri. You can do better than that,' Nash prompted. 'How come you know anything at all? It was news to me until a couple of days ago.'

'We only heard about it ourselves quite recently. We thought there may be something there that could be of use to us so we were keeping track to see how they operated.'

'Are any of your people members?' Nash asked.

'Not as far as we know, but we were approached by a former South African intelligence guy we know who offered to sell us some details of Iraq's planned procurement needs for the next ten years. The offer wasn't surprising but the timing was. We'd just been drawing up a paper for the Ministry of Defence on that exact subject and here we were being offered better information than we had found ourselves. It's pretty obvious that Spandau have inside knowledge. Either someone who's still with us or someone who's recently left. Perhaps both.'

Nash grunted. So, Spandau was doing to the Russians exactly what they had been doing to the Brits and perhaps to the Americans and everyone else as well. Smart people.

The car slowed, turned on to a side street and stopped. The rear door opened and Pyotr leaned in.

'Good morning, David, Yuri,' he said, his teeth white in the darkness. 'Very pleased you were able to make it. This way, gentlemen.'

The two men got out of the car and followed Pyotr across some wasteland that sloped up towards a small stand of trees silhouetted on the horizon. A tall, slim figure stepped out of the woods and moved towards them. Nash recognized Veronika, but a very different Veronika from the woman who had entertained him to dinner earlier that evening. The fashionable clothes had been replaced by a black catsuit that clung to her body, outlining her stunning figure. Like Yuri, she wore a bulletproof vest, the base coming down in a tongue to cover her crotch. There was a pistol secured by a Velcro strap resting on her left hip. Any memory of his first impressions of her were dispelled by the rifle she cradled professionally across her chest.

It was a rifle all right but one of such dimensions that Nash could hardly imagine firing it, let alone hitting anything.

'It's not as bad as it looks,' Veronika laughed. 'The Pauza .50 calibre sniper's rifle. Accurate to a mile and powerful enough to knock down doors, go through light armour and generally cause some serious trouble.'

The Pauza rang some distant bells in Nash's memory. Something about the Gulf War where the SAS had used them to pierce the fuel tanks of Scuds at 1,500 metres. Then when the missile launched the leaking fuel exploded, destroying the missile and the crew servicing the weapon. Since then, among long-range shooters, it had become something of a weapon of choice.

'And she knows how to use it, too,' Pyotr added. 'Veronika will knock on the door and we will push it open. Let's go.'

The men followed her back into the woods and Nash immediately sensed the presence of others, the shuffle of boots against earth, the rustle of clothing, the smell of sweating bodies and camouflage paint. There was a considerable force hidden here and he was now a part of it. His heart began to thud in his chest, the familiar feeling of fear and anticipation filling him. He could remember all too clearly the instant when Spitz had been gunned down and the moment when the assassin's finger had tightened on the trigger with him in his sights. The difference then was that he had had no choice and no time to think. Now, it was clear that some horrific, pre-planned event was about to unfold with him in the middle.

'Down in the valley is the headquarters of the Boolas,' Pyotr explained, his arm gesturing to his right. 'They are one of Moscow's more successful gangs, run by a woman named Alla Raikin. She's been causing me a certain amount of irritation recently. She is also the source of the erroneous information you have been hearing about me. I thought it might be helpful to stop by and have a little talk with her.'

Pyotr handed round small earpieces and throat microphones which Nash and Yuri plugged in, strapping the batteries to their chests. Concerned that Nash had no bulletproof vest, Pyotr muttered something into his mike and a man appeared out of the darkness carrying the protection he needed, together with an armband. The man placed the vest over Nash's head and tied down the buckles. Its security was comforting but its weight was crippling. Nash hoped that no sprint exit would be necessary and resolved to work out more often.

'OK, here's the plan,' he heard Pyotr's tinny voice through his earpiece. 'The grounds are circled by a high wall with cameras mounted every fifty metres or so. They are low light and so will see us as we come down the hill. To take care of that, we sent in a team a few hours ago who have videoed the scene outside the walls and will patch their image into the camera's transmission. That way the security people inside will see what they have been used to while we make our move.

'The wall has razor wire on top of it and we have scaling ladders to climb up and then put down the other side. The microwave alarms are more of a problem, but they'll go down along with all their electricity as we go in. My people know what to do. Your job is to stick with me.'

Nash saw that Pyotr was drawing out a pair of night-vision goggles from a small pack on his hip. If the action was going to start, he had better prepare himself, he thought.

He reached into his own pack and strapped on the webbing belt that had come over in the bag from Alex. The pouches held some extra ammunition and a few additional items that she thought might be helpful. He too had his own set of NVG and he slipped them over his head, tightening the straps so that they wouldn't fall off in the firefight that was about to ensue. He could see Yuri and Pyotr quite clearly and noticed that the armbands which they were all wearing were picked up by the goggles. Always a good idea to be able to tell friend from enemy in the dark, he thought.

The scene through the goggles was also being recorded by a miniaturized camera and transmitted to the laptop back at the hotel. The signal would alert the computer to encrypt and then transmit it back to London. There would be a record of everything that occurred tonight should he fail to report or should the operation unravel.

He plucked his pistol from the shoulder holster, snicked off the safety catch with his thumb and slid back the sleeve to chamber a round. Two more magazines were in his belt. If that were not enough to defend himself, he reckoned, it would probably be curtains.

'OK. Let's go.'

On Pyotr's instruction, there was a collective shuffling as shadows took form when the men separated from the cover of trees and bushes or stretched up from their positions on the ground. Nash thought there must be over a hundred men in the party, a small army. A force of this size meant that they were probably facing opposition of around fifty, all armed to the teeth and as willing to kill as these people.

Nash moved off, following Pyotr's ghostly green shape which moved steadily ahead of him. As the ground began to slope down, Veronika peeled off to lie prone in the brush, the long barrel of her rifle probing ahead of her towards the building that he could just make out below.

There was a pause while Pyotr waited for his men to do their work with the cameras. Nash saw him put his hand up to his ear as if he were listening intently to the message that was coming through the communications net. Then he looked up, his body filled with tension.

'We have a tap on their lines,' he said abruptly. 'We've had a leak. She's just had a call that we're about to attack. Let's move it. Everybody. Now! Now! Now!'

He turned and ran down the hillside, his men following, spread out in a wide arc that swept like two horns to surround the building. There was a sharp crack off to his right and the building and compound below were suddenly plunged into darkness. Another crack from behind and the first of Veronika's rounds went crashing overhead to hit God knew what inside the target area. Behind him, he could hear her firing steadily, as round after round poured in, the high-powered scope no doubt picking out every detail of the people moving to defend their territory.

Nash rushed on, down the slope and then on to flat ground, his feet driving forward, the excitement pushing him on, all fear forgotten in the rush to the target. Ahead, the first men reached the wall, pushed their light aluminium ladders against it and began scuttling up. At the top each man paused, reached down and pulled up the second ladder which clipped to the first, forming an arch over the razor wire and into the grounds.

Now he was on the rungs, hands following Pyotr's feet. There was a pause as he straddled the wall – the perfect target for a well-placed sniper, he thought anxiously – and then he was down and in. Gunfire was everywhere now, bullets crackling around him, the trail of tracer from some heavier weapon searing across the lens of his goggles. A man popped out of the grass ahead of him. Without pausing, he fired once and then again, the blood from the man's punctured body arcing away in a parabola of eerie green in the half-world of thermal imagery in which he was now operating. Another target. This time it was Yuri who fired, the stutter of his machine-gun distinctive in the darkness.

Then there was a man in front of him, his gun levelled. There was no time to raise his own weapon and Nash knew that this time he was too slow, too late. The gun bucked and the flame of the explosion briefly blacked out his goggles. Instantly he felt a giant hand push him in his chest, lifting him up and driving him backwards. He landed on his back, the air driven from his body in an agonizing ooomph. He lay for a moment, dazed, his mind tumbling, thinking for a moment that death felt remarkably painless. Then he realized that he could see and hear the sounds around him. He looked up and watched the man who had shot him moving towards his prone body to finish the job. He tried to move his pistol up into the firing position but knew that he would never make it. Then came the distinctive crack of a heavy calibre bullet passing overhead and his enemy took the round full in the chest. The force of the shot was such that it passed right through him, taking much of his chest cavity with it in a trail of life become death.

Thank you Veronika, Nash thought as his hands probed his chest for damage. He found the indentation where the bullet had hit the vest and been deflected. The thought that every moment he lay there he was a perfect target propelled Nash back to his feet. He stumbled, unable to regain the momentum of his forward rush, each breath a painful stab from his ribs which felt as if they had been crushed.

Nash could hear the excited babble of the invaders through his earpiece. The imprecations matched by the occasional scream of pain as a bullet from the defenders found its mark. It was a terrifying world of darkness and half-light, of fear and fantastic excitement. Nash felt himself driven on, seeking new targets – they seemed hardly to be people now, just threats to be seen, indentified and eliminated like so many pop-up ducks at a shooting gallery.

They were at the front door and Nash could see that Veronika had done her work well. The lock was still intact but the powerful, penetrating rounds had made short work of the hinges. The door sagged inwards and the combined force of the two men ahead of Pyotr was enough to push it flat against the entrance floor. The bang of its falling was answered by a burst of heavy fire from inside and the vanguard were lifted up and pushed back through the door, their bodies levitated by the bullets that seemed to hold them suspended for a moment until they fell limply to the ground.

The crack of bullets passing over Nash's head was matched by the screams from within as Veronika continued to pour in covering fire. Pyotr led the second wave with Nash, expecting to feel the bullets of the guards at any second, following closely on his heels. The devastation caused by the fifty-calibre rounds in the confined space of the hallway was extraordinary. The three men who had been manning the Minimi machine-gun had been destroyed. One had lost most of his chest to a round that appeared to have exploded on impact, another was staring dazed at his leg which had been severed at the thigh and was lying three feet away from his body. As Nash watched, the last of his blood pumped out into the enormous pool that was staining the white marble floor, his eyes glazed and he rolled gently over on to his side. The third man had been flung backwards by a bullet which appeared to have passed straight through his stomach to pulverize a statue that had once rested on a plinth against the far wall. Now it was the guard who sat there, a bloodied overseer of the destruction.

It was a scene so grotesque that Nash could feel the bile rise in his throat. He turned away, stomach heaving, and vomited once and then again on the floor of the hallway. His revulsion was somehow relieved by this cleansing and he felt able to confront the reality of what they had done. He was ready to go forward once more but the simple act of gaining entry to the house appeared to have drained the invaders of their energy. It was Pyotr who galvanized them again.

'This way,' he shouted and ran off down a corridor to his left, Nash and Yuri at his heels. His men fanned out behind him and he heard the flat smack of grenades and the stutter of machine-guns as they moved through the rooms, clearing each one and despatching its occupants. The room at the end of the passage was defended by a single large wooden door. Pyotr muttered something into his mike and one of his men ran up carrying a small satchel. He reached in and produced three small oval packets. He peeled off some backing tape, stuck them in the likely location of hinges and lock, inserted small timers with tiny aerials, made a fist with his right hand and brought it down sharply twice.

'Fire in the hole,' Pyotr shouted, the Russian words instantly recognizable as the universal warning to stand back. Pyotr made a dash for a room that had just been cleared by his men. The old cry of demolition men from a previous era struck Nash as comical but nobody laughed. The explosives man picked a tiny transmitter from his pocket, paused for a second and then pressed a button. The brief glow of a light showed that the signal had been transmitted. Then there came a tremendous explosion followed by a huge cloud of dust as part of the ceiling collapsed.

In the passage, the door had been blown inwards as if by a giant wind and the group followed swiftly in its wake. Compared with the rest of the house, this was a small oasis of calm.

The room was bathed in the eerie red glow of the emergency lighting that had activated when they took out the electricity. Nash flicked the switch on the side of his goggles that changed them from thermal imagers to simple protective glasses. He could have taken them off but now, more than ever, he wanted the scene recorded for the analysts in London.

There were five people in the room: a woman dressed in a tight-fitting red outfit that emphasized her over-generous curves; two Orientals, one young, the other old; and two other men both dressed in some kind of livery – servants or bodyguards perhaps.

Pyotr must have reached the same conclusion. There was the bark of a gun on Nash's right and first one and then the second bodyguard fell, dead before they touched the ground. Nash swallowed, the sharp taste of cordite like acid in his throat. The ruthless execution was somehow shocking, made starker by the driving, rushing charge on the house when it had been kill or be killed, fire on or be fired at. What he had just witnessed was the simple elimination of a threat carried out with no more compunction than Pyotr might have in snuffing out candles on a dinner table.

'Now we can talk without fear of interruption,' said Pyotr. He bowed ironically to the woman in red. 'How good to see you again – and in such different circumstances.'

He turned towards Nash and Yuri.

'May I present to you Alla Raikin, otherwise known as Golden Arm, leader of the Boolas. Alla, this is David Nash, of whom you may have heard, and Yuri Parashvili I am sure you know.'

The woman stood silent, giving no sign that she either knew Pyotr or had heard of her other two uninvited guests.

'Perhaps you would like to complete the introductions,' Pyotr continued, gesturing towards the two Orientals who also stood silently watching the scene.

'I think not,' the woman replied. Her voice was tight, the anger in her flushed cheeks quite clear. She obviously wanted to call in her attack dogs and have this impertinent group killed in front of her. But for now, she appeared powerless, her anger contained.

'Very well,' Pyotr replied. 'We will find out soon enough.'

He turned back to Nash.

'This woman is the source of all that you have been hearing about me and Ukraine. A short time ago, she tried to kill me. Having failed miserably, she is now trying to make me a target of every intelligence agency in the world so that I will either be killed by them or arrested and kept out of her way.'

He turned back to the woman. 'As you can now see, my dear, your little scheme has failed again.'

Raikin turned to Nash.

There was a noise behind them and the guards parted to let Veronika through. She had left behind her rifle and instead carried a small automatic pistol, perhaps the same one that she had pointed at him, Nash reflected. Her black outfit made a striking contrast with her blonde hair. She was a stunning sight.

The distraction was only momentary, but it was enough. Kiko's hand flashed up to the collar of his jacket and then swept out and down. The movement was a blur, so fast that Pyotr, Nash and Yuri had no time to respond. What left his hand appeared to be a curling snake that made a gentle sighing sound as it moved rapidly through the air. Somehow, the flight of this bizarre object was so riveting, its purpose so elusive, that they simply stood and watched. In the microsecond it took to reach its target, Nash suddenly understood what he was seeing. This was no snake. It was a deadly, curling garrotte similar to the bolas used by cowboys in South America, but this one part of the ninja tradition in

Japan. Nash made to shout a warning but got no further than drawing breath for the cry before the weapon struck.

In a horrible and deadly embrace it whipped round Veronika's neck, the two weighted ends using all the momentum behind Kiko's violent throw to wind around, once and then again. The razor-sharp edge of the wire cut deep, severing through skin, larynx and neck muscles with the ease of a sharp butcher's knife through dead meat. The trickle of blood betrayed the deep incision. Veronika tried to express her pain but with her severed vocal cords produced only a throaty gargling sound. As she tried to shake loose from the terrible ligature, the movement widened the wound. The circular incision that seemed so slight now became a ghastly dripping chasm as Veronika's head slowly parted from her neck. As if reluctant to accept the end, the lifeless body slowly toppled to one side, the head hitting the floor first, breaking from the spinal column, to slither away in the spreading pool of blood.

The transformation of that beautiful woman into a bloody, lifeless corpse had been so sudden and so horrifying that for a moment there was no reaction from the three men. Then with a snarl of anger, Pyotr turned back to confront the man who had destroyed his lover so brutally and so ruthlessly. But he was too late.

With a shout of warning, Kiko brought a small, flat box out of his jacket pocket, flicked a switch at the side and placed it on the table. His shout had been enough for the others to place their hands tight over their ears and he did the same. A second later, a piercing, agonizing whistle filled the room. It was like nothing Nash had ever heard; a mixture between a dog whistle, a scream of agony and a flute, yet so pitched that it seemed to vibrate every single nerve in his body. No, not just the nerves, his very being was being shaken and stirred like some new cocktail. He felt a crushing weight inside his head, as if his brain were being squeezed in a vice. His fingers were on fire, his stomach spasming in what felt like the beginnings of another round of vomiting.

Dimly, through his blurred vision, he saw Raikin sweep up from a table what looked like a Thermos jug, move to the wall and press a switch in the panelling. A door opened and she stepped in, closely followed by the two men. There was nothing he could do. He tried to raise his pistol but there was no force left in his arm. So, this is what death feels like, he thought. Complete impotence and absolute pain.

He felt himself falling and as he fell, he found the strength to squeeze the trigger of his pistol, once, twice and then again. His target was not the escaping prisoners but the infernal machine that was sending him into pain-filled darkness.

14

After all the drama, the hotel bedroom was a blessed refuge. He had left Yuri at the bloodbath and accepted the offer of a lift from one of his men. The journey had been made in silence, each man alone with his thoughts, adjusting to life after near death, both grateful for Nash's lucky shot which had taken out the sonic device. By the time any of them had regained their wits Alla and her friends had been long gone.

He opened the mini-bar, poured himself a whisky and lay back on the bed, sipping slowly. He could feel the alcohol coursing through his body, evening out the knots, unwinding the tension of the past few hours. In the depression that frequently follows violent action, he felt low, dispirited by the killing. The memory of Veronika's mutilated corpse lingered before him, as he suspected it would for months and years to come. Is this what my life has come to? he reflected. Killing, killing and then more killing.

It was supposed to be about doing good, saving the world from the bad guys, something like that. Instead, he felt like just another hired gun who spent half the time terrified and the remainder being carried along on the tide of events with bodies falling to left and right. It was the finality of what he had done that day that was so shocking and so difficult to accept. The men he had killed that morning probably had families who cared for them. Friends, drinking partners, people who worried whether they lived or died. A simple squeeze of the trigger and they became just a bundle of bones and oozing blood, husks for others to mourn.

They never told you about this side of life during the training, he thought sourly. This was a numbing, shattering, destructive process where he was squeezed of all emotion. Like the people he had killed, he felt drained of the lifeblood that gave him energy and optimism.

He drained his glass, the final bite of Scotch giving a brief fillip to his tired mind, a buoy he could cling on to: Spitz. He cared because of Spitz. And because of Veronika. And, more than anything, because of Jaimie. There were people out there, wanton killers, turning things of beauty into matter of almost unbearable ugliness.

The inner rage that the shrink had detected after Jaimie died had driven him on. Now it seemed that rage had become the dominant force in his life. He didn't want it to be like that. He didn't see himself as a man who fought and won with violence, but the strength his intellect had once given him was being winnowed away by the force that was driving him forward. It was a force that he seemed almost powerless to control. Perhaps he should just let go? No, he would never be able to live with himself. Better to drive forward through the mire and hope that on the other side something worthwhile was waiting. Meantime, he wondered just how much of himself would be left. He could feel himself becoming like the people he was fighting. The fact that he cared was the only thing that set him apart from the enemy. He hated what he did but they relished it, killing without scruple. He despised them far more than he would ever despise himself. He would fight them. And he would win.

The connection to London was crystal clear. It was mid-afternoon there and he could see Alex's image perfectly on the screen. After all the drama, her face, even at this distance, was a comfort and an assurance that out there somewhere a normal world was following its usual routine.

'David. Thank God,' Alex said. 'We hadn't heard anything and the last we saw on the film was a shot of the floor, presumably before your head hit it.'

Nash put his hand up to his forehead and touched the egg-shaped bruise. It throbbed but was bearable.

'I thought it was all over for a while, too,' he replied. 'I had a lucky shot as I went down and hit whatever it was that knocked us all out.'

'We've been looking at the footage here and some of the S and T people thought it might be an infrasound system, though none of us has ever seen anything that small.'

'I've no idea,' said Nash. 'All I can tell you is that it hurt like hell, like every cell in my body was in some giant blender being whizzed up for a huge milkshake.'

'Yeah. That's infrasound all right. It's a very low frequency sound tuned to the body's own vibrations. Like a perfect pitch is supposed to be able to shatter glass, so this can destroy people. It's part of a whole batch of new non-lethal weapons everyone's been working on for a while, though just how non-lethal your pal's gizmo is is debatable. This is the first time I've heard of it being deployed in the field. These people are smart.'

Nash had heard of non-lethal technology. It had become something of a buzz phrase in intelligence and defence circles in the last year or two. Some enthusiasts held it up as the perfect answer to warfare for the squeamish. Use the right modern technology and you could win wars without actually killing people. Needless to say the whole concept was anathema to the military.

Both the Agency and the Office had developed a range of weapons that could be used and were remarkably effective.

There was anti-traction technology (known as slickum) that could be sprayed on runways or roads and make them too slippery to be used. There were the superglue variants (stick-ums) that could be sprayed to ensure that anyone walking or driving over the surface would be stuck in place. Grime-from-hell could totally block all light while supercaustics could rot anything they touched. They had all seemed pretty bizarre to Nash but he now had personal experience that such systems were deadly in use.

'What happened to Raikin and the Japanese?' Alex continued.

'By the time we recovered, they had vanished,' Nash explained. 'There was a lift that went directly to the roof where they have a helicopter pad. But we did find some interesting stuff inside the house. In the computer in Raikin's office there was a bunch of software that Pyotr's people were able to make some sense of. Aside from all the financial returns and the bank transfers to accounts in just about every corner of the globe, there was a message file.' He held up a disc in front of the camera. 'It seems she was keeping in touch with Spandau through the Internet but who the mes-sages were addressed to and what they contained is impossible to decipher at this end. It's all encrypted and presumably only she has the key. If we can tap into that network then we'll be able to get a handle on the organization. Find the addresses and we'll find the people.'

'Can you download what you have from that file?' she asked.

'Ha,' he laughed. 'I was going to suggest that very thing.'

Nash slid the disc into the A drive below the keyboard, brought up File Manager and instructed it to copy and send all the files to Alex's terminal in London. The machine made the satisfied hum that indicated his commands had been understood and moments later Alex confirmed the informa-tion had arrived.

'What about the two Orientals?' Nash asked.

'We've had a bit of success there,' Alex replied. 'Tokyo station has been doing some work on underground crime as part of the Pliny investigation and they had just sent us a bunch of material.' Pliny was the Foreign Office's current pet project; a massive trawl around the world to generate a huge dossier on the links between international organized crime. 'When I queried Miss Piggy, she immediately gave us a match. Your man is Ken Yamana, probably the most powerful of Japan's Yakuza and the man who heads up the Yamaguchi-gumi. The young one is his henchman, chief killer and favoured acolyte, Kiko Katsura. By repute a very clever operator.

'I've prepared a file on them both which I can send you when we've finished. Meantime, the Chief wants to have a word. Hang on, and I'll patch you through.'

The screen cleared and then Spedding's face floated before him.

'Afternoon, David,' said the Chief. 'Been in the wars again, I see. Glad to see you've survived intact.'

The formalities over, Spedding patted his head reflectively a couple of times and then got down to business.

'This Spandau group is serious stuff, David. They may have been sweeping up everybody we've let go in the past few years. The same applies to the Americans, the Israelis, everyone. In theory, they could have an organization as big as ours and with as many resources. I need more intelligence and I need it fast.'

'I'll do my best,' Nash replied. 'But the information's pretty sketchy. We know they have access to the Office. We can assume they are inside Langley as well. We know they're offering themselves for hire and have been bought by at least one criminal group in Moscow. But that's the extent of it. No names, no headquarters, no sources or methods. Nothing.'

'I know it's a tall order,' said Spedding, 'but we need to know more. Not least because we need to plug the leak here.'

'That leak is still operating,' Nash continued. 'Someone tipped off Raikin we were on our way in. These people know what we're planning to do almost as soon as the decision is made.'

Nash paused for a moment, debating whether to pass on his suspicions about Teller. It would be a high risk allegation to make: the Chief's deputy a traitor. It would be certain to get back to Teller even if the leak was found to be elsewhere. Nash could just imagine the conversation: 'Do you know what young Nash was saying about you during that business in Russia,' Spedding would say to Teller over a glass of Burgundy in the executive dining room. 'Thought you were the leak, you know. No, really. Seemed quite plausible at the time but of course I didn't give it any currency.' Teller was Spedding's heir apparent so that conversation would surely mark the end of my career, Nash thought. Better to keep quiet until there was more evidence.

'The leak's not our only imperative,' said Spedding. 'Ministers are much more concerned with the political situation which seems to be unravelling at speed. The game players say that civil war in Ukraine would almost certainly involve some kind of nuclear exchange between Moscow and Kiev. It may be only a couple of SS-24s back and forth but nuclear is nuclear and the fallout, both literally and politically, is incalculable.

'To keep a lid on it, the boys in Brussels say we need to begin mobilization now and be prepared to deploy around 40,000 troops as part of a UN force to keep the warring factions apart. And that's just the down payment. If the shooting really starts then the ante gets upped to full mobilization and the possibility of war between NATO and Russia. God knows what happens then.'

'Is there any hard intelligence about Ukraine or is this all based on what the Americans are saying?' Nash asked.

'Until yesterday, the answers to those questions were no and yes. However, in the last twenty-four hours the overhead has picked up both communications traffic and imagery of troops on the move. It seems some of the Russian Guards regiments in the west are heading towards the border with Ukraine and there have been communications between them and some of the Ukraine border units in the east. Something's definitely up and it seems to support what the Americans have been saying. There's a meeting of NATO defence and foreign ministers scheduled for Brussels this evening and my bet is that a partial mobilization will result. It will depend on what happens in the next few days as to what further response we make.'

To Nash, the whole business seemed to be running out of control. All his instincts, everything he had seen, told him that all this was a huge bluff, a giant piece of disinformation to convince the major powers that something was about to happen in Ukraine. If this was disinformation, though, what was the truth? It was so frustrating to have one side of the equation while the other remained blank. For now, he could do nothing but urge restraint.

'From what I've learned here, the Ukraine is all a blind, a diversion for something else,' cautioned Nash.

'A diversion for what?' asked Spedding. 'We can hardly go to NATO with just an agent's hunch. We need facts.'

Nash recalled his last glimpse of Raikin, a woman with her back against the wall, with only seconds to make her escape. He could see her now as she reached out to sweep the Thermos up before she stepped into the lift. What did it contain? If Pyotr was right and she was the source of the rumours about Ukraine, then maybe she was behind the murder of Spitz and it was she and her Japanese cohorts who had stolen the biological weapons. But why?

'What about the BW?' Nash asked.

'We read what you sent over with great interest and we're checking it out now,' Spedding replied. 'We've spoken to Washington and their man Thomas in Moscow is pouring cold water all over it. But it's early days. We need more facts before we can really ring the alarm bells.'

'We've got all the questions in place but none of the answers,' replied Nash, the frustration clear in his voice.

'Right,' agreed Spedding. 'Raikin's gone to ground and I assume both Pyotr and Parashvili's people are trying to find her. You, I can use elsewhere. Alex will send you the dossier we have on this fellow Yamana. Get yourself to Tokyo and see what you can find.

'I want total security on this. There's to be no contact with Tokyo station. Only Alex and I know where you are and what you are doing. That way, we should control the leaks, wherever they're coming from.

'We need answers, David. And we need them yesterday.'

The Internet works like a post office where a letter has a destination address which the carrier uses to make sure it gets to the right person. The letters we send are not carried individually but collected in a bundle from the post box, then sorted and re-sorted until the final packet contains all the letters that will be delivered on a particular postman's round. Internet messages work in roughly the same way with the exception that every message sent identifies not only the destination but also the sender. The computers that manage the Internet automatically decide the most efficient way of getting it through the system. Sometimes to go a short distance a message might be sent halfway round the world because the shorter journey has access lines that are busy. Or, a long message can be broken up into different sections which will all go by different routes to be married together just before they arrive in the destination computer. All this takes place in fractions of a second with messages and other data passing through systems known as routers, which decide the optimum path, and repeaters, which ensure the message has enough computer power to get where it's going.

In the whole world there are no more than 5,000 repeaters and in the targets of vital interest to the United States and Britain there are only 275. The task of planting bugs in these units was undertaken entirely from Cheltenham and Fort Meade by computer software engineers sending messages to the different waystations on the Internet. These waystations became hosts to software that was instructed to make routine copies of all messages going through the system and then route those copies back to America where the vast NSA database is fully accessible to the specialists at GCHQ. Alternatively, specific instructions could be sent for the software to look out for special messages with certain identifying characteristics (for example, all those with the prefix RU, denoting Russia) and bring them to the attention of operators in Britain or America.

There is a general belief among the computer enthusiasts who use the Internet that it is somehow an inviolate space and that the technology is not available to pluck data and messages off the system. While that ignorance remains, the intelligence community continues to hold a significant advantage.

For Alex, the copy of the file from Alla Raikin's computer had been all she needed. The file contained every message that had been sent from or received by Alla's terminal in the past three months. They identified her computer address but little else. The serious players have always understood that messages might be intercepted. Such people routinely place all their traffic into ciphertext which is precisely what Raikin had done. The list of random letters and numbers that scrolled across Alex's screen made it clear that this was a job not for Miss Piggy but for the huge supercomputers belonging to both NSA and GCHQ.

In theory, high-grade ciphertext is impossible to break, being generated entirely by computers. At one end an algorithm breaks the clear text into an incomprehensible jumble. Only the person at the receiving end has a similar lengthy algorithm which is required to decode it. There is no way for any human being to crack such a code and even ordinary computers programmed to test different combinations of numbers would find it impossible.

To break such ciphertexts, GCHQ have several Cray supercomputers that match those at NSA. These are capable of more than a billion calculations a second and are fast enough to crack any code eventually. Of course, 'eventually' can mean anything from a few minutes to more than a year.

For Alex, the task of getting GCHQ to intercept all messages to and from Raikin in the future was simple enough: a message to Cheltenham with the prefix Umbra for the highest level classification followed by the single word Bikini for the highest priority would suffice. Within five hours she had a file from the database that largely duplicated the one in her computer. That the messages had gone to and from Moscow she already knew. That they had been sent all over the world she already knew. That Cheltenham could give her no idea of just how long it would take to decipher, she already knew. Now it was a waiting game.

Even in these difficult times, being a member of the Glavnoye Razvedyvatelnoye Upravleniye, the GRU or military intelligence had its perks, reflected Colonel Nikolai Muraviev. Unlike those pussies in the SVR, the GRU was still a powerful force. A flash of the green identity card still provoked a click of the heels and a snappy salute. And well it might. The military understood the effective use of force and the GRU were the last bastion of the old regime. They were happy to keep it that way.

Muraviev had travelled by military transport down to Kursk on the Russian side of the border and then hitched a ride on a convoy en route to Ukraine to resupply the 56th Guards Regiment. He was used to working alone, acting as the point man for his military masters in the operations they wanted done but didn't want to handle themselves. This mission was just another in a long list and he was happy to do it because this time he was helping set his country back on the long road to recovery.

Muraviev was a lifer, a soldier who had decided a long time ago that a life of duty and service was what his country deserved from him. In that he was following a family tradition that could be traced back to the last century and a distinguished record with the Czars and then with the communists. It was military service in the finest sense: duty to the country above all. Muraviev believed in that absolutely and had faithfully served the old regime and the new. He was one of the few who had remained untainted by service in the west, despite an affinity for the language and the culture that had made him completely fluent in English and equally at home in London or Moscow. He had watched with revulsion the way the Union had been dismembered and Russia herself reduced to a squawking puppet of the Yankees and their allies. Well, this should change all that and bring about a restoration.

The operation had begun six months earlier when one of the generals had been talking with the woman Raikin about the future. They had tentatively reached some common ground and after a week or two of delicate jousting the scheme had been hatched, matching military capability with financial muscle to produce real hope for the future. He had his reservations about Raikin and the Japs, but alliances like that were made to achieve goals. After they had been achieved, then who knew? With their forces, they would be able to dictate the terms of any future deal.

It had taken some time to get all the forces in position, shifting the loyal commanders and their troops from one base to another on what appeared to be simple rotations but were all part of the complex plan. Sending the Guards Regiment here was just part of the mix. They were now ready to play their small part but first he had to light the fire that would send the flames spreading across the Ukraine.

Leaving the convoy at the barracks, he borrowed a jeep for the eight-kilometre drive to the base of the 16th Field Regiment of the Ukraine armed forces. What he was about to do would be considered an act of war but, if everything went according to plan, a brief civil war would be just the distraction the operation required.

The fact that he was about to murder fellow-Russian officers and troops was only a small consideration for Muraviev. He had killed often for his country both at home and abroad. He had killed his own countrymen, too, when the need dictated: the execution of an embarrassing traitor here, the elimination of a terrorist team there. Once he might have questioned the nature of orders but these days he had become almost inured to the detail of killing. It was the big picture he was concerned about and this time the picture could hardly be bigger: the restoration of Russia as a world-class military and political power.

He passed the gates of the regimental headquarters and drove up the road that wound into the hills behind. After three kilometres he pulled on to the side of the road and left the jeep, pulling a small suitcase behind him. He set it down on the ground and flicked the catches. Inside, nestled between foam padding, lay a single black Thermos flask. It might have been filled with coffee were it not for the curious attachment fitted to the top that looked not unlike the spray nozzle from a garden hose. Muraviev peeled the padding from the lid of the case to reveal a metal frame which he lifted out. Legs opened from the central ring to form a perfect stand for the Thermos which he then placed in the centre. He squinted down into the valley at the lights from the barracks below and made a small adjustment to make sure that the nozzle was facing in precisely the right direction.

From his pocket he brought a small case which contained a miniature timer and detonator which he fixed next to the valve. When the timer dictated, the minute explosion would open the valve and release the gas inside the Thermos. He stood back and looked down at his handiwork, thinking ahead. Amazing, he thought, how something so small and so apparently innocent can wreak such destruction.

Getting into the jeep, he drove back down the hill, past the barracks towards the 56th Guards Regiment's base. He glanced at the luminous dial of his watch. With luck and a bit of arm twisting, he might be back in Moscow by dawn.

The tiny pop two hours later was so small it disturbed neither the rodent foraging for food nor the owl carefully judging its moment to pounce from above. The hiss of escaping gas, too, was inaudible for the fifteen seconds during which it was expelled from the container. But the breeze coming off the back of the hill picked up each little spore and carried it down the slope, spreading the millions of droplets into an enveloping, invisible cloud.

History would never give him the recognition he might have wanted, but Private Pavel Molody was the first soldier to experience the effects of RD-74, the deadly biological weapon that had been so ably perfected at the All-Union Research Institute of Applied Microbiology at Klin.

Inhaling deeply on the cigarette carefully cupped in the

palm of his hand, he stamped his feet, fighting off the boredom of guard duty. That single drag of smoke pulled with it microscopic amounts of the poison, easily enough to kill him.

He thought at first it was a coughing fit, a puff of smoke that had gone down the wrong way, and he doubled over, trying to draw breath. But a simple need for oxygen swiftly turned into the agonizing fire of real pain accompanied by the paroxyms of retching as his body fought to reject the invader. It was a struggle he was never going to win. The spores had control now and Pavel could feel his body erupting as his skin burst outwards and then his stomach and intestine voided as every nerve and every muscle struggled to survive.

In the seconds it had taken Pavel to die, the deadly mist had floated through the barracks invading buildings, bunkers and vehicles, killing with complete certainty every soldier who drew breath on that terrible night. In five short minutes, the only people out of the 3,500 in the camp who were left alive were the four-man crew of a T-72 tank who just happened to have chosen that moment to practise their nuclear, chemical and biological drill and were sealed tight in their vehicle. By the time they emerged fifteen minutes later, they found a scene of awful carnage. Bodies were strewn everywhere as men had tried to escape from the invisible and all-embracing horror that had engulfed their comrades. For each, it had clearly been a painful death. Bodies were bent in the most unnatural positions: some bowed with back arched and only feet and hands touching the ground, others hanging out of windows and doors dangling in the posture of a discarded marionette, others suffering the double indignity of a frightening death only to be run over by one of the many vehicles which had gone out of control as their drivers died.

As baptisms go, RD-74 had performed exactly as advertised. A silent, completely deadly and untraceable weapon with a life of minutes. It had done its work and died. But, as Muraviev had planned, the real effects of the weapon would linger on long after the spores had done their work.

The one advantage of being a successful gangster, thought Nash, is that the problems of ordinary mortals get swept away in the face of that great persuader, money. He had called Pyotr and explained that he was heading for Tokyo on the trail of Raikin's accomplice. The offer of the Falcon II executive jet had been unsolicited but very welcome.

There had been none of the boring formalities that affect ordinary travellers and none of the constraints of airline schedules or the terror of relying on Aeroflot to get to the destination. Instead, he had been chauffeured to the private compound at Sheremetyevo II airport. The aircraft had come complete with liveried captain and crew, a selection of delicious food and fifty videos of first-run movies. He had selected the new Grisham and promptly fallen asleep to awaken just before the aircraft landed at Osaka International.

There was no welcoming committee as only Spedding and Alex had any knowledge of his movements, so he found his own way through passport control and customs. There was no difficulty, especially as he had left the Glock in Moscow and everything else in his luggage seemed innocuous enough. In the old days, a taxi from Osaka to Kyoto would have been considered a legitimate expense even if it did cost 10,000 yen, but in today's budget-conscious era, Nash knew that the pink expenses form would be rejected by the bean counters so he took the shuttle bus for the ninety-minute journey and saved 9,000 yen.

If Nash had chosen the Hotel Kyoto, he would have found his hotel overlooked the headquarters of the man he was seeking. Nijojo Castle dominated the vista in that part of the city, its façade a constant reminder of the country and the city's proud heritage. But once again, budget constraints placed Nash at the less-expensive Three Sisters Inn Annex on Rakutoso Bekkan near the Heian Shrine. Nash actually preferred this kind of accommodation to the larger, more opulent places. This hotel placed its emphasis not on making the western visitor feel at home but on making him feel welcome in a Japanese environment. Despite the thin walls separating the different parts of his room, this was a private place with all the security he wanted and the international links he needed.

He felt remarkably rested after the journey and after the first decent sleep for as long as he could remember. The sharp pain in his ribs had faded to a dull but constant ache, a sure sign that he was on the mend and reassurance that it was bruising rather than broken bones that had been caused by the bullet his body-armour had stopped. Despite the rest he felt disorientated, the leap from Moscow, still vaguely European, to completely alien Japan was difficult. He clearly stood out as a foreigner. He was literally head and shoulders above most of the crowd and must have been glaringly obvious to anyone who sought him out. It was all very well for the Chief simply to send him to Japan, he thought to himself. There was little chance of blending in here. He would simply have to adapt. But first he needed to understand the dimensions of the problem he was confronting.

He hoped that some of the answers lay with Alex. She had clearly been waiting for him to call as she came on screen as soon as he accessed the London system. Even at this distance, he could tell that there was news, her enthusiasm reaching across the ether to embrace him.

'We have just about everything you might want to know about Yamana,' she began. 'I've prepared a file for you which I'll send over in a minute.'

Her smile of greeting disappeared and her face became serious.

'But this guy is very bad news, David,' she continued. 'He controls an army of thousands which runs whole areas of the government and sees himself as some kind of modern Samurai out to reclaim Japan's rightful heritage. I'm not sure just what the Chief thinks you can do against him. He's bigger than you, me and the rest of the Office combined and we don't exactly have much leverage.'

'That was always going to be the case, Alex,' he replied. 'If he's as capable as you say, no doubt he'll know already that I've arrived and I'll be getting an invitation soon enough. Then we'll see. He'll want to know what we know. He's survived because he plays the percentages. Maybe I can persuade him that the game is over.'

Alex looked doubtful.

'What luck have you had with the files I sent you?' he continued.

'Well, we've retrieved some additional ones from the database but as you probably noticed everything is in ciphertext so we're stuck. Cheltenham told me a few minutes ago that they expect success within days rather than months but how many days nobody knows.'

'And what do I do in the meantime?' asked Nash. 'Learn to cook sushi?'

'I'm pleased to see your sense of humour's intact,' said Alex, sarcastically 'but I think we can find something a bit more productive. You've tested the VR system, right?'

Nash replied in the affirmative although 'testing' in this case meant one go round with the virtual reality system just before he left for Moscow. Anything more complicated and he would be out of his depth. Even that one test had been a revelation. He had donned the goggles and first flown in an F-15 on a bombing run in the Nevada desert. He wasn't just watching, he was actually participating. He had felt every lurch of the aircraft, every twitch of the controls through the special gloves and had even decided on the direction to fly and when to launch the missiles. Finally, he had had to cope with an emergency loss of oil pressure and had emerged a sweating, shambling wreck. He had been there, flown the mission and come out the other side and he would have sworn that every step of the way he was in the cockpit instead of sitting in a London basement.

Virtual reality was the latest tool that had the S and T people jumping up and down with enthusiasm. They argued that here was a training resource that used no bullets, required fewer instructors and was hundreds of times more realistic than anything the Fort could devise. They were right, too, but as usual the traditionalists had fought the change. Nash saw the arrival of VR as inevitable and had been one of the first to experiment with it. Now apparently it was going to be put to some use.

'Yamana has two main places. One's in Kyoto not far from where you are now, the other is at Gifu, about an hour's drive to the north. According to our sources over there, he's currently at his country place. We've got the satellites of the area, done some research of our own and got a pretty fair idea of what you'll find. We've put together a little VR for you.'

This was supposed to be the modern version of the SAS's SPY system which they had originally devised as a database to store the designs of all British Embassies around the world and of most common design parameters. The theory ran that if they were ever called to a hostage rescue, they could do a reconnaissance of the target building from the outside noting the location of drainpipes, waste pipes, windows, etc. and from that data the computer would be able to generate the likely interior layout. It had proved sufficiently effective for them to use in operations in Bangui, Baghdad and Hong Kong.

'If you seriously think I'm going to walk into his base of operations on the basis of some computer images, you're crazy,' Nash protested.

'No, no, it's nothing like that,' Alex laughed. 'All you have to do is watch and listen. It will give you a flavour of what's out there and it may actually help you make the right decision at the right time.

'If you put on the kit, I'll fire things up at this end. Once the connection's made give a thumbs up to the screen and I'll know you're getting the transmission.'

Nash took the square box from his case, opened it and lifted out the helmet which he pulled over his head. A second, smaller, rectangular box unfolded to fit over his eyes and nose with stems to fit on the side of the helmet. He turned on the power switch at the side and waited in his dark, soundproofed world.

Suddenly, he was in a car, driving along a winding mountain road. He raised his hand in a thumbs-up to Alex and its image appeared before him. He could see ahead of him hills, capped by a snowy peak which he recognized as Mount Kinka. To his left, deep in the valley, a wide river flowed while ahead lay what looked like a large town, its peaked roofs labelling it clearly as Japanese. Before they reached the outskirts of the town, the car turned to the right, through large metal gates and up a winding drive. He stepped out of the car, leaving it silent behind him, and walked up stone steps. The door opened and he was greeted by a bowing Japanese footman, immaculate in a flowing red kimono. He followed the man through the entrance hall which was lined with Samurai armour mounted on plinths, ghostly guardians of a lost honour.

The tour through the house was bizarre. He could hear the sound of his own footsteps, almost feel the movement as he walked from room to room following his silent, smiling escort. He went up the stairs, noting the seven bedrooms, the locks on every door, the key pad into the master bedroom suite. He registered the guardhouse and saw the patrols making their rounds in the garden; saw, too, that everyone appeared well armed and prepared to repel invaders.

When the VR finished, Nash felt familiar with the house, but not yet familiar enough. The helmet's recorder had stored the images and he was able to scroll back and forth seeking the confirmation of a guard's position here, the make of a lock there. It was a laborious business but such attention to detail marks the difference between the professional who survives and the amateur who dies.

He turned the machine off and removed the helmet, eyes blinking in the sudden bright light. He stretched his neck which felt tight after such a long period trying to peer into the moving image. He lay down on the bed and played the complete image back in his mind once more. He was pleased that he had retained it all and was confident he could walk through the corridors of the house in the dark. But how much of this was reality and how much fantasy?

15

THE CALL FROM Yamana came with a hand-delivered message soon after he had signed off. It was simple enough:

I feel that we would both benefit from a meeting. May I suggest you come up to my villa at Gifu for dinner tonight. My driver will collect you at 5.30.

It was signed simply *Yamana*.

Nash looked at his watch. An hour from now. Just about time for a bath and a change. This was a man who was either supremely confident or insufferably arrogant. Nash suspected it would be a combination of both. He didn't hesitate to accept the invitation. What choice did he have? He had been charged with finding out what was happening and he could either prance around on the outside looking in or go and see for himself. He was reassured by the fact that the message had come to him direct and that he had been invited rather than simply swept up and made to disappear. That meant Yamana wanted to talk. So this was going to be a trade. Exactly what he was going to bring to the party was not clear. A good poker hand perhaps. Or rather the ability to play poker with a bad hand.

The car, a subdued Nissan, was driven by a chauffeur who either spoke no English or preferred not to. The journey out of the city on the Meishin Expressway took them from the compressed suburbia of urban Japan into countryside that had remained largely unchanged for centuries. Orchards flowed into rice fields and then, as they climbed out of the delta and past Lake Biwa, the terrain became more wooded and the area more beautiful. It was hardly credible, but the country reminded him of Scotland. It had a similar grandeur, colour and textural beauty with the rich greens and browns that he thought he would never see outside the Highlands.

He watched for the vista he had already seen courtesy of VR. After about an hour he saw the river to his left with the identical pattern of hills and snow-capped mountain ahead. They came up to the turn-off but drove straight on towards the town. Nash leaned forward to look at the driver but there was no reaction from that round, stony face.

Instead, the car continued for a further five minutes and then turned down a narrow track that had an incomprehensible Japanese sign guiding the way. After three hundred metres the car pulled into a small parking area, the driver got out and gestured for Nash to follow him. Ahead lay a bamboo-covered entrance to a large cabin. Nash entered, ducking his head under the lintel, and stopped, waiting for his eyes to adjust. There was a rustle in the darkness and, before he had time to move, he felt a sharp pain at his neck. His hand instinctively moved to his gun but before his fingers could close around the butt, oblivion had enveloped him.

The first sensation when he woke was one of warmth. He thought for a moment that he was back in the bath-house still submerged in water. Then he felt movement, then a sense of invasion. His eyes fluttered open and he found himself in darkness that was complete, black, absolute. A noise invaded his senses, a powerful buzzing that was so loud and intrusive that it seemed almost to be inside his head.

He flexed arms and legs tentatively, checking that he could still feel toes and fingers. He was reassured that he could but with that awareness came the feeling of being surrounded by something soft and pliant. There was a sensation of movement, not just around him but over him, in him, even through him. He could feel tiny, almost delicate, nips on his exposed flesh and he realized that he was naked, his body completely open to whatever it was that now surrounded him. He moved his hands up from his side towards his face and could feel the crawling movement of animals; dozens, hundreds, thousands of animals. They were small, soft and yielding, each movement of his body crushing them beneath his weight. He could feel them crawling over his face, exploring every orifice, moving inside his ears, up his nose and when he opened his mouth to let out a cry of revulsion, they swiftly entered that space, too.

He swept his hand across his face but the movement brought with it dozens of clinging beasts to replace those that he brushed away. Now he could feel them on his head, in his pubic hair and slithering between his toes, his fingers and the cleft of his buttocks. It was so invasive, so all-encompassing that his mind refused to grapple with the horror. For a moment, he had a glimpse of the abyss, that screaming darkness where panic and atavistic fear take control of the conscious mind. Then he clawed back and tried to rationalize what had happened.

Drugged certainly. Moved. Where? No idea. What? Some kind of nest of insects. What kind? Small, huge numbers, sightless, soundless. The buzzing? Then it came to him and with understanding came revulsion and an overwhelming urge to vomit. His stomach heaved once and then again, the bile acid in his throat.

He was lying on a bed of maggots, a breeding house of fish bait. Those that were allowed to complete their life-cycle were hatching into flies which were laying their eggs so that the cycle could be repeated endlessly.

Knowledge fathered its own fears. He could imagine now that he was adrift in this enormous warehouse filled with the creatures, that in the darkness he had no way of finding an exit, that he was doomed to lie here driven inexorably mad by the pervasive buzzing and the gnawing hunger of the maggots. But in those thoughts, too, lay madness. Passive acceptance of his fate would mean certain death and as he recalled the ease with which he had been trapped, he grew deeply, terribly angry. How dare these bastards take his mind and his body and use them like this?

He rolled over and put his hands underneath his body, then levered himself upright. Better. Now the crawling mass were at his ankles and he could brush his hands over his body sweeping the clinging covering away from his skin. He reached into his nose and ears, plucking out the more adventurous individuals. He took pleasure in crushing them between his fingers although the rational side of his mind understood that this was a futile gesture that had no discernible effect on the threat. Now it was the swooping, hovering buzzing of the millions of flies that threatened to overwhelm him. They clearly loved the smell of his now putrid body and wanted to sample every morsel that their sensitive antennae could detect. But he resisted the temptation to stand and swat the air. Each movement would have netted a handful of dead flies but this was an army where reinforcements were queuing up to join the front line and he knew that he could never win.

Instead, he began to move forward in a sliding, crablike shuffle, arms outstretched, searching for a wall. After twenty-five carefully counted paces, his fingers touched what felt like the rough surface of a wooden wall. Turning to his right, he kept his left hand sliding along the wall and resumed his pacing, questing for the door that would provide an escape. It seemed forever before his fingers touched a vertical crack that marked the outline of a door. Pausing, he faced the wall again and his hands reached out to trace the full rectangular shape. Around waist height, his right hand curled over a wooden latch which he moved up. With all his strength he drove his shoulder against the door.

He plunged out into a brightly lit room. The contrast was so great between the darkness of his prison and the light of freedom that he closed his eyes tight shut against the glare. He heard a movement beside him. Once more, there was a brief flash of pain and then he was returned to the darkness.

'Kuchma is completely off the reservation,' the Secretary of State said in that decorous tone he used, however dire the circumstances. 'The President of the Ukraine calling us and asking for air strikes, for God's sake. He wants NATO intervention. An emergency meeting of the Security Council. You name it, he's demanded it.'

'Well, under the circumstances, you can understand that he might be a little upset,' his deputy, Dorsey, replied.

The President intervened. 'What circumstances?' he asked. 'I've seen CNN. I read the reporting from the Agency but it's all mush.' He turned towards the DCI, clearly expecting the kind of clear answer he felt he so rarely got from the intelligence community.

'We have had both overhead and satellite information on the incident at Romny,' the DCI began. 'What we see is some extraordinary devastation. Thousands of troops dead. Our photo analysts say they are all wearing Ukrainian uniform and they all died with no sign of battle – no bodies blown apart, no limbs taken off, no large pools of blood. Nothing like that. A spectral analysis of the air turned up nothing so it wasn't radiation.'

'So what was it?' asked the President impatiently.

'The deaths are consistent with some kind of very fast-acting poison. Nobody had time to escape and there seem to have been no survivors. Our best bet is some kind of biological weapon.'

'Shit.' The expletive from the President carried with it not just the distress of a man who genuinely cared about the dead but the instant response of a consummate politician. This was a disaster and it had happened on his watch. The press would have a field day. Just as certain would be an inquisition into why America had allowed Russia's biological weapons programme to continue. It was going to be a real mess. But that was for the future. Now, there was a real crisis to address.

'What's happening on the ground?' he asked.

It was Dorsey who picked up the ball. 'The Russians are seriously pissed. Several of their officers died in whatever it was. They're claiming it's some kind of Ukrainian ecological disaster. Apparently, that part of the country has seen several nuclear leaks plus a whole raft of the usual environmental accidents. It's plausible enough except for the speed of the deaths and the way they died. Anyway, that line doesn't accord with what the Agency has from its sources.

'Both Moscow and Kiev are saying that the incident is a deliberate provocation. Both are starting to mobilize and both are claiming they must take action to protect their people – whatever that means in this mess.'

'What's our friend in the Kremlin saying?' the President asked.

'Our ambassador talked with the Russian President this morning,' the Secretary of State replied. 'He says he's trying to keep the situation under control. But the judgement of our people is that he's pretty powerless. After the Chechnya disaster, he's sold his soul to the military. He promised them a quick victory there and failed them miserably. He's hardly in a position to hold them back now if they want action.'

'Options?' The President looked round the room. Already the choices seemed terrible. Do nothing and appear impotent;

mobilize NATO and risk a wider war; call in the Security Council and risk nothing happening for weeks or even months.

'We could always send Carter,' the Secretary of State suggested. There were groans from all the others. Carter had interfered in Haiti, North Korea and Bosnia and each time had successfully hijacked American foreign policy and diminished the Presidency.

'Don't even joke about such a thing,' the President shuddered in mock horror. 'Next thing he'll be on the phone offering to fly out there and invite all the generals to come and teach Sunday School at his church.' That had been one offer that Carter had made to the Haitian military dictators which had cut deep.

'The Joint Chiefs have given me a series of options which I reviewed with the Chairman yesterday,' the President continued. 'All of them are tough calls, but we have to be seen to be ready to commit and I propose convening a meeting of the inner cabinet for later today.' He paused, flicking through a low pile of papers on his desk, each of which had the distinctive blue diagonal stripe of a Top Secret document.

'NATO's Rapid Reaction Force is designed for this kind of crisis and they should be put on alert and ready to move within twenty-four hours. They'll need air support from here and we'll have to begin pre-positioning both the heavy lift and the fighter cover. But the Chiefs are insistent – and I agree with them – that we must be ready to escalate if the deterrence doesn't work. From today we'll have to begin bringing the reserves up to speed and developing surge production capacity in the right industrial sectors.'

He picked up one of the files and waved it back and forth.

'It's all in here. I suggest you read this before this afternoon's meeting. For planning purposes this is known as the 5726 plan but for public consumption the Chiefs, with their customary optimism, have called it Operation Provide Peace.'

He turned to the Secretary of State. 'We need a diplomatic track here, too. See if we can arrange a trip to Moscow. Say we want to discuss the crisis or the aid programme or any damn thing you want. Speak to the Brits, the French. See if we can organize some kind of mini-summit. We'll try Moscow first and then Kiev.'

He liked the sound of all this. The new world order's international diplomacy at work. Better than leaving it to the buffoons at the UN.

'Force is a last resort,' he stressed. 'Diplomacy first. Action last. Right?'

The enthusiastic nods from around the room reflected the desperate hope of all concerned to avoid a commitment to a war that nobody wanted and whose outcome was too uncertain for comfort.

The memory of the maggots leapt to the front of Nash's waking mind. His eyes jerked open, searching again for the sensations that he had just left. He was relieved to find that there were no squirmy little animals beneath his fingers and toes. His feet were encased in his own shoes, his body in his own clothes, his hands resting on the arms of a comfortable chair that was covered in what felt like a conventional wool fabric.

'Good afternoon, Mr Nash. I'm afraid we weren't properly introduced at our previous meeting. I am Ken Yamana. I believe you wanted to see me.'

The speaker was sitting opposite Nash, the gap between them covered by a beautiful Persian carpet, its delicate weave of browns, reds and golds seeming to shimmer in the afternoon light that flooded the room. Nash looked at the elegant old man wearing a perfectly cut dark linen suit. He had a silk tie with a subdued pattern of green and black checks that set well against the simple white shirt. The shoes were black, lace up, hand-made, while the socks were plain and dark. It was an expensive, tasteful ensemble that made Nash feel cheap and shabby by comparison. While he realized this was probably Yamana's intention, there was little he could do to reassert his sartorial confidence when faced with such a combination of money and style.

'Let me introduce you to my associate Mr Katsura,' Yamana continued before Nash had a chance to speak. Katsura was standing off to one side, eyeing Nash with the clear look of a predator. This is a killer, Nash thought. A man waiting to be unleashed. A man to watch very, very carefully.

'I am sorry that you had such a difficult journey here,' Yamana said. 'I have been watching your progress with interest for the past few weeks. You are an intelligent man, Mr Nash. A man with many of the qualities I seek in those who work for me. A man who might find a welcome in my organization.'

'I think not, Mr Yamana,' Nash replied. 'As you must know, I work for my government and it is my country which deserves my loyalty,' Nash found himself mimicking the Yakuza's formal cadence.

The Japanese gangster smiled, mocking Nash's simple judgement.

'Oh, really?' he queried. 'And just what are you loyal to, Mr Nash? Queen? Hardly, these days. People? And just who are your countrymen? A collection of minorities all despising authority and refusing to take responsibility for their own lives; hardly worth your own life, I would have thought. Your organization? Too stupid to listen to you and too slow to understand the real nature of the new game they are playing so badly. To yourself? Ah, now perhaps there we have reached the real question.

'I arranged the little demonstration before you arrived here to show you just who you are. You now know how easily I can take both your body and your mind. I am sure there were moments in there where you nearly lost control. I can assure you I can make those moments last a very long time indeed. One can so easily be betrayed by one's own mind, don't you think? It makes the whole question of loyalty so ephemeral.'

Yamana was describing the very doubts that Nash himself had been feeling since he had been confronted by the harsh reality of life in today's world of espionage. This blurring between right and wrong, good and evil was difficult to accept. It was difficult too, to see just why he should offer his life for a cause that was uncertain and a country that didn't seem to care. But he knew that the issues were deeper than that. The arguments were not just about the elimination of the threat of communism that had given everyone a reason for fighting. The goalposts may have shifted, the touchlines become a little blurred, but his job was still to fight for democracy against the march of the dictators and the fascists; the bastards who would stop him and his kin living a life of comparative freedom within the boundaries set by society. Yamana and his ilk might demonstrate their ability to destroy and present the opportunity to participate in a very different world but what value was there in that?

'Why didn't you simply kill me?' Nash asked. 'Or are you just some kind of power junkie?'

'I can assure you I have all the power I require, Mr Nash,' replied the Yakuza. 'I spared your life because you could be of use to me. Indeed, an alliance could work to our mutual advantage.'

This was the reason he had been summoned, then. Yamana obviously had no thoughts of deals and percentages – his only interest in Nash was as a potential ally. If Nash refused the offer there would be no reason to keep him alive.

'What are you proposing?' Nash asked, running his hand through his hair, scratching at his scalp as if to rid himself of imaginary maggots.

'Probably everything you might have wished for in the last few weeks, Mr Nash.' Yamana's voice was soft and soothing, the tone of a seducer confident in his power. 'An organization that appreciates your talents, would welcome your ability to work outside a bureaucracy, would, in fact, encourage you to exploit the very talents you have demonstrated so well: initiative, persistence, courage. And, of course, working with me there would be material rewards that would allow you to fulfil your wildest dreams.'

Nash picked at his teeth, reflecting as he did so. In the end it always came down to this. The choice. Kill or risk being killed. Fight or roll over. Compromise or stick with some bloody principle you were sure existed but couldn't quite remember. He was sure that what Yamana had said was true enough. There would be another life, maybe in some ways a better life, if he took the bait. But betraying Jaimie, and the poor, hapless Spitz who'd trusted him and died because they'd both made a mistake: that was unthinkable. This was a fight, not some prissy little game. It was winner take all and the loser dies.

'I'm not sure that your organization quite reflects my values,' Nash said, trying to spin out the conversation.

'I would also just like to show you how badly you and your colleagues have judged recent events,' Yamana continued, apparently encouraged by the fact that Nash had not rejected the offer outright. He glanced at his watch. 'Have you seen the news today?'

He picked up a remote control on the side table by his chair and pressed a button. A section of the wall to Nash's right moved to one side to expose a television set that was just flickering into life. It was the opportunity Nash had been waiting for.

Nash's self-grooming during the past few minutes had been prompted by more than simple vanity. Post-glasnost, the

Office had developed a new range of imaginative – and lethal – weapons made possible by miniaturization. Nash had a few of these in his bags which were out of reach back at the hotel. If all else failed, the Office had given him a final fall-back designed not necessarily to kill but to buy time. It was known by the acronym FAW for Fire At Will or, more colloquially in the Office, as Fucking Awful Weapon. The transplants had been painful but nothing like his attempts to remove them. As Yamana had been talking, Nash had been running his fingers through his hair in a nervous, unmemorable gesture, his fingers feeling for the hair roots that felt out of place. After some minutes he had isolated first one and then the other. He pulled hard, bringing them out in his hand. On their own, the two hairs, slightly thicker towards the base than normal, were nothing. Loosely woven together and pulled hard, the surface coating parted to form a thin magnesium strip. Inside his mouth, his fingers had found the rough edge of a false molar and levered it free, secreting it in the palm of his hand. The root stump of the tooth formed a tiny detonating cap with the tooth itself a modest explosive charge, sufficient to ignite the magnesium.

Binding the hair and the tooth together, Nash twisted the bottom of the tooth, counted to three and then tossed it lightly in the direction of the killer standing next to him. Even with his eyes tight shut, the glare of the magnesium flash was almost blinding, burning bright and then dying almost as quickly.

He opened his eyes and saw that both Katsura and Yamana had their eyes shut in agony, faces screwed up in pain. He knew the effect would last only seconds but it was the chance he needed.

He pushed himself out of the chair and ran for the door, praying that the corridor outside was empty. He paused, looking to left and right, searching for a way out. The scene was familiar from the VR that Alex had prepared. If memory served him right, this was the ground floor, to his left was the front door, to his right the kitchens. The scene was the same, the dimensions of the corridor exact.

Nash heard a shout of anger behind him and knew that sight had returned to Katsura's eyes. He had only seconds now. The image of the Samurai warriors lining the entrance hall came to mind and he moved quickly to his left, slamming the door behind him. He had gone just a few paces when he heard the door crash back. He suspected that this was not an occasion for some esoteric Eastern weapon to come winging his way. He felt sure that Katsura was professional enough to rely on the speed and accuracy of bullets to do the job for him.

Nash jinked just as the roar of a gun filled the corridor. He jinked again and watched the second bullet tear into the wall in front of him. He was at the corner now, angling his body to the right to get round it at the earliest possible moment. In brief sanctuary he looked left and right, searching for a weapon with which he could meet his would-be killer.

His eyes fell on a huge Samurai sword grasped in the hand of the warrior nearest to him, which he immediately rejected as being too unwieldy.

In the side of the warrior's boot, however, was a short stabbing sword. He withdrew it from its scabbard, then moved back to the corner just as the running footsteps came to meet him. Katsura had been relying on speed of movement to overwhelm his opponent, aware that Nash was unarmed. Both assumptions proved wrong, and fatal.

As Katsura came round the corner, gun arm extended, Nash struck with a long sweeping downward motion from above shoulder height. The sword met the gunman's wrist with a solid clunk, the shock of the blow running up Nash's arm so that he almost dropped the weapon. The gun was driven from the assassin's hand, clattering across the floor to stop at the feet of one of the sightless warriors lining the hall. There was a groan of agony from Katsura, a reflection of the pain of the blow and the surprise of its occurrence.

But Katsura was a Yakuza trained to resist pain, to use it in the service of his master, to turn it against his opponent. He pivoted to face Nash. Nash was on fire now, certain that hesitation would kill him. He made another downward scything motion with the sword and then quickly swept it upwards in a looping curving arc.

The blade was moving with all the force of Nash's fury and frustration behind it as it cut deep up between Katsura's legs, ripping through fabric and flesh, through testicles and penis to embed itself deep in the crotch of his victim. His attacker stopped abruptly, completely disabled by the instant and terrible pain running deep inside to enclose his heart with the fire of agony and the ice of certain death.

He tried one last time to struggle forward but there was no power left in his muscles, his energy all focused on trying to fight the steel invader. Nash watched as the fierce eyes grew cloudy with pain and then seemed to darken as existence drained away with the blood that Nash could feel running over his hands. Katsura fell to the floor, lifeless.

With the immediate threat removed, Nash paused, uncertain what to do next. He had barely got to first base; the remainder of the house and grounds were certain to be guarded and as soon as his faithful killer failed to return carrying Nash's head, that evil old bastard was bound to order him hunted down. He hesitated only momentarily before turning back the way he had come, the bloodied sword pushing ahead searching out its next target.

The message had begun to scroll down Alex's screen that

evening. It had arrived faster than she had hoped. One up to the geniuses at GCHQ.

She had spent three hours reading through the traffic which dated back nine months and involved Raikin, Yamana and the lunatic who was running North Korea. There were messages, too, about Nash: instructions to follow him; instructions to kill Spitz; instructions to kill Nash. She shivered at the memory of just how close they had come to her and David, struck by the difference between the monochrome starkness of the message and the Technicolor reality of the action that resulted.

The reports made clear for the first time the full extent of the operation that had been planned. It was undeniable now that the whole Ukraine crisis had been a bluff, planted to shift the focus of the intelligence community away from the real goal. That part had worked brilliantly and she guessed much of the credit for that must go not to the organizers but to the mercenaries they had hired. There were plenty of messages to and from Spandau but even the decrypt gave little clue as to who they were or where they were based.

The country codes of the messages narrowed things down a little, but it would take time to match computer addresses to people. Still, as understanding grew so did the need for action. Alex knew that it was only a matter of time now before the source of the leaks that had killed Spitz and might yet kill David was identified.

Yamana was sitting calmly when David entered the room, confident that it would be his faithful servant and not the British intelligence officer who walked through the door. The gangster had spent too many years relying on others to work at the sharp end of his business. His reaction to the return of Nash was simply too slow. He reached underneath his jacket but in two quick strides Nash was across the room, sword raised. As the gun came free of its holster and reached out towards him, he brought the blade slicing down. There was a cry of agony from Yamana who dropped the weapon and covered his wrist with his other hand. The blood bubbled between his clenched fingers and Yamana lolled back in his chair, the pain of the wound clearly coursing through his body and driving out all thought of further action.

Nash looked on, surprised to note in himself a degree of objectivity, as if he were an observer of his own actions. He shook himself mentally. There was no time to waste. This was his opportunity to get some answers and he wanted them right now.

His attention was distracted by the television. He glanced over and recognized the face of Bernard Shaw, the CNN anchor who won his spurs during the Gulf War and was routinely wheeled out at times of national emergency.

'We have more on the crisis in the former Soviet Union,' he said in the sepulchral tones that American newscasters reserve for occasions when they try to be especially pompous but obviously want to jump up and down in excitement. 'The White House announced today that the President has agreed to attend a summit meeting with the Russian, British, French and Chinese leaders in Moscow tomorrow. Top of the agenda will be the worsening crisis between Russia and Ukraine, where forces on both sides are reported to be on full alert. Meanwhile, NATO has placed the 40,000 men of the Rapid Reaction Force on notice that they may be deployed to the region. The five permanent members of the United Nations Security Council will meet in Moscow in an attempt to defuse the crisis.

'Meanwhile, the situation in eastern Russia is reported calm and there have been no official statements from either Tokyo or Pyongyang beyond the initial declaration of the new republic.'

'*Eastern* Russia? New republic? What the hell is all that about?' Nash muttered. He was baffled by the broadcast. Only hours ago, the whole focus had been on Ukraine and now it had switched to somewhere completely different.

'Ukraine,' Yamana grimaced with pain but could not disguise the satisfaction in his voice, the pleasure he was taking in Nash's consternation. 'There was never anything happening in Ukraine. It was all a giant bluff, a distraction that would ensure that everyone was looking one way while we moved another.'

'Tell me something I don't know,' said Nash. 'What's this about a new republic?'

'Ah, that,' Yamana said. 'Of course, I was forgetting that you have been out of touch for the past few hours.

'There was a revolt of the officers and men of the eastern military district in Russia headquartered in Vladivostok. They have declared an independent republic from mother Russia and have set up an interim government. The Japanese government has quietly suggested that they will recognize this new state and so have their neighbours in North Korea. The new republic is a creation of myself and my two associates, Alla Raikin and Kim Jong-Il, the Dear Leader himself in Pyongyang.'

Nash tried to grasp the enormity of this plan. At a stroke, these crooks had used an unholy alliance with the Russian military to create a new nuclear state. It would leave the balance of power in the Far East in tatters and the future of Russia in doubt. And God knows what the economic consequences would be. It was almost unthinkable. And yet it had happened.

'Surely the Russians will simply move in,' Nash observed.

'With what?' Yamana replied. 'Their military will take days, perhaps weeks to get organized. The President can't afford a civil war which would destroy him politically and economically so he has turned to America for help.' He gave a satisfied smile.

'But America and NATO have been planning for a different war. Their people in Brussels have been drawing up scenarios for intervention in Ukraine and now they're having to shift their focus several thousand miles. They lack the aircraft or the men to do anything in the short term and there is no political will to do anything in the long term.'

It was so complacent, so self-satisfied and so true. Nash felt impotent this far away from the action, yet the solution to all the questions that had been nagging him for the past few days were probably within this room, with this man.

'Where does the nerve gas fit in with all this?'

'That was the distraction, the spark that caused the Ukraine to go to war – or at least to look as if it was going to go to war. A few people died. But it was a cheap price for a new country.'

The old man groaned and fell back in his chair. The blood had gathered in a deep, dark pool around his feet and Nash could smell its sickly sweet odour filling the room. It reminded him of Spitz and suddenly he felt sick. He moved past Yamana, leaving him slumped in the chair and headed towards the desk by the picture window with its stunning view of the valley below.

The computer was blinking unhelpfully at him, the screen blank and only the single winking eye of the cursor telling him that it was alive. He wished Alex were there. She would have been able to prise its secrets open with only a few delicate touches. But he needed a different key.

He moved back across the room and lifted up Yamana, dragging him over to the desk. He pushed him down into the chair in front of the keyboard.

'I want the file,' he ordered.

There was no reaction. Nash hefted the sword in his hand,

debating just how far he was prepared to go in the search for the truth. Probably not far enough, he thought to himself. Well, if this little toad could bluff, maybe he could too. He unzipped Yamana's fly and pushed the sword point between his legs. The Japanese cringed away from the razor-sharp point, imagining the slip that would leave him without his manhood. Nash pushed down slightly and Yamana moved his hands to the keyboard and began to type with quick, darting stabs.

The screen cleared for a second and then filled with images that translated into words. They were not Japanese, as he had feared, but English. He leaned forward, peering over Yamana's shoulder. He recognized the words. This was his traffic, his cable to London. The little bastard had been intercepting his e-mail.

It was the moment of distraction that Yamana wanted. He pushed his chair back, away from the sword point and at the same time pulled open the desk drawer and lifted out a tiny aerosol. He squeezed the top and a spray of gas emerged. Nash pushed himself back, the fear of cyanide or something just as deadly giving his legs a raw power. The clawing at his throat and the stinging in his eyes told him that this was CS gas. Powerful, crippling even, but not deadly.

Yamana levered himself out of the chair and moved towards Nash who backpedalled desperately, trying to keep out of range. Every time Yamana advanced, he risked entering a cloud of his own gas, so he had to move sideways round the room, spraying slightly to one side to try and keep Nash at bay. Nash had the upper hand now. Where he led, Yamana must follow.

Then he tripped, sprawling full length on the Persian rug. Yamana advanced, spray in hand to administer a telling dose of the disabling gas. Nash glanced sideways and saw the pistol that Yamana had discarded earlier lying just beyond his reach.

There was no hesitation. He switched his grip on the sword and hefted it with all his force directly at Yamana. Nash rolled over, reaching for the pistol. The butt fitted snugly in his hand, his thumb found the safety catch and flicked it off. He stretched his arm out in front of him and began firing. Once, twice. Again. Then he saw Yamana and his arm fell back to his side.

The sword had taken Yamana in the stomach and driven him back against the wall. One or perhaps two of the rounds from the gun had followed, hitting him in the neck. His eyes had already begun to glaze with the blindness of death and the arcing blood had slowed to an unsteady dribble down his side and on to the floor.

Nash picked himself up and with a final glance at the dead man moved back to the computer. He scrolled through the file that Yamana had brought on to the screen and as he read, his heart sank. File after file that he had sent to the Office or which had been sent to him had been intercepted. He realized that this was more than a simple act of betrayal. This was very specific indeed. All the information had come from the files that had been sent to and from Alex's laptop. Here was the leak. This was how they had tracked him down, how they knew exactly where he would be and when. And it was Alex who had assured him the system was completely secure. Alex who had given him the special communications that would work outside the normal channels. Alex who had been so helpful in making sure he had all the technology at his fingertips. Alex.

He sat back in the chair and ran his hands through his hair. He felt completely isolated, but more than that he was burning with anger. Everywhere he turned there were traitors, liars and crooks. And now he had been betrayed by the one person he thought he could trust. He replayed his conversation with Yamana. The bastard thought he had had it made, that the party was over. Well, how wrong he was. It was only just beginning. For the first time since this operation had begun, the enemy had been given some real shape and substance. An alliance that Yamana had described brought back all the demons of the Cold War: nuclear weapons in the hands of amoral tyrants; a world held to ransom by corrupt and ruthless men and women who cared nothing for life, civilized society or moral codes. This was an enemy he could understand.

But, there was still the unanswered question of Spandau's role in all of this. And Alex. Had Alex betrayed him? Both his head and his heart told him it couldn't be true, but the evidence on the screen was damning, irrefutable.

He turned back to the computer and continued scrolling through the file. The messages ended with their recent conversation from Tokyo. Then a new file began, this time about Spandau. There was less detail here, less information about people and places but the instructions to kill him in England and Moscow were carefully laid out. Then he stopped. Two canisters of bio weapons, one for Ukraine and the other for Moscow. If the file was right, that meant there was more to come.

There was no further detail, just a final message from Spandau to say that the mission was to proceed.

He sat back, thinking. Should he tell London? Who could he trust? Was Alex the only leak or were there others involved? And if he did tell them, what could he say? Not much except that Alex was a traitor. First he must find some answers, then he could decide what to do.

Pavel Lukyanov had thought the mission would be both simple and fun. A sea trip to New York, a visit to the city for the handover and off he would go for a two-week jaunt in a country he had never seen. Life as a courier in the Moscow underworld had become increasingly treacherous of late; he could do with a change of scenery and rumour had it that there was a good life to be made in the States. None of the problems of Moscow, a decent apartment, all the food you could want and the girls. The girls. More than a man could handle – or so he'd heard.

The ship had berthed at Long Beach and the customs and immigration had been a formality. He was simply a sailor about to enjoy a few hours' shore leave and the city welcomed him and his spending money. He had taken the package out of the ship's deep freeze, hefted the silver-coloured metal briefcase under his arm and headed ashore. His instructions were clear, take a cab from the dockside to Astoria, the suburb north of Queens where many of the new Russian immigrants had settled. He neither knew nor cared what was in the package. His business was simply to deliver it and go on his way. That's what a courier did. Ask questions and you ended up dead. Pavel wasn't the type to cause ripples, he preferred the quiet life.

He had thought that Moscow traffic was bad, but New York was a hell of mad drivers, huge shiny trucks and seemingly endless lines of stationary cars, all heading in to the city to start the day. And he could sense a thunderstorm coming. So much for the beachwear he had packed for the trip.

It was one of those unfortunate incidents that are a part of everyday commuting life that spelled the end of Pavel and his mission. They had reached the Triboro Bridge and the Haitian driver had turned to try to tease a response from his dour passenger when the car in front braked. The taxi driver's reaction was just a millisecond too slow and there was a crunch of metal as the car in front was rear-ended. A classic New York scene ensued. The driver in front – a fat, cigar-chomping, aggressive man who had been wanting to vent his spleen ever since he got up that morning – dragged himself out of the car and moved towards the taxi.

Both drivers began shouting, the taxi driver in a language Pavel did not understand and the other man in what the Russian assumed was a New York version of English. It was clear that neither man was interested in what the other was saying, clear too that the conversation was going nowhere fast. Such arguments were routine enough in Moscow and Pavel was confident that once both had had their say, each would go his own way amid a barrage of departing insults. But this was New York and within thirty seconds of the incident, there had been a dozen calls from car telephones to the police. Two minutes later a motorcycle cop was on the scene. Pavel watched in horror as the policeman kicked the stand in place and then swung both feet down to the ground. As the cop went to calm the two drivers, Pavel regarded the case on the seat beside him. Whatever it contained was sure to land him in trouble if discovered, and not just with the NYPD. His bosses at home were unforgiving of failure, a bullet in the head being the usual reminder to do better next time. Pavel decided that discretion was by far the better part of discovery.

He pushed open the door on the side further from the policeman and lurched out into the road, clutching the silver case to his chest. He took three paces into the commuter lane, heard a brief, blaring blast from a bus horn and then was lifted into the air as the front of the bus scooped him from the road. For a moment he was held in place by the forward momentum of the bus and he looked up into the horrified open mouth of the driver. Then, as the bus slowed, he slid down the front of the vehicle, slowly at first, and then as his feet touched the ground, he was sucked underneath. Even then, he might have survived were it not for the case which he still held faith-fully to his chest. As he hit the ground, the case landed first and he rolled off it to one side, directly into the path of the rear wheels.

Pavel felt nothing as the huge bus rolled over yet another bump in the road. His body was squeezed like a ripe orange, his midsection bursting under the pressure to spread an ooze of blood and slime across the road. The case, too, was destroyed. If anybody had been listening, they would have heard a cracking sound as the metal frame broke, then the hiss of escaping air. A small cloud of steam formed briefly over the case as the freezing air inside met the warmth of the New York traffic fumes. The container nestled inside the case made no sound at all as its seals were broken.

Pavel's death was a momentary distraction for the trio gathered round the taxi and they immediately ran after the bus which had pulled up forty yards beyond next to a car containing a young family of four who were off to the big city for a day of fun.

The policeman was hit first, the taxi driver next. There was no warning, just a paroxysm followed almost immediately by the boils and the bile. The family in the car looked on in horror as the men's bodies were apparently taken over by some kind of alien force that was eating the flesh from within. They looked in vain for the cause of the violent death, blessedly unaware that within thirty seconds they would suffer an identical fate. There was no escape. They, and the thousands of other commuters on the Triboro Bridge, had nowhere to go.

The spores had risen from the surface of the road and been absorbed into the air. Like an invisible wave breaking over the beach of cars, the cloud was slowly carried forward on the wind. Every window and air-vent was an opportunity, every living thing a target. Within a few short minutes, what had been a normal scene of everyday commuting folk became a picture of total carnage. The road was filled with screaming dying people. Those who chose to stay in their cars died where they sat, vomit-covered windows mute testimony to the horrors within. There was no sanctuary and no mercy.

It was the wind that helped spread the sickness and it was the wind that killed it. The storm that Pavel had sensed blowing up arrived only minutes after the carnage began, torrents pouring from the heavens, pounding the cars and the road. The rain washed the air, picking up the spores and carrying them away. Without such divine intervention tens of thousands would have died. As it was, New York got off lightly. In eight minutes, seven hundred adults and twenty-eight children died.

Before he had left Yamana's villa, Nash had pocketed Katsura's machine-pistol – a Calico M-950 with the 50 shot magazine. Now he was fighting to stay awake as the aircraft droned on through the night sky.

He picked up the telephone by his left elbow and dialled Pyotr's number in Moscow. The line was as clear as if he'd been dialling from his apartment in London to the Office.

'David, my friend,' Pyotr's cheerful, booming voice came over the line. 'You will have heard how that woman has made fools of all of us.'

'At least it proves you were right and the Americans were wrong,' Nash consoled him.

'Maybe so,' Pyotr replied, 'but you realize that the same people who were planting the lies must be behind subsequent events.'

'I know it and I can prove it,' said Nash. 'I'm on my way to you now. It's time we took some direct action.'

There was no need for Nash to spell out the details and the anticipation in Pyotr's voice was obvious when he continued.

'So all we need now is to eliminate the Raikin woman and we can get back to a normal life of crime.' His hearty chuckle forced a smile even to Nash's exhausted face.

'It's not as simple as that I'm afraid, Pyotr,' said Nash. 'They've bought themselves a little insurance. We need the woman alive. Get hold of Yuri. Pull in all the favours you can and find her. Do whatever you have to, but by the time I get there I want to know where she is.'

The two men hung up, the task clear. Nash sank back into his seat, imagining Pyotr and Yuri setting in motion the kind of manhunt Moscow had not seen since Beria's day. There was enough at stake for everyone to ensure that no snitch was left unquestioned, no source untapped.

It had gone remarkably well, Muraviev thought to himself. He had always known that the military would play their part, but you never knew quite how the politicians would behave. Fortunately they had performed true to type and vacillated long enough for the operation to be completed. He sat back in the rear seat of the fighter. There would be no combat on this mission and no need of the weapons officer. His presence was required in Moscow both to brief the generals and to make sure that the operation continued to be secure. Nothing must go wrong now and he wanted to be there to make sure that Raikin didn't fuck it up.

Thinking back over the past few hours, he felt a thrill of excitement course through his body. They had done it. Against all the odds, they had begun the formation of a new country. And what a foundation. A sea port, a nuclear-capable military and a BW capability that would be up and running in another few hours and would be impregnable a few hours after that. With the military's backing and the input from the Japs and the Koreans, there would be no holding them.

The foundations had been there since the collapse of the Empire; the politicians who had been 'elected' to power in the provinces were all old party hacks who owed their survival to the intelligence services. Their files were a rich account of human frailty that ensured loyalty. The rise of capitalism had cemented even the most fragile of bonds with the cash from crime melding with the profits of privatization to corrupt even the most steadfast. Muraviev and his allies had used their power wisely to establish their government of straw men in Vladivostok. Apparently democrats, these men and women were owned, body and soul.

With the government in place and ready to rule, it was a short step to control the means of production. The Yakuza had all the experience needed to run a secure and profitable operation while Alla and her people understood the Russian way of doing business. And when the gold, diamonds and other raw materials were combined with cheap and experienced North Korean labour, the beginnings of a new industrial powerhouse were taking shape.

It would be the foundation for a new empire. Out of this great day would come a new Russia – it would only be a matter of time before that disorganized rabble in Moscow saw the light. They would mutter and moan for a few weeks, but they would have no choice. The new republic had the raw materials that Russia needed and they had the people and the discipline. Above all the discipline.

The whole operation would be made totally secure once the Americans understood what awaited them in New York and once they had been dealt the blow that he was about to administer in Moscow.

He leaned back in the seat, savouring the moment, a small smile of satisfaction playing about his cold lips.

'Don't give me any more excuses.' The President's voice was tight with anger, his face flushed. 'All I ever hear from you is fucking excuses. Haiti, Somalia, North Korea and now Russia. My one foreign policy success. Mine, not yours, and now even that's all fucked up.'

The President had insisted that the DCI come on board Air

Force One for the flight to Moscow and the DCI believed that he was there for no other purpose than to serve as a whipping boy for the President's anger. From the moment his boss had heard about the new republic he had been loaded for bear. And the easiest target had been the Agency for failing to warn him.

This had come like a bolt from the deep blue, but the President never seemed to understand that intelligence was hardly ever about certainties but usually concerned probabilities and likelihoods. Now he expected a ready-made plan for a way forward, explanations. And the DCI didn't have any. Worst of all, the fucking Brits had been on the horn saying that they'd known all along and if you'd just refer to memo xb/2493/dn/ds you'd see, old boy, that if you'd just listened, old boy, you wouldn't be in this mess. And they were loving it.

'I'm afraid, Mr President, that we've not yet heard the worst of it.'

'Christ, you mean there's more?' the President replied, his face seeming to grow longer and more lined with every passing minute.

'The Brits believe that these people may have developed their own BW capability, or at least have one under construction. They had some intel, which looked pretty thin a couple of days ago, that over the past few months, equipment has been shipped to build a BW plant somewhere near Vladivostok. Before we left, I ordered a bird over the area. We should get the results any time.'

Right on cue, one of the communications specialists appeared from the lower deck bearing a sheaf of colour photographs which he handed to the DCI and a single sheet of paper which he gave to the President.

'Oh my God!' the exclamation was stark, the voice filled with horror. Every person in the cabin looked at the President whose hand had dropped to his side, the piece of paper with the report of the New York incident hanging between thumb and forefinger. He read the question in the eyes of those fixed on him.

'Read it for yourself.' He held the paper out to the DCI.

The report of the casualties was all the more chilling for its clinical detachment. It was the assessment at the bottom that caught the DCI's attention.

There is every indication the incident was caused by the release of a highly toxic agent, possibly a biological weapon. Both the Pentagon and the Department of Energy have teams on the scene. More later.

It was too much of a coincidence. The DCI had learned that coincidences in his business almost always revealed a plotting hand.

'If this report's right, Mr President, that's the second release of BW. And if the Brits are right, these people – and they think it's some of the organized crime barons – they'll have a complete production facility ready in the next few days. Then God help us all.'

He glanced down at the sheaf of pictures in his hand. They showed aerial shots of Vladivostok and parts of the surrounding countryside. He turned to the accompanying typescript.

Reconnaissance reveals large-scale troop movements around an area 35 miles NW of Vladivostok. In the past 12 hours, SAM sites have been developed and new radars brought on line. We best-guess that within 24 hours the site will be ringed by a series of concentric missile batteries. This is the only area where this level of activity has been observed and the site is clearly considered by the leadership to be a high-value target. Analysis of previous overflights suggests this to have been a research facility for the Ministry of Defence, purpose unknown.

'There's your plant, Mr President,' the DCI said with the total confidence of a man desperate to get out of the hole in which he finds himself. 'These reports say they are fortifying as we speak. We'll have to move now if we're to negate the threat.'

To the President, battered by circumstances spiralling out of his control, the idea of taking firm action was very appealing.

'What are our options, Dorsey?' the President asked the Deputy Secretary of State for the umpteenth time.

'It's a tough one, Mr President,' Dorsey replied. 'This is too far removed even for NATO's out-of-area forces. It would take at least six months to get them in position. The Russians are pretty impotent, not least because they're worried about the nuclear weapons the new republic may have acquired. The Chinese, who might be most affected, seem happy to let things ride. Maybe they consider a divided Russia to be less of a threat.'

'Well, that's just fine and dandy for them,' said the President sarcastically. 'So it's all left to Uncle Sam again.'

He turned to his communications officer. 'Get me the Chairman.'

In moments the face of the Chairman of the Joint Chiefs of Staff appeared on the video screen before him. The President outlined the threat while the soldier listened attentively.

'We have two possibilities,' said the Chairman when the briefing had finished. 'One, ask the Russians to do the job. It's still their country, even if they do appear to have lost control for the moment.'

'That could end up making things even worse,' said the President. 'Or?'

'Or, we go in and burn the target using FAE. We have F-117s in Japan. They can be there within hours.'

'What the hell's FAE?' asked the President.

'Fuel Air Explosives. Used in the Gulf War. Highly effective. Ethylene oxide is sprayed over a wide area and then ignited. What you get is a huge fireball hot enough to burn any living thing to powder, including any virus or bacteria that may be at the site. Best thing we have, sir – short of a nuclear device,' he said with some satisfaction.

'Could we get in and out safely?' asked the President. 'Be a hell of an embarrassment if one of our pilots is captured.'

'There are no guarantees, of course,' replied the Chairman. 'I'd rate our chances better than even. Things have got to be pretty chaotic over there right now. The longer we wait, the harder it will be.'

The President paused for a moment, reflecting. Swift action might diminish the political flak he would face for letting these people acquire biological weaponry in the first place. Be tough in a crisis, he thought, it always sells. And if he could pull this off before the summit, it would give him something to bring to the table. Threat of blackmail removed, America to the rescue, brownie points for him both at home and abroad. Yeah, FAE might just do the trick.

'I want a plan delivered to me within the hour,' he told the Chairman. 'Gentlemen, I think it's time to kick some ass.'

His hand reached forward, delving deep into the bowl of M&Ms on the table in front of him. He began popping them into his mouth one by one. Each was stamped with a silhouette of the White House and the DCI watched as the President's large teeth bit down on the image of his own home. There must be a message in there somewhere, he thought, but I'm damned if I know what it is.

16

'THE CHIEF WANTS to see you straight away, Alex.'

The call was from Joan, Spedding's personal assistant.

Alex reassured herself that there was nothing to fear but she couldn't help the butterflies fluttering in her stomach. The outer door was open and Joan waved her straight through. She walked into Spedding's lair and pulled up short. Graham Smart was standing facing her with Richard Teller sitting just behind him.

'Alex. Good of you to come.' Spedding came round his desk and gestured towards one of the chairs facing Teller. He sat next to his deputy with Smart on his right so that Alex was neatly bracketed. The whole tone was frightening. She was certain that this spelled trouble.

'Thank you for your work on Spandau,' said Spedding. 'The reports made interesting reading.' He paused, coughed, nervously touched his hair.

'I'm afraid we have some bad news. I know that both you and Nash have been concerned for some time about the source of the leak in the Office. From the way Nash was acting, we even thought he might have suspected Richard.' His eyes flicked to his left and he smiled thinly, dismissing the idea.

'Despite Nash's reluctance to assist Mr Smart, he has made considerable progress.'

Alex's eyes flicked involuntarily towards the ex-policeman. There was a hungry look to him, like a dog about to get started on a particularly juicy bone. He could contain himself no longer, interrupting Spedding's calm discourse.

'We've found the source of the leak all right. It's you.'

Just half an hour's drive from Red Square is one of Russia's best kept secrets, the presidential retreat at Novo-Ogarevo. It is to Russian leaders what Camp David is to American Presidents or Chequers to British Prime Ministers. The difference is that this building has never been photographed. Through the turbulence of two Russian revolutions it has remained a hidden symbol of privilege.

The President had only heard of it because of the briefing he had received from the Agency. And they had only heard of it because Mikhail Gorbachev had invited George Bush there for the signing in July 1991 of the historic bilateral accords that had effectively marked the end of the Cold War.

Air Force One had landed forty minutes earlier and the President had been met by the armoured Lincoln that the Air Force had flown in a few minutes ahead. The usual entourage of the American Ambassador, sundry secret servicemen with their flesh-coloured earpieces and cufflink microphones, ringed the steps leading down to the Tarmac. But there was no welcoming band playing the 'Stars and Stripes' and no head of state. It had been decided that there would be no pomp around this visit, no gladhanding. This was to be a working meeting where, for a change, the principals would actually make policy rather than rubber-stamp agreements worked out long before by their officials. This was a crisis they were going to have to solve themselves.

It was a weighty responsibility but the President had been looking forward to it. He had a feeling that his time had finally come.

There was no delay at the large wrought-iron gates that barred access to the dacha and the Lincoln followed the Secret Service Jeep Cherokee along the half-mile drive that led deep into the Rasdony Woods. The autumn colours were lovely, reminiscent of Camp David with birch leaves turning that rich red that contrasted so well with their silver bark. He caught an occasional glimpse of a camouflage uniform in the trees, but otherwise they were alone. The President could feel his adrenaline beginning to flow in anticipation of the next few hours.

The car pulled up in front of the dacha, which had been designed in a mock Palladian style. Four columns covered a rectangular portico which was flanked by two turrets, the whole façade painted a creamy yellow with white edging. The effect was peculiar, a mix of Victorian kitsch, fifties innovation and passing references to previous eras.

'Schlock architecture,' muttered Dorsey dismissively. He fancied himself a cultured man and never missed an opportunity to pronounce, usually disdainfully, on the excesses of foreigners.

The Russian President bounded down the front steps to greet his American counterpart, his arm outstretched. The American braced himself for a crushing bear-hug. As the Russian approached, the President sniffed warily. Well, at least he's not drunk yet, he thought to himself.

'Great to see you,' the Russian said. 'Come in. Come in.'

He ushered his guests along the central hallway towards the back of the house. Turning to his right, he entered the drawing room and ushered the President towards some arm-chairs that were set out facing a set of bay windows. It was a stunning view with the broad, silvery expanse of the Moskva flowing by just thirty metres away. As the President sat down and absorbed the view, he thought how unreal all this seemed. It was hard to believe that once the others arrived, they would be forced to try and resolve a drama that could decide the fate of the world. Yet here, everything was calm.

Everything was calm, too, inside Factory No. 17. For the previous three months, the place had been chaotic with endless shipments of supplies arriving under armed escort. Scientists had flooded in from across Russia and in the last few days, with the arrival of the canister from Muraviev, the guards had been tripled and everybody had been confined to base. Such restrictions mattered little for the staff as their instructions were clear and time was short. They were required to replicate the virus they had been given and then begin immediate development of a delivery system that would give the weapon a longer life and a method of reaching its target by either air or land.

For the past twenty-four hours, the quiet of the factory itself contrasted with the bedlam outside the perimeter. There, hundreds of soldiers had been digging trenches, erecting fences and mixing the concrete for the missile batteries that had begun to pepper the surrounding hills. It was all very reassuring for the inmates. They had no reason to believe they were any more vulnerable here than they had been at the other sites around Russia where they had played their part in the Biopreparat programme. But then they had no idea either that they were each playing a key role in a grand political game that had the future of their country as the main stake. Media broadcasts and newspapers did not reach Factory No. 17. None of the occupants ever knew why they died.

The four FAE bombs fell from the sky just seconds after each other. The bang as the airburst fuses fragmented the bombs and spread ethylene oxide in an enormous cloud over the area might have woken up a few light sleepers. But there would have been no time for conscious thought as the detonator almost immediately ignited the cloud. The explosive overpressure swept across the ground at Mach 6 with a force comparable to that of a nuclear explosion. Every building was razed and every body instantly incinerated in the huge fireball that erupted to envelop the site. In three seconds, temperatures at ground level had reached 20,000 degrees Fahrenheit. Nothing survived.

It had taken a few seconds for Smart's words to sink in and then the denials had begun. Now, back in the solitude of her own office, she contemplated the destruction of her world. Not only had she betrayed David but Spedding had spelled out in stark terms that he was heading straight into an ambush. Confronted with that reality, she felt devastated. As her stomach knotted, she leaned forward in front of her computer, her hands wrapped tight around her chest as if she alone could supply the reassurance she needed.

It was not just the betrayal but the understanding that even with their knowledge, Spedding and the rest of them were willing to allow Nash to go on. She had finally understood that all he had ever been to these people was a blunt instrument, a battering ram to force open the doors of this conspiracy. They knew that his tenacity and his loyalty would make him follow the leads wherever they went, irrespective of the danger or the odds stacked against him. Poor, stubborn David. She thought about him in Moscow. Alone. Slaying the Dragons.

Nash was relieved to find both Pyotr and Yuri waiting outside the airport.

'You asked for results and we've got them,' said Pyotr.

He beckoned to Nash and walked over to a Mercedes. Pyotr bent down and muttered something into the car. He waved Nash forward and he bent, too. Inside, two enormous bodyguards had sandwiched between them a thin, almost emaciated, little man, who was clearly in a state of abject terror. His teeth were chattering and a thin dribble of spittle was hanging from his lower lip. His gold-rimmed spectacles had one lens missing, making him look almost insane with one eyeball apparently three times larger than the other. His lips were swollen to perhaps twice their normal size and one ear had been torn from the side of his head to hang limply against his neck.

'We found this piece of filth at the computer at Raikin's house,' Pyotr explained. 'He's one of her bookkeepers. One of the scum who keeps the cash coming in. We have been persuading him to tell us what we need to know,' Pyotr continued, the satisfaction evident in his voice. 'Alla Raikin is holed up in a railway siding. Not just on any old train, of course, but one of the grand tourers that the *nomen-klatura* used in the bad old days. All the comforts of home, apparently, and surrounded by her own people in every building and railway arch and on every street corner.'

Nash turned to Yuri, knowing that nothing would happen without his official sanction.

'So, what's the plan?' he demanded. 'Storm the place?'

'No, a frontal onslaught would be suicide. After Pyotr's raid she'll be determined not to be caught out like that again. Some of our people have had a look from the outside. Apparently it's better defended than the Berlin Wall was.'

'Well, that was breached often enough,' said Nash, unable to resist the dig.

Yuri smiled indulgently. 'As always, the key for us is surprise and the way to achieve that is from above. We're going in by helicopter,' he said.

'But, they'll hear us as soon as we get within range,' Nash protested.

'By the time we get within range the damage will have

been done. First we're going to send in a couple of motorized hang gliders packed with explosives first to open the door for us. They'll cut their engines well away from the target, then silently glide the rest of the way to land on top of the train. After the "boom" we come in down fast ropes and clear up the mess. At the same time, Alpha teams will be going in hard from ground level to take care of the guards and clear our exit.'

Yuri opened his arms in a gesture of enthusiasm at the brilliance of his plan that was supposed to invite applause from his audience. The whole scheme seemed crazy to Nash. The timing would have to be precise and the execution close to flawless for the mission to succeed. And he could imagine just who was going to be hanging off a fast rope.

'I assume you've done this kind of thing in your training, David?' Yuri asked, nonchalantly.

In fact, Nash had never jumped from a helicopter down a rope and had hoped never to do so, though he could hardly admit that now. These people were risking their lives for him and the least he could do was play along.

'Sure,' he replied, deliberately casual. He hoped that the iron grip fear now had on his bowels wasn't showing in his face.

Nash couldn't help remembering the footage he had seen a year or two earlier after the Russian special forces had attacked a helicopter at some airport to which gangsters had flown with their ransom money and hostages. It should have been a simple operation but something had gone wrong. All the crooks had died along with the hostages in the inferno that had consumed them and four of their rescuers. He hoped this wasn't going to be a repeat of that.

Two MiL Mi-34 helicopters appeared over the airfield and touched down alongside them. On the rear aircraft, four special forces men were hanging on to the skids, their bodies held to the fuselage by a length of cord and spring clips. Each man was in a black one-piece jump suit with the soft black leather boots that gave a firm grip in all weathers. The body armour was distinctive enough but the helmets were light-weight Kevlar with none of the accoutrements they would have needed for night fighting. They seemed to have a mix of weapons, one man carrying a big shotgun, another a machine-pistol and another a rifle. Each also carried a pistol in a shoulder holster and the distinctive shapes of phosphorus and fragmentation grenades were also visible. If looks could kill, Nash thought, these people would do the business.

Yuri gestured Nash forward under the sweeping blades of the first helicopter. He reached inside and passed out a bundle of clothing and weapons which Nash swiftly donned. He retained the Calico machine-pistol he had taken from Katsura, feeling with the superstition of the truly nervous that the gun had become a kind of talisman. Soon he felt like a giant crab, weighed down by the shell of armour and defences that he now wore. It was difficult to move and frightening to have such little mobility. He placed his feet on the skid, clipped himself to the fuselage and waited for the lurch as the helicopter lifted off.

'Pyotr is going in from the ground,' Nash heard Yuri speaking through his helmet microphone. 'He says he's not cut out for this kind of rough stuff.' It was the sort of feeble joke that men make before they go into battle but Nash didn't feel like laughing.

He could hear a gabble of Russian in his ear as the men in the assault team exchanged information with the reconnaissance unit and the people on the hang gliders. The chatter stopped as Yuri broke in.

'The recce team say that Raikin has just gone into the centre carriage of her train. ETA three minutes.'

They were flying very low over the city, perhaps fifteen

metres above the high rooftops so that the projection forward of their engine noise would be kept to a minimum. He looked around, watching the lazy curl of the Moskva river pass by, then the red roofs of the Kremlin complex. Then they turned north, away from the heart of the city and he saw the railway tracks, the engines idle in the shunting yards. The helicopter rose briefly to clear the arched roof of Leningrad station. For a moment the sun striking the hundreds of glass panes in the roof was blinding and then they passed into a different area of darkness.

'Look,' Yuri shouted, his arm pointing ahead. Nash could make out the ungainly shape of two hang gliders circling down into a vast area of trains, containers and carriages. It looked an impossibly complicated target zone but the helicopter pilot was clearly following the path of the two men ahead. The pilot had swooped even lower now until he was only a few metres above the ground. It was a stunning piece of flying. Nash was so close he could see the blur of white as people stared upwards at the helicopters passing over them, their features indistinct because of the aircraft's speed.

Then a swift lurch up, a swoop down that left his stomach somewhere near the tracks and the helicopter was hovering above the end of a railway carriage with a jolly red and yellow roof.

'Nearly time to go,' Yuri yelled, flinging a coil of rope down towards the ground.

Any hesitation Nash might have had disappeared with the first explosion. The shaped charge left there by the hang-glider pilot was precisely designed to take off the end of the wooden carriage and it did its job. The wooden structure fractured in a cloud of smoke and flame, driving the planking in and leaving a huge hole. Something similar was happening at the opposite end of the carriage.

Nash reached into the belly of the aircraft, pulled out his

rope and threw it down. He unclipped himself, placed both hands around the rope, muttered a brief 'Oh, shit,' and flung himself backwards. The downwash from the rotors seemed to drive him towards the ground and the rope slid through his fingers, the heat burning through his gloves and seeming to lift the flesh off his hands with each centimetre he travelled.

Nash's feet hit the ground and he found himself running, following fast on Yuri's heels. The Russian launched himself in a dive into the wrecked carriage and rolled to his knees, his pistol pointing forward. He squeezed the trigger twice and then scuttled off to his left to lurk behind what had once been a desk.

Nash levered himself after Yuri and crawled off to his right taking in the long expanse of carriage. There was nothing ahead of him except a single corpse, presumably the result of Yuri's shooting. His eyes smarting from the residue of the explosives, Nash tried to pick out any other threat and could see none. Relief was tempered by the instant concern that they had hit the wrong target, that Alla had escaped. Then he saw the door at the far end of the carriage. Signalling urgently to Yuri, he ran forward, jumping over the body and stopping against the far wall. He undid the chinstrap of his helmet, cast it to one side and pressed an ear against the wall. He could hear nothing.

Then, he saw the handle of the door begin to turn. He waved his hand at Yuri, drawing the Russian's attention to the movement and signalled to him to wait. As the door eased open, the first thing Nash saw filling the gap was a thick gold stick – Alla's famous cattle prod, he realized – then a hand with long red fingernails and finally Pyotr Sakharovsky's head secured in place by her other arm.

'This little toy is set to kill,' said Alla from beyond the door. 'Of course,' she continued conversationally, 'Kill is sometimes an exaggeration. You never can tell with people.

The stronger ones just have their brains fried. Is your friend Pyotr strong, do you suppose?' She waved the weapon close to Pyotr's face. Pyotr spat, the saliva hitting the prod and evaporating instantly with a hiss of steam. 'I advise you to do nothing stupid.'

Nash watched as Pyotr was pushed through the doorway to be followed by Alla Raikin. He wanted to fire, simply to blow her away, but he knew that a dying reflex could easily trigger the cattle prod and kill Pyotr. It was a risk he daren't take.

'There is nowhere to go, Alla,' said Yuri. 'We have you, we have your people, we have your organization. You have nothing left.'

The woman laughed, head thrown back, throat pulsing as she drew breath between each guffaw.

'You think you've won, Parashvili? How can you when your stupid leaders are playing right into my hands? The game has only just begun.' She turned towards Nash. Her eyes flicked to the digital clock that was hanging on the far wall. 'It's too late for all of you. After today, there will be nobody left to stand in my way.'

She focused on Nash.

'And you, Nash. We should have killed you a long time ago. I suppose that fool Yamana thought he could buy you like he has so many of your former colleagues. I told him you were too stupid to accept. How is my Japanese friend, by the way?' she asked.

'Dead,' Nash replied.

'Ha. Well, that's saved me a job,' she laughed. 'Now, stand back. I'm coming through.'

Raikin was at the end of the carriage now, and her body stooped to ease Pyotr out and down to the ground while she prepared to follow. As she was bending down, Pyotr's hands fell slackly towards the floor and Nash saw that blood was dripping from the fingers of his left hand. Then he noticed the movement of the captive's other hand, a brief, almost imagined glimpse of the handle of a knife secured in a sheath on his calf. In a blur of movement it was in his hand and flashing up between Raikin's legs. The strike had all the force behind it that Pyotr could summon. There was a huge whoomph of pain and expelled air and a crackle of electricity as Alla reflexively tried to use the cattle prod, but Pyotr had already pushed himself back and away from the deadly instrument.

Alla tottered on the brink of the carriage and then fell forward, landing on the still-live weapon. Her body spasmed convulsively and there was a smell of burning flesh as her screams of agony rent the air. Alla was clearly not one of the strong ones. Within seconds she was dead, the cattle prod's low warning hum replacing her cries of anguish.

Nash ran forward and knelt over Pyotr, feeling for a pulse in his neck. At the first touch of his fingers, the Russian opened his eyes, grinned and began to get up.

'Thank you for that, my friend,' he said, accepting Nash's helping hand up. 'That was a bit too close for comfort.'

'Are you badly hurt?' Nash asked.

'No. A guard got off a shot that hit me in the shoulder. It's OK. At least the bitch is dead.'

'If only we could have taken her alive,' said Nash. 'She's the one who held the key to all this.'

The words that Raikin had spoken just before she died had been nagging at Nash's subconscious. Both she and Yamana had appeared so complacent. What was their ace in the hole? Then it came to him – the summit. He turned towards Yuri.

'We must go. Quickly. There's no time,' the words tumbled out, the need to communicate overcoming rational thought process.

'Go? Go where?' Yuri asked.

'The summit. The summit. For God's sake hurry. She had a plan to kill them all.'

Yuri stared at Nash in horror as the truth of what he heard became apparent to him.

'Yuri. The helicopters. Can we fly them out of here to the summit?'

'No chance,' the Russian replied immediately. 'Clearances for that kind of thing take days. Fly anywhere near it and we'll be taken out by missiles.'

Nash turned to Pyotr. 'Pyotr. We need your car. Now. Yuri. Come with us. Get on the radio to your people and tell them we're on our way. By the time we get there, we must be cleared for access to the grounds.'

Pyotr ordered his chauffeur from the car and sat behind the wheel himself.

'When you want a serious job done, do it yourself,' he said with a tight smile. Yuri sat in the front and immediately began talking urgently into his radio.

They had been driving towards the ring road with Pyotr sticking firmly in the outside lane, headlights on, horn permanently blaring. It was an effective tactic. Years of subservience ensured that the general population made way for those they automatically assumed had any kind of authority.

'We'll be there in ten,' said Pyotr.

It was a brief respite. Nash recalled the triumph he had seen in Raikin's eyes. She had been so certain. The biotechnology. It all came back to the biotechnology. Spitz had known: buy the weapon which has been secretly developed by the military in defiance of the President's orders and use it to kill the Russian President and his allies. Who gets the blame? The Russian military. Meanwhile, set up a new republic in defiance of the big bad Russian bear. The government would be able to do nothing and the world would be queuing up to be friends with the new republic which had been far-sighted enough to break free from this old military wolf in democratic sheep's clothing.

'You might need this,' said Yuri, reaching over the front seat to hand Nash his Glock. 'A little more discreet than your Japanese friend's Calico.' There was no shoulder holster so he simply stuck it down the front of his trousers in what was euphemistically and obviously known as the Eunuch's Draw.

The car pulled up at the dacha as Yuri talked urgently into his radio. There was a brief pause and then they were heading up the drive, the car tyres skidding on the bends. In a final flurry of squealing rubber, Pyotr pulled up outside the portico. Nash pushed open the rear door and ran up the steps. At the top there was a phalanx of secret servicemen guarding the way. He noticed the friendly face of Nick Bayes, the SIS Station Chief in Moscow.

'What the hell's going on, David?' Bayes asked.

'Assassination at the summit. No time to explain.'

Assassination. It was the one word that every person in every guard detail in the world had come to dread. These men and women were nicknamed the bullet catchers for obvious reasons, but they trained very hard to avoid having to live up to their title.

As he finished speaking, Nash saw cuffs move to mouths as each secret service detail spread the word. Guns appeared magically from beneath coats, behind jackets and in cars. Where he had been greeted by a smartly dressed group of young executives, Nash was now at the head of a phalanx of hard, tough and very well-armed people.

Yuri appeared at his shoulder as a tall man dressed in civilian clothes arrived at the top of the steps. There was a burst of Russian between the two men. Yuri turned to Nash.

'The colonel in charge of security,' he explained. 'He'll take you in.'

Nash followed the colonel up the steps. He was certain that

an assassination would be attempted, but as yet he had no clue as to the method to be used. A bomb perhaps? A timer would be unlikely as the killers could not have known exactly when the summit would start. Some kind of remote detonation, then. The device would have to be in the room where the meeting was taking place.

The colonel gestured for Nash to move ahead of him into a sitting room. Nash walked forward and then stopped, surprised to see that the room was empty.

'Hello again, Mr Nash.'

That voice. Instantly he was transported back to the monastery. To Spitz and to that terrible death which had been haunting him for so long. It was a scene he had replayed in his mind so often that the memory was as fresh as if it had happened yesterday. He had imagined how he would respond when he eventually found the owner of the voice that had so casually ordered the execution of his friend. Now he knew.

He flung himself to one side in a long, arcing dive, turning his body as he fell. His hand reached for the Glock. By the time he hit the ground, he and the gun were facing back towards the door and his finger was tightening on the trigger. He felt the gun buck once, twice in his hand. Each bullet found its mark in the body of the man who was still standing behind him, his right hand inside his jacket. The speed of Nash's response had taken him completely by surprise.

Colonel Nikolai Muraviev stood for a moment contemplating the hole that had appeared in his stomach, looking with apparent interest at the blood and matter that had already begun to flow from the gaping wound. Then he slowly crumpled to the floor.

The door to the room burst open and both Beyes and Yuri appeared in the frame.

'Traitor. Dead. Summit. Where are they?' Nash was up and running for the door.

Following Yuri's lead they arrived at the dacha's elegant conference room. Nash pushed open the double doors and was greeted by startled looks from the leaders he had come to save. He briefly registered the fear that floated across each of their faces, the sound of the gunshots bringing to life the nightmare of assassination that every politician dreads. His eyes swept the room, taking in the huge glass chandeliers, the solid ash table, the carafes of water, the Thermos of coffee.

The Thermos. Not a bomb, then, but something much more deadly.

It was of the same black and white design he had seen Raikin sweep up off the table just before he had collapsed unconscious at her house. It was the container she had deemed so valuable that she had risked a few vital seconds' delay to ensure that it left with her.

He dashed forward and swept it up off the table from under the nose of the startled Russian President. There was a small bulge on its lid, a timing device Nash guessed, no doubt primed by Muraviev when he placed the flask. He realized that at any second they could all be killed. Water. He must find water. No spore could rise through water and most would be killed by it. The river was his only chance.

He ran to the end of the room, pushed the swing doors open and stepped out on to the concrete patio, the river glinting serenely beyond. He briefly registered a shadowy form off to his right and his hand was moving to his gun even as he began to turn. He saw the frightened face of Philip Thomas, the CIA man who had briefed him about the looming crisis in Ukraine. Here was the final piece of the puzzle. Thomas was the visible face of Spandau.

Nash realized that he had been wrong about the timing device as he noted the small radio transmitter in the Agency man's hand. Thomas had clearly been about to send the signal which would release the gas, but, confronted by the weapon he hoped to detonate at a distance, he now thought only of escape. His hand, too late, was reaching for a gun concealed under his arm. Nash fired once, twice, three times. Thomas was lifted up and thrown back over a glass table on which Presidents and Prime Ministers normally rested their drinks as they took in the view. He slid across the surface, leaving a bloody trail in his wake, and came to a halt, his head on the concrete and his feet still resting on the glass.

Nash ran forward, curling his arm back in a throw he had not used since his days on the cricket pitch. He thrust his arm forward and the Thermos curled out, up and over the water, landing with a small, satisfying splash.

Epilogue

NASH LOOKED UP at the sand-coloured building outlined against the afternoon sun. Journey's end, he thought. But there was none of the satisfaction that he knew he should be feeling; no sense of coming home. Instead, he felt drained and depressed. In part, he knew it was simply his body's reaction to the stress of the last few days. After the battering he had received, both physically and mentally, his systems had finally started to rebel and for much of the flight back from Moscow he had slid from deep sleep to startled wakefulness as his subconscious processed the horrors. His waking moments brought no respite, filled as they were not by triumphal recollections of a successful mission but by the certainty that he had been betrayed.

Alex. As he began the walk up the short path to the glass doors of the Office, he pictured her face once again. Kind, tender Alex, the woman who had dressed his wound at the cottage and who had seemed for a while to be something more than a simple colleague. She had betrayed him, taken him in like a fool.

Since the events at the dacha, he had contacted the Office merely to confirm his ETA. Of Alex he had said nothing, unable to admit the reality of her perfidy, sure that there must be some other explanation. Now he must face that truth which was as solid and unyielding as the building standing before him.

There would be an endless stream of probing questions from the appalling Graham Smart in Internal Affairs and, no doubt, barbed remarks from colleagues who had sensed the closeness between Alex and David and who would either revel in his discomfort or, worse still, offer sympathy. And, of course, Spedding would be furious that Nash had let himself be taken in. No matter that Alex had pulled the wool equally effectively over the Chief's eyes; Nash would be the fall guy. Again. All that would be bad enough, but what he really dreaded was the inevitable direct confrontation with Alex: the laying out of his suspicions and the answers to his questions that he didn't want to hear.

As he pushed open the glass door and reached for the plastic card that would allow him through the security gates, he felt a hand on his arm. Its owner's voice was deferential. 'Mr Nash?'

Nash turned to meet the eyes of Frank, one of the security guards. 'The Chief has asked if you would go directly to his office.'

Straight into the lion's den, then.

Joan waved him through. Was there more sympathy than welcome in her smile? Clearly, Spedding was obviously eager to have at him. As Nash stepped through the doorway, his eyes took in the room's occupants. Spedding, Teller, Smart and – oh, God – Alex herself.

'David, great to have you back,' Spedding moved out from behind the vast oak desk that was the legacy of Captain Sir Mansfield Cumming, the original 'C'. Spedding's normally thoughtful face was unusually animated, his mouth split in a wide, open smile to reveal a row of discoloured teeth. His dark and forbidding eyes were surrounded by the laughter lines of a man both amused and happy. This was going to be even worse than he thought, Nash reflected.

'Great job. Just great,' Spedding enthused. 'Presidents

prime ministers queuing up to congratulate me. Enough in the bank with Number 10 to keep us in funds and enough leverage with the Americans to get anything we want from the vaults at Langley. That's what I call a successful operation.'

He ushered a bemused Nash to one of six grey armchairs that surrounded a rectangular glass coffee table. Sitting down, Nash briefly met Teller's eyes and saw there a reflection of Spedding's humour, the man's slight nod a reinforcement of the Chief's congratulations. There was no hint of the calculation that had marked their previous meetings, and Nash found it hard to remember just why it was he had been so convinced that Teller was the man who had been selling him out.

Nash looked at Alex. Her gaze briefly met his and then slid down towards the table in front of her. He read the gesture as the confirmation he had been looking for but had secretly hoped would not be there.

Spedding sat down next to David and leaned back in the chair, the picture of relaxed contentment.

'I'd better fill you in on what's been happening, David,' said Spedding. 'The Russians have used all this as an excuse for a good old-fashioned purge – the FSB have been lifting people left and right. Of course, whether they've got any of the real villains we won't know for months. Probably not would be my guess.'

'And what about the new republic?' Nash asked.

'What indeed?' replied his boss. 'You won't have seen this morning's newscast.'

Spedding picked up a remote and flicked it towards the television in the corner of the room. The screen filled with images of Russian fighter-planes taking off and then cut to a picture of tanks in the streets of Vladivostok. The voice-over recited a story of firm action dictated by Moscow and rapid capitulation by the rebels. Both the military and intelligence services in the new republic obviously understood the political reality and had quickly returned to the fold. The segment closed with a flak-jacketed reporter standing outside the gates to a factory guarded by men dressed in cumbersome chemical and biological warfare suits. 'It was here,' the journalist reported with the enthusiasm the media reserve for the truly macabre stories, 'that the leaders of the new republic had been preparing to manufacture huge quantities of a devastating new biological weapon . . .'

'That was a little something laid on by us and the Americans,' Spedding said with satisfaction. 'We passed on the intelligence to the right people and they turned up in the right place. Now we'll have the bloody Russians by the balls. No more delays, no more lies and no more keeping us out of their BW plants.'

'Talking of the Americans,' Teller interrupted, 'this has given us some leverage there, too. It turns out that the Agency had the intelligence on the BW threat all along, but as per usual the bureaucracy ate it. The NSA intercepted a call from the Russian Biopreparat plant near Klin which went straight to the office of your friend Colonel Muraviev. It was the signal that the first samples of BW had been passed on – probably the same samples that were tested in Russia and then used in New York. There was plenty of other intelligence around that could have tied in with that message and set the alarm off, but the intercept didn't get out of the computers until yesterday. Apparently, this bug of theirs only sends once every five days.'

'Typical,' Spedding sneered. 'This time it was their traitor and their cock-up. Good to have the boot on the other foot for a change.'

Nash looked at Teller and Spedding, understanding for the first time just how different their lives were from his. He had been out fighting a war, putting his life on the line. His job was done and he had succeeded. These people fought battles about turf, cash and control. Revulsion swept over him. This was not his world. It might be more dangerous out there, but at least what he did *mattered*. The men facing him would be more interested in who sat in which chair or who had leverage over whom in the next UK–US tussle over status and power. Without people like him in the field, their petty squabbles would mean nothing. They were tied to their symbolism, but Nash at least had his freedom.

That very freedom brought with it different choices and costs, however. He glanced at Alex and saw again the tension in her body. But this was not a time for mercy. Her betrayal had killed Spitz, and had nearly killed himself and God knew how many others; it was she who would have to pay this time, not him. Time to bite the bullet.

'That just leaves one bit of business to settle, then,' Nash said. Spedding looked at him, one eyebrow raised questioningly.

'We know this operation was compromised from the very beginning. At every turn there were people on my tail who seemed to know what I was doing even before I did. The cottage, Japan, Moscow. I'm only alive now because we cut everyone out of the loop.' Spedding nodded, acknowledging his part in the conspiracy. Smart opened his mouth to say something, then thought better of it.

'The only people who had access to all the information are in this room,' Nash continued. He paused, then swivelled in his chair to confront Alex directly. For the first time since he had entered the room, Alex's eyes rose to meet and hold his. For a brief moment he looked into them, as if seeking the answers he knew must lie there.

'It's Alex. Alex is our traitor.' He was speaking to the three men in the room, but his gaze never left the eyes of the woman he had once thought he could love.

The abrupt guffaw of laughter from Teller was immediately followed by a small smile of satisfaction from Smart. The response was so unexpected that Nash looked from one face to the next, searching for a reaction to the bomb he had just dropped in their midst. Instead, he saw only wry amusement.

'Don't you understand?' he asked, his voice rising with the tension he could feel knotting his stomach. 'This woman betrayed me, betrayed us all, and damn nearly got me killed.'

'David. You're forty-eight hours too late,' Spedding interrupted. 'We'd already worked that out. Or rather Graham here had,' he gestured towards the head of Internal Security. 'He did his homework and came up with Alex's name.'

'In that case, why is she sitting here?' Nash demanded.

'It's not quite as simple as you might think, David,' Spedding continued. 'You're right in that it was Alex's computer which was the source of the leaks, but Alex had nothing to do with it. When she was talking to you, someone outside the building was tapping in to the conversation. She's as much a victim of all this as you are.'

Someone? 'What do you mean, "someone"?' Nash asked, trying to digest this new information that destroyed the careful tower of betrayal he had constructed around Alex. His relief at this news was swamped by his fury that there were people at work out there who had tried so hard to catch and kill him. He swore to himself he would one day make them suffer for the hell he had been through, whoever they were.

'That's the question we've yet to answer,' Spedding replied cautiously. 'It has all the hallmarks of our friends from Spandau, whose fingers seem to stretch into just about every aspect of this case.'

Spandau. Spandau. Everywhere he turned he heard that bloody name. An apparently all-powerful enemy which fought on equal terms and with equal intelligence. They had set him up time and again, and now they had set up Alex.

Alex.

The shock of that thought as it entered David's mind had all the force of a thrust from Alla Raikin's cattle prod. Finally, there had appeared in his life someone who might take the place of Jaimie. No, that was wrong; not take her place perhaps, but make her a treasured memory alongside a happy present rather than a yawning chasm in his life.

Dismally, he reflected that the realization had come too late. He had accused Alex of treachery – in their business, the most heinous transgression imaginable. How could she ever feel anything for him now? For the second time in two minutes he looked into her eyes.

'Alex, I'm so sorry. There just seemed to be no other –'

'It was what Spandau wanted you to think,' she replied, taking his hand in both her own. 'They nearly destroyed us both.' She gazed back at him and for the first time in a long time Nash found himself looking forward to tomorrow.

Spedding coughed self-consciously. It was the first time David had ever seen him embarrassed. 'Speaking of Spandau,' he said, regaining some authority as he spoke, 'we may have foiled them this time, but they're still out there; nameless, faceless – the worst kind of enemy. We're going to have to do something about that, David.'

For 'we' read 'me', Nash thought wryly, and Alex's small smile told him that she had interpreted the Chief's words in the same way.

Still, he had taken them out in Moscow, hadn't he? Perhaps they weren't quite so all-powerful as they thought. One thing was certain – Spandau would be back.

Well, so would he.